MUSIC FOR TORCHING

Also by A. M. Homes

The End of Alice

In a Country of Mothers

The Safety of Objects

Jack

Appendix A: An Elaboration on the Novel "The End of Alice"

MUSIC FOR TORCHING

A.M. HOMES

ROB WEISBACH BOOKS
William Morrow and Company, Inc. New York

Published by Rob Weisbach Books
An Imprint of William Morrow and Company, Inc.
1350 Avenue of the Americas, New York, N.Y. 10019

Library of Congress Cataloging-in-Publication Data

Homes, A. M.
Music for torching / A.M. Homes.—1st ed.
p. cm.
ISBN 0-688-16711-X (alk. paper)
I. Title
PS3558.0448M87   1999
813'.54—dc21   98-55252
CIP

Printed in the United States of America

First Edition

1 2 3 4 5 6 7 8 9 10

BOOK DESIGN BY CHERYL L. CIPRIANI

www.robweisbachbooks.com

In Memory

ONE

IT IS AFTER MIDNIGHT on one of those Friday nights when the guests have all gone home and the host and hostess are left in their drunkenness to try and put things right again. "Too much fat," Paul says, carrying in dishes from the dining room. "The potatoes were swimming in butter, the salad was drenched in dressing."

Elaine stands at the sink, in an apron, in Playtex gloves, trying to protect herself. She doesn't see it yet, but despite her prophylactic efforts, her clothing is stained. Later, she will wonder if the spot can be gotten out, if her clothing can be made clean. She will regret having bought the outfit, having cooked the dinner, having made the enormous effort to make everything good again.

Paul goes into the dining room, this time returning with the wineglasses, the bottle tucked under his arm.

Elaine scrapes plates into the trash can.

Paul puts the glasses down, brings the bottle to his lips, and finishes it, swishing the last sip round and round before bending over her shoulder and spitting it into the sink, splashing her.

"Watch it," she says.

"Gristle," he says. "You're doing it on purpose. Poisoning me. I could taste the fat—going right to the artery."

Again, she doesn't say anything.

"I should be eating legumes."

"I can't make legumes for eight."

She loads the dishwasher. "What about her?" she asks.

"Who?"

"The girlfriend, the date." The woman Henry—who recently left Lucy, whom they all liked a lot—carried around all night like a trophy.

"Nice," he says, not telling his wife that when he asked the date what she did—as in what her occupation was—she said, What would you like me to do? And when he asked, Where do you live? she said, Where would you like me to live?

He doesn't tell his wife that before she left she said, Give me your phone number, and he willingly jotted it down for her. Paul doesn't tell Elaine that the date promised to call him tomorrow. He goes back into the living room for the dessert plates.

"How old do you think she is?" Elaine calls out.

Paul returns, his hands filled with wadded-up napkins. He shakes crumbs into the sink. "How old would you like her to be?"

"Sixty," Elaine says.

She finishes loading the dishwasher, mumbling, "Hope it's fixed, hope it doesn't flood, hope the gasket isn't gone, hope you were right."

"Hope so," he says.

She adds detergent. "Sink's stopping up," she says. "The house is falling apart. Everything is made of shit."

"It only lasts so long," he says, thinking about the date. How many children do you have? she had asked him. Two, he'd said. Isn't that below average? Aren't you supposed to have two point three?

"We need so many things," Elaine says.

Paul doesn't hear her. Aren't you supposed to have two point three? she'd asked, seriously, as though it were a possibility. He hadn't responded. What was there to say? He had poured her another glass of wine. Every time he hadn't known what to say, he'd poured her another glass of wine. They'd had two bottles between them. You really know how to get to me, she'd said, drinking it.

Paul looks at Elaine—Elaine from the back, Elaine bent over the sink. He looks at Elaine and lifts up her skirt, he presses against her, he starts to pull her pantyhose down.

"Is this supposed to be funny?" she asks, still washing dishes.

"I don't know," he says, looking at the pan where the roast had lain; the bottom is thick with congealed white fat, veined with bloody juice. He looks at the pan on the counter, imagines dipping his hand into the grease, smearing it over Elaine's ass and fucking her.

Her pantyhose are down, just above her knees. The water is running, the dishwasher is running.

Unbeknownst to them, the slipper-feet of his pajamas making him stealthy, silent, undetectable, their older son, Daniel, has slipped into the room. The kid opens the refrigerator door.

Paul turns, sees him, quickly pulls Elaine's skirt down. Elaine stands, embarrassed, at the sink.

"What are you doing?" Paul demands.

"Is there any caviar? Mom said that if there was any caviar left over, I could have it."

"You should be asleep," Elaine says.

Paul points to a small dish on the counter. The kid takes white bread out of the fridge and smears caviar over a piece.

Elaine, trying to pretend everything is normal, walks around the kitchen putting things away. She walks with peculiar half steps, the pantyhose holding her legs together like a big rubber band.

The kid makes himself a second caviar sandwich. "Enough," Elaine says, taking the dish away from him. "It's a delicacy, not a snack. You don't make a meal of it."

"Do you think I'm weird?" the kid asks; suddenly again, as if he were two again, everything is a question. "Is it weird that I'm eating caviar in the middle of the night?"

"Go to bed," Paul says.

The kid leaves the room. Paul goes back to Elaine and lifts her skirt again. She turns around.

"Don't fuck with me," she says, grabbing a carving knife from the counter and pressing it against his neck.

"What do you mean?"

"You insult me, my cooking. I *am* my cooking," she says. "I'm a good cook. I tried hard, very hard, to make a nice dinner. You used to like lamb roast, you once said it was your favorite food. Even tonight you ate it, you took four pieces—there almost wasn't enough to go around. Luckily, Ben is a vegetarian." She holds the knife against his neck. Her pantyhose are still bunched between her legs. She feels exposed.

"I was teasing," Paul says. "Musing about whether anyone had ever been charged with murder by *The Joy of Cooking*."

"If I wanted to kill you, I would just go like this." She pulls the knife across his neck, and the blade breaks his skin, making a shallow slash like a paper cut. A thin line of red springs up on his neck.

He runs for the bathroom. She follows him, doing her awkward duck walk. He slams the door, locking her out. The loose molding around the doorframe falls to the floor.

"It's nothing," she says, through the door, pulling her pantyhose up—just in case they have to go to the hospital. "Let me see, I'm sure it's fine. It was an accident. I'm sorry. I didn't mean to really cut you."

"Bitch," he says, opening the door.

"I said I was sorry." She pours peroxide onto a Kleenex

and dabs his wound. He winces. "Don't be a baby," she says. "We were playing your game."

She finishes in the kitchen. He holds an ice pack against his neck. "To keep the swelling down," he says.

"What swelling?" she asks. "It's a cut, not a bite."

"What do you know about it?"

They go upstairs. "The light in the hall is out," she tells him.

"We're out of bulbs," he says.

"Put it on the list," she says.

They undress. There is nothing more to say.

In the morning, in her half sleep, Elaine's thoughts race, speeding through a giant checklist, a litany, all she has ever done, all she has never done, all she meant to do, all her ideas and good intentions. Her thoughts spin until there isn't anything left. She looks up at the ceiling. The paint is cracked and peeling. It needs to be scraped, redone. Exhausted, she gets up.

"Did you see Ben's gut?" she asks. "And what about Henry's hair, who does he think he's fooling? It's awful. And what about Joan? That's who I'm really worried about. She's so depressed she can hardly speak, and Ted doesn't even notice."

"He notices," Paul says, still sleeping.

"And what does he do?"

"Fucks the secretary."

"The assistant," Elaine says.

"Sorry."

Elaine pulls up the sheets and blankets on her side of the bed. Last year they traded in their bed; they went from queen to king because they wanted more room. "After so many years," the salesman in the mattress store had said, "it's hard to sleep on top of somebody else." Now they sleep easily, without touching.

"If our friends are disgusting, does it mean we're disgusting?" Elaine asks.

"Probably," Paul says.

"Disgusting," Elaine says, going into the bathroom. "Horrible, hateful, and ugly." She closes the door and then opens it again, immediately. "Don't forget," she says. "The Nielsons' barbecue is this afternoon. We get to see everybody again."

The phone rings. Paul dives across the bed to Elaine's side and answers it. "Hello," he says, breathlessly. Then he calls to Elaine, "Your mother."

"Can I stay at your place tonight?" the mother asks Elaine.

"What do you mean?" Elaine says.

"Your father is driving me crazy. I thought I'd come and stay with you, unless of course you tell me I can't."

"I would never tell you you couldn't."

"So I can," she says. "It's all right?"

"Yes," Elaine says. "We have a barbecue this afternoon, but we'll be home early. The sitter will be here."

Mother is coming—without Father, which is a little odd, but who cares? Mother is coming—that's what counts. Mother will make everything all right.

"Oh, don't worry," the mother says, "I won't even get there before nine-thirty or ten."

"My mother is coming," Elaine tells Paul, already stripping the bed. She goes down the hall to the linen closet and gets clean sheets.

Sammy comes out of his room. "Did you wet your bed?" he asks.

"Grandma is coming," Elaine says.

Sammy goes back into his room and closes the door. "I don't like Grandma," he says through the door.

"If she's by herself, do we really need to give her our room?" Paul asks. "Couldn't she sleep in one of the boys' rooms?"

"Let's not make a thing out of it," Elaine says. "Let's just do it the way we always do it, otherwise it'll mean something that she came alone and we didn't think enough of her to give her our room. Help me," she says, pulling the fitted sheet across the bed. "Help me."

In the bathroom mirror, Paul looks at himself. He rubs the cut on his neck, rubs until blood seeps out. He wonders if the date will call, wonders what he will do with her if she calls? Will they make a plan to meet? Where will he take her—the Carlyle? Or Ardsley Arms, the motel by the highway that advertises cozy cabins? No. He can't spend the money. If he spends any more money, Elaine will find out—she's better at math than he is; she does the bills. They'll go to the date's place or they'll meet somewhere public, like Rye Playland. He'll buy lots of ride tickets. They'll go through the haunted house, rushing to be finished, released, and relieved before their car kicks through the double doors and back into the daylight. They'll go through two or three times. The first time they'll kiss, long and tenderly, as though they mean it. He'll fondle her. The second time his head will be in her crotch, her mouth on his cock. The third time she'll straddle him—she'll sit so tall that her head will bang against the fabricated fiberglass rafters, the pseudo-timbers, which will crack at well-timed intervals over their heads. The things that go bump in the night will be entirely real.

"And what about Henry's hair?" Elaine had said. Paul looks at himself in the mirror and wonders what's wrong with Henry's hair. Paul is just like his friends, as is Elaine. Their friends are just like them. They like it that way. When one of the friends changes, when something is different, they all get nervous, as if it will be contagious—as if this bit of bad luck, or poor fortune, will now be visited upon the rest of them. Elaine's words echo in his head: "Who does he think he's fooling?"

The phone rings again. "I'll get it," Paul screams through the house. "I'll get it! Hello?" he says.

"What are you wearing?" the date asks.

Elaine picks up the phone downstairs.

"Hello?" she says.

"I've got it," Paul says. Elaine hangs up.

"You didn't answer me," the date says. "I asked you what you were wearing."

"What if my wife had gotten it?" Paul says.

"She would have answered me already."

"What are *you* wearing?" Paul asks her.

"What would you like me to wear?" she asks back.

"Very little," he says. "Something, but not much."

"Are you a doctor?"

He starts to say no, but then stops himself. "Would you like me to be a doctor?"

"I'm in pain," she says.

"Tell me about it," he says.

"Examine me and I will."

"You were on an awfully long time," Elaine says when Paul finally comes downstairs. "I made pancakes. Daniel spread caviar on his. It's out of control."

They look out the kitchen window. "Grass needs cutting," Paul says. The children are playing in the yard. Daniel has Sammy trapped, with a butterfly net over his head.

"Big-game hunt," Paul says. "Next he'll try and attach a tag to Sammy's ear."

"You were whispering," Elaine says.

"Big deal," Paul says. It's unclear whether he means big deal as in "none of your business," or big deal as in "a large business transaction."

Elaine stuffs clothes into the washing machine.

"Aren't you supposed to separate the coloreds and the whites?" Paul asks.

"Segregation ended," she says, closing the lid.

"But I thought—"

"If you want to do the laundry, feel free." She picks up her purse. "I'm going to Liz's. I need some time to myself. Keep an eye on the kids."

"Why do you go to Liz's? Isn't she there? And what about Jennifer? Isn't Jennifer there? Is that time to yourself?"

"Jennifer stays in the basement," Elaine says.

"You spend more time with Liz than you do with me."

"I like her better," Elaine says, leaving.

Saturday afternoon at the cookout, regardless of the fact that they were all together the night before, they act glad to see each other. Perhaps they are not acting, perhaps they are genuinely glad to see each other. Perhaps it was that difficult being left to their own devices for twenty-four hours. Who knows? But they are in surprisingly good spirits; they are the kind of people who believe in putting on their party clothes and a party face, or at least starting off with a smile.

"Can I get you a drink?" George Nielson, the host, asks at regular intervals. "Freshen that? Are you running out? Pour you another? More ice? Splash?"

Henry is there with the date.

Paul sees her from across the yard and blushes bright red.

"Are you all right?" Elaine asks. "Are you ill?"

He sips his drink. "Spices," he says. "Bloody Mary."

"Joan is here without Ted?" someone says.

"He's not well. He ate too much last night."

"Call him, tell him to come anyway," Pat Nielson says. "We miss him. He doesn't have to eat, he can just drink. He can still drink, can't he?"

Ted's wife, Joan, shakes her head. "He's better off in front of the TV."

"And where are the Montgomerys?" Elaine asks. "They didn't come last night either." The tsk-tsk, don't-ask face is made.

"Lost his job," Joan whispers. "They don't know what to do. They're living off Catherine. A mortgage, two in prep school, one in that special place—it's a lot, an awful lot."

The subject is changed. "You have such a beautiful home," Elaine tells Pat, knowing it is the right thing to say. "Everything you do comes out perfectly." She neglects to add how intimidating the perfection is.

"Thank you," Pat says. "It means so much to me to hear you say that. It's all I do. House, house, house," she says as though nothing else matters, as though that's all there is in the world.

"It's breathtaking," Elaine says.

The Nielson twins, Margaret and Mary, play waitress. They wear little black dresses with white aprons tied on. The guests applaud their servitude and wonder aloud how much Pat and George are paying them. The guests can't tell the girls apart and so just call them Mmmm . . . , and the girls each fill in the rest accordingly.

The men hover around the grill, their faces slowly turning red, hot with the heat, charcoal glow. The women bathe in the cold blue fluorescent light of the kitchen. Each side eyes the other, hoping the gossip being traded doesn't really give the goods away.

Henry's date stands in the dark, in a kind of no-man's-land between the two groups, with only the citronella torch as her guide. Paul keeps her company.

"How are you feeling?" he asks.

"I think I'm having a recurrence," she says.

"Stubborn case," Paul says. "You probably need further treatment."

The date looks at Paul. "Your hair," she says. She starts to say something about Paul's hair, but Elaine comes between them.

Later, when they are roasting marshmallows, when he's got the date eating off his stick, Paul will try to touch her. He'll rest his hand high on her thigh.

"I'd rather you not," she'll say. "For now, I prefer to touch myself."

Far away there is the sound of another party, voices in a distant backyard. Through the trees they can see lights in other houses. Every lit window is like a small stage, a miniature color television set where little dramas play themselves out.

"Shall I put on some music?" George Nielson asks.

"That would be lovely," Pat says, and George goes into the house, throws open the living-room windows, and Sinatra wafts into the night.

"Sinatra," Henry shouts to George. "Why are we listening to Sinatra? Are we our parents?"

The Nielsons begin to dance.

"Isn't it nice?" someone says, watching Pat and George go cheek to cheek across the yard. "They still enjoy each other so much."

Henry pulls Paul aside. "So," he asks, "what do you think of the girl?"

"Nice," Paul says. He doesn't tell Henry that she telephoned, that they played doctor, that he scheduled her for a return visit. Paul doesn't tell Henry that chances are good the date has a serious problem, something thoroughly beyond both of them. He doesn't tell Henry that he's beginning to think she's incurable. Instead he asks, "Where'd you meet her?"

"In an elevator," Henry says. "Can you believe it? Isn't that unbelievable?"

"What does she do for a living?"

"You won't believe it," Henry says, pausing. "Psychic."

"Psychotic?"

"No, psychic."

"And she makes a living that way?"

Henry nods.

"Unbelievable," Paul says, looking at Henry's hair. Henry runs his hand through what's left of it.

"Who sits where?" Joan asks when the hamburgers are ready. "Is there an order, a special plan?"

Pat Nielson tells everyone exactly where to go. She seats Paul next to Elaine's best friend, Liz.

"Long time no see," Liz says, kidding.

"I keep forgetting exactly what it is you've gone back to get your Ph.D. in," Paul says.

"Women's Studies," Liz says.

"So I guess you don't want to get married again?"

"Prick," Liz says—her ex-husband, Rich, used to be best friends with Paul.

"Asshole," Elaine says later when they're walking home. "You did it on purpose."

Paul doesn't say anything. He ducks behind a tree and urinates.

Elaine waits for him. "The Esterhazys have done something to their house," she says.

Paul peers out from behind the tree. "Porch? They glassed in the screen porch?"

"Nope. Deck," Elaine says.

Paul comes out from behind the tree. "Looks good," he says, zipping up.

They have walked to the Nielsons'. Walking and drinking is the way it is done. That way they can drink too much, eat too much, and get home still feeling decent about themselves. It could have been worse—at least they got a little exercise, a taste of the night air; at least no one got killed.

The problem comes a few minutes later, when Paul has to get into the car, when he has to drive Jennifer, the baby-sitter, who is Liz's daughter, home. He sits in the car waiting for Jennifer. He sits gazing up at the house, thinking it looks shabby. Even in the dim glow of the streetlights it appears less promising, less hopeful than the other houses up and down the block.

Jennifer comes out of the house and gets into the car.

"Was that incredibly painful?" he asks, gesturing toward the side of her head, which is shaved as though she's been prepped for surgery, moving on to her eyebrow and lip, both of which are pierced—silver rings split the flesh. He touches his own lip and eyebrow as if he's speaking sign language.

"Only equal to the pain I'm already in," she says.

He nods. Jennifer was five when he and Elaine moved in. She is his first memory of the neighborhood.

He spotted her playing on the lawn of what was then Roger and Liz's house, and somehow the sight of her, staging a party with her Raggedy Anns—dressed like a Raggedy Ann herself—made him think that they could live there, that everything would be okay. He doesn't know why.

"Great scar," she says, pointing to the red line on his neck. "Did you do it yourself?"

"No," he says. "I had help."

"Cool."

He makes a turn. "Can I ask you a question?" he says, and then, without waiting for a reply, goes on. "What does my wife do at your house all day?"

"She fucks my mother," Jennifer says, without a pause.

His fantasy. His nightmare. He has no idea whether she's lying or not.

Elaine is in the living room, waiting for Paul. She is in the living room talking to her mother, who has apparently run away from home. As Elaine talks she rearranges the furniture as though this will make all the difference.

"What's wrong?" Elaine asks, pushing a chair across the floor as quietly as possible. "Why are you leaving Daddy?"

"I'm not leaving," the mother says, helping to switch a lamp from one end table to another. "I'm taking a night off. After fifty-three years, every now and then you need a night off. By the way," the mother says, "when I got here, Daniel was puffy like he was having an allergy. So I gave him an antihistamine."

"Fish eggs," Elaine says, plugging the lamp in. Her words come off with the same annoyed connotations as someone saying "Fiddlesticks!" The mother looks confused. "He eats too much caviar."

The mother shakes her head. "I'll never understand."

Paul comes in, makes himself a drink, and carries it into the living room.

"You drink too much," Elaine says, pushing the coffee table farther away from the sofa.

"I'll call it a night," the mother says, going upstairs. "See you in the morning."

Paul quickly finishes the drink and goes back for another.

"It's fattening," Elaine calls after him. "I thought you were watching your gut."

"Cunt," Paul says to Elaine, who is now remaking the L-shaped sofa into a bed for the night.

"Are you flirting with me?"

Paul does a strange and suspicious dance, circling around the sofa, around Elaine—like an animal, like a boxer. He circles and drinks. "Fucking whore."

He grabs her with his free hand. He is drunk, his breath scotchy, tainted with bitter belches, barbecue gone sour. "Show me," he says, squeezing her. "Show me what you do."

"Go to hell," she says, eyeing a chair she thinks would look better on the left side of the room.

"I'm there already."

"So leave." She tries to twist away from him. He holds on.

He bends to put his glass on the coffee table, but the table has been moved. The glass lands on the floor, and the drink spills.

"You're hurting me," she says.

"You hurt me, too," he says.

The mother comes to the top of the stairs. "Keep it down," she whispers loudly. "Or I'll have trouble sleeping."

"You're ruining my life," he hisses. He tears at her clothing. He bites her. He does to Elaine what he'd like to do to Henry's date.

"I hate you," Elaine says when Paul is on top of her. "I used to like you, I thought you were cute. But look at you now," she says.

He fucks her, his feet pressing against the armrest, using the sofa for leverage.

She begins to cry. "I'm bored," she says. "I'm so bored, it's not even funny." She digs her fingers into his back; her nails sink into his flesh and stay there.

"I'm unhappy," he says, still humping her. His few remaining strands of hair come unglued and fall forward, hanging in his face. He stops humping her for a moment, flips them back, then starts humping her again. "I'm unbelievably unhappy," he says loudly and begins to cry.

They stop fucking.

They don't finish, they simply stop.

"Remember when we smoked the crack?" he says. "Right here in this living room. You were the fountain, the fountain in front of the Plaza hotel? You were a Roman candle. What could we do now that would be like that?"

"Nothing," she says. "There's nothing we can do."

"Do you want a drink?" he asks her.

"No," she says. "Nothing."

"Have you had enough?" he asks, rolling off her.

They are both crying.

* * *

Sunday morning, Paul is in the bathroom, looking at himself in the mirror again. He looks at his hair. He takes Elaine's nail scissors and cuts it all off. Embarrassed, liberated, gleeful like a little kid, he runs his hand over his head. He is ruining something, actively destroying it. He hasn't felt this powerful in years.

All the neatly combed strands are gone. He squirts Barbasol over his head; he looks like a transvestite wearing a bathing cap. He scrapes the razor over his scalp, round and round he goes. Paul finishes, thinking he looks better, healthier, more accepting of what he's become.

"Damn it," Elaine shouts. "Damn it to hell." She has tripped on a loose board on the stairs, spilling clean clothing down the stairs.

Paul comes out of the bedroom. "What happened?" he asks. All of the clothing has been dyed pink on account of a red shirt that was mixed in with everything.

"Fucking floor," Elaine says, collecting the clothes, handing Paul his pink underwear. Then she notices his shaved head. "What the hell were you thinking?" she asks.

"I'm equal to it," he says. He looks at his underwear. "You're crazy," he says. "You can't even do the laundry."

"So fire me," Elaine says, going down the hall to wake Sammy and Daniel.

"I'm not wearing this underwear, and I'm not going to soccer—and you can't make me," Daniel says.

"Fine," she says. "Don't go to soccer, don't wear any underwear either. It's your life. I'm only your mother."

Paul leaves for the father/son soccer soirée with Sammy, promising to stop at the five-and-ten and buy new underwear on the way.

"But I like pink, pink is good, pink is pretty," Sammy insists.

"I don't care what you like," Paul says. "What you like doesn't matter here, it's what's good for you. Pink is not good for you."

"Don't worry," Elaine's mother says. She sits at the kitchen table, checking her reflection in a kitchen knife. "It happens." The mother tilts the knife back and forth, making strange, exaggerated expressions with her eyes and mouth. She puts the knife down. "It happened to your father and me. And we survived."

"What did you do?" Elaine asks.

"We went to Italy," the mother says. She finishes her coffee, draws a breath, and clasps her hands together. "Time for me to get myself together and go home."

"You're leaving already?"

"Your father is lost without me."

"But I thought we might be able to spend some time together," Elaine says.

"You'll be fine," the mother says.

Elaine starts to say something, but the mother holds up her hand like a stop sign, silencing her. "You'll be fine," she says again. "I'm telling you."

"But, Mama," Elaine says. "Mama."

"Elaine," the mother says, getting up from the kitchen table, "grow up."

The mother has come, the mother has gone; everything is the same as it was. She didn't make it all right again—she was no help at all.

The telephone rings. Elaine answers it; the caller hangs up.

Elaine goes from room to room, thinking she should clean, she should dust, she should vacuum. Elaine thinks she should sit down, make some calls; she should get the dishwasher re-paired, the disposal replaced, the leak under the sink fixed, oven tested, shower regrouted, floorboard fixed, house painted. She should go to the nursery and buy flowers for outside. She should clean out all the closets and give away what they don't need anymore.

Sunday—the day of rest—Elaine goes from room to room lying on every bed, sitting in every chair, room to room, think-ing. Upstairs, downstairs. Faster, faster. She makes mental notes: what is missing, absent, or in need of attention.

She makes notes until she feels sick, then she goes down-stairs, opens the refrigerator to get a drink. The bulb blows out while she is trying to decide what she wants. It is enough. More than enough. She goes outside and sits on the steps. She can't go back in the house. She can't go in the house again.

She sits on the steps. The air is thick. A neighbor, whose son died long ago, comes collecting for the Kidney Foundation. "It's too soon for this," he tells her, gesturing to the invisible air. "Hot, humid, and it's only the beginning of June."

Daniel comes out of the house; Elaine had forgotten he was home.

"I'm bored," he says. "And there's nothing to eat. All the caviar is gone."

"Go to your friend Willy's," she says. "You'll get there just in time for lunch."

"Fine," he says defiantly. "I will," and he heads off down the driveway.

Elaine sits on the steps all day. She sits until Daniel comes home.

"Go in and bring me a Coke, will you?" she asks Daniel, and he does, delivering the ice-cold can apparently without no-ticing that the refrigerator light is out.

He drags a beach chair out of the garage and sets it up for her. She lies down in the backyard.

Elaine hears the car door slam, as Paul and Sammy return. Paul goes into the house, makes himself a drink.

"You want one?" he yells out the kitchen window.

"Please," she says.

He comes out into the yard, drinks in hand. He takes off his shoes and socks. He wiggles his feet in the grass.

"I can't cook dinner," she says. "I just can't do it."

"We'll grill," he says. "We'll just slap everything on the grill."

She doesn't say more. It's Sunday night, a holiday weekend, the beginning of summer. They have their drinks and they have more drinks. The bleating bellow of mothers calling their children home echoes up and down the street. "Wendy, Jonathan, Danielle, Michael, dinner's ready." Elaine's stomach growls; she hasn't eaten since breakfast. Paul sets up the grill—a little too close to the house, Elaine thinks, but she doesn't say anything. He lights the coals.

"I don't think you realize what I'm saying," Elaine says. "I can't do it anymore."

"What do you want to do about it?" Paul asks.

"Where are the children?"

"In the front yard."

Elaine and Paul are silent, listening for Sammy and Daniel's game. The static of the children's walkie-talkies cuts through the air.

"What are you wearing?" Daniel squawks.

"Blue shorts," Sammy squawks back.

"And what color are your socks?"

"Mine are red," Sammy says, and then, as if they know the parents are listening, the children begin beeping each other with the Morse-code button, talking in an unintelligible language of longs and shorts, dots and dashes.

Paul picks up the can of charcoal-starter fluid and squirts it against the house. "Is this what you want?" he asks.

Elaine sucks in her breath; she can't tell if Paul is joking or not.

"Tell me," he says, emptying the can against the house, spraying a swath over the grass, a line that leads straight to the grill. "You have to tell me."

"I don't know," Elaine says.

The briquettes are almost ready; the coals are orange-edged, glowing. Elaine goes to Paul, puts her arm around Paul's waist. She balances herself, then raises her leg, her foot, her toe, and taps her toe against the leg of the grill.

"Harder," Paul says.

Elaine pulls her leg back and kicks the grill. The coals fly up and out, the grill tips over. Everything sputters and smokes for a minute, and then slowly the fire builds up from the ground and moves toward the house. They stand watching as fire creeps up the back wall of the house. Wordless, each wonders if it is a game—a dare to see who will run for the garden hose. As the fire builds, their nervousness and excitement grow. Elaine begins to laugh and then stops herself. In the early evening light, the blue flame is nearly invisible. Fire seeps into a crack in the wall. A line of white smoke rises. Elaine watches, wishing she could hurry it, wishing she could be sure.

Paul leans on Elaine and puts his shoes back on. "Get the kids and get in the car," he says.

Elaine walks away, turning back to see Paul blowing on the fire, fanning it with his hands, encouraging the flame.

"We're going out for dinner," Elaine tells Sammy and Daniel.

"Roger," they say into their walkie-talkies.

They get in the car and wait for Paul. A few minutes later, red-faced, breathless, he joins them. They drive to a nearby restaurant. The waitress fills their water glasses. Paul and Elaine smile at each other.

"I'll have the steak," Paul tells the waitress, "and the baked potato with sour cream."

"The fat," Elaine starts to say.

"I just want to live," Paul says. "Live and not worry. Is that possible?"

"I'll have the same," Elaine says, closing her menu.

During dinner they hear sirens. They linger over coffee. The children eat ice-cream sundaes. When the check is paid, they get back into the car and head home. The street is blocked off, fire engines and police cars. In the distance, they can see their house, engulfed, flames shooting out of the roof.

In the backseat, the children are oddly silent.

"Is that our house?" Daniel asks.

"Yes," Paul and Elaine say.

They watch for a few minutes, and then, worried that someone will recognize them, they drive away.

They check into a motel. The children, stunned by the spectacle, stoned on hot fudge, go quickly and quietly to sleep.

"We're awful," Elaine says, crawling into bed next to Paul. "Really bad."

"We have to try harder," Paul says.

"We have to be nicer to each other," Elaine says.

Paul plays with the blankets, pulling them up over their heads. "We should build a fortress to protect ourselves from the world," he says.

"To protect us from each other," Elaine adds.

"From ourselves," Paul says, letting the blankets fall down over them.

They are quiet. Paul curls up against Elaine and wraps himself around her. "What are you wearing?" he whispers in her ear.

TWO

IN THE MIDDLE OF THE NIGHT, Paul wakes up. "We have to go home. We have to go home, we have to go home," he says, knocking his head against the headboard like Dorothy clicking her heels in *The Wizard of Oz*.

Elaine is asleep. For the first time in years, she is sleeping well, without fear or worry. She sleeps well because the bed she is sleeping in is not her own, because it belongs to someone else, because it belongs to no one. They are in a motel room. There are no expectations, no demands. She sleeps well because she went to bed thinking she would never have to go home, thinking it was over and done—gone.

"We have to go back to the house," Paul says, waking her.

"We set the house on fire."

"Did we?"

Elaine looks at the digital clock on the nightstand. "It's only twelve-thirty," she says, disappointed. "I only slept for two hours."

Paul and Elaine are in the bathroom of the motel room. Paul has brought in the phone, pulling the short cord taut. The door is closed, the light is on. Elaine puts down the lid of the toilet and sits. Naked under the frail, flickering light, the poor fluorescence, they look at each other and at themselves, then look away. Elaine looks at the thin white towels, cracking grout, sink, commode, glasses wrapped in paper bags: SANITIZED FOR YOUR SAFETY, PROTECTION AND PLEASURE.

Paul hitches up his cock and balls and sits on the edge of the tub, one leg crossed over the other. "We have to do something," he says.

Their nakedness is like a joke, something contrived to make them seem more exposed, only it fails—their skin is only another ill-fitting layer, like clothing. It has lost its memory—the landscape of the body hangs loose, shapeless. They make no effort to disguise themselves, to hide themselves, and there is something to be said for the honesty, the extreme humanity of all this faulted flesh—it is heartbreaking.

"We need help," Paul says, further adjusting himself. "We have to do something, call someone."

"Who?"

"Someone we don't know, someone we don't see. Tom. I'll call Tom."

"Your college roommate?"

Paul is already dialing.

"And what are you going to tell him?"

"Tom," Paul says. "It's Paul." And then he stops. There is silence. He begins again. "I burned down the house," Paul says. "Now what do I do?"

"If you've done something horrible, don't tell me about it until I tell you the consequences," Tom says. "Arson," Tom says. "It's arson. Or if the fire spread, if other people's property was damaged, it could be worse. If someone was killed, if lives were lost, it could be murder."

Paul stands in the bathroom of the cheap motel—where in fact he has been before, but he can't tell Elaine that, he can't tell Elaine that he's done this all before, that at the motel across the street they know him well, but they know him as someone called Mr. Melon. He can't really tell Elaine anything, but there's no point in getting into that now. Paul stands listening to Tom's litany—the potential charges against him—all the while examining himself in the medicine-cabinet mirror, touching the scar on his neck from where Elaine nicked him with a carving knife.

"What if it was an accident?" Paul asks. "What if it was all a terrible accident?"

"They might knock it down to negligence."

"And do you go to jail for negligence?" The word "negligence" comes out sounding like "negligee," and Paul blushes. The hot pink of his face against the green glow of the light is not a good combination, and now Elaine is watching him, worrying that his blood pressure is up, worrying that he's having a heart attack, worrying that he'll die here and now in this bathroom and she'll be left with all the explaining to do. "Are you all right?" she whispers, and Paul waves her away.

"You won't go to jail for negligence, unless it's criminal," Tom is saying. "But your homeowner's won't cover."

Paul's anxiety level has affected his hearing—instead of "homeowner's" Paul hears "homo," and out of the blue, like some memory released, he remembers that all through sophomore year Tom would crawl into his bed at night, and although he had forgotten it, long since put it behind him, he suddenly misses Tom incredibly. He wishes Tom were with him now—Tom would take care of this mess, Tom would comfort him, Tom would forgive him. Instead he is with Elaine, who is looking at him peculiarly—as though she hates him. He turns away. He steps into the empty tub, pulls the shower curtain closed, and whispers to Tom, "What do I do?"

"Get your story straight," Tom says. "Then call the police."

"I really appreciate it, Tom," Paul says. "It's really good

to talk to you. How have you been? Have you been good? Have you been well?"

"Fine," Tom says.

There's a knock on the door and Paul pulls back the shower curtain and glares at Elaine, who's glaring at him. They're both frightened, thinking they've been caught. Again, there's the knocking, this time followed by Sammy's small voice pleading, "Let me in, let me in, I have to go."

"If you could just keep this under your hat," Paul says to Tom. "If you could keep it between us, I'd really appreciate it."

"Call me," Tom says.

"I will," Paul says, hanging up.

Elaine opens the door, lets Sammy in, flips up the lid of the toilet, and together she and Paul stand watching the little boy about to pee.

Sammy glares at them. "Don't look," he says, and they turn away.

When he is done, they open the door to let him out. Sammy peers into the dark motel room, asking, "Where do I go? Which bed is mine?"

"We have to go home," Paul says again an hour later when they're still sitting naked and speechless in the bathroom and the glow of the fluorescence is casting a moldy shadow over them. "There's nothing else to do."

They dress in the dark. The swish-swishing of fabric, the furtive rustle that should be so sexy, is only sad.

"Time to go," Paul says, waking the children. "Time to go."

"Am I dreaming?" Daniel asks.

No one answers.

"Can they trace the motel?" Elaine asks as they're driving away.

"I paid cash and registered under a false name."

"How did you think of that?"

He doesn't bother to add that he didn't mean to register

with an alias, but rather did it reflexively. There's a large out-
door fruit market down the street. He thinks of this whole strip
as Produce Way. He is the man with the big fruit basket, and
his ladyfriends are Mrs. Apple, Ms. Pear, and Mrs. Plum. He
looks at Elaine, Mrs. Lemon.

"What about the key?" Elaine asks.

"We'll drop it," he says. And when they pass a mailbox,
he stops, and Elaine tosses the key in, trusting the tag that reads
RETURN POSTAGE GUARANTEED. The key lands with a loud,
metallic plunk, and it's as though she's paid the toll—been
given the green light, go.

Paul drives fast, rushing to return to the scene as though
there is some prospect or possibility that he can undo what they
have done. He drives fearing the worst—not only have they set
the house on fire, they have set the world on fire. He looks at
the sky expecting to see it filled with the flames of subdivision.
Turning a corner, swerving to avoid a cat, he is sure that every
house will be burning, every tree consumed, the neighbors will
be streaming out into the melting, molten streets, their arms
thrown into the air beseeching the houses to smite themselves,
to simply put themselves out. He drives toward his imagined
inferno, asking himself, Why? Why? What is wrong with us?
Why are we so unhappy? Why?

"Slow down," Elaine says, "slow down."

He ignores her. Tires squealing, he makes the turn that
puts them on their final approach. The streets are empty, the
sidewalks bare, the night itself calm and clear. On the surface everything is as it was, as it should be. Paul pulls into
their driveway. The sound of gravel under the tires is thoroughly familiar—echoing safety and soundness. The headlights come to rest on the house, standing still against the
night.

Paul pulls up the emergency brake and turns off the engine.

In the backseat, the two boys stir.

"We're home," Paul says.

Elaine had half hoped there would be nothing; a pile of coal, a load of smoldering cinder, the stem of the chimney. But instead, it is all there, no different, only dark, very dark. She stares at the house. "Now what?"

Paul gets out. The house is wrapped in yellow ribbon that reads CRIME SCENE, POLICE LINE, DO NOT CROSS. He tries to remember what yellow ribbon means—it is a song, "Tie a Yellow Ribbon," and it is something else, something about hostages or prisoners of war. He ducks under the tape and reaches for the doorknob, hesitantly, as though it might be hot, as though he might burn himself. It is neither here nor there, neither hot nor cold. He turns the knob and pushes against the door. Nothing happens.

Elaine cracks her window open. The air smells like an old campsite, damp cinders, musty smoke. "Maybe it's locked," she says.

He goes into his pocket for the key.

"Is it safe?"

"It's our house," he says.

"We tried to burn it down."

It is night and silent, and they don't have to speak very loudly in order to be heard—they call back and forth to each other in stage whispers to keep from disturbing the peace, to keep from waking the children.

"Should I call the police?" Paul asks.

"What did Tom say?"

"Call the police," Paul says.

"I'll wait here," Elaine says.

Paul takes off on foot, jogging in the direction of a pay phone.

Elaine sits in the car, thinking she is back to scratch, zero, square one. She's back to where she started, only now it is worse.

Now she will have to take care of the house, tend it like a sick person. She imagines running away; where would she go? Into the woods to live like a wildwoman on berries and nuts? Into the city to sleep on a steam grate? She thinks of running. She undoes her seat belt. She is reaching to unlock the door when she sees Paul coming back. She sees Paul coming and pictures herself taking off down the street—the streetlights like searchlights, constantly catching her. She sees Paul chasing her, not knowing why she is running, why he is chasing, except that it is his instinct to catch her, to drag her back.

A police car pulls up behind the car, blocking it—Elaine isn't going anywhere.

The cop aims his flashlight at Paul, cutting across the lawn. She wishes the cop would yell "Freeze!" and like in the game of Statues Paul would have to stop. But Paul would think it was a joke, he would keep coming. The cop would yell again, then pull his gun and take a couple of shots at Paul, and Elaine's problems would be over—or if not over, at least different.

She sits in the car tempted to scream: Rape! Fire! Murder!

She rolls down her window.

"May I see your license, sir?" the cop says, moving to meet Paul halfway across the lawn.

"I'm the one who called. Paul . . ." he says, breathless from his brief exertion. "From the corner, from the pay phone, by the school." He points back behind him as though that says something.

"May I see you license, sir?"

Paul pulls out his wallet and hands over his license. The cop turns his flashlight on it.

"Is this your car, sir?"

"Yes. Why?"

"And your wife and children?"

"Yes. Why?"

"And is there anybody else living with you at this address?"

"No. Why?"

"Just filling out the paperwork."

"What happened?" Paul asks, a sharp edge in his voice. "We came home and the house was like this. What happened here? That's what I have to find out."

Elaine is impressed; Paul is playing upset very well. Then it occurs to her that he might not be playing, his distress may be entirely real, his questions genuine.

"I need to understand what went wrong," he demands. "Is that asking too much?"

"Where were you this evening?" the cop asks. "What time did you leave the house? Did you stop anywhere along the way? What time did you return? Were you and your wife and children all together? Was your house on fire when you left it?"

"Is this routine?"

"I can see that you're upset, sir, but I have to fill out the report."

"Everything I dreamed of, up in smoke." Paul's voice cracks. And while Elaine's sympathy was with him a minute ago, now she thinks he's making a spectacle of himself. She remains unmoved in the front seat.

The cop comes to her window. "Pardon me, ma'am," he says. "I just wanted to say hello. I believe we met one night a few years ago."

Elaine remembers.

"How have you been?" he asks.

"Fine," she says. "Just fine. And you?"

"I'm real sorry about the house," he says. "Thankfully, the damage is largely cosmetic."

"Really," Paul says, edging in. "So you think it's superficial?"

The cop shrugs. "I'm a cop, not a contractor. But I could walk you around it." He waves his flashlight.

"Good," Paul says. "That would be good. Are you coming?" he asks Elaine.

Elaine glances at the boys, sleeping in the backseat.

"They're safe enough," the cop says, answering a question that hasn't been asked.

The cop leads them around the perimeter of the house, the beam of his flashlight cutting back and forth across the grass like a tail wagging.

"I feel like a spy," Elaine says. "Like I'm sneaking something."

"It's like one of those historical house tours," the cop says, trying to add something. And they all fall silent.

They're in the backyard. The ground is damp, soggy. With every step there is a thick sucking sound. Their feet sink in. The charred, curdled smell of something gone awry hangs in the air.

"Burnt toast," Elaine says.

"Barbecue," the cop says, and again they are quiet.

The back of the house is black, the stone scorched. Ten feet above their heads the dining room window is blown out, the frame torn from the house.

"This is the worst of it," the cop says.

Elaine sees the grill on the ground, spilled onto its side, the debris of what earlier in the evening seemed so promising lies there like rot. She looks at Paul. "Remember," she says, thinking of seven o'clock when the fire was so thrilling, full of possibility. "Remember?"

Paul says nothing. He was the one who lit the match, who started the fire. Elaine leaned against him to kick the grill, to tip the flames onto the grass. Together they burned down the house, or so it had seemed—so they had hoped.

Elaine moves closer, poking at the grill with the toe of her shoe; the metal has been cooked, baked brittle. Now it is cold and crispy like it could crumble. Are houses like cars? she wonders. Do they ever declare them totaled?

"Can we go in?" Paul asks.

"Water and smoke," the cop says repeatedly when they are inside. "Water and smoke." And where Paul is comforted by the fact that the house has not been completely destroyed, Elaine is depressed. All their huffing and puffing barely blew the dining-room wall down. While Paul and the cop poke at the wall examining the damage, Elaine goes upstairs. There is a dim glow at the end of the hall—Sammy's ducky night-light running on backup batteries. She takes the duck by the neck, holds it in front of her like a candle, and makes her way back downstairs.

Outside, the horn beeps, cutting the night like a blast.

Paul, Elaine, and the cop hurry back to the car.

"Where am I?" Daniel asks. He's sitting up in the front seat.

"Home," Paul says.

"Why aren't we inside?"

"There was a fire," the cop says.

"Did I know that?" Daniel asks. "Am I awake? Am I weird?" Daniel drones.

"Shhhh, don't wake your brother," Elaine says, putting the duck down on the dashboard. It takes a nosedive, landing between the seats, the orange rubber feet poking up.

"Go back to sleep," Paul says, urging the boy into the backseat.

"Is there someone you'd like to call?" the cop asks Elaine. "A friend, a neighbor? Is there somewhere you'd like to go and spend the night?"

"We'll stay here," Paul says. "It's our house, our home."

"First thing in the morning you'll want to call your insurance agent, and then come down to the station. This'll be typed. You can just give it your John Hancock."

What is it, Paul wants to know, a report or a confession? He wants to know but doesn't ask.

"Again," the cop says, handing Elaine his card, "I'm sorry about the house. If you need anything, if there's anything I can do, just call."

"What was that all about?" Paul asks when the cop takes off.

"Community service," Elaine says.

She and Paul get back into the car, they roll up the windows and lock the doors. Elaine turns off the duck. They tilt the seats back and close their eyes.

Elaine dreams that she is on a plane. She is on a plane at night, she is alone, she is happy, she is going, going, gone.

When she wakes up, Joan Talmadge and Catherine Montgomery are staring at her through the windshield. They tap on the glass.

"We thought you were dead," Catherine says.

Elaine tilts her seat up. Paul and the children are gone, the backseat is empty.

"We thought you were dead," Catherine repeats.

Elaine rolls down the window.

"Are you all right?" Joan asks.

Elaine nods.

"It was awful," Joan says. "I smelled smoke. 'Is something burning?' I asked Ted. 'Is something burning?' I asked Ted. 'Is something burning? I smell smoke.' "

"We heard the sirens," Catherine says. "I could feel the rumble of the fire trucks. 'Search,' we yelled at the fire chief, 'search.' "

"I thought of you and the boys," Joan continues. "The car was gone, but that could have been Paul. Paul could have taken the car."

"Where is Paul?" Catherine asks.

"Right behind you," he says, coming up from the rear.

"You frightened us," Joan says, and it's not clear whether she means last night or now.

"Where were you?" Elaine asks, opening the car door.

"I took the boys for breakfast. I called the insurance agent. It's Memorial Day—there was a parade. I bought this legal pad. I'm making a list."

"What can we do?" Catherine asks.

"And I got a camera so we can document the damage," Paul says, waving a disposable camera.

"Oh," Catherine says, reaching for the camera, "let me take a picture of the two of you."

Paul stands next to Elaine, puts his arm around her, and Catherine snaps. Later, when Elaine picks up the film, the last picture, the thirty-sixth exposure, will be of a breast.

"Whose boob?" she'll ask Paul. "Do you recognize this tit?"

"Tit for tat," Paul will say, looking at the negatives. "It's the last frame. Maybe the guy at the store fired off the last shot. Who can tell?"

It is a holiday. Their friends and neighbors are slow to rise, they sleep late, paying the price for the night before.

"Cooler today, warmer tomorrow, then rain. That's the forecast," Paul says.

Mrs. Hansen from across the street brings over a mug of coffee for Elaine. "I would have been out earlier," she says. "But I drank too much last night. Sugar? Milk?" Elaine shakes her head. "I'm so sorry," Mrs. Hansen says. "About the house. I would have been out, but I drank. It's a federal holiday today," she says. "No bank, no mail, and the liquor store is closed."

In the front yard, the boys play competitive Houdini. They alternate tying each other to the maple tree with pieces of the crime scene tape, timing how long it takes each one to get free. So far, Sammy is winning with a minute thirty-seven.

In a kind of dislocated fugue, broken off from each other and themselves, Elaine and Paul wander back and forth, in and out and around the house, surveying the damage, the aftermath.

"Where does one begin?" Elaine asks.

"Not over the mouth," Paul shouts at Daniel, who's taken the game a bit too far and is now not only tying Sammy to the tree and blindfolding him but taping his mouth as well.

"Let him live," Elaine says, and it's not clear to whom she's talking.

Pat and George Nielson arrive, presiding over the situation like town elders. Even though they are all the same age, the Nielsons did everything first: married, had children, bought a house, a boat, a summer place.

"I don't know where to start," Elaine tells Pat.

"Why don't we go inside and see where you really are," Pat says, leading Elaine and Paul back into the house.

Inside, Elaine notices things she hadn't seen before: melted curtains, the dining room table cleaved in half, singed chairs, bubbly walls, blistered paint. She plucks a broken candlestick off the floor. "Broken," she says. "Everything is history."

"It can be fixed?" Paul asks.

"Who knows? I'm not an expert," Elaine says.

"Almost everything can be put back together, if you've got the pieces," Pat says.

George puts his hand on Paul's shoulder, steering him into the dining room, while Pat takes Elaine's elbow, easing her away. Like trainers, or chaperons, they take Paul and Elaine into separate corners and give them a few pointers, helpful hints, ways of winning, the art of war.

"Let's go upstairs and leave the big things to the boys," Pat says.

"They sure knew how to build 'em," Paul says, showing George the hole in the dining room wall. "If it was new," he says, "you can bet the whole thing would have gone up like a wad of paper, but these old ones, they're built to last."

"Smoke damage," Elaine says, opening the closet doors. "Everything stinks."

"Spring cleaning," Pat says, opening windows. "Make the best of the worst. Make two piles—one to go to the dry cleaner and one to give away. Remember, tax deductions for donations. My golden rule: If you didn't wear it this year or last, you certainly won't wear it next."

"Give it away," Elaine says in a sudden burst of enthusiasm. "Give it all away." She begins pulling things out of the closets and throwing them onto the king-size bed. And then she is down on her knees digging through old shoes, flinging them out behind her, pair after pair. "If the shoe fits, wear it," she says. "These never fit, none of these ever fit, fucking shoes, fucking everything."

Pat Nielson, stunned by Elaine's enthusiasm, her new-found freneticism, picks a navy Dior dress out of the pile. "When did you get this?" she asks.

Elaine stands, takes the hanger from Pat, and presses the dress against herself. "Just after we moved in, first cocktail party. I paid more for this dress than for any since. Fifteen years," she says. "It's a lifetime." And her hand goes to her throat as though she can silence herself by choking herself. She drops the dress back on the bed and turns away, overcome. "I'll never wear it again. It's a six, and I'm not even an eight anymore, more like a ten."

"You can't collect everything," Pat says, putting the dress in with the giveaways. "Life is not a hobby."

Elaine moves to take down the curtains. At first she is

gentle with the rod, but then she yanks, harder, ripping the brackets out of the wall. "I hate these. I don't even want to clean them, I want to burn them," she says.

The windows are curtainless, the closets half empty, the drawers half full. Elaine is throwing away the past, the weight of it. What's left is only what's necessary, what they need to live right now, today.

Pat carries load after load downstairs. Elaine stays upstairs. She looks out the front window and sees Mrs. Hansen arranging things on the lawn, the broken candlesticks, her Dior dress, the boys' baby clothes. Embarrassed, Elaine hurries down to stop her. The house is filled with people—a fireman stands blocking the hallway, talking to Paul. What is Paul saying? Elaine imagines him telling the fireman, My wife did it. She didn't feel like cooking. There were hot dogs in the freezer, but instead of grilling them she decided to grill the house, to burn it down.

"Excuse me," she says, pushing past Paul, out the front door and into the yard.

The sun is high, the grass richly green. Mrs. Hansen has arranged things in neat rows like departments: men's, women's, boys', and household.

A stranger walking by turns to Elaine and says, "Fine idea. It's a beautiful day for a tag sale."

A woman picks up one of Elaine's old sweaters and holds it against herself. "What do you think?" the woman asks. "Is it me?" And before Elaine can answer, she continues, "I'll give you seven dollars for it? Enough?"

Elaine nods.

"Why don't we spread out the rest?" Mrs. Hansen suggests.

Why not?

Elaine goes back into the house. In the living room there's an end table that she hates, and a lamp, and then there's Daniel's broken toy chest, the old TV, and the love seat that used to be in the den.

"Can you give me a hand?" she asks a man she's never seen before.

"Sure," he says, helping her bring things out. "Here, let me get it, you go on ahead and open the door."

"I didn't feel like cooking," Elaine tells Mrs. Hansen, who, in addition to doing a brisk business at the yard sale, has found time to make another pot of coffee.

"That's the beginning and the end," Mrs. Hansen says, raising the pot. "Refill?" she asks.

"I lost my cup," Elaine says.

"No matter," Mrs. Hansen says, taking one off the dollar table and filling it. "Anyone else for coffee, fresh cup? There's a great Dior dress on aisle three," she tells someone.

"What size?" a woman asks.

"Six."

Daniel and Sammy stand by the maple tree drinking mugs of Mrs. Hansen's French roast.

"Isn't there anything else?" Elaine asks them. "No juice."

They shake their heads, rest their mugs by the roots of the tree, and take off, chasing each other around the yard.

"That can't be good for you," Elaine calls after them.

Friends and neighbors mill around, rubbernecking. "Terrifying," they say. "The flames were taller than the trees." They're frightened because as far as they're concerned it was an accident, an act of God, something that could happen to anyone at any time, no warning. And simultaneously they're relieved because it's not their house, it's not their stuff spread out on the grass, it didn't happen to them. Relief fills them with advice, ideas for renovation and redecoration. They go through the house pointing out the possibilities. "You could put in an island, a Subzero, more cabinets—there's no such thing as too much storage." A postmodern barn raising, the neighbors come bearing the names and numbers of contractors, carpenters, plumbers, and painters.

Elaine looks at Paul; he seems to be taking it all in his stride. Enjoying himself, soaking up the attention.

Henry arrives in tennis whites and stares at the black-ened edge of what used to be the living room wall. "Oh, oh," he says. "This is a nightmare. What happened? Don't tell me." His brow furrows. "Bomb?" he asks, and Paul shakes his head. "Hot-water heater?" Again, Paul shakes his head. Henry sweeps his racket through the scorched grass. The racket goes ka-thunk against something. Henry bends, plucking the can of starter fluid from the night before out of the grass with his free hand. "Dangerous," he says. "This is a four-hundred-dollar racket."

Paul's heart has stopped. He puts his hand to his chest and bangs. He does self-start CPR. He bangs and then he coughs. He clears his throat. He breathes. Paul is looking at the can in Henry's hand, thinking that now it has fresh prints, Henry's prints. If the investigator isn't happy with Paul and Elaine's story, Paul can always finger Henry. He coughs again, correcting the irregular rhythm of his heart.

"Choking?" Henry asks.

"Cinder."

"We had a date, a plan for a game?" Henry says, shaking the can; it's empty. He carries it to the trash and deposits it.

"The house burned down," Paul says, as though Henry can't possibly understand the responsibility involved.

Daniel and Sammy run by, trailing endless ribbons of cas-sette tape. "We're tying up the house," Daniel says.

"Holding it hostage," Sammy screams and then asks, "What's hostage?"

And Paul thinks of the yellow ribbon, the crime scene tape, the song, and still can't remember what it's all about.

"We've already gone around twenty-three times, haven't you noticed? Haven't you seen us?"

Henry's cell phone rings in his back pocket. He ignores it.

"Hey," Daniel says, running around again. "Hey, Henry, your butt's calling you, aren't you going to answer it?"

"It's her," Henry tells Paul, and immediately Paul knows it's the date. "She's the only one who has the number."

The phone stops ringing and then starts again. Henry takes the phone out of his pocket and hands it to Paul. "You talk to her," Henry says. "I think she likes you better."

Paul takes the phone. He turns away. He stands in the yard talking softly—it's like urinating in public, you try to be discreet. "Hello?"

"What are you wearing?" the date asks.

"Same as yesterday," Paul says, wondering if the date knows that it's him, not Henry.

"Is that a telephone in your pocket, or are you just glad to hear from me?" she asks.

"Can we call you back in a few minutes?" Paul asks.

"Don't call us, we'll call you," the date says, hanging up.

Paul hands the phone back to Henry.

"Keep it for a few days," Henry says. "Until your service is restored."

"Thanks," Paul says, slipping the phone in his pocket. "It may come in handy."

"It was a mistake," Paul says, passing Elaine in the upstairs hallway—it's the first moment they've had alone all day.

"Was it?" Elaine asks.

Paul has no answer. "I'm going to get the policy," he says. "The adjuster should be here any minute."

"If we lie, we could get caught, we could go to jail," Elaine says, tormenting him.

"We deserve to go to jail."

"And who'll take care of the kids? Who'll pay the bills? Someone has to earn a living around here, and it's not going to come from making license plates."

"We have to pay for our mistakes."

"I'll send you an itemized statement," Elaine says.

She goes back into the bedroom, rummages through Paul's drawers, his closet, and picks out a few suits, things she never wants to see him in again. She takes them down and lays them out on the front lawn.

"Times like these really pull you together," one of the neighbors says. "I'd like to buy your melon baller," he adds. "Will a dollar do it?"

Paul pulls Elaine aside. "The investigator's over there," he says, nodding in the direction of the State Farm man.

"Have you spoken with him?" Elaine asks.

"I told him we went out for dinner. I told him I set up the grill and then you went into the kitchen and there were only three hot dogs—three hot dogs, for four people. And we decided to go out."

"Yes, but how did the fire start? Isn't that what they're asking?"

"The boys must have been doing something, playing with matches," Paul says.

At first, Elaine is horrified that he would blame it on the children, but then it's a relief—at least he's not blaming her. "Playing, trying to get dinner ready?" she says.

"Yes, they were very hungry," he says.

"Starving," Elaine says. "And how did the grill tip over?"

"Wind," Paul says, shrugging, holding his hands up as if to say, go figure.

And for the moment they are together again, bound by their secret.

"Do you think everyone knows that we did it?" Elaine asks Paul.

"They're more interested in themselves than us."

"I was hoping we wouldn't have to come back."

"What did you think we'd do?"

"I didn't think."

"Well, what did you imagine?"

"I thought it would make us change," she says, "but we're the same. The same as we were yesterday."

"Worse."

"It has to get better," she says, and begins to cry.

"You can't control everything," Paul says.

Pat and George Nielson appear. "We've got to go," George says. "We have a little event to attend—a lunch for The Sons of the Fallen."

"Don't forget you're staying with us for the duration. If you get there and we're out . . ."

"Key's under the mat," George says, finishing her sentence.

Suddenly, there's screaming, a high-pitched howl. It's Mrs. Hansen. In their exuberant efforts to tie up the house, to choke it with cassette tape, Sammy and Daniel have roped in Mrs. Hansen. She'd gone in to get something, and now she can't get out.

"Call the police," she's yelling. "Call the police. Do something. Somebody do something."

Paul goes in through the basement, gets his hedge clippers, and quickly cuts her out. The boys are nowhere to be seen.

"Oh," she says. "I thought I was going to die. I have that, you know, death in small places, claustrophobia. I think I need a drink. What time is it? Is it too early to have a drink?"

"What would you like?" Elaine asks. "What would do the trick?"

"Oh, a splash of gin and maybe a whisper of vermouth— that's all I need, just a whisper."

Elaine makes Mrs. Hansen her drink and brings it out to her. Mrs. Hansen sits under the maple tree, her legs stuck straight out in front of her, and sips quickly. "Thank you," she says. "That's better now. That's much better. It's a beautiful day, isn't it? A good day for a sale." She digs into her pocket, pulls out a pile of cash, and presses it into Elaine's hands. "Buy yourself a secret something," she says. "You earned it." When her first drink is gone, Elaine makes her a second one and then a third, and by then the crowd is thinning and business is slacking off. The sky is getting dark, and it looks like rain.

Paul temporarily patches the hole in the living room wall with pieces of plastic. A police car comes by and closes down the sale, threatening to ticket Elaine for littering or loitering, she's not sure which. Elaine stuffs the leftovers into Hefty bags that she leaves at the end of the driveway. The wind billows, and the sky gets darker still.

Mrs. Hansen takes her empty coffeepot and toddles home. "I would have been over earlier, but last night . . ." she tells Elaine.

Elaine nods. "Thank you," she says. "Thank you for everything. The sale was a great idea, an inspiration."

"Thanks for the drink," Mrs. Hansen says.

And it begins to rain.

They are alone in their house: Paul, Elaine, Daniel, and Sammy. The children rummage through the kitchen like mice. They're crabby, coming down from their caffeine high. "We're hungry," they whine. Everything is damp and smells like smoke. Elaine is emptying the shelves, throwing boxes and cans away.

"You don't have to get rid of everything, do you?" Paul asks.

"Expired in 1994," Elaine says, hurling a can of beans into the trash.

Outside, a horn honks.

Daniel goes out. "It's Willy Meaders's mother," he says, coming back. "She invited me to their house, she said I can sleep over. Can I go? Can I?"

"Why not?" Elaine says.

Paul, Elaine, and Sammy are left in the kitchen. The wallpaper is suddenly peeling, the tiles have started coming up. As the hours pass, the damage gets worse, as though the house, having held itself together for so long, is finally relaxing from the spasm of the fire, letting go, giving up.

Where will it stop? Elaine wonders.

In the background, there is a strange drip-dripping sound.

"Is the adjuster coming back?" she asks.

"They said that in a few days it'll stabilize, it'll start to dry out. They'll check back," Paul says.

"A house is not a home," Elaine says.

Paul looks at Sammy. "How come no one's rescued you yet?"

"Dunno," Sammy says.

"Don't worry," Paul says, "someone will come." And like some slick bit of comic timing or psychic summoning, as he's saying it, the doorbell rings and it's Sammy's friend Nate and his mother.

"I'm sorry," Nate's mother says, so earnestly that Elaine is confused. "It's so awful," the woman goes on. "You must be devastated."

Paul comes up from behind.

"It's Nate's mom," Elaine says, introducing the woman, trying not to let on that she can't remember the woman's name.

Paul shakes the woman's hand. "Hello." She is his Mrs. Apple, his biweekly afternoon entertainment. They met at one of Sammy's soccer games; Elaine was down with the flu, and Nate's father was at a meeting in Minneapolis. Together they took the children to the McDonald's drive-thru and then sat in the parking lot, talking between their rolled-down windows for an hour and a half, before making a date for the following Saturday. That was ten months ago, and as far as Paul can tell, Elaine doesn't have a clue.

"I have no idea what you're planning," the woman says to Elaine, "but if there's anything I can do . . ." She pauses.

Nate, dressed head to toe in camouflage gear, has pressed himself flat against the peeling wallpaper.

"Don't think I can't see you, Mr. Invisible," Paul says. "I've got my eye on you."

"I could take Sammy for the night. I just rented *Bambi* for Nate."

"Seen it," Sammy says, watching Nate.

"Well, maybe you'd like to see it again," Paul suggests.

"We could go to the drive-thru, I bet you'd like that," Nate's mom says. "McNuggets and fries."

"You're hungry, aren't you?" Elaine says.

Sammy nods. Paul takes out his wallet and attempts to give Mrs. Apple money for the snacks. At first she declines. "Oh, you don't have to give me anything." But the truth of it is, Paul owes her thirty bucks—last week he didn't have enough cash, and she had to chip in for the motel. He hands her two twenties stuck together, hoping Elaine notices only one, and Mrs. Apple takes Sammy away.

THREE

PAUL AND ELAINE ARE ALONE. The children have been farmed out, given away to good homes like kittens. Inside the house, it gets darker and darker, and there is less and less they can do. They have forgotten that civilization is just across the street, that there is electricity next door. Finally, when they can't so much as see their fingers in front of their faces, they step outside. An afternoon shower has cleared the air. The sky is Prussian blue going into night.

Elaine tugs on Paul's belt loop, and they start walking toward the Nielsons' house. They could have driven, but it doesn't occur to them. The act of burning down their house has sent them back; it is as if their licenses have been revoked. They walk.

"Should we bring something?" Elaine asks.

"Like what?"

"A bottle of wine, a pie?"

Paul doesn't answer. They pass under a streetlight, Paul looks at Elaine, and then reaches for her arm and pulls back on it, like a blackjack handle, stopping her. He spits onto his fingers and rubs her face, again he licks his fingers and then rubs more. "You're all smudged," he says.

They walk on, the breeze lifting their clothing, the smell of smoke rising up as though they are smoldering, as though they are still on fire.

"Shortcut," Paul says, taking Elaine through various neighbors' yards. All the things that yesterday were so familiar, so comforting, now seem thoroughly foreign. They sneak through backyards like criminals, peering through kitchen windows to watch dinners being pulled from ovens, like a magician's trick—the rabbit from the hat.

A shift in the wind fills the air with the trailing spoor of a barbecue.

Elaine sniffs.

"The scent of guilt," Paul says, stumbling, swooning, his stomach spinning with anxiety.

"We're almost there. Isn't it lovely, Pat and George inviting us to stay over like this?"

"Have you ever heard anything about them?"

"About who?"

"George and Pat."

"Like what?"

"I don't know, things."

They turn the corner; the Nielsons' house is just ahead. "What kind of things?" Elaine asks.

"Never mind."

They are at the Nielsons' door. They ring the bell. They knock.

"Is this a game?" Elaine asks. "Are you doing this just to get me?"

Paul rings again. No answer.

"They said they'd leave a key under the mat," Elaine says, stepping back.

Paul lifts the mat.

"How can you do this? They're among our closest friends. They've invited us to come and stay with them—'For the duration,' Pat said."

"Don't blame me, I'm just repeating what I heard."

"What did you hear?"

"Nothing, just something, that there was something, no one knew exactly what."

"That's awful," Elaine says, stepping inside. "That's how rumors start—when people are too good or too nice, no one can stand it, they have to wreck it, undermine everything good."

The Nielsons' house is cool and still as though today was the maid's day and no one's come home yet to spoil it. The lamp hanging over the kitchen table glows. The refrigerator hums steadily. How much help does Pat have? That's what Elaine wants to know. The spotlessness, the absolute absence of chaos is otherworldly. Elaine and Paul walk silently in a loop, a crazy eight, through the living room, the dining room, into the kitchen and back again. Without hosts they don't know what to do. They are lost, without direction.

"Now what?" Paul asks.

"I can't believe you told me that about Pat and George," Elaine hisses.

"I didn't tell you, I asked you."

They're standing in the living room. Paul moves to sit on the sofa.

"Don't," Elaine says, grabbing his arm. "Your hands are dirty, you're covered in soot, you smell."

He escapes her. He wanders into the kitchen. She follows, making sure he doesn't do anything weird or wrong. "There's some food," he says, opening the refrigerator. "Do you think we could have a little snack?" She comes up from behind and closes the refrigerator door. His handprints are on it; she wipes them away with the edge of her blouse. "Wash your hands," she says.

There are canisters on the counter: tea, flour, sugar, a

cookie jar—three-quarters full. Everything is in perfect order. It's because they have girls, two girls instead of boys; girls are neater, Elaine tells herself. At Paul and Elaine's house the cookies don't even make it into the cookie jar; they go straight from the package to the mouth—the cookie jar is always empty.

With a dull rumble, a slow roll, the icemaker spills its cubes into the storage bin.

"Sit," Elaine says, and they sit at the kitchen table.

Slowly, as if breaking down, Paul asks, "Could I have some water?"

It's as though he has no standards, no boundaries, no sense of what's appropriate. Elaine rolls her eyes.

"Is that asking too much? I'm sure if Pat and George were here, they'd give me a glass of water. I bet George would give me a scotch. Why, I bet if I asked, he'd give me a whole bottle of my own."

Elaine gives him a glass of water, running it for a minute first to let it get cold, noticing how clean the sink is, how the stainless steel sparkles. She hands him the glass, then dries the sink with a paper towel and sits back down at the table.

"Is there something to eat, maybe some cheese? Crackers?"

"Why do you ask me? Do you need my permission? Are you so crippled that you can't do anything for yourself? Just wait," she says. "They'll be home soon."

"Don't hold me hostage," Paul says, remembering the game Sammy and Daniel were playing. "What's hostage?" Sammy had asked. "Do the kids know where we are?" Paul asks Elaine. "Does anyone know where we are?"

They hear the sound of a key in the door. "Behave," Elaine says.

"Anybody home?" Pat calls.

Elaine and Paul wait in the hallway.

"Sorry we're late," George says. "Time got out of hand."

"I hope you helped yourself. I hope you're not starving."

Pat slips out of her sweater and neatly hangs it in the front hall closet. "I'm so glad you're here," Pat says, giving Elaine's arm a little squeeze. "What would you like first?" Pat asks. "To get out of those clothes? Have a hot shower? Some dinner?"

"How 'bout a drink?" George asks. "A little refreshment? How would that be? A drink?"

The perfect pleasantness of Pat and George offering only the warmest welcome, hot water, drinks, the promise of a fine dinner and a good night's sleep, is overwhelming.

Elaine and Paul stand speechless. Their sullen steam, their tension, their bitterness and disgust rises up off them, evaporating like the heat of a sudden summer storm.

Pat and George are before them, dying to be accommodating, looking at Elaine and Paul as if to ask, What can we do for you? How can we best serve you? And their two children, Mary and Margaret, are right there next to their parents, beaming at Paul and Elaine, also offering themselves.

"Scotch?" George asks.

"I'd love one," Paul says, smirking at Elaine as if to say, Told you so.

"Elaine?" George asks.

"Something a little lighter."

"I've put you in Mary's room," Pat says, leading them down the hall. "The girls are doubling up for the duration."

"We like to share," Margaret, the younger, says. A wave of nausea sweeps over Elaine.

The walls of Mary's bedroom are a shade of pink that Elaine can identify only as vagina pink. There are two twin beds with quilted pink-satin bedspreads, a white lacquer dresser, a small white desk, and white lace curtains.

Fluffy white terry-cloth robes have been laid out on each bed, there are his-and-hers slippers on the floor, and on the dresser are individual toilet kits like the kind you get when you fly first class.

"If there's anything you need, I'm sure we have it," Pat says cheerfully.

"We have everything," Mary says. "We have everything," she repeats to get Elaine's attention.

Elaine smiles.

"And more," she adds happily.

"Your drinks," George says, handing them their glasses.

The ice clinks. Paul and Elaine sip quickly.

"And you can just throw your clothes in here." Pat puts a laundry basket on the floor at Elaine's feet.

There is something oddly forced about the way they're all crowded into the narrow bedroom, drinking. It's as though they are hurrying through a program, a required set of exchanges, in order to get on to the next thing, as though they've come in late and are rushing to catch up.

"Let's give them a minute," George says, backing off. "Everything doesn't have to happen all at once."

"We're just so glad you're here," Pat says.

And then, as if leaving them to prepare for some kind of treatment or procedure, Pat and George step out of the room. Elaine and Paul are left alone, drinks in hand. Paul takes a couple of large swallows and puts his glass down on the dresser. Elaine quickly picks it up, wipes the dresser, and tucks a book under the glass. Paul sits on the edge of the bed and pulls off his shoes. Elaine is about to move in, about to suggest that he not sit on the satin spread.

"Fuck off," he says, seeing it coming. "Just fuck off."

They undress silently, awkward in the deep pink, towering over the furniture, which is scaled for a child. Here they are giants, oafish and clumsy. They peel off their clothing and see that it is soiled with the heavy soot of charcoal gone awry. Thick bracelets of grime wrap their wrists and ankles. Elaine, embarrassed, stands in her bare feet; her toes—the red-hot polish of an old pedicure three-quarters chipped away—curl into the plush pink carpet. She waits in her bra and panties, hesitant to go further, to drop her private garments into the basket.

"Take it off, take it all off," Paul says, stepping out of his B.V.D.'s.

Reluctantly, she unfastens her bra and pulls down her panties, hiding her underwear at the bottom of the basket. "They should be boiled," Elaine says, "or burned like something contaminated."

Elaine pulls the belt of her white terry robe tight around her waist as Paul opens the bedroom door. Pat and George are waiting in the hall. Elaine wonders what would have happened if she and Paul had decided to lie down for a few minutes, to take a little nap—would Pat and George have knocked and said, "We're waiting"? She wonders what would have happened if they'd had a fight—would they have rapped against the door and said, "Break it up"? She wonders if they were listening. . . .

"You look better already," Pat says, leading Elaine down the hall to the middle bathroom.

George steers Paul through their bedroom to the master bath. "Plenty of towels for you," he says, pointing to a huge stack.

They shower. Elaine washes her hair with shampoo that smells like apples. She watches the dirt running off, gray water rushing for the drain. She washes her hair three times, then slathers it with cream rinse that sings of citrus. She turns the water hotter and then hotter still, washing, washing, obsessed with scrubbing herself clean.

In Pat and George's shower, away from Elaine, Paul is unleashed, able to assert himself. His scalp, coated in a layer of fuzz, itches. He lathers up and, using Pat's Lady Light leg razor, works in strips, sweeping over his head, around his ears, and down his neck. He gets carried away and moves on to his arms and legs, trimming his chest down to the primal pattern, scraping his armpits and groin. Aerodynamic and unburdened, Paul feels free from certain worries and boundaries. Stepping out, he takes great care to rinse the tub, to wash away the evidence, the fur, the feathers that flew.

Back in the room, Elaine is famished. There are ten Hershey Kisses in the pencil tray on Mary/Margaret's desk. Elaine takes two and then two more, balling the aluminum foil into tiny pebbles, minimizing the evidence. The chocolate is melting in her mouth when Paul comes in. He grabs her and kisses her—his mouth is minty-fresh. She slips a half-gone Hershey Kiss into his mouth—the chocolate and mint combo is refreshing. They laugh. They make out until the flavor has faded. While they were showering, clothing was laid out on their beds—sweat suits, socks, underwear. They have entered a new regime, a cult of perfection and procedure.

"Wrong size," Elaine says. "It's not even the fucking right size," she blurts.

"It's about learning to let go," Paul says, pulling on his sweat suit. Extra fabric pools at his ankles. He rolls up the legs and sleeves.

There is a knock, the rap-rapping of a little fist on the door, and one of the girls calls, "Dinner."

The table is set beautifully—crystal glasses, delicate china, shining silver. Paul and Elaine sit in their sweats, in their oversize pajamas like children who have been allowed to stay up late. George waits patiently at the head of the table. And when his wife and daughters are ready, he thrusts a two-pronged fork deep into the roast. Bloody juice springs out of the browned round— tiny droplets splash onto the white tablecloth. They all notice.

George stops carving. "Do you want to get that?" he asks, his voice edged with panic.

"I can get it later," Pat says calmly, indicating that he should keep carving. "I have my ways."

She has made a roast, she has made potatoes, she has made glazed carrots and string beans almandine. She has made sure there are hot rolls and crisp salad, and that everything is just right; nothing is early or late, nothing is raw or burned.

How does Pat do it? Elaine needs to know. The roast wasn't cooking when Elaine and Paul got there, it wasn't even out on the counter defrosting. And when did Pat do the potatoes and the carrots? The string beans definitely aren't frozen—where did Pat find them? Elaine hasn't seen string beans in the store for months. She understands the rolls, and that's a comfort. They're from a tube, the kind you crack on the counter and the dough pops out, but still . . . And the kitchen isn't a mess; just before they sat down, Elaine poked her head in and asked Pat if she needed a hand, and Pat was already cleaning up, drying the pots and pans.

"Saves time," Pat said.

And so Paul and Elaine sit at Pat and George's table, in silence, as though their personas were lodged in their possessions, in their clothing, which Elaine hears tumbling in the dryer—the buttons of Paul's pants scraping. They dine, dipped in the devastating confirmation that everything they ever suspected about how much better the lives of the neighbors are has been proven true. Everyone else is more organized, happier, their lives less fraught, more satisfying. Without a doubt, other people do it better.

The fraud factor is what Paul calls it, the fear of being revealed. Paul and Elaine already knew it, and in fact, setting the fire was on some level a declaration of their awareness, the great and formal announcement: This is not who we are, we are not like you, we have failed, we are failing, we are failures. And yet, this is exactly who they are; they are not different at all. They are exactly the same as everyone else, and worse yet, they are trapped in it, entirely engulfed—this is their life.

They chew. They cut their meat. Paul eats heartily while Elaine eats dutifully. They eat their vegetables and listen as the Nielsons talk.

"If I start now, by Thanksgiving I'll be good enough to compete," Mary says, going on about skating lessons. "Joy Reckling did it. She took lessons, and now she skates all over the place. I bet if I worked hard I could skate as well as she does."

"You'll skate even better," George says.

"You'll be the best," Pat says.

All their dreams laid out, and George and Pat just say yes, and good, and great. Up, up, and away. They don't say, No, you must be crazy, and What the hell are you thinking? Nothing is out of range, everything is possible.

"I've been wanting to move the lilac bush—it's not thriving where I've got it now," George says. "If I put it somewhere else, it'll be happier. I like my bushes to be happy. The azaleas seem delirious, don't they?" Pat winks at George, and he grins back at her.

Paul is no longer smiling. He and Elaine sit staring down at their plates, ashamed. At their house things don't go like this; nothing is easy; it's every man for himself, each hoarding what little he has, each wanting his own, each wanting something different. They speak in the defensive. They wait for disappointment. They constantly accumulate proof of having been let down, misunderstood, unappreciated. They are a tense and bitter lot, and haven't even noticed it until now. Compare and contrast; the differences are so revealing.

"Decaf?" Pat stands over her with a pot of steaming coffee. "Decaf?"

"Please," Elaine says, raising her cup.

A plate of cookies is passed around. "Ummmm," Elaine says. She takes one. Paul takes one, then two, then three more.

"Delicious. Did you make these?" Elaine asks, expecting Pat to say that she whipped them up this afternoon just after she put the roast in. Elaine blithers on, spitting a slew of compliments, a kind of Tourette's syndrome in reverse. She goes on, using what she says aloud to beat herself up mentally. She should be more like Pat, she should get more done, she should be much better than she is, she should be more . . . There is no interrupting her.

In the end Pat blushes. "I didn't make them," she says apologetically.

"We did," the two little M&M's chirp.

"Well, what wonderful bakers you are," Elaine says, starting again, whacking her brain, for not baking, for not doing anything right, for not doing anything at all. "How wonderful you are," she says. How awful I am, she thinks. Elaine reaches for another cookie. "Ummm, so good," she says. You fat thing, you should be on a diet, she tells herself.

The girls giggle.

Elaine smiles.

Dinner is done. While Mary and Margaret clear the table, Pat and George lead Elaine and Paul back down the hall, getting them set for bed.

"There's a little light down here," George says, pointing to a night-light in the hallway. "If you need anything, holler."

"I couldn't cook," Elaine blurts. She is feeling as if she has to explain.

"It's all right," Pat says.

Elaine and Paul close the bedroom door. There's a nightgown on one bed and a pair of pajamas on the other. Elaine opens the door again. Pat and George are gone. Elaine doesn't understand where it comes from, how it happens. Her interest goes beyond the standard housewife competitiveness and into thinking that Pat and George must be shape shifters. Elaine was with them all evening and never saw Pat or George leave the table. Is there a hidden housekeeper? Do little Borrowers live beneath the floorboards? What explains it? Who does this?

Paul's back is toward her. He is wearing the nightgown. It stops just above his knees. She sees he has shaved his legs, there are nicks on the backs of his calves.

"You look very pretty."

"Thank you. I feel pretty."

"I've never seen you in a dress before."

"It was on my bed."

Elaine goes to the other bed, takes off her sweat suit and puts on the pajamas, dressing herself as though she's a paper doll—cuffing the bottoms, buttoning the buttons. She lays herself out on the satiny pink bedspread, resting her head gently on the pillow. She crosses her hands over her chest, closes her eyes, and imagines this is the look, the feel, of a coffin. Paul lies down next to her, squeezing onto the same narrow bed. She gets up. She puts a chair against the door and goes back to the bed.

"What about the boys?" he says. "Should we be calling them? Should we be saying good night? Do you have numbers for where they are?"

"Do you?" she asks back.

"No."

"Not even Nate's mother's?"

He blushes. Heat spreads through his face, his neck. He imagines his bald head glowing like a knob, a nut of molten glass—she can see right through him.

"No," he says.

"Liar."

There's nothing for Paul to say. He waits. "Should we check our machine at home?"

"Someone bought the machine this afternoon for five dollars."

They hear Pat and George talking through the wall—getting ready for bed, muffled voices, half sentences, arrangements, sleepy plans.

"It's a lot," Paul says.

"Too much for one day," Elaine says.

And they are quiet for a while.

"Home," Paul says. "Home," he repeats like an incantation. And then he stops. He seems to rally, to rouse himself. "Why'd we do it?" he asks.

"We did it because there was nothing else we could do."

The night-light has a pink bulb. It casts pink light on the pink walls. The room glows, pulsing like an organ. Paul is thinking of the date, of the cell phone in his pocket. He called her before from the bathroom—she wasn't home. The outgoing message on her machine said, "Hi, I can't come right now. . . ."

Paul's gown begins to puff, to rise like a tent. His cock swells, making the nightgown the big top of his three-ring circus.

"Fuck me," he hisses at Elaine.

He climbs on top of her. The twin bed squeaks.

"We're awful," she says from under him. "We're worse than we thought we were, worse than anyone I've ever met." Her breath is slightly muffled by his weight.

"We couldn't be that bad," he says.

"Couldn't we?"

They slide off the bed and onto the floor. They are in the gully between the beds, deep in the pink shag carpet. He hikes up his dress, she lets out the drawstring of her pajama bottoms. They toss and turn. She is facedown, gripping the carpet threads, thinking they are like the cilia that line the throat, the ear, the lungs. She is traveling, like in the movie *Fantastic Voyage,* she is moving through the body, the bloodstream. The satin trim of Paul's nightgown tickles her back.

When they are done, she pulls up her bottoms. She cinches the drawstring tight. His hot squirt is oozing out of her, seeping down her thighs. "Good night," she says, getting back into bed.

"Good night," he says, as though they are strangers.

She takes a book from the night table and begins to read from *A Wrinkle in Time.* " 'Go back to sleep,' Meg said. 'Just be glad you're a kitten and not a monster like me.' "

Paul is up in the night.

He is awake and he is hungry. He puts on a robe and goes tiptoeing into the kitchen. She is there, in her pajamas at the table.

"Hi, honey," he says.

"Hello, Paul," she says.

He realizes it's Pat, not Elaine. Pat is at the table wearing pajamas, making lists, graphs, working furiously in pencil. "Sit," she says, tucking her pencil behind her ear.

Paul pulls the belt of his robe tighter, worrying that somehow she will know he's wearing a nightgown. He sits.

She puts four cookies on a plate and warms a glass of milk for him. "I don't sleep," she says. "If anyone ever wants to know how I do it—that's how. I'm up all night. I work ahead. I plan things months in advance. Knowing what's going to happen relaxes me."

He nods. He eats his cookies.

"I sleep from twelve to three and work from three to six, then I nap from six to seven."

She goes back to her charts and graphs, her menus. She has it all figured out, shopping lists of what she needs to buy on what day, how long things take to cook, and, given the family's schedules, which night is better to make stew, which is better for lamb chops, etc. She erases an entire week and redoes it.

"You missed some brussels sprouts," he says, pointing to a Tuesday.

"Back to bed, mister," Pat says when Paul's snack is gone. "You've got a couple of hours to go." She leads Paul back down the hall and opens the bedroom door. He goes in without a word, and she closes the door behind him.

Morning. A borrowed suit hangs on the doorknob. A freshly pressed white shirt is draped over the chair.

"I thought I put the chair against the door," Elaine says.

"I was up in the night," Paul says, stretching. He is refreshed. Chirpy.

She resents it.

There's a knock on the door. They throw on the robes.

"Mummy asked me to bring you this," one of the little M's says, delivering Paul and Elaine's clean clothing, pressed, folded, practically packaged. "She's busy making waffles. Do you like waffles?"

"No," Elaine says, taking the clothing from the little girl. "No, I really don't."

"You lose," the little girl says, closing the door.

"What's your problem?" Paul riffles through the clothes, pulling out his underwear, still warm from the dryer. "You should be grateful."

"What's your problem?" she asks. "Since when are you Mr. Bluebird of Happiness?"

Paul tries on the suit jacket—one of George's. It's small. Paul's arms jut out of the sleeves, the shoulders ride up.

"George must be a runt," Elaine says. "You look like an idiot."

He ignores her and climbs into the pants. He likes that he is bigger than George; it makes him feel powerful. He zips up.

"You're not leaving me, are you?" she blurts.

"Leaving you?" He unconsciously mirrors her anxious tone, her flood of anxiety.

"Why are you wearing that suit? What do you think you're doing? Where are you going?"

"I'm going to work."

"Our house burned down," she says. "You helped."

"It was a holiday weekend. Today I'm going to work. I have a job. I have to earn money. This is going to cost us. I have no choice. You need to come up with a plan," he says. "That's how you'll free yourself. Act normal."

"I don't feel normal. I have an incredible headache."

"If you act normal, you'll feel normal. Get dressed and take some aspirin," Paul says. "We'll have breakfast with them, and then I'll walk you home."

"I can't have breakfast. I can't have waffles." Elaine is whining. She can't be good. She can't take any more perfection. She doesn't want to go home, and she doesn't want to be left with Pat. She can't win. She's afraid that she's going to scream. For the first time in years, she is clinging to Paul—he is what defines her, he is familiar. Without Paul, Elaine's head will explode. She can picture it: There will be an enormous and ugly eruption. Human splatter. Pat will be the witness, and without a pause she will rush to get her rags, her bottles of Fantastik and 409. As fast as it happened she'll be at it, wiping up, as though it's just another household spill, all in a day's work. Spic and Span.

"Come on, we'll have some juice and then we'll go. Why don't you make a list of things to do?"

"Did something happen during the night? Did you have a personality transplant?" Elaine asks.

"It's just common sense," he says. "You have to step back, get some perspective. Everything is fine. Nothing has changed, nothing is different."

She is silenced. Nothing has changed. Nothing is different. Is that a good thing or a bad thing?

*   *   *

"Sleeves are too short," George says to Paul when they go into the kitchen. "Other than that, you're okay."

"Waffles?" Pat asks. "With or without fresh fruit?"

Elaine looks at Paul, knowing he wants waffles, knowing he could eat two or three, doused in fruit, drenched in syrup.

"Juice and coffee," Paul says. "That's it for me, just juice and coffee."

"And you?" Pat asks.

"Coffee would be great, and a couple of aspirin," Elaine says.

Paul also has a muffin. It's there on the table in a basket. He takes it. He butters it. He looks at Elaine guiltily. She smiles. He's cute. His bald top has a shine, a glow like the dome of a state capitol. She's seeing something boyish and lovable in Paul, something she hasn't seen in a long time.

"Hurry," the little M's tell each other. "Hurry, let's not be late."

Elaine braces herself against their enthusiasm by thinking about her own children. "It's seven o'clock," she announces every morning like a human cuckoo clock. "It's seven-fifteen, you're going to be late. Seven-thirty, you're in trouble." She has to pull back the bedclothes and make them cold and uncomfortable before anything happens. "I've made you a nice hot Pop-Tart, burned on the edges, just the way you like it. Do you want some cocoa? Some chocolate milk?" She gets them going the cheap way, glucose, sucrose. If they pass out once they're at school, at least she got them there. She wonders what they are doing right now—are they behaving, are they making some other mother's life miserable, are they happy?

"Bye-bye," the angelic M's say, kissing their parents good-bye, flying off with their knapsacks strapped to their backs like ballast.

Elaine finishes her coffee and puts the cup down. Paul drains the dregs of his juice glass—fresh-squeezed.

"What time will you be home?" Pat asks.

They all stop. Who is being spoken to? George? Paul? Elaine? There is a long pause.

"We're usually home by seven," Elaine finally says.

"That works," Pat says.

Outside. The grass is green. The sky is bright. The air cool and fresh, like water. It is as though they've woken from a dream. The dew on the lawn soaks their shoes; they squeak across the grass and leave footprints on the sidewalk. They move quickly, race-walking toward home, arms and legs pumping.

They have escaped.

Paul and Elaine speak quickly, as though they haven't spoken in weeks, as though they haven't been able to talk until now.

"I had fun last night," Paul says, confessing his pleasure. "I like wearing a nightgown. It's loose, liberating."

"We'll have to get you one of your own."

"And she makes good coffee," Paul says, romanticizing their adventure. In his mind he's back at Pat's—Pat taking care of everything, Pat in her pajamas in the middle of the night, Pat with the cookies and milk.

"Better coffee than mine?"

"Not better, just good."

As they walk, they get quieter. Their conversation loses its structure; it turns into odd single words, huffed, puffed, spoken as though spit out. They are going uphill.

The school bus passes them. A face is pressed to the glass. Sammy waves. They don't see him until it is too late. They wave after the bus.

They are more together and less together than ever before. They are close, but as they get near the house, they drift. He moves out ahead of her. He is going forward. She is falling back. She is running out of air. The house is haunted, it will turn on her. She is expected to take care of it, to nurse it, to love it, to coach it back to health. She hates the house. She is afraid of the house. She doesn't want to be left there. She would rather go into the city with Paul, would rather go to a museum, wander, go shopping.

"Should I come with you?" she asks.

"Where?"

"I don't want to go home," she says.

"Things have to be fixed, Elaine. The children need a place to come home to."

Her anxiety. She is having an anxiety attack. Her heart is racing. Her hands are clammy. She thinks she is dying. Drowning. She runs. She runs across the street. Paul follows her. He thinks it is a joke, a game; she is running from him, wanting him to chase her.

She runs faster.

"Hey, hey," he says, catching her, stopping her.

Her eyes are fierce, wild.

He pulls her toward him and holds her pressed against his body. "You're okay," he says, even though he is frightened. "It'll be okay," he says, guiding her back to their side of the street. "It's just the shock. The shock is hitting you."

Home.

Her mother's car is parked on the street. He is relieved. "Your mother is here," he says. "Everything is going to be all right."

Mother is here. Mother will take care of it. Everything will be good again. An early incantation.

"Are you going to be at work all day?" Elaine asks Paul.

"Where else would I be?" He wonders what she's getting at. Does she know that sometimes he goes places—to see people, Mrs. Apple, etc.?

"I just need to be able to reach you. What if I have a question about the house?"

"Why don't I give you Henry's cellular." He hands over the phone. "My office is on autodial. I'm auto 0-2."

"Who's auto 0-1?"

"Henry," he says. It's never occurred to him that the phone has information, things it can tell him about the date. Who's 0-3? he wonders, and 0-4, and 0-5? The memory holds 99 numbers—who's 99?

Elaine's mother is waiting on the lawn. "I've been calling you since Saturday night," the mother says. "There was never any answer. I got worried, and so I came. What happened?"

"We burned the house down," Elaine says.

"I see," the mother says. "I thought something must have happened. Your yard looks like a million people trampled through. I thought maybe you had a crazy party. Well, I tried to call," the mother says. "I needed to talk. When I talk to you, I feel better."

"It's supposed to be the other way around," Elaine says.

"Whenever I talk to your father, when I try to have a serious conversation with him, he turns on the TV. You were away."

"We had a fire," Paul says. "We're staying with friends."

"What happened to your answering machine?"

"We sold it."

"Well, I wanted your opinion. I came home the other day and your father—"

"The house burned down," Elaine says, interrupting.

"I saw. I couldn't help but notice. I walked around the back—there's a huge hole in the dining room wall."

The three of them stand on the front lawn, waiting. Paul checks his watch. "I have to go," he says.

"Guess so," Elaine says.

He gives Elaine a quick kiss on the cheek. It's the first

time he's kissed her good-bye in years. "Have a nice day," he says, walking off.

"Is Paul not well?" the mother asks.

"In what way?" Elaine asks.

"What happened to his hair? He looks like he's getting chemo."

"Oh, that," Elaine says. "That's what they do. When it starts to go, they go with it. They get rid of it. Better bald than balding."

"He's a shaved fish."

"It's a control thing," Elaine says.

There's a pause.

"I was worried," the mother repeats. "I tried to call. There was no answer."

Paul walks toward the train. His mind wanders, it races. He thinks about Henry and the date; why is Henry so willing to share? He thinks about Mrs. Apple, about Sammy waving from the bus. He thinks about Pat and the pajamas and Elaine on the floor last night, pulling out a big tuft of the pink shag carpet. Fucking.

He passes house after house. From a distance Paul sees someone coming down a driveway, an old guy with a walker. He hears the wheels of the walker squeaking as if teasing. The old guy holds on tight, taking the driveway with the full concentration of a skier taking a downhill slope. Paul watches, trying to decide if the guy broke his hip, had a stroke, or both— had a stroke and fell, breaking the hip.

The man sees him, lifts his head, takes one hand off the walker, and sweeps it through the air in a large, floppy greeting.

Paul is two houses away and closing in.

"Did ya see the tatas on Miss October?" the man calls out. "Big ones. You think those were implants? Hey, what do you know about nipples? What happens to the nipples when they put in implants?" The man is shouting. His voice, cracked with age, is surprisingly strong. Embarrassed, Paul looks around; there are no people, no one can hear. He stops at the end of the driveway.

"Morning," Paul says.

"George?" the man asks, looking at him strangely, already disappointed, already almost sure that Paul is not George.

"I'm Paul."

"I thought you were someone," the man says. "I thought you were George." He leans over the walker toward Paul. "Do you know him, George Nielson?"

"This is his suit," Paul says, pulling at his lapel.

"Well, no wonder," the man says, beaming with relief. "My eyes aren't too good, but they're not too bad either. I thought you were George."

"I'm Paul."

"The fella whose house got toasted?"

"That's me."

"Good to meet you. I'm McKendrick. Walter Mc-Kendrick." They shake hands. McKendrick settles in on his walker and heads down the sidewalk with Paul. "Going to the train?"

"Yep."

"I can't stand not getting up and out first thing. Makes me feel dead. No matter what, I go out. I go down the driveway, around the block and back. Rain or shine. So, what do you know about nipples?" the old guy asks. "How do they handle that? Used to be there was no such thing as implants; you either had tits or you didn't. Now you can get 'em big as the Good-year Blimp. They got whole magazines of big tits—George showed me."

So George has some juice in him. Thank God. Paul laughs.

"What'd you say your name was?" the old guy asks.

"Paul."

"You going to the train?"

"Yeah."

"Getting kind of a late start." The guy checks his watch. "Nine-eighteen. You won't get in before ten-thirty, quarter of eleven."

"It's the day after a holiday."

"Doesn't matter what day it is. Punctuality counts. You never caught me late for work."

Paul changes the subject. "What happened?" he asks, gesturing to the walker. "Was it an accident?"

"Well, it certainly wasn't intentional, if that's what you're getting at. Busted my ass, pardon my French, but it's true. Two years ago, Grand Central Station, I was running to catch the train home. Lost my footing, fell down a flight of marble stairs, almost did myself in. Seventy-four years old—it gave them a great excuse to put me out to pasture. I got pins in my ass now, no joking. Pins in my ass, in my hip, in my leg. It's my punishment for all the nights I worked late. I would have died at my desk if I could have. That's where my life was. That's where I was happy." They come to an incline, a long rolling hill. "I can't go down with you," McKendrick says. "Much as I might like to. I did it once and couldn't get back up. I had sit down there and wait for someone to rescue me. A lady in a station wagon brought me back up to the top. He stops. "I'm exhausted. I'm going home." He starts the slow pivot, the four-point choreographed move that turns the walker around. "Stop by sometime, I'll show you a few things. I've got quite a collection."

"I will," Paul says, waiting, feeling he should keep an eye on the old guy, make sure he crawls home safely.

"Go," McKendrick says, swatting Paul away, pushing him off. "Don't miss the train."

Paul checks his watch. It's 9:27. The train comes at 9:35. Paul still has a long way to go. The old guy is right, he can't

miss the train. He can't be any later; he is already late. He starts
to run.

"Atta boy," the old guy yells after him. "That's the way
you do it."

Elaine and her mother go into the house.

"Open everything," her mother says, making grand gestures with the windows and doors. "It smells. It smells," she
shouts as she works.

Elaine is in a daze, a stew. Has anyone ever listened to her?
Has anyone ever asked what she wanted? Has she ever thought
to tell? Elaine tries to open the window over the kitchen sink.
She bangs on it, pounds at it. Bam! Bam! Her hand almost goes
through the glass.

"Work it gently," her mother says. "When something's
stuck, you have to work it gently."

Elaine does, and the old casement frame pops open.

"Do you have apples and cinnamon? That's what they do
in houses that are for sale. They put a pot of cider and cinnamon
on the stove, and buyers think the place is cozy."

Her mother opens the fridge. The stench of things going
bad pours out. She closes it.

Elaine goes upstairs, opening windows everywhere.

In the master bedroom, which is directly above the dining
room, Elaine notices a small hole in the ceiling—a puncture
straight through to the roof. It's like a pinhole camera. Through
it she can see the sky, a spot of the bluest blue. A cloud passes
over and then an airplane and then it's gone. Everything is in
constant motion, and she is standing still.

"Open sesame." She hears her mother talking to herself
downstairs.

She notices Paul's briefcase, pushed into the corner. She
pulls out the cell phone and dials the Nielsons. "Paul went off

without his briefcase," Elaine tells George. "I was hoping you might bring it to him in the city. Thank God you haven't left."

"Not a problem. No big deal. It's nothing," George says, his repetitions, his disclaimers all indications that it is in fact a favor. "I'm just getting in the car now. See you in a minute."

She pushes "End," then dials Daniel's school. "I need to leave a message. Could you please tell Daniel Weiss to come home, to his mother's house, after school."

"Who am I speaking with?" the school secretary asks, suddenly suspicious.

"His mother," Elaine says.

"And your name is?"

"Elaine. Elaine Weiss." She starts to say something about the house burning down.

"What's your address?" the secretary asks, cutting her off.

"Is there a problem?"

"We just have to be very careful. One moment, please."

She is on hold. The phone, pressed to her ear, is beginning to heat up. Her ear is burning.

"Elaine," the woman says, coming back, speaking as though they're old friends. "You're fine. I'll send the message—Daniel is to come home, to his mother's house, after school."

End. Elaine touches her ear. It's hot. Is a cell phone like a dental x-ray, something where the exposure should be limited?

The phone rings. It rings and simultaneously vibrates in Elaine's hand.

"Is that the phone?" her mother calls. "Is the phone fixed?"

Elaine flips the phone open.

"I've been trying to reach you all morning," a woman's voice says. "What are you wearing?"

Elaine looks down at herself. "Dirty clothes."

There's a pause. "Aren't you going to ask me what I'm wearing."

"What are you wearing?" Elaine asks.

"Are you speaking to me?" her mother calls in from the other room.

"Nothing," the woman says.

"Elaine?" her mother calls.

"No," Elaine says to her mother.

"Yes," the woman says.

"What number are you dialing?"

"Yours," the woman says.

"Elaine, did I hear the phone?"

"I have to go," Elaine says, starting down the stairs, briefcase in hand. "My mother is calling me."

"I'll call again later."

"I thought I heard you talking to someone." Her mother is in the kitchen. She has tied a dish towel over her nose and mouth, like a bandit. The place reeks of fire and Shalimar.

"I had to smell something decent," her mother says. "I emptied my atomizer—you'll buy me a new bottle for my birthday."

Elaine nods.

"May I?" her mother asks, taking the cell phone from Elaine. "I should call the phone company, also the electric, and I should call your father to let him know everything is all right. How do you turn this thing on?"

"It's turned on," Elaine says. "Just put in the area code and the number and push 'Send.' Could you call Sammy's school and tell them to make sure he comes home?"

Elaine flashes on the image of Sammy on the bus, waving— how could they not have seen him?

Outside, George beeps. Elaine grabs the briefcase and hurries.

"Take the trash," her mother says, pointing to the pile of garbage bags by the door.

An old blue Mustang drives by. The car passes Elaine and

then backs up. The driver is a woman wearing a navy-blue floral scarf over her hair and dark sunglasses.

"Hi," she says. "Isn't it great?"

Elaine comes closer to the car. "Sorry?" she says blankly.

"The dress." The woman pulls at her dress—it's Elaine's blue Dior, the one Mrs. Hansen sold yesterday.

"Oh," Elaine says. "It's great."

"And look what I got in Elmhurst." The woman points to a blue Dior purse lying on the car seat.

"Wow," Elaine says, "you're a great shopper." There's a phone mounted between the bucket seats. "And you have a car phone."

"Couldn't live without it. It's a lifesaver. Well, gotta go," the woman says.

Elaine is left at the curb, wondering, Was that her—the mystery caller? It makes sense; the phone, the fixation on clothing. Elaine goes back into the house.

"I've done my duty," her mother says, still holding the phone. "Sammy's coming home, the phone company is on the way, the electricity will be on before dark."

The cell phone rings. Elaine sees it vibrate in her mother's open hand.

"I don't know if I like that," her mother says. It rings again. "Should I answer it? Hello?"

Elaine watches her mother's face—is it the woman calling again?

"A blouse and a skirt," her mother says, and Elaine moves to take the phone away. Her mother brushes her off. "Gray, or more a kind of taupe." A pause. "No, I don't think we've spoken before. Are you a friend of my daughter's? She's right here." Another pause. "Dirty clothes."

"Mother," Elaine says.

Her mother holds her hand up, silencing Elaine. "Umm. Ummmmm," the mother says, listening carefully. She blushes.

"Mother," Elaine says again, embarrassed by the pink flush in her mother's cheeks.

"Well," her mother finally says, "that all sounds fine, but I don't think we're interested. Thank you." She turns to Elaine. "How do you hang it up?"

"Press 'End.' Who was that?"

"I don't know. At first I thought it was some sort of survey, and then it got a little odd."

"Did it sound like she was calling from a car?"

"No. No, I don't think so," her mother says. "Is your number listed?"

"It's not our phone. It belongs to Henry."

"Well, then that's it. Turn it off," her mother says. And she does.

Paul is on the train, watching the other men drink their coffee and read their fan-folded papers. He is thinking of McKendrick, at home with pins in his ass, flipping through porno magazines. Paul is glad to be on the train, glad to be going to work. He remembers McKendrick's papery voice—"I would have died at my desk if I could have."

Paul thinks of the house, of leaving Elaine and her mother on the lawn, abandoning everything. He hasn't told anyone, but he is afraid of the house, too. He doesn't know how it will get fixed. He's afraid that something irrevocably horrible has happened, something he doesn't yet understand. What they did was so incredibly impulsive, so willfully destructive, and so strangely thrilling that he scared himself. Everything is fine, he tells himself, repeating what he said to Elaine this morning.

Make a list. He reaches for his briefcase—he doesn't have it. He has nothing. It is as though he is seven years old and has forgotten his lunch. Naked, unprepared, panicked. The train pulls into the Fordham stop, and he thinks of jumping off, turning around, taking the next train home and getting his briefcase. He checks his watch—late. He doesn't even know where the briefcase might be. Is it in the house, in the front hall by the coat closet, or did Elaine "accidentally" sell it at the yard sale? If so, what did the price include? When he gets to the office, will someone else be sitting at his desk?

"Excuse me," he says to the fellow sitting next to him. "Could I borrow a pen?" The man hands Paul a pen, and Paul writes on his hand. Insurance. Stonemason. Painter.

"You forgot Baker, Banker, or Indian Chief," the man says.

"Pardon?"

"I used to do that all the time. I hated my job, and on my way to work I would make lists of all the other things I could do."

"Oh," Paul says.

"And then I gave up all hope of fruition." The man smiles warmly. "Bob Becker," he says, extending a hand. "CEO Pathways International."

"Pharmaceuticals?"

"That's the story—mental medication, smart drugs, target your transmitters, re-uptake inhibitors. And you are?"

"Paul. Paul Weiss," Paul says, handing back the pen.

"Ah, and Rifkind?" the man asks, as though this were a Beckett play. There is an air of unreality about him; everything means something, and then it also means something else.

"No Rifkind," Paul says. And "Rifkind" comes out sounding like a word, a word that means something, like—"Pretty good, and yourself?"

"Let's take a look at your list," Becker says, eyeing Paul's hand.

"It's not really a job list," Paul says, holding his hand close to his chest. "It's more along the lines of things I've got to remember to do, things to be taken care of."

"Well then, let's look at your palm." Becker tugs at Paul's

hand, spreading the fingers, rubbing the seat, the heart, the soft spot in the middle, blurring Paul's notes just a little bit. "Interesting . . ." Becker says. "You've got a lot going on and a lot more to look forward to."

As the train pulls into Grand Central Station, Becker pulls Paul's hand closer still, pressing his lips into Paul's palm. "Good to meet you, my friend," he says. "All good luck."

There is the rush to exit the train. Paul is jostled, caught in the moment that just passed. His palm is tickling, reeling from the kiss—was it a kiss?

He rises up on his toes and looks for Becker, but Becker is gone.

On the subway, Paul tries to forget what happened. He thinks about work. He is looking forward to hunkering down behind his desk—regrouping, organizing. He will take the bull by the horns. He will make lists, phone calls, appointments. His chest is tight. He rushes to get to the office. If he can just get to the office—tag base—he will be okay. He will talk to people. He will ask their advice, he will ask them for names of other people, people who can help him, people who can fix things. He wipes his palm back and forth on his thigh.

"Good morning," his secretary says as he comes through the door.

"Nice suit," a woman from a higher floor says.

"Thank you," Paul says, forgetting that the suit belongs to George.

He is smiling. He is glad to be there. It's morning, bright and early. Well, almost . . .

"I forgot my briefcase," Paul says, swinging his arms giddily back and forth like a little boy, explaining the lightness of his load. "Just walked out without it. Plumb forgot."

"Your friend George brought it by, about four minutes ago."

Paul stops swinging. How did that happen? Where was

his briefcase? And more important, how did George beat him into the city?

"He said he'll see you tonight at dinner, but if you have any questions or need him before then, feel free to call at the office."

George is good, Paul thinks. And he is fast. Maybe he's a little too good. Paul wants to call him. He wants to ask George a couple of quick questions: Did ya see the tatas on Miss October? Think those were implants? Hey, what do you know about nipples? What happens to the nipples when they put in implants?

"What else?" he asks his secretary.

"Warburton wants a response to the report."

Paul stares at the secretary, who's still holding the briefcase.

"The report. I put it in here on Friday." She pats the side of his briefcase.

"Never got to it," Paul says, feeling as though he's saying the dog ate it. "There was a fire. We were in a motel. I forgot."

"I'll stall," the secretary says.

"I'll read," Paul says, taking the briefcase into his office.

His secretary puts through a conference call from Henry.

"Ménage à trois," the date says.

Paul doesn't say anything.

"Come on," Henry says. "Play along. I'm Bond, James Bond."

"I'm the Russian spy," the date says.

"And who am I?" Paul asks.

"A diplomat from the UN," Henry says.

Paul's secretary interrupts. "You have a meeting in ten minutes."

He puts his hand over the receiver. "In eight minutes, knock on my door."

"Of course," the secretary says, closing the door.

He goes back to the phone. Henry is talking to the date in a poor imitation of Sean Connery. The date moans with a Russian accent.

Paul listens.

Paul thinks about his hand; the kiss is still on his palm, and he has to pee. He needs to wash his hands, and he needs to pee, and he thinks it would be odd to walk into the men's room and wash your hands before peeing. He doesn't want to act strangely, and he doesn't want to touch himself with the kiss still in hand. He will wait, wait to wash his hands, wait to pee. He will do work, he will touch other things. The kiss will wear off; it will erase itself.

He buzzes his secretary. "Could I have some coffee, please?"

A few minutes later, when she hands him the cup, he "accidentally" splashes a little on his hand.

"I'm sorry, did I scald you?" the secretary asks.

"Not at all," Paul says, smiling, blotting his hand with a napkin, wiping himself clean.

They work. Whatever room her mother is in, Elaine is out of. Her mother's presence, the annoying surety of her opinions on everything from the organization of the refrigerator shelves to the right way to fold a towel, fills Elaine with rage. The resulting chemical surge propels her. She works harder, faster, and more thoroughly than she would if left to her own devices. She strips the beds, gathers the smoky sheets, towels, clothes, etc. With a bucket, a sponge, and her own concoction of Murphy's, Windex, and 409, she erases the thick footprints of the firemen. She works her way around the house— a poor man's Pat, a person who has to be pissed off in order to be productive.

At a certain point she comes downstairs to refill her bucket. Her mother has mixed a defrosted can of lemonade concentrate with a bottle of flat seltzer.

"You and I have to have a serious talk," her mother says, pouring Elaine a glass.

This is the moment Elaine's been waiting for: the reprimand. Her mother will tell her to get her act together, straighten up and fly right.

"The other day, I was trying to tell your father something," her mother says. "I wanted his opinion on the sofas in the living room. I'm thinking of re-covering them. I found fabric, but it's expensive. . . . And then I started thinking, maybe we should just get new sofas." Her mother stops, looks at Elaine as if to ask, "Are you with me?" She goes on. "And so I said to him, 'It'll cost us to re-cover, and it'll cost us to replace. Six of one, half dozen of the other.'"

Elaine listens attentively, hoping this is a parable, hoping the punch line at the end will be filled with import and meaning.

"Now, I don't know how much you know about furniture. . . ."

Suddenly, Elaine can't listen anymore; the story is entirely irrelevant. She's busy beating herself up: Why are you so gullible? Why do you get suckered in? Why do you always think this time it will be different? Why do you always have hope? What kind of an idiot are you?

Elaine starts to cry.

"Is it the drink?" her mother asks. "You don't like the drink? It's a little sweet—maybe there's not enough seltzer."

"I'm unhappy. I burned my house down, and I'm really unhappy," Elaine says.

"What would you like me to do?" her mother asks, defensively. "You're too old for me to do anything. Do you want to come home? Do you want me to take you back to my house?"

Not "our" house, not "the" house, but "my" house. Elaine hasn't lived there in twenty years, but she still thinks of it as her house or at least *the* house, the family home.

"Do you want to come home? Do you want to bring Paul and the boys? Would it be better if we were all under one roof?"

Elaine pictures it. She pictures herself in her room at the top of the stairs, in the narrow bed of her childhood. She pictures Daniel and Sammy down the hall in the den, Paul on the fold-out couch in the living room. She imagines waking up every morning with her father and mother bickering in the background, constant natter. "We're not fighting, we're talking. It's a conversation."

"Is that what you want?" her mother asks.

"No," Elaine says, definitively.

What does she want? She thinks of herself in the third person, as though the distance between first and third will give her perspective: What does Elaine want? She struggles to answer her own question: advice, confidence, direction, comfort.

"Do you hate it?" Elaine asks her mother. "Do you hate everything? Do you hate having a family? Do you hate me? Am I awful? Are we all that awful?"

Her mother cuts her off. "Who's allowed to hate? Who's allowed to think such horrible thoughts? You think you're supposed to have feelings about everything? You don't need so many feelings." She sighs. "You have a fantasy about how things should be. Stop daydreaming. Ask yourself what do you want, and then go get it. You have to do it yourself; no one does it for you. You have to make your own life."

"I don't know how. I don't know what I want. I don't know anything," Elaine sobs. "I'm crying, and I don't even know why. I'm stuck. I'm totally stuck."

"You have a wonderful life," her mother insists.

"Maybe what I want is beyond me, maybe it's not for me."

"You're just bored."

Elaine stops crying. "Bored and boring. And pathetic. And stupid. How could I be such a fool?" she says, getting up from the table.

The doorbell rings. "You forgot fat," her mother says.

"What?"

"Boring, stupid, and fat." Her mother launches into an ancient and inaccurate litany—the things Elaine used to say about herself when she was a kid.

Elaine is not fat. She has not been fat since she was fifteen, and even then she was just chunky. She looks at her mother in horror, as if to ask, Why are you still doing this? Haven't you heard one word of what I've been saying?

The doorbell rings again. Her mother clucks. She lets the electric man in, and Elaine escapes up the stairs. There are things she needs to do, but when she gets to the top, she can't remember what.

She lies on the stripped bed, looking up at the pinhole in the roof. The sky is blue. Clouds pass over. Sky, air, clouds, the sun and moon; it's fine. It's the same as it ever was. She stares at the small spot of blue. She sleeps. She dreams. She wakes up feeling a little more and a little less like herself.

The kitchen is spotless and silent. The living room has been Endust-ed, polished, and waxed; the mixed scents of Lemon Pledge and Murphy's Oil Soap hang in the air. Her mother sits on the sofa reading a magazine. She's got her jacket on, her purse beside her. She sits like a cleaning lady waiting to be told she can go home, waiting to be paid.

"I didn't want to wake you," her mother says. "Your friend Pat called. She wanted to know if you needed her. I told her that everything was under control." Her mother smiles at her own efficiency. "Did you have a good rest? Are you feeling better? I checked on you. You were sleeping like a baby. I figured it was safe to run an errand. You didn't hear me leave, did you?"

Elaine shakes her head. "I didn't hear anything."

"I ran to the store. I had to go anyway; I had nothing to feed your father. I bought you a few things. I wasn't sure of your brands, so I just bought for the boys. I figured they're not so picky."

She is being apologetic, and even that is offensive. How does she know how picky they are? Elaine and Paul are far less picky than Sammy and Daniel.

Her mother picks up her purse and takes out her keys. She struggles to get up from the sofa. "It's a little too soft," she says, trying to stand. "You should think about getting something new, not so deep. I'm not the acrobat I used to be."

"Are you leaving?"

"Your father needs me. After a few hours, he gets lonely." She takes a deep breath. "The electric is back on, the phone is on, sheets are in the wash, towels in the dryer, dishes done. Snacks in the kitchen for the boys. I don't know what else I can do."

Elaine wants to say, What about the dining room, what about the hole in the wall? What about the way the rug goes squish, and how the dining room table is split in half like firewood? She wants to say, You can't leave yet, you're not finished—I still feel horrible.

Her mother checks her watch. "They'll be home soon," she says, walking to the door.

Elaine wants to throw herself down on the floor and grab her mother's leg. She wants to plead, Don't go. But instead, she walks her mother to the door. She waves good-bye.

Mother was here. Mother is gone. Everything is as it was. Elaine closes the door.

The late-afternoon light creeps into the living room, sweeping over the furniture, seeping into the hall. Orange. Blood orange. The red swell of the setting sun pours down the walls and across the floor, all of it reminding Elaine of flames, of fire.

The house is empty.

Elaine takes off her clothes, throws them into the washer, and puts the wet towels in the dryer. Naked, she ascends the staircase like a figure in a painting. She showers, washing herself while simultaneously scrubbing the shower walls with the loofah she bought to scrape dead skin. She is in overdrive. Like Pat, every motion contains two motions—shower and scrub. She makes a mental note to buy something to clean the grout.

Dripping. She goes down the stairs, worrying that someone can see her through the windows—the woman in the blue car, Mrs. Hansen, a child walking by. The house is like a cage, a display case. She is deep in her thoughts. She does not hear the door. She does not hear his feet on the floor.

The cop is in the front hall. "Are you violating the integrity of a crime scene?" he asks.

"Am I?" Elaine asks, crossing her arms over her breasts.

"Just kidding." He laughs at his own joke. "Police humor."

They are standing in the hallway. She's naked, wet. He doesn't seem to notice her nakedness, and yet he must be aware—it is his job to be observant, to take in the details.

"So are you, like, breaking and entering?" she asks.

"Just visiting," he says, "but you'd better call a locksmith."

"Is the lock broken?"

"Apparently," the cop says.

She's standing in a puddle, a little pool of bathwater. She remembers the first time they met; she and Paul had been to the movies. On the way home they'd smoked a couple of joints in the car and parked down by the water. A light had flashed across the car and there was a knock at the window. "Roll down your window, sir," the officer had said.

"Just taking in the view," Paul had said.

"We don't do that here, sir," the cop had said, and then he asked to see Paul's license. Paul, convinced that they were about to be busted, just about had a heart attack. Elaine can still remember his color—glow-in-the-dark white, his skin covered with a slimy, cold layer of sweat.

"Go home," the cop finally said, dismissing them, but forgetting to give Paul his license back. The next day he'd appeared at the house; Elaine was naked in the kitchen, stoned, snacking. The doorbell rang, and she dropped to the floor. She crawled across the linoleum from the kitchen to the front-hall closet on her belly. She stood up inside the closet and put on Paul's black cashmere overcoat before opening the front door.

"Somehow," the officer said, "I didn't give your husband his license back."

"Thanks," Elaine had said, taking the license from him, wondering if he knew she was naked inside the coat, wondering what he thought of that.

And now, again, she is standing before him, naked—this time really naked.

He's looking at her.

The water on her skin evaporates. Goose bumps rise up. Her nipples are shriveled, pulled into hard knots that might be mistaken for desire.

"I just stopped by to see how things were going," he says.

She nods. In the background there's the tumble of towels in the dryer.

"Kids at school?"

She nods again.

"Husband in the city?"

"And my mother just left," she says.

"Yeah, I saw her car."

Elaine puts her hand on her hip. "So," she says.

"It's all coming together," he says.

There is a noise—footsteps up the back steps.

"The kids," Elaine says, making a dash for the laundry room.

She comes out with a warm towel wrapped around her body and another wrapped around her hair. He's gone. He's been replaced by Mrs. Hansen, who stands in the front hall holding a plate of cookies.

"I baked," Mrs. Hansen says.

"Oh, good," Elaine says, looking around her, over her, through her, trying to find him—and wondering where the kids are; she's sure she heard them.

"Rum cookies," Mrs. Hansen says, pushing the plate at Elaine.

"Really lovely," Elaine says, confused. Again, there's the sound of someone on the kitchen stairs.

Sammy and Daniel bang at the door.

"Hello, hello," Elaine says, opening up. "How are you? My little kiddles, my chickadees." She struggles to be enthusiastic. "Welcome home." She kisses each of the boys on the forehead.

"Good afternoon," Mrs. Hansen says, eyeing the creatures who managed to hold her hostage yesterday afternoon, trapped inside the house while they sealed it off with cassette tape like a crime scene.

"Just give me one minute," Elaine says, excusing herself to get dressed. She hurries upstairs and throws on the first clean thing she can find—a pair of Paul's khakis, a big belt, and a T-shirt. She goes back downstairs. Everyone is gone.

They are out back. Mrs. Hansen has pulled together the pieces of the picnic table and arranged an ersatz tea party.

"Rum cookies and lemonade," Mrs. Hansen says, announcing the menu.

Sammy takes a bite of a cookie and spits it out. "Yech," he says. "It tastes like medicine."

"Give it to me," Elaine says, taking the cookie. The cookies are strong and rich, drenched in alcohol—rum sponges. "Stunning," Elaine says.

Daniel eats four and starts weaving drunkenly around the yard. "More cookies, more cookies," he begs.

"I think you've had enough," Elaine says.

"There's nothing better in the afternoon than a taste of something good," Mrs. Hansen says. "I used to be such a cook. When my boys were young, I did everything. I did it all." She looks up into the sky and then takes another cookie for herself.

The back of the house is singed. Thick streaks of black rise up toward the roof, each one higher than the last—skid marks on the trajectory to tragedy, the results of a wicked rat race, none reaches the top—there is no winner.

The hole in the dining room wall is a puncture, a blasted-out circle with the same charred, chewed look you see in cartoons when a stick of dynamite goes off. Did the fire make the hole, eating its way into the house, crazy with consumption, or did the firemen punch through in their effort to extinguish the flames? Which came first, the chicken or the egg, the fire or the hole?

Her yard. Her petunias, impatiens, and geraniums have been trampled, their stems crushed. The flowers, not believing they are dead, hold their color, as though holding their breath.

Elaine goes to the wrecked flower bed. She gets down on her hands and knees and tries to resuscitate what's left. She props up the flowers. Leaning one against another, they all fall down. She starts pulling at them, violently yanking out what's been crushed. She can't stand the sight of so much gone wrong.

"Sordid," Mrs. Hansen says, getting down on the ground next to her.

Elaine thinks Mrs. Hansen has come to take her away. She imagines Mrs. Hansen saying, Come on, dear, that's enough, gently leading her off as though she were a mental patient, ripping out her hair and not just dead flowers.

"These flowers look exhausted," Mrs. Hansen says, taking a tool out of her pocket and unfolding a pair of scissors, "but I bet they'll perk right up in a glass of sugar water." She snips the stems, "My Handyman," she says, tapping the tool. "I don't go anywhere without it."

" 'You can call me Flower,' " Sammy says, repeating his favorite line from *Bambi*—a movie Daniel calls *Waiting to Be Road Kill.*

The yard is like a tar pit, a muddy mix of charred wood and stone. The grill is still there, lying on its side, leftover chunks of burned briquette crumbling into the dirt, all of it starting to harden and set—the fossilizing of America.

Daniel pokes a stick into the muck, stirring things up. "Why was the cop here?"

"Just checking in."

"How come you were wearing a towel?"

"I took a shower. How was your day?" she asks, changing the subject. "How was school? Did you get off to a good start? Did Mrs. Meaders make you something good for breakfast?"

Daniel looks her in the eye, sizing her up. "You don't usually take a shower in the middle of the afternoon."

"I was dirty," she says.

He scratches through the dirt with his stick. "What's this?" he asks, uncovering a pack of burned matches, picking them up with his stick, instinctively not touching the evidence with his bare hands.

"Looks like matches," she says.

"Maybe it means something," he says.

"Are you doing some sort of an investigation?" Elaine asks, wondering whose side he's on.

"Don't know," he says, stirring the dirt miserably.

"Did I do something wrong?" Elaine asks.

"Did you?" he says.

Elaine sees in him the same disdain she's seen in Paul. Her stomach tightens. She tries to find her way past it. "You look so much like your father," she says, reaching for his cheek. He pulls away.

"Are you fucking the cop?"

The thought had not occurred to her.

"Are you?" he asks.

She hears Daniel say "fucking the cop," and she thinks yes. Yes, she will fuck the cop, if the cop wants to fuck her.

"Don't say 'fuck,' " she tells Daniel.

Elaine is wiped out. She feels fragile, as though she's been ill. She looks at Mrs. Hansen, hoping Mrs. Hansen will do something. She has summoned her children for a visit but can take only so much. Their needs overwhelm her. She has no idea how to connect with Daniel; nothing she does is right. She is hoping Paul will come home soon and collect her. Together they'll drop the children off, and he'll take her back to Pat and George's. The day has been impossibly long. She's playing house in a broken home.

There's a thundering, bright, metallic bang, the ground-shaking slam of metal, like the sound of a car accident. They feel it in their feet and up their legs, like an explosion, a burst followed by a fat puff of air, the breeze of something displaced.

"What was that?" Elaine shouts.

Mrs. Hansen goes around front to look. "The Dumpster has arrived," she announces.

Paul is on the train coming home. It has been a lost day. He read the report and gave his opinion, which seemed to go over well, but the bulk of the day was spent worrying.

"Wash your bowl." That's what the guy on the train, the palm kisser, told him that morning. "When you're stuck, when you don't know what to do—just go on, do the next thing. If you ate cereal for breakfast, you wash your bowl."

Paul walked the corridors of his office looking for advice— "Do you own your house? Did you buy or build? Brick or wood? Flat roof or pitched? Any experience with stonework? What about fire insurance? Painters? Restoration? Reconstruction?"

"What happened? Couldn't wrestle your Weber?" one guy said, mocking him, as if to say, real men don't let their houses catch on fire.

"Things got out of control," Paul said.

"I bet," the guy said.

Three times he tried calling Elaine on the cellular and got a recording—"The cellular customer you're trying to reach is temporarily out of the calling area. Please try your call again later."

Paul thought of his friend Tom; Tom from college, Tom whom he hadn't seen in years. The other night in the motel room, Paul felt incredibly close to Tom. It was Tom he called, Tom who comforted him over the phone while Elaine watched.

Paul looked up the name of the company where Tom worked and gave him a call. "How are you?" Paul asked.

"How are *you*? is the question."

"I'm all right," Paul said. "Listen, I was just thinking about you. I wanted to thank you for the other night."

"Not necessary," Tom said. "So, where is it now? What happened with the police and the insurance investigator?"

"We're waiting to hear," Paul said, wishing they could talk about something else, about where they've been all these years, about their lives, their fears and failures.

"Any idea of what it's going to cost you?"

They talked in numbers, pluses and minuses. They talked without talking, without saying anything, all facts and figures.

"It'd be great to see you sometime," Paul said.

"Yeah," Tom said. "I'm a little bogged down, but when the fog lifts, definitely."

"We'll do it then," Paul said.

"If I can be of any help . . ."

"You've already been a help. Enormous. An enormous help."

"All right, then," Tom said.

Paul hung up feeling farther rather than closer. He hung up and immediately dialed Mrs. Apple. He dialed Mrs. Apple, desperate for a dose of connection. Things with Elaine were good this morning, which was nice, but he didn't want to push it; he couldn't expose himself, he couldn't ask her for comfort. He called Mrs. Apple and got her machine. He punched in the first bar of "Mary Had a Little Lamb"—their private code—and hung up.

Paul is on the train. Every day he rides back and forth with the same people. He knows what towns they live in, what kinds of coats they wear, what they eat for breakfast, but he has no idea who they are. They go in and out together and are entirely anonymous. Do they recognize him? Do they notice that some days he looks better than others? The train lurches, a woman he's seen every day for years comes down the aisle, he nods. She nods back. See, he tells himself, it's easy to make friends.

Paul sneezes. He reaches into his pocket for Kleenex, wondering what he's doing; he has never kept Kleenex in his pocket. But it's there, he uses it. This is not his jacket, it's George's. He goes through the other pockets; a ticket stub from a concert at the community center, an empty cellophane wrapper, pink pocket lint, and three-quarters of a roll of Life Savers—Wint-O-Green. He peels one off.

Paul walks home from the station. The sky is still bright with the cool static light of a sun neither ascending nor descending but seeming to fade slowly, withdrawing into the horizon. He walks, surprised by the number of thoughts he has, curious

whether anyone has ever studied the speed of thoughts and why
worrying runs faster than thinking. He pulls out his pocket
calculator and tries to count the thoughts; every time he has
one, he pushes plus one, and if he has the same thought again,
he does it again exponentially.

Stop thinking, he tells himself, stay in the moment.

The air is nice, he tells himself. It is room temperature,
neither too hot nor too cold, perfectly pleasant. As he walks,
he's inclined to whistle—the refrain from Otis Redding's "Dock
of the Bay." The world is his mirror. The mood is even. Nature
is benevolent.

Ahead of him a squirrel is crossing the street, carrying a
large nut in its mouth. It goes back and forth, unable to decide
whether to make a dash for it or not. The squirrel goes forward;
the treasure in its mouth slows it down. The station wagon
doesn't see the squirrel; there is a small crunch. Paul looks at
the car, he sees the driver, a woman, looking back in her rearview
mirror. He watches the squirrel, its tail flapping, the last moments of its life a fast and frenetic attempt to escape what has
already become inevitable.

Paul hurries the rest of the way home.

Mrs. Hansen sits at the picnic table in the backyard, staring into space.

Sammy is next to her. "Who do you think you are, mister?"
He talks to himself and then waits for a reply. "Hey, hey, you,
I'm talking to you."

"Evening," Paul says.

"Elaine's in the house," Mrs. Hansen tells him.

The house smells. The air is thick with an olfactory fog:
fire, smoke, foul water, and her mother's perfume—all of it
dipped in a thin film of Murphy's Oil Soap.

"Elaine," he calls.

"Upstairs," Elaine says.

Paul goes into the dining room. What's left of the curtains

has cooled into a thick, fibrous blob. The hole in the side of the house is covered in heavy plastic. The walls are streaked, as though someone tried to wash them with a dirty sponge. Paul is seeing the damage thrown into the full relief of daylight—it's better and worse than he thought it would be. It is not global, the house does not need to be razed, but what's there is there—it's real. The room is a ruin.

The house is not something Paul can make a virtuous and manly show of Mr. Fix-it with. There's no reaching a hand in to turn a loose screw—saving them a handyman's house call and seventy-five bucks. The house isn't even like a radio he can pluck apart with the enthusiasm of learning how things work, sure he'll be able to put back every diode. Paul has never fixed anything. And he reminds himself that he did this, he brought it on; without a moment's pause to wonder whether or not it could be reconstructed, he destroyed it. Worse yet—and this is the part he's admitted to no one—he got a kick out of it. It felt invigorating, it felt fucking fantastic.

He goes upstairs.

Elaine is lying on the stripped bed.

"It looks better already," he says.

Elaine grunts. She doesn't mean to grunt. She means to say something, but the grunt is all that comes out. All day she's had things to say to Paul, things ranging from the incredibly warm and generous to the horrific: I adore you, you're the best, we can fix the house, we can make it better, you were so wonderful this morning. But then I remembered what an asshole you are and how you're screwing God knows how many women, and I hate you, I despise you. You're a disgusting, vile shit, and I want out. I just want out, whatever that means.

"I tried a hundred times to call you on the cellular," Paul says. "But you had it turned off."

"It was on, but we started getting strange calls—a woman

who wanted to know what I was wearing. At first I thought it was a survey, but then she kept calling, so I turned it off."

Paul blushes.

"Sorry. Our phone's fixed now anyway. My mother took care of it."

She points to the hole in the ceiling. "Do you think they saw it? Should we report it to someone?"

"We should take a picture," Paul says. "Where's the Polaroid?"

"In the dresser, bottom drawer, on your side."

Paul gets the camera, hangs it around his neck, and lies down on the bed next to Elaine. He aims the camera at the hole and shoots. A print spits out.

"Oh," Daniel says, coming into the room, finding both parents, fully dressed, lying on an unmade bed, staring at the ceiling.

Elaine checks the Polaroid—it's coming out dark, with a spot of light in the middle. "Maybe you'd better take another shot," she says.

"Do we have any Ziploc bags?" Daniel asks.

"For what?" Elaine asks.

"Something."

"Something like what?" Paul asks.

"Do we have any?" Daniel asks.

"If we do, they're in the drawer downstairs next to the aluminum foil."

"I already looked there."

"Then we don't have any."

"Could you get me some?"

"Your wish is my command," Elaine says. "What size?"

Daniel shrugs "Medium, I guess."

Paul stands on the bed, aims at the roof, and clicks again. "On my way home, I saw a squirrel get run over," Paul says.

"Should we get a ladder and try to stuff it, in case it rains?" Elaine says.

"Stuff it before it rains?" Paul asks. "The squirrel?"

"The hole."

"No," he says, stepping down off the bed. "Let's just move the bed. What time do we have to be at Pat and George's?"

"Seven."

"We'd better get going. I need clean clothes," Paul says.

"I did laundry."

"Good." They push the bed out of the way.

Elaine packs the bag to take to Pat and George's, wondering, are they moving in or are they moving out?

On their way out the door Paul remembers the Life Savers in his pocket. "Hey, come here for a minute," he says, gesturing to Elaine and the boys. This is all he has to offer them, and it is nothing—stale candy, a desperate attempt to win them back. He steps into the half bath by the kitchen door.

"Into the bathroom?" Daniel asks.

"Yes."

"All of us?" Elaine asks.

"Yes."

They crowd in. Sammy stands on the toilet-seat lid. Paul pulls down the window shade. "Close the door," he instructs Elaine. "I heard something once; I just want to see if it's true." He throws a few disks of Wint-O-Green into his mouth. "Watch for sparks," he says, rolling his lips back and crunching down, teeth bared. He has a split second to charm them.

Sparks fly.

"Wow," Sammy says.

"Weird, really weird," Daniel says.

"How'd you do it?" Elaine asks.

Paul passes out the rest of the roll, and they all crunch down, and their mouths light up like little sparklers, a spray of glittering phosphorescence. It's Paul's moment to feel like a father, it's the first thing they've done as a family in a really long time, and it's perfect; no heat, no flame, no risk of injury.

"Pretty great," Elaine says, stepping out of the bathroom.

"Weird, really weird," Daniel says again.

"Have a lovely evening," Mrs. Hansen says. "See you tomorrow."

In the car, buoyed by the success of the Life Saver display, Paul throws out an idea. "How would it be if one night this week the four of us went out for dinner, someplace nice?"

"Why?" Daniel asks.

"So your mother and I don't get lonely."

"You'd better check with the Meaderses," Daniel says. "They're very organized about things."

"Should I call what's-her-name?" Elaine turns to Sammy. "What's Nate's mother's name?"

"Mom?" Sammy says.

Daniel hits him. "Butt plug."

"Help me, what's her name?" Elaine asks Paul.

"Susan," he says. "I'll ask her when we drop Sam." It's a convenient excuse to get out of the car, to talk to her—Nate's mom, Susan, Mrs. Apple. Paul pulls into the driveway and toots the horn.

The front door opens. The hall light frames Mrs. Apple's head like a halo. Glorious dinner smells waft out into the twilight. Paul fights the urge to push Sammy out of the way, to run into the house, slam the door behind him, lock it, bolt it, wedge a chair up against it, and hold his fingers over his head in an X, a cross protecting him from Elaine, from his children, from his life.

He wants to go home. He wants to rest. He wants the comfort of a bosom that expects nothing of him. He wants his mother.

"I missed you today," he says to Mrs. Apple.

"My time is not my own," she says, annoyed. "I called you."

"Did you get my message?" he asks.

"I did," she says, putting her hand on Sammy's shoulder, bringing him into the house. "I drive car pool tomorrow."

"Does that mean no?" he asks.

"It means I haven't figured it out. I'll call you," she says, closing the door.

"Night, Dad," Sammy says through the crack.

Paul walks back to the car. It's getting dark, that odd hour when earth and sky merge, when it's hard to see clearly.

"What night did she say would be good for dinner?" Elaine quizzes.

"I forgot to ask," Paul says, backing out of the driveway.

"What were you talking about?"

"Would you like me to turn around and go back?"

"No. You can call her tomorrow," Elaine says.

"Fine."

They pull into the Meaderses' driveway.

"Don't forget my Ziplocs," Daniel instructs Elaine. "And I might need a few other things, supplies and stuff," he says, getting out of the car.

"No doubt you'll let me know," Elaine says. "Have a good night. Do your homework."

"And don't forget to find out what night is good for dinner, or your mother will kill you," Paul says.

They are on their own, on the road to Pat and George's. They ride in silence—not the steely silence of anger or the censored silence of frustration, but the simple silence of a pause, a moment alone, a quiet calm.

When they get to Pat and George's, the lights are all on,

the house is filled with music. Pat and George and the two little M's are dancing around in costumes of the islands with plastic leis around their necks.

"Tuesday-night dinners are theme nights. We put on a show, and between courses we dance," George says. "You're a few minutes late, we started without you."

One of the little M's offers them pineapple cubes on toothpicks, while the other M takes center stage in the middle of the living room.

"She's been rehearsing all afternoon," Pat whispers.

"Tonight we're doing *South Pacific*," George says. And as if playing ringtoss, he throws plastic leis over Paul's and Elaine's heads. Elaine stands holding the bag she packed at home, feeling like a traveler who got off at the wrong stop.

The little M opens her mouth. " 'If they asked me, I could write a book,' " she croons.

They can't compete. Paul and Elaine's few good moments—Mrs. Hansen's tea party in the backyard, Paul and Elaine lying on the bed looking up at the hole, the glow-in-the-dark Life Savers in the bathroom—their tiny flickers of hope can't go up against the Nielsons' full-scale production. Paul and Elaine are back to square one.

Elaine looks at Pat, thinking she must have had a very different day. Elaine is exhausted—the afternoon felt three weeks long—and Pat is exuberant, sitting on the sofa with her two little girls, pantomiming "I'm Gonna Wash That Man Right Outa My Hair."

"We're always doing things like this to keep from getting bored," George says. "That's how you conquer it, head it off at the pass."

The girls do their song and dance, and dinner is served on trays in the living room—something hot and sour and poi, "which is made from taro roots," one of the M's explains. And the show goes on.

FOUR

PAUL IS UP EARLY. He is out of his nightgown, into his suit, and out the door. "I have to get to the office," he whispers in Elaine's ear.

"Are you talking in your sleep?"

"No, I'm all dressed, I'm ready to go."

"Have a nice day," she says, rolling away from him.

"I have to get to the office," Paul says again as he passes Pat in the hall.

Pat is in her robe, unkempt, uncollected, not at all her usual self, who by now would be dressed, set, made for the day.

Paul checks his watch. "It's seven A.M.," he says, figuring if he hurries, if he keeps to it, he can make the 7:33—it's mostly downhill from Pat and George's.

"Oh, I know," Pat says. "Some days are just like that. Would you like me to fix you a go-cup?"

"A what?"

"A cup of coffee you can take with you?" She nudges Paul into the kitchen, whips open cabinets and cupboards—coffee, milk, sugar—and gets it all into a brew. She flashes a shelf filled with sip/no-spill mugs covered in logos: FRANK'S HARDWARE,

7TH ANNUAL CONFERENCE ON HOME AND FAMILY, a gigantic one from National City Bank Corp.—THINK BIG—YOUR DEPOSIT IS YOUR FUTURE.

"Pick one," she says as she writes his name on a piece of white Johnson & Johnson adhesive tape.

Paul pulls out the one marked MUDSLIDE BAKERY AND BREWERY.

She slaps his name on the side, fills it with coffee, and tops it with milk. Her aim is off; milk splashes across the counter.

"Shoot," she says, grabbing a dish towel. The milk runs over the edge, dripping down the cabinet and onto the floor.

"Are you all right?" Paul asks.

"Is it so obvious?" Pat asks.

Paul looks at her, thinking, She looks deranged. It's her hair; she didn't brush her hair—that's the first giveaway. "It's not like you to spill the milk," he says.

She fits the nonspill sip-top onto his mug. "I'll be better soon," she says, walking him to the door. "Have you got everything? Have you got your briefcase, your papers, your good thoughts to start the day?"

"I'm good to go," he says, gesturing at her with the coffee mug.

"Something special you want for dinner? Wednesday is grab bag. Everyone puts in their wishes in the morning, and each person ends up getting at least one thing they want."

"Anything is okay with me," Paul says.

"Nope," Pat says. "You have to name it. Name it now, or I'll have to hunt you down at the office." She stoops to pick up the morning paper. "What's your favorite dinner?"

Food. He is being asked to think of food for dinner when he hasn't even eaten breakfast.

"What do you crave but never get?"

He gives Pat a strange look, as though she's changed the subject.

"Things you eat for dinner," Pat says, prompting him—it sounds like a category on *Jeopardy:* "I'll take meat and vegetables for two hundred."

"Pot roast, mashed potatoes," he blurts. "Yellow cake with chocolate icing."

Pat smiles. "That's nice. That's so nice. I knew you'd be good under pressure. Go on now," she says, stepping back into the house. "You don't want to miss that train."

He checks his watch again, it's 7:07. He has the jump on things. Out the door and into the air, carrying the warm mug of coffee in front of him, slightly ahead of him, he travels, trots toward the train, struggling to master the combined arts of race-walking and coffee-toting. He feels like an ancient warrior woman trying to balance a jug of water on her head as she hurries back from the well to her village. He tries to take small sips along the way but finds it only slows him down—he saves it for the train.

As he passes McKendrick's place, Paul looks up at the house, thinking he might spot the old guy starting his slow roll down the driveway, white knuckles gripping the bar of his walker. McKendrick isn't out yet, but there's a light on in the kitchen. Paul is tempted to press himself against the glass and say, You were right, old man, work is where it's at. I'm on my way, getting a good start, bright and early, out of the gate and down the straightaway. He is tempted to knock on the window, but there are high thorny hedges blocking him, and he's carrying his coffee, and if he's not careful, he'll be late. He makes a mental note to do a little something for the guy, buy him a magazine, a tape, or some sort of a toy—would an inflate-a-mate mean anything?

Paul walks on, counting the sidewalk cracks, watching the ground in front of him, not letting his eyes get too far ahead, not wanting to see too much—thinking of the squirrel from yesterday, again hearing the crushing crack, picturing the tail flapping its frantic last gasp. Paul doesn't want anything to upset him or throw him off. He doesn't want to know too much.

At the station he buys himself a pack of Kleenex and a roll of Life Savers. He takes out a tissue and wipes the morning dew off his shoes. He is perfect and is taking pride in his perfection. He sips from his go-cup. He is buoyant and bouncy and filled with big ideas. All night he was thinking about the house, putting French doors in the dining room where the hole is, having them open out onto a deck. Maybe glassing in the side porch. . . . Why just repair, why not rethink, remodel?

"Don't you just love your mug?" the woman sitting behind him on the train says. "I couldn't get to work without it."

"Yes," he says, sipping. "It's my first time, but I'm loving it." He sips some more, all the while staring at his name taped to the side—Pat's clean print. He tilts his head back and drains the mug, realizing that it reminds him of Sammy's old teething cup. A drop of coffee runs down the corner of his mouth; he blots it with the back of his hand.

The cup is empty. Now what? What do you do with it when you're done? It's too fat to fit inside his briefcase. Do you just hold it, or do you tie it to your belt and let it hang off you, banging like a beggar's tin cup? He has the urge to throw the cup away, to abandon it on the train and tell Pat that he lost it. Suddenly he hates the cup. It is not his cup, it is not his friend. He feels none of the attachment that a man can form for his regular mug.

The train pulls in. He gets off, carrying his briefcase in one hand, the annoying cup in the other.

TERMINAL BAKERY: FREE REFILLS. LET US PUT OUR COFFEE IN YOUR CUP. That's what the sign in the station says. The woman from the train is waiting in line, her mug extended. He gets in line behind her, thinking, Why not? He could use a little more; a little more might make everything all right.

"Java joe?" the guy behind the counter asks.

"Fill 'er up," Paul says.

"Hi and low? Tall and light? Wet or dry? Sauce on the side?" the guy asks.

Paul has no idea what the guy is getting at. "Milk and sugar," he says, looking around, noticing that a lot of people are carrying cups. That's how they do it, he thinks, that's how they keep going day and night; guzzling gallons of joe and eating muffins bigger than their heads—muffins like intestinal sponges that soak up all the coffee, muffins with names like "Wendy"—a blend of apple, oat bran, and mandarin oranges; or "Todd"—with the weight of cappuccino cheesecake; and "George"—pure corn.

Filled to the brim, he is out of the station, into the subway, and then up the stairs, onto the streets, and into his office building. He pushes into the crowded elevator just as the door is closing. He presses 44. As the elevator rises, it fills with the volatile vapors of hot-coffee farts, the fumy flatulence of breakfast cereals, of All-Bran and yogurt, of Egg McMuffin, of sausage on a biscuit. The gaseous display becomes all-encompassing. No one speaks, no one knows who let loose—at least it wasn't Paul. Was it by choice, a kind of kamikaze welcome-to-work terrorist attack, or did it erupt involuntarily? It just gets worse. The noxious intestinal output, the rear-end rocket seems to be of the variety that explodes in sections on a kind of timed delay. Laughing gas, tear gas, mustard gas. Napalm. Paul stops breathing. The elevator rises. On the forty-fourth floor, Paul bursts out, gasping, hoping his clothing hasn't absorbed the spoorish scent, hoping he doesn't stink.

"Good morning," his secretary says.

"Morning," he says, his tongue tasting the hazelnut afterburn of the joe that the jerk at the Terminal Bakery poured him. His stomach is starting to gnaw, to chew on itself.

"Can I get you anything?" his secretary asks. "Cup of coffee?"

"How about something solid," he says, "something like a roll?"

"A doughnut?" she says. "I saw a big box of doughnuts in the kitchen this morning. Krispy Kreme."

She brings him a doughnut on a paper napkin and sets it on the edge of his desk. It has been glazed, dipped to a dull shine, doused in a white icing, splashed with brightly colored jimmies, a visual antidepressant that a four-year-old would find appealing. He goes at it and then licks the crackly glaze off his fingers. He is sick. He is stoned. He checks his watch: 8:57. Off to a good start.

Elaine is awake. She is embarrassed to have slept late. She lies in the bed, feeling the strange absence of her morning panic—a panic she didn't know was panic, until now. Usually Elaine wakes with the full force of a high-voltage electrical shock. She is ejaculated from the bed, thrown down the hall to Daniel's room, to Sammy's room, rebounding back to Paul, then bounced down the steps to the kitchen, to the coffeemaker, the orange juice, the toaster tarts, lunch money, permission slips, pushing and packing to have the three of them out the door before seven forty-five.

She breathes deeply.

How are you? she asks herself.

Fine.

It's interesting, this absence of anxiety. She didn't wake up whistling, but it's okay, things are not so terrible. She has the feeling things are possible; there's room for improvement.

And she is actually thinking—not worrying, not racing—thinking. She is thinking that what she has to do now is get up, get dressed, and go home. She has to fix the house, fix herself, and focus on what comes next. She has to plan for the future. And she has to call her friend Liz—she meant to do it last night, but felt funny calling from Pat's house, like she was cheating on someone—she didn't know who.

She glances across the room. Paul made his bed. He hung up George's suit. Looking down the length of the bed, she notices that the blanket is dotted with Post-its. Elaine is decorated with notes from Paul, each one with a message, something to do: Pick paint. Repair or renovate? Contractor. Do you want a deck? Roofer—ask Pat. French doors? Make dinner plans. The car is for you—keys on the dresser. Insurance company will come. Measure.

It is as though he couldn't contain himself, as though he had to relieve himself before leaving for work.

Elaine gets out of bed, carefully collecting the Post-its and putting them in a pile. She makes the bed, brushes her teeth, combs her hair, and washes her face. The house is quiet. She puts the Post-its in her pocket and slides into a clean white shirt that Pat pressed for her yesterday. Elaine's plan is to go into the kitchen, have a quick cup of coffee, and then go home.

"Wash your bowl," she remembers Paul saying as they were going to sleep. Wash your bowl. He was going on about something—a man on the train who had kissed him and then told him to clean up his room. Was Paul talking or dreaming? Elaine wonders.

Pat is in the kitchen. She is on the phone and also ironing. "Eight-four-nine-oh-X Azalea in a medium," she says, spraying starch on a shirt.

"Good morning," she whispers to Elaine.

"Seven-four-oh-seven-Y, two size smalls, one Tangerine, one Pistachio, and if you've got it, a four-three-oh-six-A in Sapphire."

"Morning," Elaine says.

Pat smiles. "Is there a belt for that? Something brown would be perfect," she tells the operator.

"I have big feet," she whispers to Elaine. "Did you sleep well?"

"Very," Elaine says.

The coffeepot is on. Elaine pours herself a cup and leans against the counter. Pat is still in her robe. Her hair is a mess. On the table is a bowl of pineapple slices, left over from the night before—no muffins, no warm morning pastries, no fresh-baked bread. Elaine checks the clock—10:00 A.M. How odd. Pat in her robe, Pat serving leftovers. If Pat can't keep it together, who can?

Pat is smiling at Elaine, practically grinning. Why?

"What?" Elaine asks.

"You're so lovely," Pat says, and Elaine isn't sure if Pat is talking to her or the woman on the phone.

"No four-three-oh-six-A in Sapphire? Well, do you have it in Ruby?"

The kitchen table is stacked with how-to books, fix-it manuals, handy, helpful hints. There's a big fat one opened to the page on clothes dryers. Elaine sits down with her coffee and begins reading the part about testing the switches: "Set VOM on RX 100; clip probes on leads, look for moderate resistance. . . ."

In the background Pat is placing another call—she's ordering lamb. "Page forty-three. Could I have three racks and then one leg?"

Elaine had never heard of anyone having meat mailed to them.

"And page fourteen, the cans of colored sugar, one set."

"For decorating cookies," she whispers to Elaine.

"Ummmm," Elaine says.

"Over the phone. Door-to-door. Hardware, underwear,

shoes, food, everything," Pat says as she's hanging up. "It saves me so much time." Pat sprays starch on the last of the shirts and digs in, wrestling the wrinkles.

"I slept late," Elaine says sheepishly.

"Every day isn't perfect," Pat says. "Some days start strangely."

Is that why she's still in her robe? Should Elaine ask more?

Pat taps the repair book Elaine's been looking at. "My favorite," she says.

"I thought George was Mr. Fix-it," Elaine says.

"George couldn't fix his way out of a cardboard box. He's not mechanically competent," Pat says.

"I never would have known."

"Life's little secrets." Pat sits down next to Elaine. "Looks like I'm going to have to replace an idler pulley on the dryer. And I'll probably go ahead and do the drum belt as long as I'm in there. It's pretty well worn. Twelve years already. Can you believe that? You can't control everything."

Elaine has no idea what Pat is talking about. She sips her coffee while Pat studies the diagram. As she reaches across the table for the newspaper, the coffee sloshes, it splashes onto Elaine's clean white shirt. "Shit," she says, jumping up, running to the sink, blotting it with a kitchen sponge.

"Take it off," Pat says.

"I'm not dressed," Elaine says, pulling the stained fabric away from her skin—she's braless.

Pat takes something out from under the sink, squirts it directly onto the shirt, and rubs thoroughly with her bare hand. The spot disappears. "Will you let me iron it?" Pat asks.

Elaine hesitantly unbuttons the shirt and slips it off.

Pat moves to the ironing board to press the blouse dry. Steam rises from under the iron. Goose bumps come up on Elaine's skin. She crosses her arms over her chest.

Pat holds the shirt open for Elaine, like a bullfighter's cape. Toro.

"Thanks," Elaine says, sliding her arm in.

There's something delicious about the shirt, crisp, bright white against her skin. The cotton is hot on the spot where the coffee spilled, the place where Pat worked it. Hot against cold. Elaine closes her eyes and lets the warmth soak in. "Thanks," she says again.

Pat is moving in a slow circle around Elaine, lifting Elaine's hair out from inside the neck of the blouse.

Something brushes against Elaine's neck. What? What was that? A prickly tingle. Elaine turns toward it, turning toward the trouble, wanting to see what's what. It's Pat. Pat kissing her. Pat kisses her again. Pat kisses her on the lips. "Ummmmm, ummm," Pat murmurs.

A whirl, a dizzying spin.

The purple press of Pat's lips is insistent and sure. Pat is kissing her, and Elaine isn't sure why. She pulls back and looks at Pat. Pat's eyes are closed, her face a dissolve coming at Elaine again. Elaine turns slightly to the side, avoiding her. The kiss lands on Elaine's cheek. Pat's eyes blink open—baffled. Something. Guilt. Confusion. Elaine can't think, can't see, can't breathe, but she doesn't want to give Pat the wrong idea, she doesn't want to say no, she doesn't want Pat to be hurt. Elaine kisses Pat.

The kiss, unbearably fragile, a spike of sensation, shatters the frame. Everything Elaine thinks about who she is, what she is, is irrelevant. There are no words, only sensation, smooth sensation. Tender, like the tickling lick of a kitten. Elaine feels powerless, suddenly stoned. Pat is kissing her. She is kissing Pat. They are standing in the middle of the kitchen, giving and getting every kiss they've ever gotten or given; kissing from memory. Kissing: fast, hard, deep, frantic, long and slow. They are tasting the lips, the mouth, the tongue. Elaine puts her hands to Pat's face, the softness of Pat's skin; the absence of the rough-scruff and scratch of a stale shave is so unfamiliar as to seem impossible. Pat rubs her face against Elaine's—sweeping the cheek, the high, light bones, nuzzling the ear, the narrow line of the eyebrow, finishing with a butterfly flick of the lashes.

Elaine's mind struggles to make sense, to find familiar coordinates—it spins uselessly.

Pat reaches for Elaine's hand. "Come," she says.

"Where are you taking me?" Elaine asks in an airless voice.

"Bedroom."

"No," Elaine says, fast, firm. Bed, that's breaking a rule—a rule she didn't know she had. It is like being a teenager again. There are things you will and won't do. Bed is too much. Pat and George's bed, the twins' twin beds—no. Bed is out of the question. So far it is a kiss, just a kiss, nothing truly unforgivable. "No," she says again.

"Am I frightening you?" Pat asks, coming in close, whispering the question right into Elaine's mouth. Kissing. "Am I?" Pat's hand is on Elaine's shirt, on the buttons.

Elaine, not wanting to offend, breathes, "No," even though she is terrified.

Pat undoes the buttons. It feels amazingly good. Pat is unbuttoning the blouse, brushing her lips against Elaine's neck, her clavicle, going lower.

Elaine fixates on the blouse, holding it against her body, worrying it will get wrinkled.

"Don't worry," Pat says, pulling the blouse away. "I'll iron it. I promise, I'll iron it again when we're done."

The shirt falls to the floor.

Elaine bends to pick it up. She stops to drape it over the back of a chair.

It's fine, Elaine tells herself, if it's only a kiss. Fine as long as the clothing is on, fine if only her shirt is off, fine if . . . She's making rules and instantly breaking them.

Pat is at her breast. A noise escapes Elaine, an embarrassingly deep sigh—like air rushing out of something. Elaine can't believe that she's letting this happen; she's not stopping it, she's not screaming, she's enjoying it. Pat is kissing Elaine's belly, tonguing the cesarean scar that no one ever touches. Elaine reaches for Pat—there's an incredible strangeness when they touch simultaneously. Elaine can't tell who is who, what is what—Marcel Marceau, a mirror game, each miming the other. Phenomenal confusion. Elaine touches Pat's breast, pressing. Her knees buckle, she collapses to the floor. Pat goes with her.

They are in the kitchen, down on the linoleum floor. It is fine, Elaine tells herself, fine as long as Pat is dressed, fine as long as Elaine keeps what's left of her clothes on.

"Is this all right?" Pat asks.

"Nice," Elaine manages to say.

Luscious. Delicious. Pat is smooth and buttery, not like Paul, not a mass of fur, a jumble of abrasion from beard to prick. Pat is soft—enveloping rather than insistent.

Elaine is thinking that it'll stop in a minute, it won't really happen, it won't go too far. It's just two women exploring. She remembers reading about consciousness-raising groups, women sitting in circles on living room floors, looking at their cervixes like little boys in circle jerks, women taking possession of their bodies. Only this is far more personal—Pat is taking possession of Elaine.

Pat is pulling Elaine's pants off. Elaine is lifting her hips, her khakis are tossed off under the kitchen table. Pat is still in her robe. Elaine reaches for the belt, half thinking she will use it to pull herself up, she will lift herself up and out of this. The robe opens, exposing Pat.

Pat spreads herself out over Elaine, skin to skin, breast to breast. Pat against her, hot, ripe, repulsive. She almost screams—it's like a living thing—tongue and teeth.

And Pat is on top, grinding against Elaine, humping her in a strangely prickless pose. Fucking that's all friction.

She reaches her hand under Elaine's ass to get a better grip. Crumbs. There are crumbs stuck to Elaine's ass. Horrified, Pat twists around and begins licking them off, sucking the crumbs from Elaine, from the floor, and swallowing them like a human vacuum cleaner. "I sweep," she says, wiping dust off her mouth. "I sweep every day. I'm sweeping all the time."

"It's all right," Elaine says. "It's fine."

Fine if it's only on the outside, fine if it's just a hand. Fine if it's fingers and not a tongue, and then fine if it is a tongue. Fine if it's just that, and then it's fine. It's all fine.

They are two full-grown women, mothers, going at each other on the kitchen floor. A thick, musky scent rises, a sexual stew.

Pat reaches up, pulling a pot holder shaped like a bright red lobster off the counter, tucking it under Elaine's head—from above Elaine looks as if she has claw-shaped devils' horns sticking out of her head. "That's better," Pat says.

"Thank you," Elaine says. "I was starting to get a headache."

"Mmmm," Pat says, spinning her tongue in circles.

"Mmmm," Elaine echoes involuntarily.

Pat's fingers curl between Elaine's legs, slipping in.

"Aooww," Elaine says, combining "Ah" and "Ow," pain and pleasure. It takes a minute to figure out what hurts. "Your ring," Elaine pants.

The high diamond mount of Pat's engagement ring is scraping her. Pat pulls off the ring, it skitters across the floor, and she slips her hand back into Elaine, finding the spot. She slips in and out more quickly, more vigorously.

Elaine comes in cacophonous convulsions, great guttural

exaltations. She's filled with a flooding sensation, as though a seal has broken; her womb, in seizures, squeezes as though expelling Elaine herself.

And just as she thinks it's over, as she starts to relax, Pat's mouth slides south, and Elaine is flash-frozen at the summit of sensation, her body stun-gunned by the flick of Pat's tongue. She lies splayed out on the linoleum, comparing Pat to Paul: Paul goes down on her because he saw it in a porno movie, because he thinks it's the cool thing to do. Paul goes down on her like he's really eating her, like she's a Big Mac and he's got to get his mouth around the whole burger in one big bite.

Elaine is concentrating, trying to figure out exactly what Pat is doing. Every lick, every flick causes an electric surge, a tiny sharp shock, to flash through her body.

She is seeing flashes of light, fleeting images. It's as though she's losing consciousness, losing her mind, dying. She can't bear any more—it's too much. She pushes Pat away.

"Stop," she says, closing her legs. "It's enough."

Pat lies next to her. Pat kisses her. Elaine tastes herself on Pat's lips, a tart tang, surprisingly slick, a lip-gloss lubricant. Their mouths move over each other, hungry.

They begin again.

She owes Pat something.

Elaine's hand moves down, over the rolling hill of Pat's belly, the slow arch of her pelvis. The absence of balls, of the ropy, rock-hard root, is strange, simultaneously familiar and un-. Elaine rubs Pat, working fast and furtively in the swampy heat, doing what needs to be done, not lingering. Pat fills with blood, becoming thick, fibrous, seeming to swell, to tighten on Elaine's hand. Out of character and undignified, Pat writhes athletically, enthusiastically, on the floor. She comes with a long, low moan.

They are finished.

Elaine looks around the kitchen—at the cabinets, the

counters, noticing that the coffeemaker is still on and that they kicked the kitchen table, knocking some of the do-it-yourself books to the floor. Her thigh is stuck to the linoleum; she peels it up; it makes a thick sucking sound. She is naked on a kitchen floor with a pot holder tucked under her head as if she's had some strange household accident. Her underwear is across the room, by the refrigerator; her khakis are under the kitchen table; her blouse, draped over the chair. She is doused in the queer perfume of sex, drowsy—as though awakened from a dream before it ended.

"You're a treat," Pat says. "A delicacy. I never get to kiss. George doesn't like it."

Elaine is crawling around on all fours, rounding up her clothing, wondering, What do you do now? How do you bring yourself to standing? How do you get up, get dressed, and move along?

"How about a bath, a long, hot bath?" Pat asks.

Elaine pulls on her underwear and looks at the kitchen clock. "I can't," she says. "Look at the time; it's eleven-thirty. Aren't you worried about having gotten off schedule?"

Pat shrugs. She finds her ring on the floor and puts it in her mouth, sucking it to clean it.

Elaine is dressing as fast as she possibly can. She can't believe what she's done: Okay, so Pat kissed her—George doesn't like to kiss, and Pat needed a kiss, but what about the rest—did it really happen? Has Pat done this before? Does Pat think it was all Elaine's fault? And why is Elaine thinking fault? Why is she blaming herself? Pure panic.

"Are you all right?" Pat asks.

"It's fine," Elaine says, hurrying.

Elaine needs to be in her car going home, she needs to be someplace familiar and safe, she needs a few minutes alone. She is suffering the strange anxiety of having risen so far up and out of herself as to seem entirely untethered. She's scared herself—as though this has never been done before, as though she and Pat invented it right there on the kitchen floor. She wonders if she's suffered some odd injury—did she hurt herself? Did Pat scrape her? Will she get an infection? Will she have to tell someone—explain it? She fumbles frantically with the buttons on her blouse.

"You seem upset," Pat says, slipping back into her robe.

"I just feel . . . like I'm running late. I slept late, and then, well, this happened. And now I'm really late. I should go." Elaine practically runs for the door.

"Something special you want for dinner?" Pat calls after her. "What's your favorite food? Wednesday is grab bag. Everyone puts in their wishes, and each person ends up getting at least one thing they want."

Nothing, Elaine wants nothing.

"You can't leave without naming something," Pat says.

"Beets," Elaine says, racing.

"Oh, that's good, that's great. I never would have thought of that," Pat says.

Elaine throws the car into gear and pulls away—she hates beets. Why did she say beets? She drives around the block, pulls up in front of the house, and blows the horn. Pat opens the door, thrilled that Elaine has returned. She leans forward, as though expecting Elaine to make some declaration along the lines of I love you, or at least Thanks, that was fun. Elaine rolls down the window and shouts her confession across the lawn. "I hate beets. I don't know why I said that."

Pat's face takes a fall.

"Asparagus," Elaine says. "Asparagus is fine."

"Oh," Pat calls back, recovering. "Oh, good. Asparagus is a good thing."

She drives. She stinks like a skunk—the funky musk of sex. She rifles through her purse, looking for something she can spray herself with—an olfactory cover-up. She douses herself with a perfume sample. The car fills with a vigorous, bright fragrance, which works like smelling salts, bringing Elaine back to her senses.

She pulls into the shopping center, parks, and goes into the hardware store. She has no idea what she wants: hammers, files, the common nail, precision blades, wires, switches, paints, and polishes.

Pure panic.

She hasn't felt this strange in thirty years, not since the afternoon in the maid's room of Charlie Thornton's house, when she touched, then kissed Charlie's penis—she remembers it; hot, fat, and rubbery, like something in a house of horrors. His voice changed when she touched it. "Kiss it," he'd said, and she did. Kiss it.

"May I help you?"

"Just looking." Self-consciously she walks the aisles. The salesmen's heads turn—they smell the perfume. She dips her hands into huge bins filled with clevis pins, cotter pins, and thumbscrews. Her body is still flooded, confusedly dilating and contracting, her breasts rubbing against her shirt, sore.

Pat. Pat would never have occurred to her. The cop occurred to her—occurs to her now—but Pat? Not Pat.

Elaine buys something, just to buy something. Screwdrivers, pliers, and a retractable tape measure. There's a lot she has to do. She has to take responsibility, she has to learn how to fix things.

"Women love hardware stores," the cashier volunteers as he's ringing her up. "By nature they're solution-oriented—everything here solves a problem. That'll be fifty-two fifty." He flashes a gap-toothed smile.

She dashes into the supermarket and throws a few things into a basket—soda, cookies, Smokehouse Almonds—she has to be a better wife, a better mom. Daniel asked for Ziploc bags; she can't remember what for. She drops a box into the basket and checks out. She dips into the liquor store, picking up a few bottles of wine. She is in and out of every store in the shopping center, and then she is ready to go home—she can't think of anything else to do.

The phone is ringing.

Elaine is standing outside, at the kitchen door, holding her grocery bags, her wine.

"Morning," Mrs. Hansen says, coming up the driveway behind her.

"Good morning," Elaine says.

The phone rings—its raucous rattle passes through the house, punctuating the air, splitting it, dividing it, defining it; comma, period, exclamation point.

"Your phone is ringing," Mrs. Hansen says.

"Yes," Elaine says, holding her bags, making no move to open the door.

"We sold your answering machine at the yard sale," Mrs. Hansen says.

"I remember," Elaine says. "I have to get a new one. I'm just wondering if I should run and do it now before I even go inside."

"It stopped," Mrs. Hansen says. "The phone stopped. You missed your call."

"It's fine," Elaine says, drawing a deep breath, feeling freed to find her key and step inside.

The house still stinks.

Mrs. Hansen follows her in. "Are you by chance wearing perfume?" Mrs. Hansen asks.

"It spilled," Elaine says. "It was a sample that spilled."

"It's intense," Mrs. Hansen says. "I couldn't tell right away if it was you or the house."

"The house stinks, and so do I," Elaine says, exasperated. "That's why I came home—I need to take a shower and change."

The phone starts to ring again.

Elaine stares at the wall. What looked all right yesterday is blistering, bubbling today.

"I'll get it," Mrs. Hansen says, taking the bags from Elaine and gesturing toward the stairs. "Go on. I'll get it."

Elaine can still feel the press of Pat on her body, her weight, her swampy sex. She showers, scrubbing herself with the loofah, imagining putting the long loofah up inside herself, like a bottle brush, to scratch the itch, the tingling lick of Pat's tongue, scraping herself clean. In her whorish fog, she lathers her breasts with soap, massaging them, and using the long neck of a shampoo bottle, makes herself come.

The phone keeps ringing.

Elaine dresses. Clean clothes are like fresh bandages, covering everything, making it smooth, easy, nice. She transfers the pile of Post-its into the clean pocket and goes back downstairs. Burnt toast. Today the house smells like wet burnt toast.

"Just two calls," Mrs. Hansen says. "A painter is coming to measure. And your mother—she wants you to call her back."

If anything can penetrate her fog and remind her of who she is, or more likely who she is not, it's her mother.

Elaine dials.

"Hello," her mother says, drawing the word out, dividing it in two, making it into a faux melody, like the NBC chimes or a doorbell.

"Hi, Mom."

"Your father is driving me crazy. I'm not the kind of woman who wants to walk out on a seventy-two-year-old man, but who does he think he's kidding? I open my mouth, and he says, 'I don't want to hear it.' "

"Is Daddy home? Do you want me to talk to him?"

"Of course he's home. Does he have a life? Does he have anything to do? No, and still he can't take a minute. He can't talk to me."

"I'm here, I'm here," her father says, taking the phone. "Twenty-four hours a day she wants to talk. I want one minute to think, and it turns into World War III."

"Be nice," Elaine says. "She's all you've got."

"So she says." He takes a breath. "I hear you have problems with the house."

"We had a fire."

"That's what your mother tells me. Are you insured?"

"Hopefully. They're coming today."

"Make sure you keep your receipts. Get a fireproof box; that way if anything happens, at least you have the receipt."

"Okay, Dad."

"You want your mother back, I can tell. Here she is."

"So," her mother says. "Help me with the sofa. Clearly your father isn't going to."

"I can't," Elaine says. She is determined to say no, to put her foot down. "Everything is falling apart. I have to take care of things. I'm sorry."

"How about tomorrow?" her mother asks.

"We'll see," Elaine says.

"What about your mother? Someone has to take care of your mother."

"Is it too early for a glass of wine?" Mrs. Hansen whispers while Elaine is on the phone.

"I'll call you in the morning," Elaine says, hanging up.

"Too early?" Mrs. Hansen asks again when Elaine hangs up.

"It's perfect, just perfect," Elaine says.

Mrs. Hansen uncorks the bottle.

"Have you eaten breakfast? We have to eat a little something with it," Elaine says, digging crackers out of the grocery bag.

"I don't really like to snack," Mrs. Hansen says. "It ruins the appetite."

* * *

Elaine's friend Liz pulls into the driveway, beeping her horn.

"I came the minute I heard." She rushes toward the house as though it's an emergency, as though the fire is still raging, as though she's going be the one who puts it out.

"We just got back, twenty minutes ago," Liz says, scurrying up the steps.

Liz grabs Elaine, hugging her. Elaine braces herself. "How are you?" she asks "Are you all right? Is everyone all right? What happened?"

"We had a fire," Elaine says, pulling back.

She feels so far away from Liz, from herself—she burned down her house, she had sex with someone other than her husband, she is losing her mind, and Mrs. Hansen, who she never really knew before, seems to be playing the role of full-time housekeeper. It's been less than a week, but it's like forever.

"Jennifer heard about it first. When we got home, her friend Mo was there feeding the cats, and the first thing Mo said was that your house caught fire. I ran right over. It wasn't clear whether you'd just caught on fire or what. So what happened?" Liz asks pausing for breath. "And when?"

All week Elaine's been waiting for Liz to come home; in her head she's been telling Liz everything, laying out what led to what, how it all turned to shit. But now that Liz is there, Elaine's need to tell, to confess, to relieve herself of the burden of the awkward events has evaporated. Other things, perhaps even more unbelievable, have happened. A stranger, even more unlikely scenario is unfolding.

The house burned down—worse yet, it didn't even really burn down and was only moderately damaged. Does it matter that Elaine tipped the grill? Which matters more, that Elaine tipped the grill or that she fucked Pat for breakfast? A breeze blows the plastic covering the hole in the dining-room wall. The house fills with a wingish, flapping sound.

"How was your trip?" Elaine asks. Liz and Jennifer have been touring colleges, visiting schools for Jennifer, who is going to be everything Liz and Elaine are not: doctor, lawyer, movie star.

"Wonderful," Liz says. "Jen is amazing. They all want her. Oberlin is lovely, Chicago isn't what I thought it would be. Yale was incredible, and an entire floor of the Barnard dorm is filled with girls with pierced tongues. But Jennifer wants to go somewhere far, far away, maybe Berkeley, which would be fine. We'll see. She could change her mind. Tomorrow she could become a young Republican, who can know?"

I set the house on fire, Elaine imagines herself saying. If it would make sense to anyone, it should make sense to Liz; after all, this is what she went back to school to study—the lives of women in relation to what's around them. She recently wrote thirty pages on "The Male Gaze as (Dis)played in Your Grocer's Dairy Case." Elaine remembers there being something in Liz's paper about the significance of the live-lobster tank in the fish department. She imagines Liz writing a paper on "The Burning House," finding some sociocultural explanation for what happened, revealing the truth of Elaine, not as a person but a phenomenon.

"How are Paul and the boys?" Liz asks.

Elaine pulls herself back into the conversation. "We're a little scattered," she says. "The electricity was off, and there's the smoke, the smell, and the hole."

"Come stay with me," Liz says. "We'll pack up your stuff, and you'll all come to my place until it's fixed. It'll be fun, like a slumber party."

"We've been with Pat and George," Elaine says.

Because Liz was away, because she missed the moment, she's been deposed. Now Pat has Elaine, and Elaine can't tell

Liz, because it's all so crazy. And so even though Liz is supposed to be her best friend—because they once were best friends and the assumption is that the assignment is permanent—and even though Liz is standing in front of her, asking, What can I do? practically begging, Elaine can't say anything. There's something about the new and improved Liz that annoys Elaine. Liz is making a career out of the parts of life that Elaine loathes—she found a way out by going farther in. Elaine doesn't want to celebrate women's lives, she wants to smash her life, to pummel it into a powder. And she can't deal with Liz's pronouncements, her judgment, her need to read something major into every situation.

Mrs. Hansen comes out of the kitchen and hands Elaine a glass of wine watered down with seltzer. She puts a small dish of almonds on the coffee table in the living room. "Can I get you a drink?" she asks Liz.

"We're having wine," Elaine explains.

"Yeah, sure, that'd be great," Liz says, and Mrs. Hansen goes back into the kitchen.

"New cleaning lady?"

"That's Mrs. Hansen from across the street—she's been here since the fire."

Mrs. Hansen delivers a spritzer for Liz and heads back to the kitchen.

"She's shy," Elaine says, sipping her drink.

"I've never seen you drink during the day."

"It's just a glass of wine," Elaine says.

Liz checks her watch—just past one—and takes a sip. "So," she says, "what're you going to do? You need a goal, a project."

"What's this?" Elaine asks, gesturing around the house.

"Repair work," Liz says.

There's a pause, a silence. In the kitchen something drops. "Sorry," Mrs. Hansen calls.

"It's fine," Elaine calls back. "It's fine," she says, and remembers the kiss—the satiny feel of Pat's lips, Pat's hands sliding over her skin—it's fine. Fine as long as it's only this. It's fine—if it's just one time. Fine.

"Let's get out of here," Liz says. "I'm taking you shopping. I start a summer internship next week, and I need a few things." That's another thing about the new Liz that Elaine could never have been: a convert. Liz has abandoned the cult of the home for the cult of the classroom and become an academic fanatic.

Elaine pulls the pile of Post-its from her pocket and thinks of her khakis bunched up on the floor, under Pat's kitchen table. Pick paint, repair or renovate. Contractor. Do you want a deck? French doors? Roofer—ask Pat. Make dinner plans. The car is for you—keys on the dresser. Insurance company will come. Measure.

"Paul asked me to take care of a few things. I should stay here and deal with them," Elaine says.

"Fuck Paul," Liz says, taking the Post-its, going through them as though they're a flip book, a slow-motion show of two people doing a dance. "Okay," she says. "We'll go to the paint store, we'll get chips. Definitely renovate—why just repair when you can improve? Contractor—call Ruth Esterhazy; they just did a job on their house. Yes, deck. Yes, French doors. I have a roofer, Ric. 'Ric's Roofs—We don't let it rain on you.' I'll give you his number. Measure. What are you supposed to measure?"

"I have no idea," Elaine says. "Measure up?"

"Come on, I'll drive."

"Should I ask Mrs. Hansen to join us?" Elaine whispers.

"Whatever."

"Mrs. Hansen," Elaine calls as she's getting her bag. "We're going to do a little shopping, would you like to come?"

"Oh, no," Mrs. Hansen says, stepping out from the kitchen. "You go. I'll just stay here. That painter is coming to look around. And maybe I'll do a little work in your garden, if you don't mind."

"I don't mind. Should I leave you a key?"

"Oh, I don't need a key; the lock is still broken."

"Right," Elaine says. "Well, we'll see you in a little while."

As they're pulling out of the driveway, Elaine notices the cop car parked just across the street—the cop waves.

"Community service," Elaine says.

They shop. The get paint chips and a couple of quarts of colors to try out. They go to the mall in White Plains. They go in and out of the stores. Elaine starts to feel more normal, more like herself. In Nordstrom's, Liz buys a linen suit for her summer job: assistant to the assistant director at the Center for Women in the Humanities at NYU. "I thought it would give me broad exposure—no pun intended," Liz says. "Now I just need shoes."

Elaine motions toward the lingerie department. "I've got to pick up something," she says. "Why don't I meet you in twenty minutes?"

Elaine is looking for a nightgown for Paul. Something large, something long. Not a nightshirt, he made that clear. "Silky," he'd said. "With a little lace. I like lace, it tickles." She finds one she thinks will look good on him. "It's got to cover my ass," he'd said. "Nothing baby-doll—that makes me feel too exposed, like I'm going to get poked." She finds one for Paul and the same one for herself in a smaller size and then is looking at the bras and panties.

Panties. She never wears panties. She wears underpants— but that sounds so generic, almost medicinal, like a mustard plaster.

"Do you have these panties in black?" she asks the salesgirl.

"Are they low-cut, high-cut?" she asks when the girl brings them out.

The girl shrugs. "Depends on how *you're* cut."

Elaine slips into the dressing room and tries on a few

things. She had sex with a woman—how could that have happened? It has the surrealistic quality of a dream. Why did she do it? Will she do it again? She doesn't think so, and yet she is shopping for lingerie—sexy things in black, things that will make her look good for Pat. Elaine studies herself in the mirror—her left breast is a third the size of the right, her pubic hair is thin. And her thighs, her thighs seem to be melting, pulling away from the bone and pouring down, dripping over her knees. She needs to get in shape, to lose a few pounds. She is looking in the mirror comparing herself to Pat. Horrified. She thought this kind of thing didn't happen between women— that's why lesbians look the way they do—they don't make comparisons.

The salesgirl stands outside the dressing room. "Can I get you anything? Do you need different sizes?"

"I'm fine," Elaine says, passing the undergarments out over the top along with her credit card. "Just ring me up."

"The grill tipped," Elaine says in the car on the way back to the house. "That's what started it."

"A Weber?"

"No, just a crappy thing we got at the grocery store last year."

"Unbelievable," Liz says. "That's what started the fire?" she asks, and Elaine wonders if Liz doesn't believe her.

"Yeah."

"Wow."

"It seems so strange," Liz says, pulling into the driveway. "What can I do? What would be helpful?"

Elaine has no answers.

"Are you all right?" Liz asks.

Elaine shakes her head no.

"Do you want me to come in with you?" Liz asks. "I'm back. I can do whatever you need."

Elaine smiles. "Thanks," she says; her tone is somewhat

lost, somewhat resigned. She doesn't want to go home. She is fine—or if not fine, at least better—when she is out of the house.

"What is it? You and Paul? The boys?"

Elaine can't answer. What if it's not one thing? she thinks. What if it's everything?

"I'm sorry," Liz says, sort of catching on. "I'm sorry, I always think of you as being so fantastic."

"You do?" Elaine gets out of the car. Her head is a sour soup, a confit of confusion.

FIVE

IT IS A PERFECT JUNE DAY, the sky is a hearty blue, the trees are freshly green, the air is cool and sweeps over Elaine's skin, drawing her out of herself and into the day.

It is the kind of afternoon that people notice. They look up at the sky and say, "What a blue," and, "You ought to get outside—it'd be a shame not to." "Enjoy!" they implore each other. It is the kind of a day that brings on a good mood; the air is pregnant with promise.

She is in a whirl, a dizzying spin.

It is Elaine, all Elaine. The darkness, the rot is inside her, like poison, consuming her—death eating flesh.

With a terrific echoey bang, Daniel pops up out of the Dumpster like a jack-in-the-box unsprung. "Where have you been?" he demands. "You're late. You're always home when we get here."

A startled shout escapes Elaine. "What are you doing? Are you stuck? Did you fall in? Is this some sort of a game?"

"I was looking for something," Daniel says as he starts to climb out.

"What would be in the Dumpster?"

"Stuff," he says, crawling out over the top, lowering himself to a stepladder he's parked alongside.

"So where were you?" Daniel asks again. He rolls down the sleeves of a white dress shirt that Elaine has never seen before.

"I was with Liz, if you must know."

"Oh," he says, buttoning the cuffs. "I thought maybe you'd gone off somewhere."

"Like where?"

"Dunno, somewhere."

"Why would you think that?" she asks, sensing his suspicion, his constant disappointment in her.

He shrugs.

"Where's Sammy?"

"Inside."

"And Mrs. Hansen?"

"Right here, never fear," Mrs. Hansen says, coming around the corner of the house, rubbing her hands together. Her hands are a rich dark brown to the wrist; it looks as if she's wearing leather driving gloves. Her apron is muddy. "Don't say it, don't say it," she says, waving away Elaine's stare. "Use a trowel, that's what everyone says, get a good gardening outfit, but this is how I like it. I like getting down in the dirt, in deep with the worms, et cetera, et cetera," she says, her speech ever so slightly slurred. "Isn't it a beautiful day?" She holds her face up to the sky. "Glorious," she says.

The boys are home. Mrs. Hansen is home. The yard is hardening, pulling itself back together, forming a firm and crusty surface. The world has held its shape. Everything is as it was. Elaine is both comforted and disconcerted. She is glad things are the same, but it throws into relief how very strange she's feeling—there is an enormous distance, an unbridgeable electromagnetic force field between Elaine and everyone else.

"Pat called. And Paul called. And your father called looking for your mother—he says she escaped, he's afraid she's run away. He last saw her folding laundry, and then she was gone. He says it's no joke."

The phone rings. Sound turned inside out; a gentle trill comes from the garden. Mrs. Hansen hurries around back. Elaine and Daniel follow her.

"Hello," she says, picking up the blue Princess phone that used to be in the hall and is now resting in the dirt near the flower beds. A long line of telephone cord trails out the kitchen window. "Hello," Mrs. Hansen says. "Hello, hello."

"It's your father," she whispers to Elaine.

Elaine shakes her head.

"I'm sorry, she's not back yet. Can I take a message?"

"Oh, that's good," Mrs. Hansen says. "That's wonderful. I'll give her the news." She hangs up. "He found your mother. She was there all the time, but she was hiding. So nothing happened, nothing is wrong. Isn't that nice?" She smiles.

Elaine imagines that her parents have been playing a constant and peculiar game of hide-and-go-seek for the last forty-seven years.

"She was hiding," Mrs. Hansen says.

"Where's Sammy?"

"He's inside," Mrs. Hansen says. "And the insurance man is somewhere around here—that's his car down by the curb—he's been lurking for about an hour, canvassing the neighborhood. He caught me as I was crossing the street. I went back for the long phone cord—I was sure we had one—and he stopped me. He asked me, 'How long have you been friends?' I told him, 'We really weren't friends at all, until the fire.'" She gets down on her hands and knees. "I've got my planting to do," she says, digging in the dirt. "He'll be back."

Mrs. Hansen, the nanny they never had. Who could ask for more? An older woman with experience, mature and a little tipsy. You couldn't get a better one from an agency.

Elaine goes into the house.

Surrounded by soot and ash, Sammy sits on the floor in front of the TV, playing a video game, ignoring the fact that the TV screen has been dimmed by smoke.

"How come you're in here all by yourself?" Elaine asks.

"I don't stand a chance at Nate's," he says, manically flicking his thumbs on the controls.

Elaine looks past him at the hole in the dining room wall—bandaged but still looking like the entrance to a cave.

The zim-zam careening sounds of the video game blast. Elaine goes over to the TV.

"You're blocking me," Sammy says.

"This might help," she says, pressing her palm to the TV and moving her hand in an arc like a wiper blade across the screen. The picture brightens—her hand is covered in black soot.

"Don't stay in here," she says to Sammy. "It's too cruddy, and it's a beautiful day outside."

Sammy jiggles the controls, and two buildings blow up and fall into an animated heap of rubble. "Yes," he screams at the TV set. And then the pieces miraculously grow legs, scramble together, and run away. "Go," he screams. "Go."

Elaine goes upstairs. She looks at herself in the bathroom mirror. The face is familiar, not contorted—not twisted into an anxious knot. One eye twitches, but that's it. The dense fog of anxiety, the cloud cover of guilt is invisible.

Daniel stands at the bathroom door.

"What are you doing?" he asks.

"Nothing," she says.

"Do we have a waterproof marker?" he asks.

"In the drawer in the kitchen," she says.

He stands in the door.

She turns toward him, wanting to reach him, to find a point of contact. He's wearing a suit. Elaine has never seen him

in a suit before. He doesn't even own a suit. Her confusion is
obvious.

"Mrs. Meaders gave it to me," he says. "It was in their
basement, in the GoodWill pile. I like it." He holds the lapels
and turns as if modeling the outfit.

There's a huge stain on the back of the jacket—Elaine
debates whether to tell him or not.

"Take off your jacket," she says.

"Why?"

"It's got a stain."

"No, it doesn't."

"Yes, it does."

"This is like a joke," Daniel says. "You're making fun of
me because I'm wearing a suit and you think it's funny."

"Daniel," Elaine says, "mothers don't make fun of their
children—or at least not to their faces. That's why mothers and
fathers sleep in a double bed, so they can make fun of the kids
all night."

"Not true," Daniel says, taking off the jacket, checking
the spot. "They sleep in the same bed so they can fuck."

"Watch it, mister," Elaine says.

"Like I'm telling you something you don't already know."

What *does* he know? Elaine is uncomfortable, somehow
threatened.

Daniel pulls a notebook from his pocket, a long narrow
notebook like a reporter's steno pad, only it's a grocery list.
Instead of lines, it has categories: fruit, vegetables, meat, poul-
try, fish.

"How old were you when you married Dad?" he asks.

"Twenty-six."

"How old were you when you got pregnant with me?"

"Thirty-one."

"And how old are you now?" he asks, doing the math.

She has the feeling that he is trying to stump her. "Is this a test?"

"Just answer the questions."

"Forty-three," she says.

There is a sound from downstairs—Sammy laughing, Sammy entertaining himself. She is heartened. She smiles. She looks at Daniel, who is still fixed on her with an impassive stare. The noise continues—what she thought was laughing becomes more frenzied, more like barking, and Elaine realizes that Sammy is wheezing. She races down the stairs, grabs him by the arm, ripping him away from the television set. Moving through the house, as though she's flying, she grabs the spare inhaler from the drawer in the kitchen along with the pills for severe occasions and rushes Sammy out of the house. He is breathing as though he's choking, as though there is no air. She shakes the inhaler and holds it to his mouth. "Breathe," she shouts, squirting a puff into his mouth.

"Hold it," she says. "Exhale." She shakes the inhaler again. "And breathe," she says, shooting another puff into his lungs. She hands him a pill and goes back in for water.

They sit on the kitchen steps waiting for the drugs to take effect. She rubs his back and encourages him to breathe slowly, deeply. The wheezing subsides.

"Are you okay?"

Sammy nods.

"As soon as that starts to happen, you have to use the inhaler. Don't wait. Ask someone to help you. Do you know how to use the inhaler?"

He nods.

Her heart is racing. "It's my fault. I shouldn't have let you be in there. The house is too dirty for you. You have to stay outside until we get it all cleaned up. Okay?"

He nods again.

The house is like a ruin; you can only dip into it. Sammy's attack proves to Elaine that the house can't be trusted, that she can't be trusted. She should have known better, she should have pulled him out as soon as she saw him there on the floor. Around her children, she feels the most helpless kind of love, achingly inadequate. What if she hadn't been home? What if it had just been Daniel and Mrs. Hansen—what would have happened then?

Daniel is walking around the front yard, scribbling pages of notes.

"Dad's home," he announces before Paul reaches the driveway.

She is nervous. She's not even sure what to feel guilty about: cheating—that it was with another woman, does that even count?—or enjoying it?

Paul comes into view. "What a fucking incredible day," he says, coming up the driveway.

Sammy starts to rattle again. Elaine rubs his back slowly. "Breathe," she encourages him.

"I'm home," Paul says, beaming up at the family.

Elaine looks at him as though he is a foreigner. Her memory of him is distant, divorced, like déjà vu—Paul who? "What puts you in such a good mood?"

"I just had the best walk home from the train. It's a beautiful day. We're fixing up the house. We're going to have a deck and French doors."

"The house is giving Sammy an asthma attack," Elaine says.

"Oh."

"And the insurance guy is around here somewhere. He's interviewing our neighbors. He could tell us we have no coverage at all. He could say, 'Sorry, folks, you're on your own.' "

"Why are you being so negative?"

"Somebody has to be," Elaine says.

"You're ruining it," Paul says. "For all of us. We're having a great time." He nods at Sammy. "Right, Sammo?"

Sammy closes his eyes and breathes.

"You might be having a great time," Elaine says. "What did you do today?" she asks.

"What do you mean?" he asks defensively.

"Never mind," she says. They take swipes at each other, scratching, clawing, fighting to hit a nerve, to get a reaction. Elaine pats Sammy on the back. "It's much better now, isn't it?" She rubs a dirty spot on his leg. "What's that?"

"Nate peed on me," he says. "I put dirt on to clean it."

"Nate peed on you?" Elaine asks. "That's disgusting."

"He must have missed," Paul says.

"Uh-huh," Sammy says, getting up, going down the steps and into the yard.

"Take it easy," Elaine calls after him. "Don't go wild."

"All day I tried calling you," Paul says. "You weren't home. Did you get my messages? Did you get my Post-its from this morning?"

"Got 'em all," she says. "Got your Post-its and I got your paint chips, got your names and numbers, shapes and sizes. I got it all like a good little wife."

"Good little wife?"

The insurance guy bursts through the bushes, taking the shortcut through the neighbors' yard. "I'm Randy, your State Farm man," he says, shaking Paul's hand. He is younger than they are, maybe thirty or thirty-five, a baby-faced blimp with a strangely thin coat of fine brown hair like feathers. His belly presses against his pale-blue short-sleeved shirt, straining the buttons. Elaine imagines that when people describe him as a "big fella," he thinks it's a compliment.

"I've got your file right here with me," he says. "I hope you'll be able to clue me in, fill in the missing links so we can dot the I's and cross the T's. I hope we can get it over with here and now."

Elaine and Paul nod.

"I've taken a look around and talked with your neighbors," the investigator says. "They weren't much help. And I've also gone over your claim history. There isn't much."

"We had a flood once," Elaine says. "A pipe broke."

"Yes, I know," the investigator says, looking through his file.

"Give me an idea of how this works," Paul says to the agent nervously. "I always need to know how things work."

The investigator holds up a finger, keeping Paul at bay. He pulls a fresh pen from his shirt pocket. "Things good at the office?" he asks Paul.

"Good," Paul says. "Good. Everything is good."

"Any debt?" the agent asks.

"Not much. The house, the car, and a little home-equity loan we took out a couple of years ago to fix up the bathroom," Paul says.

"We redid the master bath," Elaine says.

Daniel comes around the side of the house and catches Paul's eye.

Paul smiles.

Daniel flips to a clean page in his notebook and writes something down.

Elaine sees it coming. She stares at Paul and shakes her head, no, no, no. She is powerless to stop it.

"Why so dressed up?" Paul asks Daniel. "You going to a funeral?"

Daniel looks at Elaine as if to say, See, you are making fun of me. He scribbles frantically in his notebook and walks away.

"Hey," Paul calls after him. "Your jacket's dirty, you've got a stain on your back."

"I hate you. I hate you," Daniel screams, breaking into a run.

"What did I do?" Paul asks Elaine.

"Let's take a walk around back," the agent says, "and see what we've got."

"Did you call Pat to tell her we'll be late for dinner?" Paul asks.

"No."

"Why not?"

Elaine doesn't answer.

"Could you call her now and apologize for not calling sooner, tell her you forgot and that we'll get dinner on our own."

"Could you?" Elaine asks.

"What's wrong with you?" Paul asks.

"Don't investigate me," she says.

"Just call. You don't even have to go inside." Paul points to the blue Princess phone in the dirt.

Elaine dials.

Perfect Pat, Pat from the night before, Pat from the kitchen floor. "Should I hold dinner?" Pat asks.

"No. We'll be fine on our own," Elaine says, pronouncing each word as though reading from a script, trying to say the minimum.

"Are you all right?" Pat asks.

Fine as long as . . . Fine if it's only . . . "I'm fine," she says. What else can she say?

"Did I frighten you?" Pat asks. "Are you avoiding me?"

"Oh, no," Elaine says, lying. "I've just been busy with the house, and then Liz was here, and then the boys, and now the insurance man." Elaine turns away from everyone. "I can't talk right now." She stares at the dirt. "I'm out in the yard."

"See you soon," Pat says.

Elaine hangs up.

"So," the agent says, pushing papers deeper into the folder.

"You asked how this works. Basically, I could investigate you upside down and inside out. I could look at your finances and your fingerprints. I could send out a questionnaire to every person on your block. I could interview your parents, your boss, and your first-grade teacher. But why would I?"

A faint line of perspiration breaks out on Elaine's upper lip. The evening air is still, slightly warm. She begins to sweat, to breathe too quickly, to panic. It feels as if the temperature is going up as the sun goes down, and the humidity is on the rise. The air is without air, there is nothing to breathe.

"You tell me you have no debts, and I believe you," the agent says. "But have you got a bank statement I could take a peek at? Do you have a retirement account? How much are you putting in? Are you maxing out?" He pauses and takes a peek at his papers. "Any health issues? Cancer in the family? Either of you recently diagnosed with a horrible, expensive disease?" The agent looks at them carefully. "Anything you don't want me to know?" He laughs to himself: heh, heh, heh.

Paul bangs on his chest. "Healthy like a hog," he says.

"Knock wood," Elaine says. "We have nothing to tell."

"We're incredibly boring," Paul says. "That's the fact. We even bore ourselves."

"I hope so," the agent says. "I hope that's the whole story."

The boys come running through the yard, walkie-talkies squawking. The agent crouches down to Sammy's level. "Do you like your mommy's meat loaf?" he asks. Sammy makes a face, pretending to throw up, then he burps in the investigator's face.

"He hates meat loaf," Paul says.

"Let's talk a bit about the grill?" the guy says, standing up. "Do you cook out a lot?"

"More in July and August, but it's been so warm," Paul says. "We've already been to three or four barbecues this year."

"I couldn't cook," Elaine says. "I just couldn't cook."

The men exchange winks—as if to say, Mine gets that way too. Elaine sees it and hates both of them.

"So this is the grill that failed you," the agent says, crouching over the remains. He tucks his file into his armpit and struggles to reassemble the parts. He tries to put it back together, and it keeps coming apart. "How does it go? What's the drill? She marinates and you . . . ?"

Who squirted the stuff that soaked the coals, who lit the match, who fanned the flames, who kicked the grill and caused it to fall? Who dared do this to the house that Jack built?

"What usually happens is that I get home and everyone's starving. I take off my jacket, set up the coals, get it started, and go in and change while they're warming up." Paul shrugs. "I feel like it's all my fault."

The guy holds up his hand. "Do you leave the grill unattended?"

"What can I say?" Paul says.

"There weren't enough hot dogs," Elaine says. "There were only three franks, and there are four of us. And Paul and Daniel sometimes eat two or three apiece." Elaine keeps thinking, It's a trap. Paul is acting looser and looser with the guy, like he can say anything, as if they're buddies, having bonded on the idea that their wives won't cook. And the agent is acting friendly, giving advice, waiting for Paul to confess. Waiting for Paul to lean in and, say, ask confidentially, Suppose a fellow "accidentally" burned his own house down?

Whatta ya mean by accidentally? the agent would say.

Well, you know, had a patch of temporary insanity and set the thing on fire—what would happen then?

Suppose a fella worked for an insurance company, the guy would say, and the fella who burned his house down asked him this question. Whatta ya suppose the fella from the insurance company should think?

Elaine can hear it in her head. She sees them losing the

deck, losing the French doors, the house, the kids, the car, losing the bonus prize behind door number three and going directly to jail.

"Tell us about yourself," Elaine says, changing the subject. "Where do you live?"

"We're in a condominium in Fordham—indoor garage, roof deck, health club, party room whenever you want it. A house is too much responsibility. All day I see what goes wrong. I know what happens. It's better to have nothing; that way you have nothing to lose." While he talks, he draws diagrams of the scene.

Elaine looks at his pictures; he sketches like a child: a square box, a triangle for the roof. The family is represented by stick figures; the grill looks like an armless, three-legged man. Elaine thinks of the "Can Dinky Draw?" ads on the backs of comic books. Everything is flat—he has no perspective. He has no vision.

"There's also a hole in the roof. You can see it from the bedroom," Elaine says. "We took Polaroids."

The agent draws a circle in the roof; he draws an arrow marking it and writes, "hole/roof." "I guess it was just about now—this time of day," the guy says, looking up. "Just about dinnertime."

"Just about now," Paul says, echoing him.

A horn beeps.

The phone rings. Mrs. Hansen answers it. "Hello," Elaine hears Mrs. Hansen say. "I'm sorry, they're busy now. Can I take a message?"

Kick the can. Sammy is kicking the can of charcoal-starter fluid, around the yard; the hollow, metal ka-thunk echoes. Where did he get it? Elaine remembers seeing Paul and Henry in the yard yesterday, Henry picking up the can, shaking it, and putting it in the trash. She remembers Paul emptying the trash can into the Dumpster. How did it get out again? Is this the "stuff" Daniel was looking for? Did he give it to Sammy on purpose? What is he doing? What kind of game is this?

"Wallace, Wallace," a boy calls. The neighbors' dog comes crashing through the yard, carrying something in his mouth that looks like underpants. On his wild ride, he brushes against the grill, which the agent has finally gotten to stand; it collapses. "Wallace, Wallace." A boy chases after the dog. "Jesus Christ, Wallace, get back here. You're driving me crazy, Wallace. Do you want a cookie, a major Milk-Bone? Wallace, come home, please."

The horn beeps again.

Daniel comes into the backyard. "Mr. Meaders is here."

"I was on my way home, and thought I'd stop by and pick up Daniel—if he's ready to go," Meaders says, appearing in the backyard. "I thought I'd save you the trouble of dropping him. I hear you folks have been having some difficulties."

"We had a fire," Paul says.

"Something in the wiring?"

"An accident," Elaine says. "The grill tipped."

"These things happen," Paul says.

"Wouldn't know," the man says. "I never grill. I don't like surprises."

"I wouldn't think so," Paul says.

"You all set?" he asks Daniel. "You have your books, your homework?"

Daniel nods.

"Tell your folks good night."

"Night," Daniel says.

"Sleep well," Elaine says. "See you tomorrow."

"I hate that guy," Paul says when they are gone. The sight of his eldest son trailing off after Meaders so willingly, as though Meaders is his trainer, his guide, infuriates Paul and is disheartening as hell. "He gives me a knot in my gut. There's something about him I don't trust. What does he do for a living?"

"He's some kind of tax investigator."

"Oh," Paul says. "I knew it was something."

There is a moment's silence.

"It isn't so bad," the insurance guy says, signing his forms. "I've seen worse. You wouldn't believe the idiotic things people do when they're not thinking." He pauses. "The other day I caught my wife brushing her teeth and blow-drying her hair simultaneously. One hand is under the water and the other's got the blow-dryer going. I'm afraid to touch her. 'Hey, hey,' I yell, 'you're underwater.' And she looks at me like I'm the idiot."

"So where do we go from here?" Paul asks. "What now?"

"I don't think it'll be a problem," the agent says. "I have the report, I talked to your neighbors. Anything could have happened. That damned dog could have done it, who knows? Do you know? I don't know. Therefore, I think it'll be fine."

"Does that mean you're going to pay?"

"Basically," the agent says. "You're covered under the stupidity clause."

"Is there really a stupidity clause?" Elaine asks.

"No," he says, closing his folder. "But here's a good example: I once had a guy whose pipes froze, and he went to unfreeze them with a blowtorch and burned the whole house down. It was an accident, stupidity. He didn't do it on purpose—that's the way it goes. Nice to meet you," the agent says, shaking their hands.

"Great meeting you," Paul says buoyantly.

Elaine smiles.

Paul turns to Elaine, beaming. "We're covered under the stupidity clause. I'm so relieved."

Sammy plays with both walkie-talkies. "What are you wearing?" he asks one walkie-talkie.

"Who is this?" he asks the other.

"It's me," he says. "Do you have your shoes and socks on? Are you ready to go?"

"Who is me? Do I know you?" he asks.

So relieved.

In the front yard Elaine and Paul have a fierce, whispering fight. "I'm in a good mood," Paul hisses. "I want to take you out to dinner. I want us to have an hour alone. Why do you have to ruin it? Why do you ruin everything?"

"He had an attack, Paul," Elaine hisses back. "He was in the house playing a video game. I was upstairs, I thought I heard him laughing, but he wasn't laughing, he was wheezing, he was wheezing horribly."

"But he's all right now," Paul says.

Elaine shakes her head. She hates Paul for putting her in this position, for making her choose, for being so fucking selfish.

"Roger," Sammy says into walkie-talkie number one.

"Hey, I'm not Roger," he says into walkie-talkie number two.

"If you're not Roger, then who am I?"

"I'm starving," Paul says. "Let's just drop him off and grab a bite."

"Fine," she says. "If something horrible happens to him, it's your fault."

"Nothing is going to happen."

"Over and out," Sammy says. "Over. Outer."

They drive Sammy to Nate's. Paul gets out and takes Sammy to the door. They ring the bell. Nate answers. "Oh, it's you," he says and walks away, leaving the door open.

Paul and Sammy step inside. "Hello," Paul calls. "Hello, it's Paul and Sam." They wait uncomfortably in the hall. There are sounds from the kitchen. Paul rubs Sammy's back. "Are you okay? Do you have your medicine in case you need it?"

Sammy nods.

"Mommy and I are only a phone call away."

Paul debates whether to go in farther, whether to look for Susan. He wonders if Gerald is home.

"Oooooo, ick pot," Nate shouts, running past them, through the house, and up the stairs.

Sammy sighs deeply.

"You'll be all right," Paul says. "Hello? Anybody home?" He wanders down the hall. "Susan?"

She steps out of the kitchen. "I didn't hear the door. I was grinding nuts."

He smiles—they had a lovely conversation earlier this afternoon, everything is good. They have a date for Friday— she has arranged for someone else, some other mother, to pick up the kids after soccer. She will be his Mrs. Apple, from four-thirty to six-thirty. "I'm just dropping Sammy," he says.

"Hi, Sam," she says, giving him a special little smile. "How are you today? It was a beautiful day, wasn't it?"

Sammy doesn't answer.

Paul pats his chest and mimes wheezing.

"Are you better now?" Susan asks. "Are you hungry? I made wieners for dinner. You like wieners, don't you?"

"He has his inhaler in case there's trouble."

She squeezes Paul's shoulder, kneading him. "How many puffs?"

"Two."

"See you tomorrow," Paul says, getting down on his knees, giving Sammy a big squeeze. "Be a good boy."

"Did you give her the inhaler?" Elaine asks as soon as he's back in the car.

"Sammy's got it."

"Well, you should have given it to her. Does she know how to use it?"

"She knows everything," Paul says, pulling out of the driveway.

*   *   *

At the Chinese restaurant, Paul is sweet, he is loving and attentive. He holds open the door for Elaine, pulls her chair out, and then tucks her in. He is acting like a gentleman, as if he wants to please her, as if pleasing her gives him pleasure. But she is in a foul mood. Elaine is the anchor to reality, the unrelenting reminder that all is not well. The happier Paul seems, the more pleased he is, the fouler she becomes. "Why do you have to ruin everything?" she hears the echo of his asking.

She looks at Paul—Paul is beaming. Why?

Is Paul happy because he has something horrible to tell her? Maybe he's going to tell her that he's having an affair—she's convinced he's having one. Maybe he's leaving. Maybe he's so damned happy because he finally found a way out.

"Am I supposed to pretend that everything is fine?" Elaine asks. "Am I supposed to ignore things?"

"Not ignore," Paul says. "But if you noticed less—if everything didn't mean so terrifically much—things would be better."

"That's all it takes?" Elaine asks.

"It's a start."

The waitress comes. "What can I get you folks this evening?"

"Oh," Elaine says, "we're not ready yet, we haven't even looked."

They open their menus. Elaine thinks of Pat. Will Pat be angry that they went out for dinner—that Elaine didn't call until the last minute?

"You pick," Paul says. "Get whatever you want. No kids. No rules. No limits."

He is thinking of Mrs. Apple, of the date, of Elaine. With Mrs. Apple he has the fantasy of himself as the caring husband, the good father—she doesn't burden him with details about money, about what needs to be fixed, about where they're going for summer vacation. With the date he has adventure—tomor-

row she has promised something that will "change him forever."
And with Elaine he has all the rest. In his mind they are not
three different women but continuations of one woman. A giant
breast. On some profound level, he can't imagine that it would
be a problem, that anyone would mind. He's aware there's a flaw
in his thinking, an immaturity that tells him what he does is
excusable. His behavior—his constant need for comfort—makes
sense to him, therefore it should make sense to others—to
Elaine. In Paul's mind Elaine is like a mother—required to
accept him completely no matter what he does; she can never
get too fed up, she can never leave. And in his mind Elaine is
always annoyed with him for not doing what he should. And
Paul is always mad at Elaine, hating her for making him feel
that he's failed.

"Did ya figure it out?" the waitress asks.

Paul looks at Elaine, helpless.

"Soft-Shell Crabs in Garlic Sauce," Elaine says. "Ginger
Chicken. Brown Rice."

"Sounds great," Paul says, closing the menu, beaming.

"Your smile is making me nervous," Elaine says.

"I'm just so relieved," he says. "I didn't realize how worried I was. I'm so happy about the insurance. It's like getting a
prize even though we don't deserve it. Maybe God is giving us
this, to teach us a lesson—not everything has to be a negative
experience. Maybe the point is, you can lose your head and not
completely ruin your life."

"I don't think we should tell everybody that it was stupidity."

"Who's everybody?"

"Our friends," she says. "It's stupidity, not a citizenship
award, it's not something to brag about."

"We're covered," Paul says. "That's what counts. Besides,
it's funny. Stupidity is funny. Hey, if you can't laugh at yourself,
then you certainly can't laugh at anyone else."

"The house wasn't stupid—we were," Elaine says.

"Would you like some tea?" he asks, still cheerful.

"Please."

He pours for her.

Paul is looking at Elaine as though she is a stranger, as though they've never met. He is looking at her with a completely open face—absent of history—like a doe-eyed idiot. He is looking at her as though he is in love with her.

Elaine is tempted to ask, Do you know who I am? To remind him that she is his wife, the one he fights with all the time. But, in keeping with the idea of noticing less, she lets it go.

"The first date I ever took a girl on was to a Chinese restaurant—on Palmer Avenue in Bronxville," he tells her. "There was a red neon sign in the window—and about ten tables. It was the only 'foreign' restaurant in town. Her name was Sally Potter. I ordered chow mein. She didn't eat anything. Not a bite. Worms, she told me later. Her mother had told her that Chinese food was made of worms."

Elaine is trying to calm down, to warm up, to allow herself to be open to Paul. She's frustrated with herself for being so angry, for making things more difficult.

"Let's pretend we've just met," she says. "Let's pretend we're on a date."

He seems surprised. "Don't you want to talk about the house?" he asks. "About what we're going to do? I thought we might talk about the deck, about the French doors."

"Should we pretend we're engaged, then?" she asks.

"That would be nice," he says. "And let's pretend we get along."

"Fine," she says. Fine.

The waitress brings the food, and they have a wonderful dinner, talking about the house, about windows and doors.

He is trying, and she is trying, and it is rare that they are both trying at the same time.

Usually he tries until he gets tired and quits, and then she tries for a while and gets mad at him for not noticing her effort, and they push and pull at each other until finally they both stop trying. But right now, for this moment, their efforts are in sync, and it seems to be working.

Near the end, Paul leans across the table and begins eating off Elaine's plate. He takes a piece of crab from her, pops it into his mouth, and says, "I love you. I love you so fucking much." And in that moment he feels it, he really feels it.

"That's nice," Elaine says. "I love you, too," she adds, pulled into the mood of generosity.

For the moment they are their fantasies of themselves, their very best selves, the people they'd like to be, and then just a minute later they are once again their more familiar selves— petty, boring, limited.

"So what did you do with Liz all day?" Paul asks.

"Not much, some shopping, the things on the Post-its." Elaine pauses. "What's the problem with you and Liz anyway? Why do you hate her?"

"She's your friend. She has you in a way I never can," Paul says. "You tell her things about me, how horrible I am, how much you hate me. I hate her because she hates me—it's simple."

"She doesn't hate you," Elaine says. "You want the truth? I hardly talk to her about anything personal. I don't know what to say. I'm afraid to say anything to anyone—they'll think I'm nuts." She pauses. "You're the one who tells people about us— you called what's-his-name, Mr. Blow Job, Tom, from the motel. Why Tom? Why all of a sudden did you think of Tom?"

Paul shrugs. "He's smart and calm, and I knew he'd help us."

"What about me? What about us? You hid in a shower stall confessing to someone who gave you a blow job in college, while I sat on the toilet waiting. . . ."

"I'm sorry."

"Sorry for what?" Elaine wants to know. "Let's stop," she says. "Let's just stop for now. We can take a night off from it, can't we? Or are we so addicted?"

They stop.

"Should I call and check on Sammy?" Paul asks.

"I'm sure he's all right," Elaine says. "It just frightened me. His attacks always frighten me."

Paul squeezes her arm sympathetically and plucks the last piece of chicken from her plate.

She doesn't tell Paul that she's always secretly glad when she misses one of his attacks, when she hears about it after the fact, when things are okay again—like over the phone from the school nurse, or in a note from the soccer coach. She is always terrified that one day the puffer won't work, one day it will be worse, one day there won't be anything she can do.

"I'll call," he says.

"Leave him alone," Elaine says.

Their fortune cookies come, they crack them simultaneously—two fortunes fall out of Elaine's cookie. "You are going places," her first fortune says. "You have come a long distance," the second says. "And yours?" she asks Paul.

" 'You are lucky in work and love.' "

As they walk from the restaurant, Paul takes Elaine's arm, pulling her close—she feels good against him, and he feels good to her, large, comforting, protective.

"Thanks for dinner," she says.

"You're welcome," he says.

*   *   *

In the car en route to Pat and George's, Elaine is remembering this morning and worrying what will happen when Pat opens the door—will Pat throw her arms around Elaine and kiss her hello? Will she make a scene? And if she does, what should Elaine do? She imagines ignoring Pat—pretending it never happened.

"Slow down," she tells Paul.

"I'm only going thirty," Paul says.

Elaine wishes they weren't going at all. She wishes they could just go home, get in their own bed, with the children down the hall, with the damned hole in the dining room wall, and call it a night.

Paul parks by the curb.

All the lights in the Nielsons' house are on. The house is radiant, vibrating against the night sky; the glow spills across the lawn, onto the neighbors' grass and brushing against the very foundations of other people's homes, drowning out even the streetlight at the curb.

They ring the bell—pealing chimes split the night. Nothing happens. They ring again. Still nothing. Paul goes into his pocket for the key; Elaine stops him. "They're home," she says. "You don't use the key when people are home." And so they ring again. And again. It starts to feel strange, otherworldly; Paul and Elaine in the night, stranded, on the small, dark front stoop while the rest of the sprawling ranch beckons effervescently.

Paul walks around the perimeter of the house, peering in the windows. He sees the little M's in a room and taps the glass. They scream. "Got 'em," he calls to Elaine.

She shifts the shopping bag she's carrying back and forth from hand to hand.

A minute later the front door opens, the glow washes over them, a blinding white light.

Pat and George are nowhere to be seen.

"You're late," the little M says. "You missed dinner."

"We called," Elaine says.

"You're in trouble."

Paul and Elaine stand paralyzed in the front hall, the front door still open, the black night still available to them.

Pat appears, a laundry basket tucked into her hip. "I was just folding," she says. "Have you been here long?"

The sight of Pat sends a hot red rush through Elaine, pooling in her crotch. For a second Elaine thinks she has had an accident, she thinks she has wet her pants. She clenches her legs together. And prays.

"Are we intruding?" Paul asks.

"Oh, no, not at all. Not at all. Come in, come in."

The door slams shut.

"I wonder where George is?" Pat says. "Must be in the basement. Deaf and dumb when he's down there. How'd it go with the insurance guy?"

Elaine is speechless, stupefied, swooning, scared. She puts down her bags.

"I can't tell you how relieved I am," Paul says.

"Well, I hope you're still hungry," Pat says. "I bet you forgot what night it is. Remember the little quiz this morning—your favorite foods? Wednesday is grab bag—I kept it warm."

"I'm so sorry," Elaine blurts. Her discomfort is enormous. She imagines running for the bathroom, throwing up, fainting, or somehow impaling herself on Pat.

"We're idiots," Paul says. "Irresponsible, ungrateful idiots."

"Leave it," Pat says, taking them into the kitchen. "You're here now, that's what counts. And I bet you're starving. You didn't eat, did you?"

"Not a bite," Elaine says, hoping Pat doesn't smell the Chinese on them.

"Starving," Paul says, rubbing his gut. "Faint from hunger."

He smiles conspiratorially at Elaine. She can't look at him.

Pat has set two places at the kitchen table. Napkins artfully folded into flowers bloom in the water glasses.

"So incredibly thoughtful," Elaine says, overcome with guilt for not having called, for everything.

Pat leans over the table and lights the candles. "Sit," she says, pulling out a chair. Her hand brushes against Elaine's, and again there is an intense flash of heat.

Paul takes the seat.

"Sit," Pat says again, pulling out the other chair. Pat ties on an apron and begins bringing things out of the ovens, announcing the origin of each item as she puts it on the table. "Fried chicken—a cornflake/buttermilk dip; the recipe is from Margaret's Brownie leader. Brussels sprouts—that's George. Mashed potatoes—that's one of yours," she says to Paul. "And asparagus—for you," she says to Elaine. "I did it with some Pecorino melted across the top, hope you like it like that— cheese on top. And, of course, a salad."

"My God," Paul says. "My God," he repeats. "This is impressive." "My God" is something Paul has never said before; it is the phrase his father used when he had no idea what to say.

Elaine is practically in tears. She slips a brussels sprout into her mouth. "Delicious," she says, and then remembers that "delicious" is what Pat called her this morning on the kitchen floor. Elaine blushes.

She has let herself take a lover. Her lover is serving her dinner, while her husband looks on. Her head is throbbing, buzzing from the MSG, her lip quivering. She remembers hearing that if you drink milk with Chinese food, that doesn't happen.

"Have you got any milk?" she asks.

"Of course," Pat says, bringing her a glass.

The light above the kitchen table is on, and the candles are burning, the effect a cross between a romantic dinner for two (or three) and an interrogation.

"What's your favorite food?" Paul asks Pat.

He is being a good guest. On a full stomach, he is eating dinner again. Elaine looks at Paul and feels herself genuinely warm toward him. Her husband and her lover.

"Oh, I like just about everything," Pat is saying.

"Your absolute most favorite food?" Paul says.

"I guess, my favorite food, is well . . . iceberg lettuce," Pat says. "It's nothing, but I love it. Give me an iceberg lettuce salad, with fresh tomatoes, onions, croutons, and I'm in heaven. There it is. Iceberg lettuce."

There is silence. There is nothing to say.

"My God," Paul says again.

"Delicious," Elaine repeats.

"Pat! Pat!" George's voice bellows from deep inside the house. It is stern and unpleasant.

"Excuse me," Pat says, taking off her apron, hanging it on a hook by the door. The kitchen door swings closed behind her.

Elaine is thinking of Pat, Pat on the kitchen floor, her robe opening, the morning light.

"Thank God we had Chinese," Paul says. "I was actually getting a little hungry." He plucks a couple of sprouts from Elaine's plate and then asks if he can suck on her chicken bones.

"Isn't it enough already?" She begins clearing the table, carrying dishes to the sink, moving as if dancing, her body searching for points of contact, for the press of Pat.

Paul sits at the table.

"You could help me," Elaine spits.

There are words in the background. George losing his temper. The little M's crying. Because it is so unexpected, so un-George-like, it is terrifying.

Elaine panics. She confesses, "It's all my fault. I didn't call. I got busy. I got caught up in things. I was with Liz, and then the children were home, and then the agent, and then you."

"Everything is not about us," Paul says. "People have their own problems."

And for the first time Elaine and Paul are glad they are not Pat and George, they are glad that the two howling little M&M's aren't their children—it is all too hard, too much to live up to.

Pat pushes back through the kitchen door.

"Is everything all right?" Elaine asks.

"We all have our moments," Pat says, peeling aluminum foil off a baking pan and turning to Paul. "For dessert we have your favorite food—yellow cake with chocolate icing. Can I get you coffee or tea?"

"You really are something special," Paul tells Pat as she eases a huge piece of cake onto a plate.

Elaine can tell that Paul means it, and she's pleased.

"Cake?" Pat asks Elaine. Elaine shakes her head no.

Elaine is in the bathroom, chewing a short stack of Tums and brushing her teeth.

Pat slips in. "I had to wait until they went to bed."

"I feel terrible," Elaine says, lathering her face.

"Why?"

"Dinner. Everything." She looks up, making eye contact in the mirror. "Does George know?"

"Of course not, why would he?"

"The fight."

"The girls didn't get into Hanford; he's annoyed. He thinks they don't work hard enough—it's crazy."

Pat takes Elaine's damp face in both hands and kisses her. They fall back against the vanity. Out of the corner of her eye, Elaine watches herself in the mirror—she has never seen two women kiss before.

"It's been the longest day," Elaine says.

"Sleep," Pat says, slipping out of the room.

Elaine goes down the hall, closes the bedroom door, and puts a chair against it.

"Everything okay?" Paul asks.

"Fine." She undresses. She rummages through her shopping bags. "I have a present for you," she says, pulling out the nightgowns.

"Wow," Paul says, "matching."

They slip on the nightgowns and climb into Paul's twin bed.

"We have to get the house fixed," Elaine says. "We can't stay here forever; it's too complicated."

"Trust me," Paul says, turning out the light. "They're glad we're here."

"Tomorrow," Elaine says. "We start tomorrow."

Somewhere in the house the phone rings. They ignore it; it is not their house, it is not their problem. There is a tapping on their door. "Phone call," George says. "Your boy is on the line. I think you can just pick up Garfield in there; his tail is broken, but the rest of him works."

"Okay, thanks," Paul says.

Elaine has turned on the light and is looking around the room. There's an orange plastic Garfield the cat on the desk. She points. Paul picks it up and hands it to her.

"Hello," Elaine says, talking into the cat's belly.

"I want to go home," Sammy says.

"Are you breathing all right?" Elaine asks.

"I want to go home," Sammy drones.

"Daddy and I aren't home," Elaine says. "Remember,

you're at Nate's house, and Daddy and I are with Pat and George."

"I want to come where you are," Sammy whines.

"Honey, everyone here is asleep. Be a good boy and go back to sleep."

"No," Sammy says.

Paul takes the phone. "Is Susan there? Give Susan the phone."

"Hi, Paul," she says. "Sorry to get you up—he had a bad dream. He wanted to call."

"I want to go home," Sammy demands in the background.

"I'll make him some cocoa," she says, "and then I'll put him to bed again."

"Thanks," Paul says. "That's great."

Susan hands the phone back to Sammy. "You and I are going to make ourselves some hot cocoa, and then I'm going to tell you the most amazing story," she says. "Tell your daddy good night."

"Be a good boy," Paul says. "Love you."

In the middle of the night, the phone rings again. George taps on the door.

"Go and get him," Elaine mumbles.

Paul picks up Garfield the cat. "On my way," Paul tells Susan, pulling off the nightgown, sliding back into his clothes.

The bug light is on, Sammy is waiting outside in his Superman pajamas. She is behind him, in a large white men's shirt, the bug light staining her a jaundicey yellow. She bends to say something to Sammy, and Paul's eyes automatically dip into the crevice of her shirt. She is naked. He can see the whole way down—her full breasts languid against her chest. He is hard. Sometimes it takes so little.

"He's a little disoriented," she whispers to Paul, her breath half fouled by sleep. He moves toward her, his fingers quick-slipping under her shirt, fast-finding her, splitting the lips.

"Oh," she says. "Oh."

He is wishing they could duck inside, wishing he could convince Sammy to stay. "Are you sure you want to go?" he asks his boy.

Sammy, staring at the car, nods.

Paul imagines having her in Gerald's Barcalounger, in the full reclining position, her legs draped over the arms, while upstairs her family sleeps.

"Do you have your things?" Paul asks, pulling his fingers out of Mrs. Apple.

She hands him Sammy's knapsack and a brown paper bag. "I already made his lunch," she says.

There is something slightly romantic about this: a father rescuing his son in the middle of the night, Sammy standing on the steps in his Superman pajamas, his superpowers having failed him.

"He wouldn't wait in the house," she says. "He went running out. I actually had to chase him around the yard."

"Maybe it's the medication. Maybe it made him hyper, it can do that." Paul is embarrassed that Sammy is acting so strangely.

"It happens," Susan says.

Sammy starts walking to the car. "Careful," Mrs. Apple softly calls after him. "Your laces aren't tied."

He kisses her cheek and hurries to let Sammy into the car.

Sammy is shivering. It's June but not terribly warm. His teeth are chattering.

"Hurry," Sammy says. "I want to go home."

As they're pulling out, Paul looks up and sees someone in the upstairs window. "Look," he says. "There's Nate, saying good-bye."

Sammy starts sobbing, wailing. "What?" Paul asks. "What is it?" He tries to comfort him while driving. "Did something happen?"

And then just as suddenly as he started, Sammy stops. "I'm hungry," he says.

Paul doesn't know how to respond. He's never seen someone start crying and stop so abruptly. Is Sammy awake or asleep? Is all of this happening in a dream?

"I'm hungry," Sammy says again.

"Didn't you eat dinner?" Paul asks.

Sammy doesn't answer. Paul pulls out the sandwich from the lunch Susan made, gives Sammy half, and eats the other half himself: his third dinner, a sandwich made by Mrs. Apple. He lingers over it, turning the peanut butter and jelly on his tongue, making it last.

"Tiptoe and not even a peep," he says, leading Sammy down the hall at Pat and George's. "Everyone's asleep."

Paul takes off his clothes and crawls back into the bed, where Elaine is already asleep. Sammy climbs aboard as well; the three of them in a twin bed, Sammy in his Superman suit sprawled across the top, laid out over them, as if he's fallen from a great height and landed with a thick splat. Tender Sammy.

SIX

PAUL IS PLEASED WITH HIMSELF. He is up and out. His sip-cup is full. He has remembered his briefcase. He is walking Sammy to school and then will catch the train. Pat has made Sammy a new lunch—with a big piece of yellow cake from the night before. Elaine is still sleeping. All is well.

McKendrick pops out from behind a bush, pushing his walker into the path, nearly tripping Paul and Sammy.

Sammy squeals.

"Scared you, didn't I?" McKendrick says, the wrinkles of his scowl slightly menacing. "I escaped. If I stayed in that house a minute longer, I'd have gone insane. Been out here since five A.M., waiting for something to happen."

"I looked for you yesterday," Paul says. "The light was on."

"Well, there I was."

"This is my son Sammy," Paul says.

McKendrick bends to shake Sammy's hand. He doesn't get down very far. "Pins in my ass," he says, and slowly straightens up. "What train are you catching?"

"Aiming for the seven forty-three."

"Well, get to it, man," he says, pulling his walker out of the path. "Stop by for a drink sometime," he calls after them. "I've got some things I want to show you, good stuff; I've been downloading little girls."

Sammy waves good-bye.

"Takes me an hour to get up the driveway," McKendrick says to no one in particular. "An hour, and what does it matter? I've got all day. I'm not going anywhere."

Paul takes Sammy to the edge of the schoolyard, to the fence; children stream in from all sides, moving across the playground, up the steps, and into the school, as though the building itself has magnetic pull.

"Can I have a drink of coffee before I go?" Sammy asks.

Paul hands him the cup. "I didn't know you drank coffee."

Sammy takes a sip. "Gross," he says, and then he takes a bigger gulp. "Gross, gross."

"Go to school," Paul says, taking the cup away.

"Hey, Dad," Sammy calls. "What's pins in my ass?"

"I'll tell you later."

Paul is on the train. He is on his way. He is rummaging through his briefcase, pulling out pads and papers, making plans.

He is thinking about his lunch with the date—he will work hard all morning, he will take the meetings and the calls, he will play the part of the go-getter, displaying a level of energy and enthusiasm that can't ordinarily be sustained. He will make sure that everyone sees him, that they notice how hard he's working—and then he will duck out for a long lunch. He will linger in the middle of the afternoon. He is thinking about his hand slipping under Mrs. Apple's shirt, thinking about how lovely it felt to be curled tight against Elaine, with Sammy lying on top like icing on a cake. Thinking.

He is swollen with a strange sense of virtue, still so glad, so deeply relieved about the insurance. He is pleased with his efficiency, his ability to juggle everything. He is determined to pay attention to all the little details, to keep his ducks in a line.

"Fine morning," his secretary says.

"Isn't it," Paul says.

"Can I get you some coffee?"

Paul swirls his sip cup around; what's left in it sloshes. "Dump it," he says, handing it to her. "And I'll have a fresh cup."

"Doughnut?"

He shakes his head. "Pass."

"You already had a couple of calls, two hang-ups and Mr. Warburton wants to see you at ten."

"All good things," he says. "Thanks."

He goes into his office, sticks his finger into his potted plant. It's a little dry. He waters it and makes a note to ask his secretary for plant food.

He makes more notes. He drinks his coffee. "All right," he repeats to himself. "All right," as in all is good, all is right.

He calls Mrs. Apple. "You were so great last night. I just wanted to thank you."

"Did Sammy get to sleep?"

"Like a log. I just dropped him at school. And how was the rest of your night?" he asks.

"Wet," she says.

"Oh," he says. "Ohhhh, you're dirty." Mrs. Apple doesn't usually talk dirty.

"Rotten," she says, laughing. "Rotten to the core."

"You looked great in your shirt," he says.

"It's not my shirt," she says. "It's Gerald's shirt."

There is a pause.

"What about you and Nate?" Paul asks. "Back to sleep okay?"

"Nate?"

"Yeah, I saw him in the window as we were pulling out."

"That's odd, I checked him when I went up—he was fast asleep."

"If I give you one of my shirts, will you sleep in it?" Paul asks.

"Does the laundry write your name on the collar?" she asks.

"I'll buy a new one," he says.

"Wear it first. Give it to me dirty."

"See you Friday."

Pat and Elaine are sitting at the kitchen table, having coffee.

They have already gone at it fast and furiously in the laundry room, with Elaine on top of the washer, clinging to the control panel as the machine frantically vibrated beneath her, whipping through the spin cycle, and then with Pat bare-assed on the dryer, tumbling, hot. Elaine remembers looking up at a shelf filled with cleaning products—Downy, Fantastik, Bon Ami—each item suddenly charged with intention, desire—housewife homoerotica.

"Has this happened before?" Elaine asks as Pat refills her coffee cup.

"Occasionally."

"It would never have occurred to me," Elaine says. "When did you think of it?" Elaine asks, as though it is some trick of the body, of the soul, that Pat has invented, as though it is something like wiggling your ears, snapping your toes, or moving one eyebrow, a kind of physical party trick.

"I've always been attracted to women," Pat says.

"So why did you marry George?"

"I've made myself a wonderful life," Pat says. "Nothing matters to me more than being normal. That's what I wanted most, a good life."

Elaine is quiet. "You're good," she says. "I love the way it feels when you touch me. Your mouth is like velvet."

Pat blushes. "Thanks. It's important to me to be good at things."

"You are, very good," Elaine says.

"I have something for you," Pat says, handing Elaine a present.

"But I have nothing for you," Elaine says.

Pat shakes her head—not to worry.

Elaine tears at the package. The wrapping is off. "*How to Fix Almost Anything*—a book on home repair?"

"It's my favorite," Pat says. "It's got everything from dishwashers to garage-door openers. If you can fix things, you'll feel better."

"I'll give it a try," Elaine says. "By the way, what kind of lightbulbs do you use?" She is remembering the Nielsons' house at night, flooded with fluorescence.

"Mail order. I'll give you the number. They last forever."

Paul is gathering his notes for the meeting, his lists of projects and proposals. He has collected a great pile of papers, hoping to make a show of things. He's heading down the hall.

"Where are you going?" his secretary asks.

"Warburton's," he says.

"No," his secretary says, "he's coming to you."

"Shit," Paul says, hurrying back into his office, rushing to clean his desk, to put his various piles in proper order.

This is the new power play, the home visit, the boss comes to you. Paul hates it. He likes walking down the hall, pulling himself together just outside the corner office. This new twist has a false informality that's really a move to catch someone off guard. Paul rushes. He sweeps everything off his desk and into the trash can—he will empty it later. He stuffs picture frames into his pencil drawer, cracking the glass on Elaine. A desk should be as impersonal as possible, no papers, no mementos, no giveaways.

The secretary buzzes. "He's on his way," she says. "And he's got Wilson and Herskovitz with him."

"Come in, come in," Paul says, ushering them in, like a stop on the Good Housekeeping tour, a white-glove inspection.

Warburton takes the chair just in front of the desk, and the two juniors, Wilson and Herskovitz, perch on the edge of the love seat.

"How's the house?" Warburton asks. "I heard about the fire."

"We're covered," Paul says, sitting. "Under a . . . a clause." He tries to get comfortable in his chair. "In fact, we're planning to take advantage of the situation and put in a deck and some French doors, do it up a bit."

"Good," Warburton says. "Forward motion."

Warburton is slick. He is also five years younger than Paul; he is what Paul will never be. And Paul has hated him from the beginning—which, for Warburton, was only three years ago.

"Let's talk about the program," Warburton says. "Where do we stand? Where are we going?"

"Well," Paul says, "I think we have to look at return. We have to think about giving less and getting more."

"Yes," Warburton says, nodding. Out of nowhere War- burton's rubber band appears. There is always a rubber band; Warburton plays with it when he's thinking, when he's schem- ing, when he's psyching out the other side. He holds it between two fingers and pulls at it, flicking, flicking.

Paul's secretary buzzes. "Phone call."

"We're in a meeting," he says, surprised she's inter- rupting him.

"Phone call," she says again.

"Excuse me," Paul says, watching Warburton with the

rubber band, wondering what it means if the rubber band snaps, splits in half, what happens if it accidentally shoots off, goes flying across the room. Does Warburton chase after it? Does he let it go? Does he acknowledge that anything happened? "This'll take just a second." Paul picks up the phone.

"Are you prepared to bleed? Are we on? I made an appointment for you with a friend of mine." The date is calling.

Paul can't answer. He can't turn away and whisper, "Your timing is lousy, I'm in a meeting." Instead he just says, "Ummm-hummm."

"Meet me at one at the Road Kill Kaffe, it's downtown."

Downtown, he hadn't planned on going downtown— that'll take forever. "Could we do it uptown?"

Warburton is checking his watch, flicking the rubber band faster.

"No," she says. "The appointment is downtown."

"Okay." He hangs up. "My apologies," he says to Warburton.

Herskovitz on the love seat starts in. "Return is fine, but what about the future? You have to look at what's ahead and not always down at the bottom line. You miss something staring at your feet."

Paul hates Herskovitz, creeping up behind him, gunning to run him over, to skip into the second spot, the big office next to the corner that's been empty ever since Sid Auerbach went into cardiac arrest during a conference call.

"Let me take this one on," Paul says. "I think we can do something here, we can go further if we go deeper."

"I want you to bring me a new way of seeing," Warburton says. "Fresh vision."

Paul nods. He checks his watch—noon.

"Good," Warburton says, getting up. Herskovitz and Wilson also stand. "Good," Warburton repeats, and it's like getting a grade—about a C. It's good, but it's not very good. It's not a

B, and it's not excellent—it's not an A, and it's certainly not brilliant—not an A plus. He has to do better, to work harder.

Before lunch, Paul calls Elaine. "How's it going?"

"Good," she says, "really good. I phoned Ruth Esterhazy, got the name of her deck guy. He's here now, and we're talking. I also got the name of an architect to help with the French doors. And another painter has come and gone—that's a second estimate. And how are you?" she asks.

"Right now, I'm in kind of a panic. Warburton was here, he had two other guys with him. It wasn't good."

"Well," Elaine says. "We're moving along here. We're talking about all kinds of things; there are decks called Resort Style, Trendsetter, Bold Angled, and Weekend Entertainer."

The deck guy chirps in, "I'll leave some plans you can look at tonight."

Elaine continues, "I also found a commercial cleaning company—they're sending a six-man crew this afternoon. They'll scrub us floor to ceiling, even the walls. And they suck the air out of the house and refill it with something better."

"Yeah, like what?" Paul says. "Laughing gas?"

She ignores him. "After what happened with Sammy yesterday, I'd like to have it boiled and sterilized."

"The painter can take care of the walls," Paul says. "Have them do everything but the walls. We don't need to pay for the same thing twice."

"We're covered," Elaine says.

"Fine, if you're feeling so fucking flush, then why don't you have one of those freaks come in and Feng Shui it? You know, point everything in the right direction. That's probably what it needs, a kind of chiropractic adjustment. Why don't you ask the deck guy if he can do that?"

"Why are you so angry with me?" Elaine asks.

"I'm not angry with you," Paul says. "I'm angry with everyone, and myself most of all. I'm having a lousy day."

"I'm sorry," she says. "I hope your afternoon is better."

"Yeah, I've gotta go," he says. "I've got lunch." He hangs up. He shouldn't have called. All of his anxiety, his stress, his guilt has been hurled at Elaine. He hopes she knew enough to duck, not to even try to catch it. Later he will apologize. He hates it when he does this, when he behaves badly.

Out of the office and into the day. The air is turning thick, like mud. Paul is fucking up. He should be at work. He should be having lunch with the boys, figuring things out. He will have to work harder to catch up. Double time. He makes notes on his palm as he rides downtown. Later they will be automatically erased, sweated away.

Exiting the subway, Paul is all turned around. He has no idea of where he is, which way to go.

"Road Kill Kaffe?" he asks someone.

The woman stops. Points. "Go east," she says, "go right. Go down a couple of blocks."

He is thinking about the date—wondering why he does exactly what she tells him to, why he can't say no. She's not living in reality; nothing is impossible to her. It doesn't occur to her that it might be difficult for him to leave the office and come downtown in the middle of a workday.

He arrives at the restaurant. She's not there. He waits. Finally he lets the hostess seat him. He opens the menu. He decides.

He plans what he will say when she finally arrives. He wants to tell her that he is overextended, that there's too much on his plate, that she is the thing that will have to go. He wants to tell her that he can't afford it on any level—game over. But he won't. He will go ahead. He will do whatever she says. He goes from hating her to being just annoyed and then slightly amused. Finally, she walks in.

"Ready?" she asks. "I want to take you somewhere."

"I ordered," he says. "I waited, and then I went ahead. Do you want something? Should I cancel it?"

"No, go ahead," she says. "I'll have a drink."

"I'm having a lime rickey, it's the house specialty. Lime rickeys and shrimp salad sandwiches. Want a sip?"

She shakes her head. "We have to hurry. The appointment was for one-fifteen."

He flags the waitress. "She'd like a drink," he says. "Iced tea? Lemonade?"

"Frozen margarita," the date says.

"In the middle of the day?"

"What's the middle of the day?" the date asks back.

His sandwich arrives; he inhales it, swallowing the baby shrimp as though they were aspirin tablets.

"What's your favorite color?" she asks "Green? Blue? Black?"

"Blue," he says, signaling for the check. "Where are you taking me—what kind of a place?"

"The kind that gives you pins and needles." She laughs.

"Can't wait." He is thinking that she'll take him to her apartment, there will be another girl, maybe her roommate. It will be the three of them, two against one. He imagines the date on top, riding him, while the roommate squats over his face. His is a pathetically standard fantasy, and yet his groin pulses with the possibility.

"How's Henry?" she asks. "I haven't heard from him in a few days."

"He's away, traveling for work."

"I keep trying his cell phone. First I got some woman, and now it's turned off."

"Oh," Paul says, thinking of Elaine at home with the cell phone. "He'll be back soon."

He pays. She leads him down the street. He's nervous. The

neighborhood, if you can call it that, is like a bombed-out war zone. Paul can't imagine that anyone normal lives there. "Who is the appointment with?" he asks.

"Gary," she says.

He begins to sweat. "Who's Gary?"

They're buzzed in. The building smells like gas and cats. They go up an endless staircase, climbing higher and higher, ascending into darkness.

"What's this about?" he says. "What are we doing?"

"I want to get you marked."

"What does that mean?"

"Tattooed."

Paul is reeling. He's thinking she's insane. He's feeling how conventional he really is. With Elaine he is the madman, with the date he's terrified.

"Did Henry do this?" he asks.

"Henry's pathetic," she says.

"I don't think I'll get one, but if you want one, I'll watch."

"I have two already," she says.

He can picture one, a butterfly just above her breast. "Where's the second?"

"Ass crack," she says, "I have a rose coming out of my ass."

"Oh," he says. "Well, get some more. Get a whole bouquet. My treat."

"No. I want to watch you," she says.

A thin, reedy guy answers the door. The apartment is a long, narrow hall, with rooms branching off to the right and left.

"Gary's in the back," the guy says.

"Who's Gary?"

"Nick's boyfriend. That was Nick at the door, he's a painter."

Gary is big. He looks like a Hell's Angel. His hair is pulled back in a high ponytail. He is bearded and his beard is gathered into a second ponytail, in front, held with a ponytail holder, the kind with the two plastic balls, just beneath his chin.

"Hi," the date says.

"You're late," Gary says.

"Sorry, he had to eat." She points to Paul.

Gary grunts. "So, what'll it be?" he asks. "Squirming mermaid, mother's maiden name, anchors aweigh?"

The date asks, "Can he look through the catalog?"

"Sure." Gary gestures at a pile of tattoo books. "You're not a whiner, are you?" he asks Paul.

Paul doesn't speak. Gary shrugs and leaves the room.

"This just isn't a good idea," Paul whispers to the girl.

"Sure it is," she says, pulling at his jacket, unbuttoning his shirt. "Just a little something right about here." She puts her mouth on his heart. "I can feel your pulse with my tongue."

"Does it really mean a lot to you?" Paul asks her.

"I like my men to be marked so I can tell they're mine." She pulls at his nipples with her teeth.

Gary returns. "I could pierce those for you if you like." He lifts up his shirt, flashing a multicolored dragon-covered belly and tits punctuated with silver rings.

From Paul's point of view, he looks like a circus act. "I'll pass," Paul says.

"Why don't you hop up here," Gary says, patting what looks like an old examination table from a doctor's office.

Paul sort of wants to get out of it, he wants to say something like—my health insurance doesn't cover tattoos, my mother won't let me, or my wife won't like it. But, on the other hand, he's into the idea of redefining the body, especially as it is changing, as it is beginning to escape him. He is thinking that if he does do it, he'll get something small, something simple, something like an ancient symbol—a hidden source of power. He'll tell himself that it's part of his training—to be a warrior.

"I'm assuming you just want one color," Gary says.

She is pulling at his zipper. "This is where I want it," she says. "Down here, a vine coming up."

Paul shakes his head. "I was thinking on the arm."

"You shave?" Gary asks.

Paul's chest is clean. And as the date pulls down his pants, no fertile forest appears.

"Straight people don't shave. It's kinky," Gary says.

"Swimming," Paul lies.

"I'm getting so excited," the date says, pulling at his pants. Paul is resisting. "Oh, come on. Don't get weird. Gary's not going to hurt you too much," she says. "Just enough."

"You use a clean needle, right?" Paul asks Gary.

"Disposable and sterile. A fresh set for each person." Gary shows him his tools.

And then Paul is lying on the table, wondering how they got to this point, how they got from shoulder, chest, or back to groin. He is nude. Gary has draped a paper towel, a sheet of Bounty, over his cock and balls—a motion toward modesty.

The stencil is applied.

Gary holds a mirror above it so Paul can look. Paul sees a curl of ivy, a leafy vein rising up from below; he sees something about six inches long.

"The right spot?" Gary asks.

"Yes," the date says. "Yes." Her breath blows the paper towel up, tickling Paul's testicles.

"If you decide to let your hair grow back, it'll just about cover it," Gary says, putting on goggles, a mask, and latex gloves.

Paul pops a sweat. His skin goes clammy.

"This is so erotic," the date says.

"So you say," Paul says.

The sensation is one of vibration, of burning, of a thousand pinpricks all at once, of a fiery match being touched to tender skin. It is pleasure and it is pain—more pain than pleasure.

"Oh," the date says. "Oh, it's amazing. Oh. It's so incredible, watching you, watching the little needle drilling. And you're hardly bleeding, just sort of beading up. Oh. Ohhh."

When they are done, Gary lathers the tattoo with antibiotic ointment, tapes a nonstick bandage over everything, and gives Paul instructions.

"Keep it clean—that's the main thing. The bandage stays on for about eight hours, then lots of ointment for ten days. Keep the scab lubricated, otherwise it'll heal peculiar. Questions?"

Paul sits up. The hankie over his cock falls off.

"How much do I owe you?" the date asks.

Paul is light-headed. He wonders why they don't offer him a little cup of orange juice the way they do when you give blood. He looks down at the bandage and thinks of outpatient surgery—vasectomy. He wonders if he should put ice on it. He eases himself off the table and gently slips into his boxers, his shirt, his pants, his jacket.

"That was incredible," the date says as Paul comes out of the room.

Paul walks down the stairs, slowly, weak, wrung out. He wishes he could lie down. He wishes he could just rest somewhere.

"I came," she says. "I got so into it. While he was doing it to you, I did it to myself. Did you hear me? I came. You were so incredible."

"Do you live near here?" he asks her.

"Why?"

"Could we go to your apartment?" he says. "Just for a little bit."

"Oh, yeah, sure. I guess," she says. "I wasn't planning on it, but, yeah, let's do it. Right now, I'm so into you, I would do anything."

Paul checks his watch, two-thirty—he should be back at the office. He will rest until three.

They walk up four flights; she uses lots of keys to open various locks. The decor is something that can only be described as demented Gypsy.

"Nothing in this apartment was paid for," she says proudly. "Either people gave me or I found it on the street."

He lies down on her bed, hoping this is one of the things someone gave her. He undoes his pants—it's hurting. A lot. "Do you have some aspirin? And some juice." She gives him a couple of Advil and some sort of herbal ginseng drink. She wants to fuck him.

"I don't think so," he says. "I don't think I should rub against anything." She starts to give him a blow job—nothing happens. He is impotent.

"This doesn't happen to me," he says, propping himself up, looking down at the limp lion. And he's telling the truth. Of all the things that happen to Paul, this isn't one of them.

She rolls her eyes—that's what they all say.

It's all about his blood, the recirculation of blood. It is pooling in the pinhead punctures that now decorate his upper deck, instead of collecting in his cock.

She pouts.

He reaches for her. "Squat over me," he says. "Sit on my face." She tries. He buries himself in the salve of her excitement, working her with his tongue, with his teeth—committed to making her come.

She is bored. She wiggles back and forth. She bounces on his nose. Finally she slides off. This is not what she wants. His face is slick, shiny with her transmission fluid, her motor oil.

"Come back," he says.

"Just stop," she says.

He is left lying there, embarrassed, ashamed. Both Elaine and Mrs. Apple adore him no matter what, sunrise or sunset, but the date seems genuinely annoyed. He pulls up his pants. "I'd better go," he says.

Elaine is working at home. She's met with the deck guy, fixed the running toilet in the upstairs bathroom, and removed the drink rings from the coffee table—using the book Pat gave her—and now, while she's waiting for the cleaning crew to come, she and Mrs. Hansen are chopping up what's left of the dining room table, using an ax they found in the basement.

"What fun," Mrs. Hansen says, taking a solid swing.

Elaine smiles, watching the wood chips spray across the room.

Mrs. Hansen hacks at it again, and a huge section of the table breaks free.

"I could do this forever," she says, raising the ax up high. "Anything else need the old chop-chop?"

"I think that pretty well does it," Elaine says.

Mrs. Hansen rests the ax on the floor and looks out the window at her own yard. "I wonder if that tree out front is alive or dead. I wouldn't mind taking a crack at it."

"It seems to have little green leaves," Elaine says.

"Too bad," Mrs. Hansen says.

Together Elaine and Mrs. Hansen haul the remains of the table out to the Dumpster, and Elaine hurls them over the top.

It is impossibly hot, all day the heat has been mounting, and the weather service has issued some sort of a warning.

"How 'bout a nice cold drink?" They are dripping with sweat. Mrs. Hansen is breathing hard.

"Let me do the mixing," Mrs. Hansen says, offering to

make a pitcher of her "special" iced tea—Lemon Zinger, vodka, and a dozen drops of something called Rescue Remedy. "My secret potion," Mrs. Hansen says. "A friend gave it me. It's holistic."

Paul is lost, he is turned around, he can't tell east from west, up from down. Out of the date's building he takes a right turn, figuring he'll walk down the block, he'll walk until he comes to an avenue, and then he'll be back on track. From there, he'll make his way uptown.

Conflict, confusion, weakness, nausea—his body is demanding attention. He has to pee. He can't wait. He tucks himself into the corner of a building and urinates. Pee splashes off the wall and onto his suit. He steps back.

He is walking. And walking. All the cabs have their off-duty lights on. It is that odd hour of the day, between three and four, when the taxi drivers are changing shifts, and it's impossible to get someone to stop.

Without warning, near the corner of Bleecker and Bowery, Paul vomits, hurling a pink, chunky mess, a pile of whole baby shrimp, into the street. He vomits violently, uncontrollably, again and again. No one stops. No one notices. No one does anything.

He walks on, thinking he might faint. He's panicked, wondering if something went wrong, maybe you're not supposed to have a tattoo done down there, maybe Gary hit something, punctured something significant—a vein, his intestines.

The air is thick, oxygenless; later there will be storms.

Paul looks for a pay phone. He calls his office. "I just got out of lunch," he blurts to his secretary. "I'm not well at all. I must have eaten something bad."

"You sound awful," she says. "Where are you?"

"I'm downtown. In the street. I just threw up."

"Poor guy," she says.

He wants someone to be informed, in case it gets worse, in case something else happens, in case something has to be done—he's afraid to call Elaine.

"I thought I could make it back to the office."

"Go home," she says. "Don't come back here."

There is a pause. A big truck passes.

"Any messages?" he asks, recovering himself temporarily.

"Nothing urgent."

"Oh," he says. "Oh, I'd better go, it's happening again." He hangs up and vomits once more, dragging the dregs of his stomach, the foamy bile that comes when there's nothing left.

Paul takes the subway from Astor Place to Grand Central. He buys a bottle of water for three dollars, rinses his mouth, and spits on the platform. He's on the 3:43 heading home. He is falling further behind. He should be at the office. Herskovitz is probably already making a plan, trying out Paul's desk chair, flipping through his files.

Paul falls into a brackish sleep on the train. His sleep is timed; an automatic alarm goes off thirty-five minutes later. When he wakes up, the train is cold, like a refrigerated compartment. He tucks his hands into his armpits and remembers that his briefcase is still at the office. He recalls the trash can—sweeping everything off the desk into the trash and then sliding it back under his desk. Shit!

From the station he will call his secretary again, he will ask her to rescue the trash before the cleaning crew comes. Notes, plans, files. Frantic, he rummages through his pocket looking for phone change.

Off the train. Paul lunges for the pay phone. He dials 0 and waits. "I need to reverse the charges," he tells the operator when she finally answers.

"I don't know what that means. Do you want to make a collect call?"

"Yes. Yes," he says.

"Moment, please." An automated voice comes on. "At the sound of the beep, please say your name."

"Paul," he says.

"Paul" echoes back in his ear

"Please hold."

There is a delay. Paul watches the taxis load up and speed off.

He hears the phone ringing, he hears the sound of his secretary's voice mail: "I'm not at my desk right now, but if you'd like to leave a message . . ." The oblivious automated voice announces, "You have a collect call from . . . 'Paul.' " Paul hears the sound of his own voice. "Say yes or press 'one' to accept the charges," the digital idiot drones.

He hangs up. He dials again, this time trying the extension of one of the men down the hall. Again voice mail. He tries another fellow, voice mail. He tries his secretary again. She must have taken advantage of his going home to go home herself; maybe that's why she told him not to come back. He dials fast and furiously, trying every extension he can think of until finally he calls Warburton's office; Warburton's secretary answers.

"Oh, thank God, a real person," he says. "It's Paul, Paul Weiss."

"Yes," she chimes, "what can I do for you?"

"I'm sick. I had to leave early. I've been trying to get my secretary on the phone." He babbles. On and on.

"Don't you worry," Warburton's secretary says, "I'll go right down there. I'll take care of it. Personally."

"Thank you. Thank you so much."

"You get well soon," she says, hanging up.

Again, he is relieved.

The sky is dark. The station is entirely empty; no taxis have returned. An odd and urgent breeze blows. Paul walks. He walks as if ducking, dashing from safe spot to safe spot, playing hide-and-go-seek, not wanting to be caught out in the open when the storm hits. Whenever he moves, his clothing scrapes his bandage, the pain makes him unsteady, his stomach rolls, his vision thins. He wonders if the tattoo might spread, if too much activity might cause the simple line, the delicate arc of ivy, to mutate, to smear, expanding into an inky-faced monster.

The sky is blacker still. The leaves turn up, flickering nervously. There is the rumble of thunder. Everything is happening at a strange pace, there is the sense of impending disaster. Paul may not make it home. There's a little hut in the playground where you go to sign up for courts and basketball games. He sees it up ahead. He aims for it. He is off the sidewalk and onto the grass, running. More thunder.

There is a pay phone at the hut. Paul will call Elaine—it is safe to call Elaine now, he is on terra firma, he is in the neighborhood, he has calmed down, and besides, he has no choice. He will call Elaine, and Elaine will come and get him. Everything will be all right.

"You have a collect call from . . . 'Paul.' "

"Paul?" she asks quizzically.

"Say yes," Paul says.

"Say yes or press the number 'one' to accept the charges," the now insanely familiar voice goes on.

"Yes," she says.

"Elaine? Elaine, I don't think I can make it home," Paul says breathlessly.

"Are you all right? You sound strange."

"I'm at the park. I had a bad day, kind of an accident." He stops. "Can you come and get me and take me home?"

"Come and get you? Take you home?"

"Yes. I just told you, I had a really bad day."

"Paul, where are you? What kind of an accident? What park are you in?"

He's watching some kids continuing to play tennis despite

the oncoming storm. "This is so weird," he says. "I think I see Daniel. Does Daniel have a tennis racket?"

"Paul, are you all right? Can you hear me?"

"It's Daniel," Paul says. "I see Daniel. I'll call you back." He hangs up. Two boys are coming off the tennis courts, looking up at the sky. "Daniel?" Paul calls.

Thunder. Lightning.

The boys walk toward him, looking at him blankly. "Dad?" Daniel finally says.

Paul nods.

"What are you doing here? Are you following me?"

"I'm going home," Paul says.

"Is it the right time for you to be going home?"

"I can go home whenever I want; I'm an adult. Why are you here?" Paul asks. "That's the big question. Why aren't you in school?"

"School gets out at three-thirty," Daniel says.

"Hi, Mr. Weiss," the other boy says.

"Hi, Willy," Paul says.

"And what are you doing now?" Paul asks Daniel.

"Scout meeting," Daniel says.

"My father is troop leader," Willy says. "On Wednesdays he comes home early to lead us. Today we're making plaster casts."

Willy's awful father is the man Paul can't stand, the guy who picked Daniel up at the house, the deputy head of the New York tax department.

"Since when have you been a Boy Scout?" Paul asks Daniel. He has no memory of Daniel's being a Scout. "Don't you have to be a Cub Scout first?"

"Since I've been at Willy's house," Daniel says.

"So, all week?" Paul says.

"You can join at any time," Willy says.

Paul wants to say, Your mother and I don't believe in

Scouts, we think they're a right-wing cult. We don't believe in anything where you have to wear a uniform. This is what we marched for in the 1960s—the right not to have to do this. Paul wants to explain to Daniel that it's not cool to be a Scout, it's nerdy as hell. And Daniel is too weird and too mean to be a Scout. Scouts are good-natured, they are honest and trustworthy, they help little old ladies across the street, he wants to say; you're not like that.

"Did you tell your mother?" Paul asks.

"Yes," Daniel says. "After the meeting I'm supposed to go home, and then Jennifer is taking Sammy and I to the school fair."

"Me," he says. "Sammy and me."

"Yeah," Daniel says.

"My father was an Eagle Scout," Willy says.

"Oh, oh." Paul suddenly runs away, ducks behind the little tennis hut, and throws up again. He comes back. "I'm sick," he says. "I came home early because I'm sick."

"Am I supposed to do something?" Daniel asks.

"Like what?" Paul asks. He sits on the curb, head between his knees.

"My mom will be here in a minute," Willy says.

"I'll be fine," Paul says.

The wind is quickening.

"I hope we don't have a tornado," Willy says.

"There are very few tornadoes in Westchester County," Paul says.

"Where did you learn to play tennis?" he asks Daniel, making conversation to distract himself from the nausea, from the odd sensation that something wet, like blood, is trickling down his leg.

"You taught me, a long time ago, remember?"

"But you're pretty good," Paul says.

"I've been practicing," Daniel says.

"We play every day," Willy says.

Mrs. Meaders pulls into the lot, tooting the horn even though the boys are right there.

Daniel taps on the window. "Could we give my father a ride home? He's sick."

"Of course," she says. The boys climb in the back, and Paul gets in the front. He is afraid to talk, afraid his foul breath will flood the car. "I came home early," he says, speaking out the window, away from everyone. "There were no taxis at the station. I thought I could walk. And then the weather."

"Where am I taking you?" she asks. "Your house or the Nielsons'?"

"Home. Elaine is home. I threw up," Paul says, frightened like a child.

"Are you feeling better now?"

"Better except for the car, the car is making me nauseated."

"Should I go faster or slower?" she asks.

"Faster." As fast as you can, he wants to say.

The rain starts. Fat splashes land on the windshield, drops the size of dinner plates. Thunder. Lightning. Wild trees. And it's only going to get worse.

Mrs. Meaders stops in front of the house; a truck is blocking the driveway.

"Thanks for the lift," he says, opening the door, making a run for it.

Men in yellow coveralls, with goggles and masks, swarm through the house like bees. Paul counts six of them. Their outfits are intimidatingly hard-core; they're dressed as though they're cleaning up a toxic-waste site, as though the house is truly contaminated. Paul wants to tell them to lighten up—it's not that bad. He wants to say, Hey, we live here, we've lived here for years, we're okay.

"You are such an asshole," Elaine says as soon as she sees him. "Where were you? What happened? You called and then you hung up. You can't do that to me—never, ever, again. You scared the hell out of me."

He heads for the stairs, in a hurry to check his wound.

"And," she says, "as soon as you hung up, you had a phone call." Paul imagines the date, checking on him, his health, his well-being, his ill erection.

"Mr. Warburton's secretary called. She said your garbage is fine and she hopes you get well soon."

Paul pictures the trash can on top of his desk, a big DO NOT DISTURB sign taped onto it, written in desperate red Magic Marker.

"What's going on? Did you get fired?"

"They're washing the walls," Paul says, watching the men in yellow. "Why are they washing the walls, Elaine?"

He goes upstairs into the bathroom and pulls down his pants. It is a mess, an oozing gelatinous mess: the dark ink of the ivy, the blood, the shine of the ointment, all conspiring to give the impression that something serious is seeping out of him, something organic and intestinal.

He starts wiping at it, frantically.

Elaine comes in. "Oh, God," she says. "What happened?" Her hand covers her mouth. "What is it?" she asks, speaking through her fingers. "Were you mauled by an animal?"

"Tattoo," he says.

Her hand drops away from her lips. "Erase it," she says. "Erase it right now."

"I don't think I can."

"Is it permanent?" She stoops to look at it a little more carefully.

"I assume so," Paul says, realizing that he didn't think to ask. There is a pause. "Do we have any bandages? Any antibiotic ointment?"

Elaine opens the medicine cabinet. She gets down on her knees in front of him with a bottle of Bactine, a tube of Neosporin, and some nonstick Telfa pads. "Don't move," she says, dabbing at him. Her annoyance is a relief, her rough handling exciting. He gets a little hard-on. "Don't even," she says.

Bactine stings.

"Elaine," he says, "it's like I've lost my mind. I feel so strange." He stops. "I'm sick," he says. "I ate a shrimp-salad sandwich. I've been throwing up all afternoon, four times, right in the middle of the street. No one did anything," he says. "I'm scared," he says. "I'm so scared."

"You're fine," she says, coating the area with ointment, putting a fresh bandage over the wound. "You're probably dehydrated; that can make you feel funny. I'll get you some tea." She picks herself up off the floor.

"Could I have juice instead of the tea?"

"Not if you've been throwing up."

"I have to lie down," he says, moving to the bed.

"I just don't understand," she says. "When did you have time to do it?"

"During lunch," he says. "I ate quickly."

"Maybe that's why you're sick."

"Dunno. Elaine," he calls after her. "It's fine about the walls. Maybe once they're washed they won't need to be painted, maybe we can save some money there."

"I just want everything to be all right for Sammy," she says.

"I know."

He lies down on the bed. There is an enormous crash of thunder. He pulls up the covers, and the heavens open. They pour. Paul lies back, and drops of rain begin to come through the little hole in the roof, they come through the ceiling and land in the middle of his forehead, tap-tap-tapping against his thoughts.

179

* * *

When Paul wakes up, Jennifer, Liz's daughter, is there by
his side, the voice of reason.

"Are you alive?" she asks.

"I don't know. Am I?"

"You were breathing strangely."

"Yeah, like how?"

"Panting," she says.

"I must have been dreaming."

"Are you sick?" She presses her punkish seventeen-year-
old Florence Nightingale hand against his forehead.

"Demented," he says, propping himself up.

"Do you want a cold washcloth?"

He shakes his head no. "It's like I've been run over," he
says. "I threw up. Four times in broad daylight, and no one
noticed."

"Chunky or smooth?"

"Extra-chunky," he says. "Shrimp salad."

"Watery," she says.

"Not really," he says.

"Watery isn't a question, it's a comment," Jennifer says.
"Watery means, like, gross."

As Jennifer talks, Paul hears a slight slurring, a little lisp
that he never noticed before. He looks at her. She starts to say
something—a small shiny spot flashes on her tongue.

"Jennifer," he says, "what happened to your tongue? You
sound strange. Did something happen to your tongue?"

"I had it popped," she says.

"Popped?"

"Yeah, pierced. I had a stud put in."

"Oh," Paul cries out. "Oh."

"What's the big deal?" Jennifer says. "It's not like I haven't
done it before."

"I'm going to be sick," Paul says. He gags and sputters and spits into a Kleenex. The idea of pain is making Paul sick. "I feel sick. I feel so sick."

"Do you want some ginger ale?"

She is his Jennifer, his hope, his promise. She is what sold him on this house, this life, a dozen years ago. Jennifer at five, dressed as a clownish Raggedy Ann, playing on the grass; Jennifer dolled up, her cheeks painted with wide circles of zinc oxide, two large rounds of her mother's red lipstick dotting the middles, making twin targets on her cheeks, somehow made him think that life here would be good. He thinks of Jennifer, solid, reliable, resilient, their beloved baby-sitter. And now, Jennifer at seventeen, about to graduate from high school and venture forth. Jennifer with her body pierced, punctuated with the grammar of her generation.

"Ginger ale," she says, handing him the glass. "Elaine left it for you."

He sips. The straw is paper, wilted, limp. It collapses.

"Where is she? Where's Elaine? Where is everybody?"

"Elaine went to the hardware store, Sammy's at Mrs. Hansen's, Daniel's at Scouts, my mother has school till five-thirty, and I'm here with you."

"Are you baby-sitting me?"

"I guess so."

"Do you know what I did?" Paul asks. "Do you know why I'm lying here? Did Elaine tell you?"

Jennifer nods. "Can I see it?"

He is careful to show her the tattoo and nothing else. He keeps his cock covered. He peels the bandage down, flashing the pulpy sore.

She is speechless. Her mouth falls open. The silver stud in her tongue shines.

Quickly, he covers everything up.

"Did you shave yourself, or did they shave you?" she asks.

"I shaved myself."

The storm has passed, and the sun is coming out again, if only temporarily.

A ladder bangs against the bedroom window, a face presses against the glass. There's a knock at the door. The men in the yellow suits are on their way up. "Sorry to startle you," the front man says, his voice muffled by his protective hood. "But you'll have to evacuate the room."

The men in yellow throw open the windows and attach thick white hoses to the house, hoses that will pump clean air in and dirty air out, hoses that will breathe for the house, like a respirator.

Paul slides out of bed. The cleaning crew moves carefully around him, giving him a wide berth, as though he's contaminated. He starts for the stairs. A yellow suit comes galumphing after him. "You forgot this," he says, handing Paul his glass of ginger ale.

On the stairs Paul passes an unusually short guy; the pant legs of his yellow suit are doubled up, rolled over into bulging cuffs.

"Are you ill?" the short guy asks, again his voice muffled by his beekeeper-style hood? "Sometimes we clean a house after someone dies or after a murder, but never when the guy is still here."

"I'm fine," Paul says, pushing past, holding his ginger ale. "Perfectly fine. Just a little nauseated. I had some bad shrimp salad."

Farther down, Paul passes the leader of the pack, the head of the yellow suits.

"Did I hear the short guy talking to you?" he asks.

"Yes," Paul says.

"He shouldn't have done that. No one is supposed to talk. It's supposed to be very quiet."

"Oh," Paul says. "Well, I guess he forgot."

"It's my company," the guy says. "I invented it. I'm the president. Deep cleaning: We suck out your vents, boil your sheets, flip your mattresses. Dust, dead skin, microscopic bacteria—there are pounds of it in every room." The head honcho speaks so animatedly, so heatedly, that his face mask fogs up.

And Paul does notice that things in the house are changing—the musty fog is abating, the soggy, charred odor evaporating. The air seems easier to breathe, and in general everything is becoming more pleasant.

"It's a great thing," Paul says. "Out with the old, in with the new." He slaps the guy on the back. The yellow suit makes a fat, puffing sound.

"I hope you're satisfied," the man says. And Paul isn't sure if the man means it or if he's being snide.

"Hope so," Paul says, going down gently, holding himself as though he'd had surgery, a hernia repaired.

Jennifer is at the kitchen table with a set of children's watercolors and paper. Paul is afraid to look at her to spy the silver dot, to set his stomach on a spin. He sits sideways, looking out the window. He can't help but notice that the kitchen is spotless—more than spotless, it is shining brightly. The cabinets have turned a shade or two lighter, and there's something thin and neat about the air—it smells like a showroom.

"You're graduating soon, aren't you?" Paul asks Jennifer.

"Next year," she says.

"Do you know what you want to be?"

"I want to run a large company, like Sony or something. I want to dominate. My plan is to major in world history and then get an M.B.A."

"Really?" Is this the Jennifer of his hopes and dreams, the Jennifer of his imagination? "I thought you wanted to be a folksinger or a potter or something."

"Not for a living. I make pottery to relax, but cash rules. Do you realize that I've worked ever since I was five years old? When I was ten, I had two jobs, and last year I had three part-time positions in addition to being an honor student."

"Can you help me with my homework?" Paul asks, genuinely awed.

"As long as it's not math."

"I'm serious. I'm having a hard time at work," Paul says. "It's like there's animal breath on the back of my neck. I feel like I'm being watched. I need to figure out a few things."

"Like what?"

"What's important right now? What makes a consumer buy something?"

"The idea of something better, something more. Fantasy. Facts are irrelevant."

Paul dips a watercolor brush into the red paint and begins a picture of his own. "Go on," he says.

"Don't compare yourself or your product by saying, 'We're not going to tell you that our product is better than theirs.' Don't announce, 'We're not going to try and sell this or that.' Take a bigger step. Assume. There's power in assumption. Assume Your Right."

"Assume Your Right," Paul says, moving from the red into the black, dipping in. "Assume Your Right"—he paints it across the page.

In the distance there is the thump-a, thump-a sound of the air pump, beating like a heart.

"Somebody? Anybody?" Mrs. Hansen calls, rapping her knuckles against the side door.

"We're in the kitchen," Paul says. "Come on in."

"He's home," Mrs. Hansen announces, delivering Sammy.

Sammy is carrying a plate of cookies. "I baked," he says, holding out the plate. "Want one?"

The idea of food gets Paul's stomach going again.

"I'll have one," Jennifer says. Sammy's cookies are strange-looking, tortured figures, maniacs with bulging cinnamon-dot eyes, crazy sugar-sprinkle hair, and cracked M&M mouths.

Jennifer chews off the head of one. "Not bad," she says, her silver stud coated in cookie crumbs.

Mrs. Hansen glances around the room. "Everything looks brighter," she says. "Did you paint the cabinets, or am I getting a migraine?"

"The walls were washed," Paul says.

Elaine comes in, carrying a bag from the hardware store.

"Where were you?" Paul asks.

"I went for a tool so I can fix the drippy pipe."

Outside, they hear Daniel shouting at one of the yellow men, "Hey! Hey, you, who are you? What are you doing here? This is my house."

Elaine hurries out. "Daniel," she says. "Daniel, stop. These are the men from the cleaning company."

"They look like they're from outer space," Daniel says, coming into the house. "What happened to Odetta?"

"She only comes every other Friday, and she doesn't do heavy work."

"And what's that noise?" Daniel asks.

"The air pump. They're changing the air in the house, making everything good again."

Elaine looks around the kitchen, she notices that the patch of crud on the hood above the stove, the spot she's forever trying to Brillo away, is gone. She steps closer. It shines. She checks the toaster oven; it's sparkling and crumb-free, even the little knobs on all the cabinets and drawers have been polished. There are no fingerprints on anything. She breathes deeply. The air is easy.

Sammy picks up two cookies. "This is the good man and this is the bad man," he says, knocking them against each other.

"And the only way to kill the bad man is to eat him." He takes a bite out of the wrong one.

Elaine presses her head against Sammy's chest. "Deep breath," she says, listening. "And another," she says. "Good. Very good."

"It's just like show-and-tell," Mrs. Hansen says. "Sammy made cookies, Paul and Jennifer painted a picture, Elaine bought a tool, and . . ." She turns to Daniel. "And did you make a paperweight in arts and crafts?" She looks down at the white lump Daniel is holding.

He looks at her as if she's an idiot. "It's a mold," he says. "A plaster cast of my left hand."

"It's very handsome," Mrs. Hansen says.

"It isn't about looks, it's about proof. You can make a mold of tire tracks so you can find out what kind of a car got away. You can make a mold of anything."

"How exciting," Mrs. Hansen says.

Daniel shrugs. "It's just a piece of the puzzle."

Mrs. Hansen checks her watch. "Best to go," she says. "Time to feed my hubcap."

"Hubcap?" Paul asks.

"Mr. Hansen," she says.

"You should bring him over for dinner one night soon," Paul says.

"Not so soon," Mrs. Hansen says. "We chopped up your dining room table this afternoon. God, it was fun. Whack. Whack." She demonstrates the motion of the ax.

"I had the sense something was different," Paul says.

The president of the yellow suits steps into the kitchen. He pulls off his helmet and holds it tucked into his hip, like an actor coming out of character to take a bow. He stands in front of them, posed—I am not a smart person, but I play one on TV.

"We're just finishing up," he says. "Disconnecting the hoses, packing up our brushes and sweepers. You'll notice a difference right away, but I find that the full effect usually takes twenty-four hours."

"I can feel it right now," Paul says. "The air is definitely cleaner."

The president smiles, as though it's all so obvious. "I'd like to leave you with a stack of sponges," he says, handing Elaine a plastic-mesh sack filled with sponges in assorted sizes and colors, each with the company's logo printed on it. "Do you know that your kitchen sponge is the dirtiest thing in the house?"

"I had no idea," Elaine says.

"Change it, and change it frequently," the man says. Elaine nods.

The man extends both hands toward Paul, smiles, and presses something into each of Paul's palms. "Petrified horse dung. It absorbs the toxins, pulling them out from your heart through your hands." He makes a gesture that's like a salute. "Be well," he says, stepping out.

The yellow suits have left the house.

There has been a surrealistic edge to the afternoon, which begins to fade once Elaine and the children are home. Each of them is an element in the equation, each is like an anchor, a weight.

"How was school?" Paul asks.

"Okay," Sammy says. "We had rehearsal."

"Rehearsal for what?" Jennifer asks.

"Play," Sammy says. "I'm the head of a rhinoceros."

"Wow," Daniel says. "Last year you were the back of an elephant."

"When is it?" Jennifer asks.

"Tomorrow," Sammy says.

"Tomorrow, and you're just telling me now?" Elaine says.

"He's not even telling you," Daniel says. "He told Jennifer."

"Why didn't you tell me?" Elaine asks.

Sammy shrugs. "I didn't see you," he offers.

Jennifer checks her watch. "Okay, guys, fair time."

"We need money," Sammy says.

"We should be there by seven," Jennifer says.

"Give them some money," Elaine instructs Paul.

Paul moves to reach for his wallet. The motion irritates his wound. He is wearing sweatpants; he has no pockets, no cash. His wallet is upstairs, in his pants.

"Never mind, I've got it," Elaine says, digging into her purse, pulling a pair of twenties off her wad, her booty prize from the yard sale.

"Give Jennifer some, too," Paul says. "She's an excellent baby-sitter."

Elaine looks at him suspiciously and pulls off another twenty. "Make sure you eat enough dinner," Elaine says. "Have some protein."

"Have some fun," Paul says, and they are out the door.

Sammy's plate of cookies and Daniel's weird mold are left on the table.

"Does Sammy seem strange to you?" Elaine asks.

"It's stress. He's picking up on all the stress. Daniel is the one who scares me."

"Yeah, why?"

"Overnight he's a Scout and a goddamned junior detective. I don't trust him for a minute. I think he's a stool pigeon."

"Paul," Elaine says. "We're talking about Daniel."

"Just you wait and see," Paul says.

Elaine turns to go upstairs. "Are you dressing for dinner?"

"It hurts to wear pants," Paul says.

"Well, I'd offer to lend you a dress, but I'm afraid you'd take me up on it."

"You never can tell," Paul says, following her. "Do you think I can get away with wearing sweats?"

"Can't you just put on a suit and act normal, even if it hurts?"

"If it would make you happy, I'd be glad to hurt myself."

"I think you're confusing me with someone else," Elaine says, and quickly turns away.

"How would you describe your mood?" Paul calls after her. "Does 'bitchy' even begin to do it?"

Elaine ignores him and picks up the phone. "I'm calling Pat and George and telling them we'll meet them at Joan's."

"Do we really have to go? I feel lousy. I've been sick all afternoon." He feels small and weak and not at all sure he can maintain the usual façade. " 'I am the egg man . . . the walrus,' " he sings to himself.

"It will be good for us to be with people," Elaine says, convincing herself. "It will remind us of who we are," she says.

"Who you want us to be," Paul says, going into the bathroom. "What was the name of the guy who shot John Lennon?"

"I don't know, why?"

"I'm trying to remember."

His suit pants are hanging from the shower rod—perfectly pressed. The tile is radiant, even the grout seems to be glowing. Paul can see his reflection in the chrome faucet handles. "How much does the cleaning guy get?"

"You don't want to know."

"I'm curious," Paul says, peeling down his bandage, squirting a little extra ointment over everything, figuring if nothing else to keep the area well lubricated. He can't look at the tattoo. The sight of what he's done to himself is terrifying, a mark of insanity, another in what's becoming a series: the fire, the date, his job.

"Did it hurt?" Elaine asks as she comes in to put on her makeup. "Did it hurt like hell?" Her eyes are rolled back into a strangely accusatory position as she puts on a face she clipped from a magazine—the page is propped against the sink, with step-by-step, paint-by-number instructions. "I'd assume that's a sensitive area," she says, piling it on.

Paul notices that the color of her eye shadow is Fiction, her lipstick is called Sheer Fraud.

"Did you even notice—or were you doing something else at the time?"

He doesn't respond. He waits. He buttons his shirt. He tucks everything in and zips his pants. "What happened to the dining room table, Elaine? Why'd you chop it to pieces?"

"The damage was irreparable," she says, finishing up, smacking her lips, dabbing her mouth with toilet paper.

"We're not millionaires, Elaine."

"Why does it always come down to money? That's how I can tell you're looking for a fight. You say something stupid about money."

Paul puts on his jacket. "Are you ready to go, or do you want to call and tell them that we're not coming because Thursday is our night to stay home and fight?"

"Get in the car," Elaine says.

"I know it's crazy to have a dinner party on a weeknight," Joan Talmadge says, opening the door, "but I thought it would be fun. Ted's leaving tomorrow for three weeks, and my book club is off tonight. I'm so glad you could come."

"I hope we're not late," Elaine says.

"No, you're it, though. The Montgomerys couldn't make it. Something happened," Joan whispers.

"How are you folks?" Ted asks, coming up behind Joan, giving her a squeeze. "What can I get you to wet your whistle?"

"White wine," Elaine says.

"Scotch," Paul says.

"Water?"

"Rocks," Paul says.

The weather is starting up again. Joan opens the front door and takes a peek. "I know it's crazy," she repeats to no one in particular. "But I thought it would be fun." She closes the door.

"Strong front pushing through," Ted says.

"Clear flying tomorrow," Joan says.

"Glasses, glasses," Ted says.

"In the cupboard," Joan says.

Joan leans in and whispers to Elaine, "The Montgomery boy tried to kill himself. Or something. Catherine and Hammy had to take a ride up and meet with the people at the school." Joan pauses and looks out the window. "God, I hope they're not caught in the storm."

Ted is down on his knees in the foyer in front of the cabinet where they keep extra wineglasses, dishes, crockery. He is holding three wineglasses in each hand, and he can't get up. "Joan," he bleats softly. "Joan, Joan."

Ted is a former football player. He works for one of the sports networks in the business office. He used to get everyone great seats to games at the Garden; now he gets them nothing, and Paul can't tell if he's been moved up or moved over.

Joan goes behind Ted, slips her hands under his arms, counts, "One, two, three, push," and lifts him enough so that he can get his footing. She turns to Elaine and shrugs. "He just folds up sometimes, and you have to unfold him," she says.

"My damn trick knee," Ted says, embarrassed.

Paul nods. He thinks he sees the date in the distance, walking from the dining room into the living room. He thinks he must be hallucinating.

"Are Pat and George here?" Elaine asks.

"Of course," Joan says.

Elaine is nervous about seeing Pat out of context, Pat with George, Pat with other couples, Pat with clothes. Will Pat speak to her? Will it be strained? She is nervous and excited—the way you get when you have a crush.

Ted hands them their drinks. They gulp. Paul leans back against the frame of the kitchen door, and Elaine goes in search of Pat.

"Hors d'oeuvres," Joan says, coming out with a trayful. "Mini-blinis." Paul pops one and then another into his mouth, swallowing them whole.

"Good, aren't they?" she asks. "Beluga."

"Ummm-humm." He blots his lips with a cocktail napkin. Again, he thinks he sees her, moving from room to room, back and forth in front of him, a hypnotic tease.

"Surprise, surprise," Henry says, sideswiping him.

"I thought you were away."

"Just flew in—and boy my arms are tired," Henry says, teasing. "I hopped the last plane." He takes Paul's glass. "You look like you could use a drink."

The date slides in next to Henry. "You remember my friend, don't you?" Henry says, winking. His wink is so strange that it looks like an overextended blink, it looks as if Henry's got something in his eye and is flapping his lid furiously trying to clear it.

She is stalking him, setting out to ruin him. She has no judgment, no limits. She is wearing a skirt that is more like an elbow patch, a Band-Aid. Bile rises in his throat. He makes a run for the powder room. The two mini-blinis he swallowed fly up and out as if jet-propelled. They land in the toilet intact, staring up, two eyes in a sea of yellow foam. He rinses his mouth, washes his face, and rejoins the party.

"We waited for you two," George says. "Finally I said to Pat, 'We've got to go on without them. They're smart, they'll catch up.' "

"Sorry," Paul says, hating the paternalistic tone, the rap-on-the-knuckles reprimand. "The kids, the storm, the house—we ran late. We called you," he says.

George cuffs him on the shoulder. "Forget it," he says, handing Paul his empty glass, disappearing into the bathroom and locking the door behind him.

Paul feels drugged, depraved. His wound burns. The date is dangerous; she could kill him. He looks for Elaine. He needs protection. He stands next to her, listening to her talking to Ted. "I've started fixing things," Elaine says. "Yesterday I fixed the disposal, and today I'm working on the toilet. Wouldn't it be great to be able to fix everything? Wouldn't it be wonderful to be an auto mechanic? Or an electrician? Or even a plumber?" She pauses. "I need to believe I can do some good, and it's too late to go to medical school."

"Fine thing," Ted says. "It's never too late."

"Sometimes it is," Elaine says. "The moment passes. It comes and goes."

"Soup's on," Joan announces. "Your places are marked."

Paul circles the table. He finds his name between Liz's and the date's—her card simply says GUEST OF HENRY.

Elaine is across the table between Pat and George.

"Odd woman out," Pat says, settling in.

"I threw up all afternoon," Paul whispers to the date as he's putting his napkin in his lap. "And the adhesive on my bandage isn't holding well—right now my pants are rubbing against a horrible mess."

"You're turning me on," she says, almost loud enough for someone to hear.

"How's the house?" Ted asks, divvying up the fish. "That's what we want to know. Do you know what caused the fire? More importantly, are you covered?"

"We're covered," Paul says, looking at Elaine, checking to see if he's allowed to tell the stupidity bit.

"Instead of just patching things back together, we're using it as an opportunity to expand. We're adding French doors and a deck," Elaine says.

"Oh, I love French doors," Joan says, putting beans on a plate and passing it down.

"Wonderful beans," Pat says.

"I just want to tell everyone," Joan says, "I was at the office all day. This dinner was whipped up in sixty minutes or less."

"And it tastes like it," George spits into Elaine's ear.

"Beautiful flowers," Elaine says.

"It's what I do," Joan says, passing plates. "It's my therapy." Actually, Joan is a financial whiz. When she was home with their first child, she started tinkering with their investments. Last year she told Elaine that she pulled in half a million, and that was when the market was slightly down.

"What about the Fourth? Does everyone have plans for fireworks?" Liz asks.

"We're already planning Christmas vacation," Joan says.

"Do we have plans?" Paul asks Elaine.

She shakes her head.

"Not to worry," Pat says. "You'll do whatever we do."

"We are so boring. I don't even tell the travel agent where we want to go anymore," Joan says. "I tell her, 'You pick it. Pick a place I would never dream of, and book us in for two weeks.'"

Outside, thunder rolls. Wild branches scratch against the house.

Joan rings her spoon against her glass. "It's a real treat to see everyone tonight. I've been instructed to tell you how very sorry Catherine and Hammy are not to be joining us, but they're looking forward to seeing everyone Saturday night."

Ted, Liz, and Pat applaud.

When dinner is done, Ted tries to get up and help Joan clear but has trouble with his legs; he stands and falls, stands and falls, and finally sits back down.

"Stay," Joan says, patting his shoulder. "Sit and stay."

An enormous crash of thunder and lightning shakes the house. "Now, that had to have hit something," George says, racing to the window.

Again, there is thunder, and the power goes off.

Taking the electrical interruption as her signal, the date reaches into Paul's lap and grabs him. He whimpers.

"What?" someone says. "What happened?"

"Nothing," Paul stammers. "I just—the chair—my toe."

The lights come back on.

"I've got cheesecake for the brave among you, angel food cake for anyone afraid of fat, and a bowl of berries for the faint of heart. What'll it be?" Joan asks. "Ménage à trois? A little bit of everything?"

Pat and Liz are talking softly. "Pregnant?" Liz says. "At forty-seven? Were they doing things?"

"They did nothing," Pat says.

"What a nightmare, preggers at forty-seven. I can't even imagine having sex," Joan says, licking her fingers. "Coffee?" she asks. "I've got a pot of decaf. Let's see a show of hands. One. Two. Three."

"Get home safe," they call to each other as they're pulling away.

"Drive careful," Joan and Ted say, waving from the door. "See you Saturday at the Montgomerys'."

In the car Paul and Elaine talk.

"Do Joan and Ted not have sex?" Paul asks.

"I don't know, why?"

"She said, 'I can't even imagine having sex.' Do other couples not have sex?"

"I don't know."

"Should we not be having sex?"

"I don't know."

"If nothing else, it seems like the one thing we do well—we fight and we fuck. That's how we know we're still married." Paul laughs.

Elaine says nothing.

"That was supposed to be a joke."

"What's the punch line?"

"You were in a perfectly good mood at the party; what happened?"

"I don't know," Elaine says.

They drive, following the red glow, the afterburn, of the Nielsons' taillights. The electricity is off everywhere—trees are down, flares are up.

"Wave," Paul says as they pass Elaine's cop, directing traffic.

"Do you think we have to check on our house?" Elaine asks.

"No," Paul says. "It couldn't get worse."

The night is ink. It is as though there's nothing out there—if they can't see it, it doesn't exist. They crawl toward the memory of home.

The Nielsons' house hovers, glowing dimly like a spaceship, burning out, low on fuel.

"Pat and George must have a backup generator or something," Paul says.

The two little M's greet them at the door.

"Were you scared when the lights went off?" Pat asks.

They shake their heads. "We played camp-out."

All around the perimeter of the room, battery-powered backup lights beam dutifully.

"You can never estimate how long the power will be out," George says, crawling around the room turning things off.

"How about lights-out for the campers? It's a school night, after all," Pat says, leading the little ones off to bed.

"Nightcap?" George asks Paul

"Have you got any pain medication?" Paul asks.

"I think there's some Percocet left over from my deviated septum. You having a problem?"

"Percocet would do it," Paul says.

George goes off down the hall and returns with a pill and a flashlight.

"Sorry about all the noise last night," George says, dropping the pill in Paul's palm. "Sometimes it just gets to you. I want so much," George says, "that's what it is, high expectations."

Paul nods.

"Anyway," George says, "I went down into the basement, smoked a little grass, and felt much better. Every now and then I do it. Don't tell Pat; I wouldn't want her to know."

Paul shakes his head. "Don't worry," he says. "I'd never tell." Pot and pornography. No one would believe me anyway, he thinks.

"It's my way of letting a little air in," George says. "Next time join me, if you're inclined. You smoke?"

"Sure," Paul says. Of course he smokes. He does every-thing. He doesn't tell George about the time he and Elaine smoked crack, how she was the fountain in front of the Plaza hotel, a Roman candle with sparks and color and light pouring out of her. He doesn't tell George that it was one of their highest moments—no pun intended—a moment of communion and communication, and that now he worries he and Elaine have drifted, and he's not sure that it's the usual ebb and flow.

"Where did Elaine go?" he asks George.

George shrugs. "She must have gone with Pat. What a lousy party, don't ya think?" George says, pouring himself a drink. "What a lousy idea, a dinner party on a work night. People can't drink enough to make it worthwhile." George has never sounded so bitter before.

"I thought it was just us," Paul says.

"It's everyone," George says. "And Christ, Ted's knee, it's depressing as hell. He's falling apart. Big strong guy, can't even pick himself up from the table."

"I wanted to stay home. But Elaine needs to see people. She feels strange if she's left alone for too long. Where'd you say she went?"

George shrugs. He tops off his glass. He hands Paul a flashlight. "Sleep tight," he says, heading down the hall into the dark.

Elaine is in the bedroom.

"Where'd you go?" Paul asks.

"Where'd I go?" Elaine repeats. "Where would I go?"

"Dunno."

The beam of her flashlight is directed down onto the page of a magazine.

"You have a flashlight, too," he says.

She ignores him.

The deep-pink walls of the little M's' room look even meatier than usual; they have the color of something oxygen-deprived, a failing organ. It makes Paul nervous. "We have to get out of here before the weekend," he says. He puts the Percocet on the night table and pulls off his shoes.

"What's that?" she asks.

"A treat."

"Mine or yours?"

"Mine," he says.

"Are there more?"

"I got it from George. It's left over from his deviated septum." Paul reaches for the water glass.

"That's my water," Elaine says, taking it away.

"What's wrong with you?"

There is no answer.

He undresses. He peels down his bandage and takes a long look at himself with the flashlight, contemplating. Things are both better and worse in the half-light. There's something about the tattoo that he likes—it's a badge of a certain kind of sick courage.

"Do me the favor," Elaine says, watching him examine himself. "Keep yourself covered. The whole world doesn't have to see what you did, and I really don't want the boys to have to deal with it. It'll frighten Sammy, and God knows what it'll mean to Daniel."

"Why are you being so awful?" Paul asks, putting the bandage back in place, in effect tucking everything in for the night.

"Why?" Elaine throws back the covers, swinging her legs over the edge. She stands up and fixes her flashlight beam on his face. "Why?" she says, coming toward him, zeroing in.

He is naked in front of her. "This afternoon you were so wonderful," he says. "You took care of me, you didn't ask questions. You were incredible. I felt so safe. Filled with hope and love."

She looks at him, stunned, amazed. "What kind of idiot do you think I am?"

"Shhhh, someone will hear you," Paul says.

"Am I supposed to think that you were at the office, working away, and all of a sudden, out of the blue, you decided, 'I need a tattoo on my crotch,' the same way you might think a cup of coffee would be nice?" she whispers viciously. "Or would it be better if I assumed you were kid-napped by aliens on Fifty-seventh Street and that the poison ivy below your belt is their insignia, the logo from their spaceship?"

"I'm not saying . . ." Paul says.

"You're not saying is right," Elaine says, wagging her light at him. "You think you can go off, do whatever with whomever, then come crawling home and I'll take care of you. You think I'm so wonderful, so marvelous and forgiving, that I'll make everything all better. Who do you think I am?" she says, loudly. "I'm not your mother."

"No," Paul says. "You're not. You're out of your mind. You're some suddenly perfect Miss Fix-it who wants to do some-thing with her life. It's not too late to go to medical school," he says, in a mean, mocky voice.

"Who are you fucking?" Elaine asks.

"Who are you fucking?" Paul throws back. "You must be fucking somebody, otherwise you wouldn't be acting like this. Are you fucking Liz? Do you like it? What's it like?"

Elaine hits Paul.

Elaine has never hit anyone before in her life. She hits him again, hard.

He opens his mouth. "Bitch."

She hits him again. Again and again, there's something satisfying about the sting of her hand against his skin.

He grabs her arms, her wrists.

A noise like a war cry comes out of her mouth.

He hopes no one hears her.

"Be quiet," he hisses.

"You be quiet."

He pushes her away.

She falls against the bed, bounces up, and rushes toward him. "Where'd you get the tattoo, Paul?"

"You're acting crazy," he says, brushing her off.

"I'm acting crazy?" she says. "I'm acting crazy?"

He picks up the Percocet and is out the bedroom door; she's after him. Their feet padding fast down the hall. She is on his back, slapping, scratching. He's turning and twisting, trying to shake her off. Sofa, chairs, side tables, lamps—it is a treacherous domestic obstacle course. Everything is in the way. They're dancing around the room, weaving, bobbing, ducking. His elbow meets her cheek. The corner of the coffee table stabs him in the leg—he cries out.

"Be quiet," she mocks.

She lunges. He trips over an ottoman and slams to the floor. There is a groan, the sound of air escaping him. She makes a fist. She punches him in the gut. He pulls her hair, as though by yanking it he will snap her out of it. She is upon him using both fists, like sticks, pummeling him relentlessly.

He is a naked man, and she is his wife in her beautiful new nightgown. She is beating him up in the dark, in the living room of a neighbor's house. He is trapped in the space between the sofa and the coffee table. They are not speaking. There is nothing to say. The only sound is the repetitive, thick thud of her hand against him and the accidental expression of his surprise—grunts and groans. And then it is done. He is curled into a tight ball. Not moving. Not fighting. She takes a pillow from the sofa and pounds him with it. She is crying now. Everything is futile; there is nothing, nothing but sadness and frustration. She puts the pillow down.

He moves to get up.

"Watch your head," she says.

He goes ahead of her, down the hall back into their room. He breaks the Percocet in half; she hands him the water glass. He swallows his half of the pill and has a sip of water, and then she does the same.

They sleep.

SEVEN

THE WORK BEGINS.

The storm has roughed up every house up and down the block—branches and leaves are everywhere, beheaded geraniums dot the flagstone path, and the potted plants look as though they've been spun around in the night.

Mrs. Hansen is in Elaine's front yard, straightening up. She is hauling branches, one in each hand. Bright green leaves frame her face; her khakis act like camouflage. She is the woman who turns into a tree.

"Hello, hello," she calls from behind the leaves. "Hello, hello," like a little girl playing peek-a-boo.

"Mrs. Hansen, is that you?"

Mrs. Hansen throws off the branches, hurling them into a pile—she's stronger than you'd think. "Wild night, wasn't it?"

"Out of control," Elaine says.

"God's night off," Mrs. Hansen says. "A house on Oak was struck by lightning, and over on Maple there's a tree down on a Mercedes. I'm not sorry for that son of a bitch; I hate German cars," she says. "At three A.M., I was making cold hot toddies trying to calm myself. The whole thing scared the hell out of me."

"Cold hot toddy?"

"Like a hot toddy, only the electricity was off so I drank it cold. The mister and I were up all night wondering what would happen next." She glances around the yard. "Thought I'd tidy up over here. The last thing you need is more mess. Your phone's been ringing like crazy—every ten minutes since seven-thirty. Expecting a call?"

Elaine shakes her head no.

"I would have put on a pot of coffee, I would have gotten the phone, but . . ."

Elaine looks across the street. The Hansens' yard is neat as a pin, the grass so well groomed that it appears combed. The stone front of the house, a perfect façade. "Your yard is amazing," Elaine says, realizing that she has no idea what the house is like inside—she pictures Ethan Allen.

"I was up early," Mrs. Hansen says. "Radio said there might have been a tornado, but it's unconfirmed."

"You really are something," Elaine says, noticing that Mrs. Hansen's tousled reddish-brown hair is dyed, aware that she's made up a little story for herself about Mrs. Hansen that may, or more likely may not, be true.

"I used to be a goer, go, go, go," Mrs. Hansen says. "But then, out of the blue, I decided I didn't want it anymore. I didn't want a schedule or a plan. I wanted out. So I stayed in. More or less for a year. I didn't leave the house. Gave everyone quite a scare, but I knew I was fine—it was what I needed to do.

"How long have you lived here?"

"Twenty-seven years last April."

"Are you happy?" Elaine asks, and immediately worries that she's gone too far.

"You're not thinking of moving, are you? Not after all this, not after we've become friends."

"I'm not going anywhere," Elaine says.

"Don't scare me. Last thing I need is another scare."

Inside the house, the phone is ringing.

"Phone," Mrs. Hansen says.

"I'll get it," Elaine says.

"Why are you ignoring me?" Liz asks. "Did I do something to offend you?"

"I don't know what to say," Elaine says. It sounds like an excuse, but she means it. "I just don't know what to say."

"Well, you're going to have to say something. I can't stand this, it's ridiculous."

"It's not you, it's me," Elaine says.

"I know it's you," Liz says. "You'll tell me all about it. I'll pick you up at noon. We'll have a lump of cottage cheese; I'm on a new diet."

"That's an old diet," Elaine says, hanging up. She looks out the kitchen window and into the Dumpster—it's filling up. There's the axed dining room table, a half dozen assorted shoes Elaine threw in yesterday, and the remains of the grill, which someone tossed in on top.

The phone rings again.

"Elaine, I'm buying you an answering machine," her mother says.

"Have you been calling all morning? Mrs. Hansen said someone's been calling."

"No," her mother says. "But last night I needed you and I couldn't get you."

"We were out." Elaine wanders into the dining room, stretching the phone cord. She stands where the dining room table used to be, wondering what should fill the spot, what comes next.

"Exactly," her mother says. "In a storm, no less. I've got to run, but I'll come by later. I'll bring a new machine."

Elaine hangs up. And again the phone rings. "Hello," she says, exasperated.

"Just checking in," a woman's voice says.

"Who is this?" Elaine asks.

"Who would you like me to be?"

"I think you have the wrong number," Elaine says, hanging up.

She takes a deep breath. The house doesn't smell. It has no smell at all. It is neither here nor there, dead nor living, it is nonexistent, without connotations. Neutral. They did an excellent job.

The phone rings.

"What?" Elaine says instead of hello.

"Hello, it's Rich Perloff, your architect. I've been calling all morning. First it rings and rings and no one answers, and then it's busy. Haven't you got an answering machine or at least Call Waiting?"

"Who is this?" Elaine asks.

"Rich Perloff. Are you home? Can I come over now?" he asks. "If you want me to do this, I have to do it now," he says.

"Fine," she says. "Come. I'm here."

Elaine hangs up. She digs through the cupboard for the Yellow Pages. It's time for her to do something for herself. Elaine is looking for information—schools, vocational programs, ways out of her rut. She lets her fingers do the walking. She dials.

"Westchester Technical Institute."

"I'm looking for some information . . ." Elaine says.

"One moment, I'll connect you."

"Bud Johnson," a man says, picking up.

"I'm looking for information—" Elaine says.

He cuts her off. "Is the student having problems in school, flunking out, has he been expelled or arrested?"

"It's for me. I'm calling for myself."

"How old are you?"

"Forty-three," Elaine says.

"Oh, I don't think so," Bud Johnson says.

"Yes, I am."

"No, I mean, our program wouldn't be right for you. It's for 'stupid' boys," he says to her. "What's your name?"

"Elaine."

"Elaine, do you know what you're looking for?"

"No," she says. "This is the first call I've made."

"Tell me about yourself."

"I'm married, I have two children, and I'm going insane."

"And I guess you've already tried to drown yourself in aerobics classes?"

Elaine doesn't answer.

"That was supposed to be a joke."

"I've never taken an aerobics class in my life."

"Okay. So what kind of educational background do you have?"

"NYU a long time ago."

"Have you worked?"

"Not since college."

"Umm-hummm."

She doesn't know who she's talking to, she doesn't know what she's looking for; this feels a little like a waste of time and a little like she's called a suicide hotline—she can't hang up.

"And what do you think you'd be good at now?" His voice is calm, soothing.

"I don't know," Elaine says.

"What have you tried?"

"The other day my friend gave me a fix-it book. So far I've

repaired the disposal and the toilet, and I must admit I got quite a kick out of it."

She wonders what he looks like. She pictures dark curly hair.

"In your wildest dreams what do you see yourself doing two years from now?"

Inexplicably, Elaine blushes. "Oh," she says. "Oh, I couldn't answer that."

"Well," he says cautiously, "I'd be glad to talk with you about your situation, and maybe we can think of something."

"I'm scared," she whispers. "I'm so scared."

"Would you like to make a time to meet later today?"

"I have to go to my son's school play at two o'clock. He's the head rhinoceros."

"Let's meet at four. I think I can get out of here by then. Odyssey Diner on Central Avenue?"

"How will I recognize you?"

"I'll be carrying a manila folder." A bell rings in the background. "I have to go," he says. "Hang in there."

The architect pulls into the driveway, just missing Mrs. Hansen, who jumps into the bushes, making a narrow escape.

"Run me down, why don't you. What's the big hurry? Fire's out," Mrs. Hansen says, climbing out of the shrubbery.

"Are you the mother-in-law?" the architect asks, ringing the bell. "Are we adding on a room for you—so the hen can come back to roost?"

Mrs. Hansen gestures across the street to her house. "I'm the lady next door," she says proudly.

"You don't have much left in the way of a roof," the architect says.

"I'm aware of that," Mrs. Hansen says. "That one's been on there seventeen years."

"All good things come to an end," the architect says.

"Thanks for being available on such short notice," Elaine says, letting him into the house.

"Did you have the walls washed in here?" the architect asks.

"Yesterday," she says.

"I can smell it," the architect says.

"There is no smell."

"Exactly," he says. "What are you covering up?"

"We had a fire." Elaine leads him to the hole in the wall. The plastic got blown around in the storm, the entire setup is looking a little soggy, the surrounding plaster is starting to show a stain, and there's a kind of weird swelling, a bulge in the wall that wasn't there the day before. "We're thinking we'd like to take advantage of the situation—adding a deck and French doors."

"Face-lift," the architect says.

Elaine ignores him and goes on. "The deck man was here yesterday. I picked this one." She shows the architect a picture and a scrap of paper with the dimensions.

The architect shakes his head. "Too square. You need something narrower, something that has a shape, some style."

And before Elaine can say anything, he reaches out, yanks the plastic off the hole, and starts poking at the edges.

"Who started the fire?"

"Grill fell over."

"I never heard that one before."

Elaine doesn't blink.

"Have you got a ladder?"

"In the garage."

The architect hauls Paul's big ladder out and sets it up in the backyard—not far from the hole. "Go on," he says, and Elaine starts to climb. He follows her up. "I want to hear your fantasy—you in your backyard, how do you see yourself? Tell me your fantasy, and then we'll talk reality."

Three steps from the top he calls out, "Stop. Turn." And she does. "What do you see?"

"Sky, trees, houses." She looks more closely. "The Mercedes on Maple being towed away."

She can see the intersection of four backyards—wood, wire, and split-rail fencing all coming together in a point. A swing set, an above ground pool, a Japanese garden.

"This is your view," the architect pronounces from just beneath her. He gesticulates, the ladder rocks. "I was supposed to start a big job this morning. At midnight last night, they called to cancel—they're getting divorced instead." He starts down the ladder, it sways. "Something else you might want to think of, while you've got me, is putting in a safe room, I've been doing a lot of them."

"Safe room?" Elaine asks. She's thinking padded walls, no sharp corners, a housewife goes insane.

"The couple I was going to do the house for was getting a safe suite: underground phone line, water supply, oxygen. I could do a single room, say, master bath for under five grand. I've got a great bulletproof door with interior dead bolts. These days you never can tell when you're going to need to just get away, buy yourself a few minutes of calm. You can't count on the police to be there when you need them."

He pulls a straightedge out of his pocket, sits down at the kitchen table, and draws on a sheet of Sammy's construction paper. He swears while he works. "Shit. Fuck. Eraser," he calls out. "Have you got an eraser?"

He measures. He plots. It takes him less than twenty minutes. "These are your French doors," he says, showing her the plan. "And that's your deck."

"Am I allowed to make suggestions?"

"Is there something wrong with what I drew?"

Elaine looks at the picture. "All the doors open onto the deck?"

"Yes," the guy says.

"Well then, I guess it's fine," Elaine says.

"Don't tell me you're getting cold feet. Don't tell me you're saying no. Don't tell me anything I don't want to hear." He starts to have a temper tantrum. He gets up from the table, flapping his arms. "Why are you doing this to me? Why are you doing this?" He goes into the dining room. He stares at the hole. He takes a few deep breaths. "Sorry," he says. "I'm sorry if I'm coming across as kind of tense. I didn't meditate this morning. I always meditate in the morning. It focuses me. And I'm so upset about the couple that canceled. It's bad for all of us, when a couple gives up. It means we all failed."

"How much is this going to cost?" Elaine says, feeling obligated to ask. "Shouldn't I call my husband?"

Paul is at the office. He has gone to the toy store and bought himself some children's watercolors and paper. The box says nontoxic, and he thinks that's a good thing. He is painting a plan, conjuring the color of success for a margarine company— lite-butter yellow.

He is behind his desk; his pants are undone. His wounds hurt, but he's cooking, feeling oddly all right. It's a long shot, but that's what's called for now—something different.

The date has called, several times, using several different names. He's not taking calls. He's busy, the work has begun. He's thinking things through, replaying last night: He sees himself talking to George, getting the pain pill, going into the room, Elaine on the bed reading. He remembers undressing; the image of his tattoo appears as a close-up, in full color, the shine of the antibiotic ointment under the thin beam of the flashlight. And then there is Elaine coming toward him, Paul throwing her off, Elaine bouncing on the bed, Paul out the door, down the hall, chased. Paul and Elaine spinning around the living room, like a twisted game of tag, tackle the marriage and bring it down.

Elaine hitting him.

Paul pulling her hair.

Elaine pummeling him.

And at some point it stops. It doesn't end, it just stops.

He thinks of what Jennifer told him yesterday afternoon—"Facts are irrelevant."

Paul dips a watercolor brush into the purple paint. "There's power in assumption," he tells himself, remembering her words. "Assume your right," Paul says aloud, moving from the purple into the pink.

"I should call my husband," Elaine says, picking up the phone.

His secretary puts the call right through.

"The architect is here," Elaine announces. "He had a cancellation. He can start now, they can bring a wrecking ball this afternoon. But I wanted to check with you."

"I was just thinking of you," Paul says, dipping his brush in water, rinsing it. "I'm sitting at my desk painting."

"I'm standing in the kitchen talking," she says.

"Are you having a good day? Feeling better?"

"Yes," she says, and she can't say any more.

"Is he right there, next to you?"

"Yes," she says again.

"This is the guy who did the Esterhazys', and they're happy?"

"Yes," Elaine says again.

The architect is huffing and puffing, pacing the kitchen.

The house is starting to have a smell; it's picking up the scent of the architect, anxiety and Irish Spring.

"Has he given us an estimate? Do we have to look for a contractor?"

"No. He has someone."

"Do you want to let him have the job?"

The architect takes the phone from Elaine. "Look," he says, "it's a small thing, it's not like you're building a house. You're just letting a little light in; don't make it more than what it is." He pauses. "I don't care what you do, but what I told your wife is that I was supposed to start something today and they canceled, they're splitting up instead of building a house—so here I am. You can do the same thing, you can procrastinate, or you can do the job. If you can say yes, you can have it right now. It's a onetime deal. This isn't something to dick around with. You see a good thing coming, embrace it," the architect says. "Don't waste my time. Everyone is always wasting my time."

"Be quiet for a minute and let me think," Paul shouts.

The architect hands the phone back to Elaine.

"What a fucking asshole," Paul says.

Elaine doesn't say anything.

"Do you think we should do it? Could you get him to write something down, some sort of an estimate, tell him we need it for the insurance?"

The guy takes the phone from Elaine again. "Are you saying yes or no?"

"Don't take a tone with me," Paul says. "I'm saying go ahead, fine, get your hammer in hand. I'm going to need something in writing by the time I get home."

"Short fuse," the architect says, hanging up. "Can I use your phone?" Elaine nods. He dials. "Joey, let's go. Here's the address—it's a deck and doors. I'm leaving a sketch on the kitchen table. You need the mini-ball; there's a stone wall that's gotta come out. I'll be in my office in an hour, I'll call you from there." The architect hangs up. "Did I tell you? The contractor is my brother-in-law, married my baby sister, it's kind of an all-in-the-family business. Safe rooms to swimming pools, soup to nuts."

"No, you didn't mention it," Elaine says, feeling slightly screwed.

Mrs. Hansen comes in, mixes herself a drink—white wine and cranberry juice in a big tumbler—and goes back out again. Elaine checks the clock. Eleven-thirty.

"Listen," Elaine tells the architect, "my son has asthma. I worry a lot about dust. Can you do me a favor and keep it clean?"

"I had asthma," the architect says. "I spent my childhood choking to death. I can keep it clean. We'll seal the whole thing off. You won't even know it's happening. Can I use your phone again?"

She nods.

"Joey, remember that roll of plastic left over from the gym job? Throw it in the truck. We have to keep the house clean; their kid can't breathe."

"Thanks," Elaine says.

"Don't mention it."

The phone rings. The architect answers it. "For you." He hands the receiver to Elaine.

"I hope it wasn't crazy to have a party on a weeknight," Joan Talmadge says.

"It was lovely," Elaine says. "It's always good to get out of the house."

There is noise in the background. "I'm in my office," Joan says. "It's completely crazy. The market's been up and down all day." She draws a breath. "Are you living at home yet?"

"Soon," Elaine says.

"Well, as soon as you're back, we'll have a welcome-home party."

"That'll be nice," Elaine says.

"Ted thinks you're wonderful," Joan says. "After everyone left, we were talking, and of all of the other wives he likes you best."

"Well, thanks. I like Ted, too."

"Are you really thinking of going to medical school? Don't you have to be twenty-two or something?"

"Have you heard from Catherine?" Elaine says, changing the subject.

"Oh," she whispers, "it's bad, really bad, worse than you can imagine. In fact, I've never heard of anything like it. He did something so horrible, unthinkable. He went insane. He bit a teacher's fingers off, the index and—what's the longer one?— the fuck-you finger. He bit them off and ate them. The hand got infected, and then something weird happened, a poisoned blood clot or something, and the teacher died. He killed someone. Seventeen years old and already a murderer, can you imagine?"

"It doesn't sound like he meant to kill anyone."

"He ate human flesh. Imagine how Catherine and Hammy must feel," Joan says, carrying on the conversation with herself. "All morning I've been trying to, and I just can't. He was a wonderful little boy. Always making things with his hands— an artist. Gifted."

"They'll be here within an hour," the architect says, waving good-bye. "Do you want me to talk to your insurance agent? I'm very good with those kind of people," he says, talking while Joan is still talking. Elaine is trying to listen to two things at once.

"No," she says. She doesn't want him to talk to anyone.

"Yes," Joan says. "It's unbelievable and it's true."

"I'm sorry," Elaine says. "The architect was here, and he's on his way out."

"I have to keep repeating the story in order to make it real," Joan says. "I'm at the office, I have to go. I want to call Pat, I'll talk to you later."

Liz arrives, pulling in just as the architect is pulling out.

He beeps. He shouts. "Hey, you're blocking me. You're holding me up."

"Ready?" Liz asks Elaine, ignoring the architect.

"Yeah, let me just tell Mrs. Hansen." Elaine waves at Mrs. Hansen, who's across the yard. Mrs. Hansen waves back.

"How old is she?" Liz asks.

"I have no idea, I'm figuring early seventies."

In the middle of the yard Mrs. Hansen has built an odd altar to the destructive forces of nature, a kind of ersatz tepee, a peculiar pile of branches, leaves, and twigs.

"I'm going out for lunch," Elaine yells. "And then I have an appointment at four—will you be around when the boys come home?"

"Of course," Mrs. Hansen says. "I was thinking I'd teach them how to send smoke signals." She nods at the pile. "I never told you, but long, long ago, I was a den mother."

"All right," Liz says once they're in the car. "What's the problem? Who's doing what to who?"

"I'm stuck," Elaine says. "I'm incredibly, horribly stuck. It's like I'm in a coma and can't wake up. Like I'm under the surface."

"That's why you're not talking to me? Elaine, women have been stuck for years. They write books about it—think of Tillie Olsen's *Silences,* think of Charlotte Perkins Gilman."

"I'm not talking about books. I'm talking about myself!" Elaine screams. "I am *The Yellow Wallpaper.*"

"Oh," Liz says. "Well, what are you going to do?"

"I don't know," Elaine says, disappointed at Liz's re-

sponse. She was hoping for something more—the offer of
a collective effort. What can *we* do, what can *I* do to
help you? "I'm so embarrassed," Elaine says. "This isn't
supposed to be happening. Women aren't supposed to be
stuck anymore. We're already having postfeminism, and
I'm in the Dark Ages. I missed the whole damn thing. Even
you did it," Elaine says. It comes out sounding like a cut. She
stops.

They sit in a booth in the luncheonette. Liz orders the diet
plate.

"I'll have the same," Elaine says, unable to make her own
decision.

"I thought you were having an affair and were too embarrassed to tell me with who," Liz says. "I know how you are, very
moral, a little naïve, and I wanted to tell you that if you've
succumbed and become a sniveling horny-hound like the rest
of us—it's all right."

"Everyone does it," Elaine says, flippantly confirming.

"Exactly," Liz says, digging into her cottage cheese.

"I don't know what to say," Elaine says. She is humili-
ated and disappointed. On all fronts, she has failed herself, rad-
ically. She stares at her plate; the iceberg lettuce reminds her
of Pat.

"I'm your best friend, remember," Liz says. "You can tell
me anything, no matter how horrible."

She can't tell Liz about Pat—Elaine imagines telling Liz
and Liz being offended, competitive, possessive. She imagines
Liz saying, I can't believe that you did it without me, that
you didn't think of me first. I would have done it if you'd
wanted to.

"Who did you have an affair with?" Elaine asks.

"An affair? Affairs. If it rang my doorbell, I fucked it, no
questions asked—like trick or treat."

"I think Paul is having another one," Elaine says. "He's

acting weird. He shaved all his hair off. I mean *all* his hair, and he's sleeping in a nightgown."

"Maybe he's hooked up with a drag queen?" Liz snickers.

"He says it's self-expression. I hope it's no one good."

"Good?"

"Someone we know or someone better than me." Elaine takes a shallow breath. "I hit him," she says. "Last night, at Pat and George's, I got so mad that I punched him."

"Oh, please," Liz says. "I used to pound Roger like I was tenderizing a piece of meat."

"Did he ever hit back?"

"No, he was 'better' than that. He had his own forms of revenge."

"Like what?"

"He left."

There is an awful silence. "Sorry," Elaine says.

"Whatever it is, work it out," Liz says. "The last thing you want to be is divorced. Everything after the first is seconds; it's a scratch-and-dent market."

"It's like I'm doing the dead man's float," Elaine says, picking up the check.

They drive in silence. Elaine's anger and anxiety are paralyzing. She doesn't know how to make herself better, how to save herself. "Do you want to come to Sammy's school play?" she asks Liz.

"Can't," Liz says. "I have to finish an assignment for a class."

Liz drops Elaine back at the house. A group of men are maneuvering a mini-crane up the driveway and around the Dumpster. Like an air-traffic controller, Mrs. Hansen is there, guiding them in.

Elaine checks her watch. Without a word, she gets into her car and speeds away—an hour to kill. Bored and half crazy, she calls Pat on the cell phone.

"Come on over," Pat says.

Elaine pulls into the driveway, parks, and hurries into the house. "Sammy's play is at two," Elaine tells Pat.

"I'll get you there," Pat says. Her kisses are insistent and sure. They taste of Crest and coffee. Pat and Elaine are in the living room, the same living room from the night before. They are on the sofa. Pat knows better than to try to get Elaine down the hall to the bedroom; it won't happen. Pat is unbuttoning Elaine. Elaine is worried that someone might see them through the windows, that the girls will come home, that an encyclopedia salesman will ring the bell. She is thinking of the night before, Paul in the dark, Paul on the floor, wedged in the space between the coffee table and the sofa. She is thinking of the soft sweep of Pat's skin across her own. She is sliding her clothing off.

"Hang on," Pat says, getting up, hurrying down the hall. Elaine sits on the sofa, waiting. She's thinking of the fight, a farcical domestic routine, dancing around the room in the dark, like a scene from an old black-and-white movie, slapstick sick. Futile. Everything is futile.

Pat comes back in her robe. They begin again. Pat kisses Elaine. Elaine is still not at all sure what it means that she is kissing another woman.

Elaine pulls Pat toward her.

The robe falls open. Around Pat's hips is a wide black belt, a silver-studded harness, with straps dipping between her legs. The whole contraption is like medieval armor, or motorcycle gear. And there is something hanging from it. "Buster," Pat says.

"I know someone whose cat is named Buster," Elaine says.

Pat has another one in her pocket. She pulls it out—a pale, fleshy fang that looks as if its skin is peeling. "I made it myself, using a candle mold and art supplies."

Elaine picks a familiar scent out of the air. "It smells like cedar chips," Elaine says.

"I keep it in with my sweaters," Pat says. She reaches into the robe and strokes the one she's wearing. "I bought this one over the phone. It's called a Jelly, a champagne-colored Jelly."

The sight of Pat in a black leather harness with a translucent plastic prick, poking up, like a faux fountain, is incredibly peculiar. Who does Pat think she is? Who does she want to be? Can Pat see how strange it looks? Has she taken a look at herself in a mirror? A thin roll of flesh curls over the harness. Is this supposed to be a turn-on?

"You don't have to do this," Elaine says. "I'm fine without it."

"Please," Pat says, her voice hungry and thick. "I want to. Just let me."

Elaine is on the sofa, and Pat is on top of her—theirs is a graceless, technical composition.

"Is it in?" Pat asks.

"Yes."

A hole is to fill. So different from a hand, from a tongue, from the real thing.

Elaine hears something. "What's that?" she asks, lifting herself up; the angle is good. She holds herself there, peering over Pat's shoulder. She is worried they will be caught. It's one thing for someone to be found doing it with the neighbor's wife, another if it's two wives doing it together, and quite a third if it's two wives and something called Buster. "There was a noise."

"The dryer," Pat says. "The dryer went off."

Pat fucks her. It's not tender. It's not two lonely women making each other feel better—it is something more, fantastically brusque, almost brutal.

Pat humps. Buster slips and slides sloppily, sometimes stabbing Elaine, sometimes poking her ass, her thighs. Pat thrusts. Buster slides out. It goes nowhere.

"Put it in," Pat says as desperately as anyone. "Put it in."

And Elaine guides it back in, a lifeless probe, a plug, a cork instead of a cock. Chicks with dicks, a pole and a tit. Pat's breasts flap against Elaine. The silky sensation of skin on skin, the motion, the rocking, the deep drilling does the job. Elaine hooks her legs around Pat, holding her there; her cunt clutches the blind, deaf, and dumb thing stuffed inside her, brainless Buster.

"Did you come?" Pat asks.

"Yeah," Elaine says.

Pat rolls away. She snaps off the harness, the dildo falls to the ground—it bounces.

There is a moment of silence, a resting place. Pat is propped up on her elbow, looking at Elaine.

"Do you want me to do it to you?" Elaine asks, hoping Pat says no. "I owe you. You didn't really get any . . ."

"I got enough," Pat says.

The contraption lies limp—not limp, but lame—on the floor.

Elaine notices a second hole, at the back of the harness. "What's that for?"

"A butt plug," Pat tells her.

Elaine has heard the expression only once before—from her children. She can't imagine what it is, how it works, and where her children and Pat learned about it.

"You know what would be great?" Pat says. "If we could go away for a weekend, just the two of us, someplace where we don't have to pretend, maybe Provincetown?"

"Oh." Elaine is putting her clothes on, hurrying to leave. "I don't think this is a good time for me," she says.

Elaine pulls away quickly. The car coasts to Sammy's school as though it is not Elaine driving, but Elaine being driven, pulled on a track that takes her back and forth from Pat to Paul, Paul to Pat, here and gone. There and back.

There is the memory of Buster inside her, her womb still contracting, squeezing the hollow core, beating out blood time.

She has been fucked.

And now she is late.

Sammy's school. High windows, low desks. In every room the alphabet unfurls, A to Z hugging the wall like molding. SPRING INTO BLOOM, the bulletin board announces. Paper flowers abound. MY SUMMER PLANS: On wide-lined paper the children have scratched their dreams—camp, Grandma's, Europe.

Elaine ducks into the girls' bathroom. She towers over everything, the mirror cuts off her head. She can see herself only from chest to knees. Another mother's head pokes up over the top of a stall. They catch each other's eye and laugh.

"I feel like I'm a giraffe," the woman says, flushing.

Library. Art room. Science lab. The auditorium is also the cafeteria; the lunch tables have been put away, and a hundred metal folding chairs have been set in lines. Elaine takes a seat at the end of a row and checks out the room. To the left is Wendy Trumble, who interviews movie stars for women's magazines. She's always catching the 12:15, "running into town for a little lunch," and barely getting back in time to collect the kids from soccer practice. There are other women, halves of couples that she and Paul had dinner with once or twice long ago and then never saw again. Elaine wonders what happened. Who didn't like who? Was there something more she should have done? Ahead on the right is Claire Roth, the shrink whose kids are the same age as Elaine's. Claire, with the fancy practice in Greenwich Village, and Sam, her perfect lawyer husband who drives her to work every morning. When the Roths first moved here, Elaine had them over for a barbecue; she thought the boys might get along. They never saw them again. Claire stares at her.

"How are you?" Elaine asks.

Claire nods. Does Claire Roth even remember?

A woman up ahead is smiling. Elaine smiles back. She has no idea who she's smiling at—could that be the one Paul's fucking? The woman smiles more broadly, her braces show, and Elaine realizes that she's a friend of Jennifer's who sometimes baby-sits.

A boy comes onstage. *"The Summer's Parade: A Fable,"* he announces. The school orchestra begins to play. "I once lived in a small village, deep in the Walnut Hills at the edge of the Honey River. It was a quiet village, until one summer when a man came to town." The curtain lifts.

"What a peaceful village," a boy wearing a beard says, shifting his big gun from one shoulder to the other. Villagers come onstage carrying baskets and hoes and begin doing chores, choreographed as dances.

Two rows up, Elaine sees Nate's mother. What's her name? Why can't Elaine ever think of her name? Elaine stares at the back of Nate's mother's head; something about her makes Elaine think she's a failure—she's the one taking care of Elaine's son when Elaine can't. She's the one who came to the door the day after the fire filled with the best intentions, good ideas. From the back of her head, she seems pleased with herself. She doesn't seem to be suffering. And she has a good haircut.

Shots are fired in the forest, the animals stampede. There is a lot of noise, animals running back and forth across the stage, through the forest, over the river, in and out of the village.

The stage clears, and a village girl—the hunter's daughter—lies dead in the rubble, and a rhino has also been shot. The hunter looks at his daughter's body. "What have I done?" he says. "I have destroyed the thing I love the most." The dying rhino lifts his head and looks out into the audience. The curtain falls.

The mothers applaud. The curtain goes up again, and the animals sing a song—"Let's all get along, every day from now on. . . ." The actors bow. There is more applause and then the clatter of metal chairs, folding.

"How are you?" Nate's mother asks Elaine.

"Good," Elaine shouts over the din. "And you?" She is stoned from sex.

"I barely got here," she says. "I raced from my aerobics class. If I don't go every day, I get so depressed."

What does "depressed" mean to her? She doesn't bake brownies in the afternoon, she drinks, she fucks the neighbor's wife—what? Elaine looks down at Nate's mother's little pink tennis shoes and impulsively wants to kick her. Susan, she remembers her name, Susan.

"Mom, Mom." Sammy tugs Elaine out of her trance. He's standing in front of her, holding the rhino's head.

"You were so great, honey," Elaine says. "The best rhinoceros I've ever seen."

Sammy takes a bow.

Nate arrives, still in his hunting gear. "You're dead," he says to Sammy.

"Play's over," Sammy says. "I'm living now."

"You're a very strong hunter," Elaine says to Nate.

"Natural-born killer," Nate's mother says. "He gets it from Gerald."

"Can we go home now?" Sammy asks.

"Actually, I thought I'd take them for ice cream," Nate's mother says. "If that's all right?"

"It's perfect," Elaine says, so perfect. She takes a deep breath; the auditorium air is stale, crusty with the fetid scent of half-eaten sandwiches, the curdled, sour smell of spilt milk.

"Will you join us?" Susan asks.

"Please, please," Sammy says, pulling at her sleeve.

"I can't. I have an appointment at four," Elaine says as they're walking out.

"I want to go with you," Sammy says. "I want to go home."

"I'm not going home, I have an appointment. But I'll tell you a secret," Elaine says, whispering in Sammy's ear. "You'll be back in your own room very soon. And I think you'll be pleasantly surprised."

"I'm getting a banana split," Nate says.

"So am I," Sammy says.

"I'm getting two banana splits and a chocolate milk shake," Nate says.

"Me, too," Sammy says. "Whatever you get, I get, too."

Paul has been at his desk all day—painting. When he went to dump his dirty water, word spread that he was up to something. And that he was walking with a bit of a limp.

"That must have been terrible with the shrimp," his secretary says, ordering him a bowl of chicken soup for lunch. He mentions that he tried to call her about not emptying the trash can. "Oh, I was gone by then," she says, unapologetically.

Herskovitz and Wilson stop by while Paul is eating at his desk, crumbling crackers into his soup. Sheets of watercolor paper are spread out all around him.

"Doing a little OT?" Herskovitz says.

"Overtime?" Wilson asks.

"Occupational therapy," Herskovitz says. "My mother-in-law does that in her Alzheimer's day-care program."

Later, as Paul is about to go wash out his brushes and call it a day, Warburton sticks his head in. "Nice colors. May I have one? Or are they only available in a set?"

"Help yourself," Paul says, quickly zipping his pants, standing, stretching his legs.

Warburton picks the one that says "Assume Your Right." "I'm feeling the need for an inspirational slogan," he says, sitting in Paul's chair, leaning forward. "You don't want that corner office, do you?" he asks conspiratorially. "Theoretically, it could be yours. But I like to keep one office empty; it keeps the tension up, gives the boys something to aim for. There should always appear to be something to aspire to. Don't you agree?"

Paul would like that office. Nothing good has happened to him at work in a long time—he's just been sitting there, waiting.

"It's got a view, it's got an executive loo. Do you know how fantastic it is not to have to go down the hall and lock yourself in a stall when you have to shit? I can't shit in public places, can't do it," Warburton says.

Paul nods. He wonders if Warburton is playing with him. He checks his watch; he's going to miss the 4:23, he's going to be late for Mrs. Apple. "It's a nice office," Paul says. "But the decor is awful. Sid Auerbach had no sense of style."

"It could be redecorated."

"Repainted? Recarpeted?" Paul asks.

"Outfitted," Warburton says. "Just the other day, I saw a desk chair with arms that were adjustable in a thousand small increments. A chair so comfortable it's like a coffin; you can sit in it for years. Something to think about," Warburton says, leaving. "Something to sleep on."

Elaine is going to meet the guidance counselor. He will tell her what to do, she will do it, and she will feel improved. She drives down Central Avenue. The traffic is heavy. She hurries. In the parking lot of the diner, she freshens her lipstick, brushes her hair, and checks herself in the rearview mirror.

He sees her immediately. He waves from a booth in the back. "Bud Johnson," he says, shaking her hand.

"Elaine."

He is dressed like a teacher: short-sleeved dress shirt, pen protector in the pocket, glasses. His hair is not dark and curly;

it is deeply receded, thinning, and largely absent. "You're probably wondering why you're here. Let me tell you who Bud Johnson is," he says. She gets the feeling that he'd done this before. "In high school I was an average student from an average family. I grew up in Yonkers. No one talked about options. At the end of high school, I joined the Army. I believed 'Be All That You Can Be.' I wanted to fly helicopters." He taps his glasses. "I have bad eyes, I couldn't fly anything. I hated it. After four years, I got out, went back to school, and studied counseling, figuring I might be a college counselor, help kids decide where to go. I ended up at Westchester Tech because I mentioned that I like fixing things. Anyway, that's where I am. I arrange internships, placement services—I know lots of good mechanics, technicians, repair people. It serves me well. If I can't fix it myself, I know who can."

"What do you fix?" Elaine asks.

"I can do most of my car, simple carpentry and electrical, a little plumbing, painting, and I like computers." He tells her this the way some people say they speak foreign languages—a little French, a bit of Italian, a few phrases in German. He pauses. "I thought we could talk about what might interest you. I did a little digging; the most obvious areas would be nursing, travel, and real estate. But I don't guess those appeal?"

Elaine shakes her head. Without warning she begins to cry. She doesn't mean to cry, but she does. She pours uncontrollably. He hands her paper napkins. He looks a little uncomfortable—hoping no one sees him with a weeping woman. "I don't think it can be fixed. I don't think you can help me. Our house caught on fire, my husband got a tattoo, the children are staying with neighbors, and you wouldn't believe the rest if I told you. This isn't just about a career. It's my life. I'm stuck." She sniffles. "You're probably wishing you hadn't come. You're probably thinking, Who is this crazy woman?"

"What does 'stuck' mean?"

"It means I should make some big decision, I should do some enormous thing. And I can't do anything. I can't stand my life, and I can't change it."

"Maybe it's not an enormous thing," he says. "Maybe you have to do one small thing and then another small thing."

"How could I let this happen? I don't remember myself this way."

"We're going to take this one step at a time," Bud says. "You reached out and called me—that's a good thing."

Elaine looks at him. He doesn't seem to want to fuck her; Elaine is relieved. Is he married, is he gay? She can't tell.

"I brought some interest questionnaires." This is his big moment, the moment he studied for. He spreads a pile of pages out across the table. Elaine picks up something called "The Fear Index—Are you afraid of the vacuum cleaner? Taking a bath? Being naked? Seeing others naked?"

"That's from something else," he says, taking it away. "It must have gotten mixed in."

She picks up another one. More questions: "Do you like numbers? What are your favorite subjects? What is your favorite time of day?"

He orders a piece of pie while she fills in the blanks. When she's done, he collects the pages. "I'll review them later."

The waitress brings her a cup of coffee.

"Some things are nearby," he says. "Iona, Sarah Lawrence, and if you're willing to travel, to go into the city, the whole world opens. You could become a polygraph expert in six weeks, you could learn dog grooming in ten."

"I just want to feel better."

"When you have something of your own, you'll feel better. Go to the library, ask the librarian for career books. Start making lists. You don't have to commit to anything, just start thinking about what interests you. You have my number, call me. And if you need someplace to go, to get out of the house, or hide out, come by the school. I'm there from seven-thirty till four."

The check comes. Elaine grabs it. "Let me get this," she says. "It's the one thing I can do."

"I'll talk to you on Monday," he says. "We'll figure it out. We'll get you unstuck."

"Thank you."

EIGHT

PAUL IS LATE. He scurries. He gets off the train two
stops past home and walks three blocks to the motel. He goes
into the office and gets the key.

Her car is parked, waiting.

"I'm late," he says.

"I thought maybe you weren't coming, I always think
maybe you aren't coming."

"I missed the four twenty-three. I tried to call."

"I took the boys for ice cream," she says. "They had banana
splits. I ate half of each one just to be fair."

This is the part he hates most—standing in the parking
lot, exposed. He wonders how many affairs come here, he imagines lots, and yet he's never seen anybody.

"Now I'm nauseous," she says.

"Do you want a soda?" He's jiggling the key in the lock.

"I brought some scotch," she says.

They close the door.

"The school play was this afternoon," she tells him, as he
pulls the curtains closed.

"How was it?"

The drapes are heavy like lead. They block out all the light, except cracks around the edges.

She turns on a lamp by the bed.

"Sammy makes a handsome rhinoceros, and Nate's quite the hunter," she says proudly.

The motel room is brown. Dank. It consists of various shades of dirt, of earth, of funk. The wallpaper is vinyl and curling in spots, the carpet is bald chocolate, the bedspreads coffee chenille. The television set is old and has rabbit ears, the phone between the beds is tan and has a rotary dial. "Our Love Cave," she calls it. Sometimes, if he gets there early, he buys coffee and doughnut holes from the place around the corner and they sit on the edge of the bed eating and talking. It's too weird to always fuck and go.

"We don't have much time," she says, pulling a small airplane bottle of scotch out of her purse. He gets a glass from the bathroom—SANITIZED FOR YOUR COMFORT AND PROTECTION—and rips off the paper. She pours herself a little and gives him the bottle. He sips.

She undresses. He takes off his shirt and gives it to her— she wears it. They lie together on top of the bedspread, the scotch between them.

"How are you?" she asks, and he thinks she really wants to know.

"I'm all right," he says. "And you?"

"Okay."

They kiss. They share the flavor of the scotch, the thickness of the tongue. He kisses her in a way that he can't kiss Elaine anymore, deep, filled with need and longing.

He feels himself getting hard and is relieved—it isn't broken.

"Were you in a fight?" she asks, sweeping her nails over his arms, his shoulders and back. He is green and yellow, purple and red, meaty and raw. He shivers.

"I had a little accident."

"So butch," she says. "I don't think of you as black and blue."

He is at her breasts. He loves her breasts; they are full and heavy and tug at her shoulders.

She reaches for his zipper.

"Be careful," he says, licking her.

"What is it?" she asks when she sees the bandage.

He peels away the tape—like pulling the cloth off a canvas.

"When did you do it?"

"Yesterday at lunch."

"How wild." It means nothing to her—it's not a testament to his infidelity. The date is irrelevant, as far as she's concerned—she is the date. "How does it feel?"

"Better today."

His dick is in her mouth. They fuck.

They fuck wildly. They fuck, and it is about fucking and nothing else—not bills to pay, decisions, resentments, failures. They fuck, and it is his dick and her tits. And there is the slap-slapping of their skin, the musical squeak of the springs. He is glad they are friends and that they talk to each other. She thinks he is wonderful, and they are both glad that they are not married to each other. "Fuck me," she is saying. "Fuck me. I want you to fuck me." His hands are under her ass, and he's pulling her open. The headboard bangs against the wall, she holds on to the frame of the bed. He is hard like marble, he is burning at the base of his balls. The light is on because she doesn't like it in the dark. He is watching her. "No, no, no," she cries. "Oh, no, don't stop. Oh, no." She is on top of him; her nipples are wide moons, purple and hot. And he is behind her. She clutches the edge of the night table. Her face goes deep red. The muscles in his neck strain. Noisy. And then it is over.

They lie in a sweaty heap.

A strange, steamy funk rises around them. It happens every

time. It is something about the room; they can never tell where it starts, if it's the bedding, the carpet, the cheap pressed fibers of the sordid walls. It smells like sweaty socks, like stale popcorn, like a dog's paws. They lie in it for a few minutes, catching their breath.

"Do you ever like one of your kids more than the other?" she asks.

"I like them differently," Paul says. "Why?"

"It's been nice to spend some time with Sammy. He's totally different from Nate, sweet, almost fragile." She rolls onto her back. "If I ever have another kid, it'd better be a girl."

"Is that something you think about?"

"Sometimes," she says.

"And whose child would you have?" he asks, jealous and possessive.

"Quit," she says, getting up. She goes into the bathroom and closes the door. That's how you can tell it's an affair—they close the door.

He pulls down the covers and rolls across both beds, rumpling them. It's something he's compelled to do—as though there's the remotest possibility of a legitimate reason why two adults would need a motel room for an hour—a shared medical condition that requires emergency naps? He hates how obvious his life is. This afternoon when he went into the motel office to check in, the guy said, "You're late, pal. You'll be lucky if you get any now." He half thought the guy said, "You're late, Paul," and started worrying that his cover was blown, that it was really Elaine waiting for him in the parking lot.

She comes out of the bathroom and presses against him. He holds her. They kiss again.

"Do you want a ride home?" she asks.

"That'd be great," he says.

"Shower fast," she says.

Paul steps into the tub and pulls the curtain—the liner is

moldy. The water—lukewarm. He peels the wrapper off the soap and lathers up. He rinses his mouth with suds, scrubbing out the scotch. The soap has a sharp, deodorant taste. He gags and spits. He tries a little soap on the tattoo; it burns. He lets the water run.

The towels, thin and rough like a medical treatment, leave him with a rash—small red dots on his back and neck.

He watches her dress. He watches her finish the scotch and fix her hair.

He opens the drapes.

"Ready?" she asks.

He picks up his briefcase.

This is the part that's tricky—the minutes in the car, when they might pass Elaine on the road. He always thinks of what he will say; his explanation changes depending on where they're discovered—how close to or far from home.

"Are you still at Pat and George's?" Susan asks.

"Yeah," he says. "But we'll be going home soon. They've started work on the house. We're putting on a deck."

There's a pause.

"So, what else is new?" he asks. "How's Gerald?"

"Gerald is Gerald. He's going to war camp again on Saturday to shoot paint balls at his friends—he wants to take Nate."

Paul interrupts. "Sammy cannot go to war camp," he says, emphatically.

"I know," she says. "And as far as I'm concerned, neither can Nate. Anyway, they have soccer," she says. "And then Monday he's off on a business trip."

Paul lifts his eyebrows—as if to ask, Does that mean special opportunities?

"We'll see," she says. "Are you picking up from soccer?"

"Guess so."

She pulls over to the curb. They are still far from home.

He opens the door. "See you tomorrow," he says. "Sorry I was late."

"I'm glad you came," she says.

"I always come," he says.

"Me, too." She drives away.

He looks around. He has no idea where he is. She always leaves him in a different place. He walks to the corner. He is on Locust going south. He turns on Hickory. He is thinking about this afternoon—replaying the scene with Warburton. "You don't want the corner office, do you? Theoretically, it could be yours. . . ." Was Warburton offering something or just tempting him? Sometimes Paul is so caught up with what's going on in his head, he misses an opportunity. Situational stupidity. He wonders what to do about it now. "Assume your right," he tells himself. He thinks of the palm kisser who he ran into on the afternoon train.

"Why you going home so early?" the guy had asked, sliding in next to Paul.

"Under the weather," Paul said. "You?"

"I always go home early," he said. "Wonder why?"

Paul shrugged.

"I'm the boss," he said, and laughed. "Feeling a little low? Sit on it," the man said, still smiling. "Sitting in a comfortable position, just following your breath for twenty minutes, can make an improvement. And if that doesn't do it, take some of these." He shook a gold vial of pills at Paul. "I believe in combining old and new. There is no one right answer."

"I've never seen a gold pill bottle before," Paul said.

"My wife had it made for me—perfect gift for a pharmaceutical man." He poured a pile of bright, shiny pills into his hand. "Mood enhancers," he said. "I can get you started, but then you'll really need a prescription."

Paul shook his head. "No, thanks."

"In a few years they'll be over-the-counter, nonprescription, I'm banking on it. A pill-pop shop on every corner, the same way there are coffee places now." He shook the pills in his hand; they were all different colors and rattled like Good & Plenty. "Mix 'em and match 'em," the palm kisser said. "You take what you need, depending on what ails you—they're very specific. He tossed a pink one down his throat. "Good Humor," he said. The train pulled into the station. "Isn't this your stop? Don't you usually get off here?"

"I'm going on," Paul said.

"Oh," the guy said. "Oh." And fell silent.

Now Paul is walking home. He still has a way to go. He's thinking about her, how she looks sipping scotch, how she looks in her beige slip, her breasts pressing against the satin, straining. He thinks of her, naked in the brown motel room, the feel of her body, still unfamiliar, still unknown. He turns right on Walnut.

Elaine is at the library. She has made a decision; she hides in the stacks and calls Pat from the cell phone. "Sorry to be so erratic," she says, and then has a flash of thinking like Paul—thinking she's said erotic instead of erratic. "Sorry," she says. "But we can't come tonight. We have to stay home." She shifts her position, and the phone makes a static sound like a wave crashing.

"Why?" Pat asks.

"There are things to be done. We have to pay attention to the house." She breathes. "It's our home, we have to go back."

"Well, you're welcome to stay with us for as long as it takes. Months even. *Mi casa es su casa*," Pat says.

Elaine doesn't want to seem hostile, ungracious, or impolite. But she can't go back—it's not just one thing, it's not just the perfection thing, perfect house, perfect family or that Pat fucked her, perfectly fucked her, not just a kiss, not just fingers, not just a tongue. It's not just that, it's all of it.

"I made dinner," Pat says.

"You always do."

"I made grouper, and the children made a movie; they're screening it for us tonight. Come back. I want you back."

"I can't," Elaine says.

A man pokes his head around the stack and gives Elaine a strange look. "Do you know where Ellery Queen is?"

She shakes her head. "I have no idea."

Pat goes on. "I'll keep the room ready, in case it doesn't work out."

"Thanks," Elaine says. "Thanks so much, for everything. You've been incredible."

She pushes "End." She goes to the reference desk. "Where would I find books on careers?"

"What kind of careers?"

"I don't know," Elaine says.

"Well, I'm not sure I can help you if you don't know what you want."

Elaine feels as if she's going to scream; it rises, a tornado in her belly. Her mouth opens, it should blow like vomit. Nothing happens. She coughs. She summons what she can, a short burst, vowelly, cattish.

The librarian punches something into her computer. "I've got something on witchcraft," she says, jotting down a call number and handing the paper to Elaine.

Elaine goes home. She sits at the kitchen table with Mrs. Hansen, having a glass of wine. Out the kitchen window she can see the wrecking ball dangling—the dull purple and gray light of early evening throws the steely black ball and chain into relief. It hangs twenty feet off the ground.

"Your mother was here," Mrs. Hansen says. "She waited for about an hour. I got the impression that she didn't particularly like me. Finally, I told her to go home. I hope I didn't do the wrong thing—she is your mother, after all. I told her you'd call as soon as you came in."

"I don't know what I would do without you," Elaine says.

"She brought you an answering machine," Mrs. H. says, patting the box on the kitchen table. "The architect was here, too. He left you an envelope. And Pat called and asked that you reconsider. You're to call her—either way."

Mrs. Hansen takes a sip of her wine.

"How is it?" Elaine asks.

"Very dry," Mrs. Hansen says.

Elaine picks up the phone and calls her mother.

"Who was that woman, that Nazi drunk? Your cleaning lady? How can you afford to have someone every day? Is she a live-in? She tried to get me to go along with her. I wouldn't have any of it. And then she asked me to leave. She put me in such an awkward position, I didn't have any choice but to go. You would never ask me to leave, would you? I'm your mother. Does she know what that means?"

"Thank you for the answering machine," Elaine says.

"Oh, you're welcome. I'm glad you got it. I was hesitant to leave it with her. I thought she might take it for her own."

"I got it," Elaine says.

"And you know how to hook it up?"

"I do."

Paul comes in. He makes himself a drink.

"She's talking to her mother," Mrs. Hansen whispers loudly.

"Mother, I have to go, Paul just came in. I'll talk to you tomorrow."

Mrs. Hansen finishes her wine and stands up. "Hello and good-bye," she says. "I bid you adieu."

"You don't have to rush off," Paul says.

"Oh, but I do," Mrs. Hansen says. "I've got to feed the hubcap, and I'm sure you two unrulyweds could use a few minutes alone. Don't forget—call Pat," Mrs. H. says on her way out.

"Thank you, Mrs. Hansen," Elaine says. "For everything."

"Don't thank me," Mrs. Hansen says. "Thank God."

Paul adds a little more to his drink. He and Elaine look at each other tentatively.

"Hi," she says.

"Don't forget to call Pat," he says.

"Why?"

"Because Mrs. Hansen said so."

"I called this afternoon and told her we weren't coming back, and she still wants us—it's like she's chasing us. I can't go there," Elaine says.

"If we don't go to Pat and George's, what are we going to do for dinner?"

"She made grouper."

"I hate grouper," Paul says.

"And the girls made a movie—what do you think that means, they made a movie?"

He shrugs. "What are we going to do?"

"Fend for ourselves."

"The Dumpster is full of rocks," Paul says, looking out the window, surveying the situation.

Elaine nods.

They take a tour of the house. The dining room has been sealed off floor to ceiling with multiple layers of plastic wrap and duct tape. Outside, around the back of the house, there are deep tracks, like dinosaur prints, where the wrecking ball came through. The back wall of the house is gone—metal support columns have been put in place.

"The architect mentioned that taking advantage of natural disasters was one of his specialties," Elaine says.

"It's going to be good," Paul says. "French doors, a deck—we can barbecue." He catches himself. The word "barbecue" is complicated. Paul goes back into the house. He makes himself another drink.

"Here's the estimate," Elaine says, handing Paul the architect's envelope.

He opens it. "Do we really need French doors?"

She looks over his shoulder; eighteen thousand and some—Elaine has no idea if that's high or low. "You smell," she says, sniffing him.

"Like what?" he asks, nervously.

"Deodorant soap."

"I washed my face in the men's room at work. That's probably what was in the dispenser."

"Hard on sensitive skin," she says.

Paul notices that the hole in the ceiling has been left off the estimate. "You'll have to tell him," he says.

They sit in the kitchen with one light on. Drinking. It is not dark, not day, not night—twilight.

"Just think, last Friday we had people in for dinner, I made lamb, you ate four slices."

"And look at us today," he says. "The dining room table is in pieces at the bottom of the Dumpster."

"Are you starving?" she asks.

"Not yet," he says.

"We don't have any food. There's nothing for me to prepare."

He remembers the Peppermint Patty that he bought for Mrs. Apple at the blind man's stand in Grand Central—it was meant to be a door prize for his tardiness. He forgot to give it to her, and now he hands it over to Elaine. "Get the sensation," he says.

She bites into it.

"I made you a picture," he says, giving her a watercolor of

the house, a split view, one scene with the whole family standing in a line out front; the second is the house from the back with the French doors and deck—all fixed.

"Nice," Elaine says. The painting looks like folk art, flattened, unrealistic. She tacks it on the fridge with a magnet.

It is getting darker.

"Are you in the mood to go out?" she asks. "We could go to the supermarket."

"Sure." He is glad to get out of the house. The house was built before either of them was born, and the fact is, they tried to level it, to burn it. He's a little uncomfortable now, home alone—unsupervised. "Let's go."

"I'll drive," she says.

They are on Central Avenue. Elaine passes the Odyssey Diner and says nothing. Who is she: Paul's wife, the boys' mother, Pat's lover? Who is she for herself? What would she like to be doing in a year? Can she talk to Paul about it—can they have a real conversation?

"How was work?"

"I made watercolors all day," Paul says.

"Is that a good thing?" Elaine asks, thinking of the one on the fridge.

"Warburton thought so."

"Good," Elaine says.

"And you?"

"The architect, lunch with Liz, school play—Sammy was great."

"Sammy is great," Paul says.

The supermarket is deserted. It is frigid and bright. Paul squints. Elaine fumbles through her purse for her sunglasses. The long fluorescent tubes blast them with an unearthly white light. Elaine takes a cart, pushing it up and down the rows. The wheels rattle. Paul trails behind. Aisles and aisles, brand names, variations on a theme: Buy me, try me, new and improved, better color, texture, flavor.

Elaine has a long list; she's written down everything they need. Butter, sugar, milk, happiness, comfort, satisfaction.

Milk, OJ, coffee. There is a row for everything. On some aisles she shops well, planning ahead, buying the economy size in anticipation of desire, need to come. On others she takes nothing from the shelves; expiration dates make her anxious, the dairy case upsets her enormously—too much pressure.

She imagines not being married to Paul. Could they live without each other? Without the weight, the pull of one against the other? This is the fabric they are made of—they are a knit, like Siamese twins. What would ending it mean? She can't imagine it over. What is "over"?

"Do you even like me?" she asks Paul in the produce section.

"Oh, Elaine," he says.

"I thought so," she says. "Do you like fruit?" she asks.

He looks at her oddly—Mrs. Apple?

She flashes a few plums in a bag.

"Fine," he says.

The squeaky wheel. The wire basket. She throws things into the cart. What does she want? What does Sammy like? What does Daniel need? What does it take to keep them happy?

Cookies.

Paul goes for the sugar. In aisle 19, the cell phone rings. His pocket rattles like an alarm.

"You're ringing, sir," the stock boy says.

He ignores it.

It rings twice more.

"Ringing," the boy says again, loudly, as if Paul didn't hear him the first time.

Paul hands him the phone. "You answer it."

"Price Slasher, may I help you?" the boy says.

Pause.

"I'm in baked goods, near frozen foods."

Pause.

"No, ma'am, I've never had a Hungry Man Dinner."

Pause.

"Five-seven, blond hair, green eyes, zits. I get off at ten." He hands the phone back to Paul. "Cool, very cool," the kid says, and goes back to pricing angel food cakes.

"Don't mention it."

Elaine is on the other side of the store, searching for spray starch. Pat used it on everything; it kept the fabric stiff.

If the marriage is falling apart, is there anything they can do to stop it? Or should they just let it go, let it completely unravel? Elaine wonders. She wheels past a display of Jell-O letters laid out on Styrofoam boards like chicken parts. An edible alphabet in orange, red, or green. Elaine imagines writing a Jell-O note: Welcome Home. Back at four. Help me. She imagines writing something in Jell-O and wonders how many packs it would take to say something substantial. She throws four into the cart.

"What do you want for dinner?" Elaine asks Paul when he comes back, a pound of sugar in hand.

"Why don't we each have whatever we want, a free-for-all?"

"I'm sick of whole meals," Elaine says. "Let's just have appetizers, all appetizers—gherkins, Stilton, smoked salmon."

"Kippers and cream," Paul says. "A big antipasto. Artichoke hearts. Miniature egg rolls, cheese puffs, pigs in blankets."

"Whatever you want."

"I'm thinking martinis," Paul says.

Elaine puts a jar of jumbo olives into the cart.

"Do we have gin?"

"I hope so," Elaine says.

"I hope Mrs. Hansen didn't drink it all."

"Do you want to run to the liquor store?"

"Maybe." He goes off.

If Elaine and Paul divorce, how will they pay for things? They will be two poor households instead of one. Elaine will have to work—who will hire her? Will she be a saleslady with swollen ankles, folding clothes at Bloomingdale's, or will she become a travel agent and plan other people's exotic adventures, or sell Avon products door-to-door? The career counselor said nothing about working in retail.

She wanders through the bakery department. There are half cakes for sale. There's something depressing about half a cake, the cut frosted over as though no one would notice. A cake isn't something that's supposed to be split; it can be bigger or smaller, but not cut in half.

Paul has her paged. "Elaine. Elaine. Please meet your party at the Customer Courtesy Counter."

She pushes her cart to the front of the store.

"May I help you?" the courtesy lady asks, leaning over the counter as Elaine approaches. "Have you reached your party?"

Paul is there in his raincoat. He has dashed to the liquor store and is holding a paper bag, a bottle of gin and some horrible blue carnations wrapped in cellophane.

"Where were you?" he says. "I went up and down the aisles, I looked for you everywhere. I thought you'd evaporated."

"I'm stuck," Elaine blurts. Neither the courtesy lady nor Paul has any idea what she is saying—is it about the cart, the wheels? "If I don't do something soon, something horrible is going to happen to me." She had no intention of saying any of this here, now, but there it is.

The courtesy lady has politely turned away.

"Me, too," Paul says. "I think that's why I got the tattoo. I thought it would wake me up—like electroshock."

"We're all we have, and we're not enough," she says.

"It's good we noticed," Paul says. "We can go on from here."

"Do something," she blurts.

"What?"

"I don't know."

"Home," Paul says. "It's time to go home."

"You got gin?"

He nods.

It is almost ten o'clock. They still haven't eaten. His stomach is growling. They check out.

In the car on the way home, Elaine thinks of Paul, Paul when he was young, when he had hair and enthusiasm and energy, Paul when they first were together, when they talked about the future, when the boys were born, when they moved into the house—ascending. She thinks of Paul—there was supposed to be more, and now there is less.

Home.

"Doesn't look so bad, does it?" Paul says, pulling into the driveway. The house is dark. They sit in the car for a few minutes. Elaine doesn't want to go in; she doesn't want the house, she hates the house.

She remembers the last time she was happy with the house—it was the day before they moved in, the house was big and empty, and they hadn't started to pay for it yet.

Paul opens the door and unloads.

"It is a bottomless pit," Elaine says, getting out.

She turns on every light. She turns on the radio in the kitchen; they usually only use it on stormy mornings to listen for school closings.

Paul unpacks. Elaine goes upstairs to put toilet paper in the bathrooms.

There is a padlock on Daniel's door.

"Paul," she calls, her voice quizzical, curious.

A hasp and staple have been fixed to the wall. A metal loop and bracket, shiny, galvanized, bound by a thick padlock.

"Paul," she calls again.

"When did it happen?" he asks when she shows him the door.

"Can't tell."

"Do you think he did it, or was it the workmen?"

"Why would the workmen do it?"

"Well, he can't put a lock on the door. What has he got to lock up? What's he hiding?"

"Maybe it's just normal adolescent behavior."

"I'll take care of it," Paul says. "Do you have a hairpin?"

She gets him one and stands watching while he picks at the lock. He wiggles and jiggles, trying to get the innards to drop, to let go. It gets him into a frenzy. "I told you he was up to something." He slams his shoulder against the door. He kicks it hard. The door strains against the frame.

"Do you think it's drugs?" he asks frantically—his tone half implying that it wouldn't be the worst thing, maybe they'd get a discount.

"I doubt it," she says. "He's been wearing a suit. Drug dealers don't usually wear suits."

"Then what is it, Elaine? Banking? Do you think he's become a banker and that's why he's got the place locked up like Fort Knox?"

Elaine stands back. Paul is heaving, banging, pounding. Finally, the molding gives way. The hasp and a great chunk of wood rip off. The staple flies. A screw skittles across the floor. The door pops open.

The room is undisturbed. Nothing looks out of the ordinary. Elaine picks up a shirt and folds it.

Paul goes to the desk. He reads aloud from an open notebook. " 'On my honor I will do my best to do my duty to God and my country and to obey the Scout Law; to help other people at all times; to keep myself physically strong, mentally awake, and morally straight.' My patrol call is Slithering Snake. I make a rattling hiss."

"I bet something's in here," Paul says, picking up a chunk of plaster from the desk. "I bet it's buried in here." He drops the mold on the floor and stomps on it with his shoe. White plaster powder rises like smoke. There is nothing inside.

"I'll tell him it's my fault, it fell while I was cleaning up his room," Elaine says, sweeping up.

She opens a dresser drawer to put away the shirt and feels something. She pulls out a Ziploc bag—her lipstick, Strong Persuasion, is inside. She reaches in again and pulls out a handful of Ziploc bags. Each contains a single item: a sock, a pack of matches, a chip of red enamel.

"Evidence," Paul says.

"Evidence of what?"

"I don't know."

They sit on Daniel's bed.

"Does he know about the fire?" Paul asks. "Does he know not to talk to anyone about it?"

"You'd think he'd know instinctively," she says.

"That's what worries me, he has no instincts." Paul stops. "Do we have to be scared of him?"

Elaine thinks of Catherine and Hammy's son eating the science teacher.

"Do you think he's going to bust us?"

"Why would he do that?" she asks.

"He hates us. Kids get hung up on right and wrong. They get very righteous and moral. We have to find out what he's got," Paul says, ransacking the room, dumping dresser drawers on the floor, turning the place inside out.

"Enough," Elaine shouts after a few minutes of frenzied

chaos. "Enough," she shouts. "We're overreacting. Let's clean up. Let's put it all back together."

She goes to make the bed, to put on clean sheets and the new comforter she bought him the other day—black on white, a repeating figure of a man in a suit carrying a briefcase. She lifts the corner of the mattress; magazines slide out: *Chunky Bunch, Big Jugs*. Fat-girl nudie magazines. Big women. Enormous. Elephantine. Not just chunky but oozing flesh.

"Have you ever seen anyone who looks like this?" Paul asks her.

"Never."

"Not even in the Loehmann's dressing room?"

"No," Elaine says, horrified. She turns the page and begins to read the story of a woman so fat she can't get out of bed, a woman whose legs have to be held open by a special machine in order for her to have sex.

The doorbell rings. They jump. Paul gets up to go. Elaine puts the magazines back. She puts them in a neat stack under the mattress. She folds all the clothing, puts it back in the drawers, puts the drawers back in the dresser, and tucks in the Ziploc bags.

Who is she cleaning up after, Daniel or Paul?

Jennifer is downstairs. "Is Daniel home?"

"No, why?" Paul asks.

"He called me," she says.

"Not here," Paul says, wondering if Daniel often calls Jennifer, if they have some sort of relationship he's not privy to. "Do you want a snack? We're just about to have dinner." They go into the kitchen. He preheats the oven, gets a cookie sheet, and lays out the delicacies, a row of pigs in blankets, a row of mini–egg rolls, a row of cheese puffs. He gets the pitcher and starts to mix the martinis.

"I'll just have a gherkin," Jennifer says.

"Have two, they're small," Paul says. "Why did Daniel call you?"

"I guess he had a question or something," Jennifer says, eating gherkins. "Do you realize that in two weeks I'll be a high school graduate?"

"Yes," Paul says. "Elaine and I would like to get you something special for graduation. Something that would really have meaning—any ideas?"

"A Chanel suit," Jennifer says.

"Oh," Paul says. The thought would never have occurred to him—or anyone. "What size?"

"Like an eight," Jennifer says.

Paul jots down "Chanel 8" on a piece of scrap paper. Later, he will see it and wonder if there was something he was supposed to watch on channel 8.

"I should go," Jennifer says, looking up at the kitchen clock. Light glints off the silver ring sticking out of her eyebrow.

"Where do you go at eleven at night?"

"Out," she says.

"With who?"

"People."

"Well, have a good time," Paul says, pulling the cookie sheet out of the oven.

Elaine comes down. "Who was that?"

"Jennifer," Paul says. "Here and gone."

"Where does she go at this hour?"

"Out," Paul says.

"With who?"

"People."

"You don't have to be so rude," Elaine says. "It's not like I'm going to tell her mother."

Paul ignores her. "Where do you want to eat?"

"Upstairs in bed, with the TV?"

They load things back into grocery bags and carry up the loot. Paul brings a tray of hot snacks and the pitcher of martinis.

"God, I'm glad to be home," Elaine says, settling in on the bed, arranging an assortment of jars and boxes in front of her—olives, onion, crackers, Stilton.

The phone rings, the machine answers.

"Hi, Elaine, it's Mom. That's nice you're using the new machine. All right, I guess you're not home, otherwise I'm sure you'd take pity on your poor mother and pick up." She pauses, waiting for Elaine to answer. "All right, I'll talk to you tomorrow."

Paul pours martinis.

"Our kid is a pervert," Elaine says, dropping olives in. "We have to do something about it."

"Tomorrow. We'll fix it tomorrow."

They gorge. They eat pigs in blankets, cheese and crackers, sardines—stinky things that will make them steam and smoke. They flip channels—going round and round, 1 to 99, backward and forward; basketball, old movie, sitcom, sitcom, Headline News, The Weather Channel. They dip their fingers into jars, pulling out tastes of this and that—juices drip everywhere. Paul refills their glasses—his homemade rocket fuel splashes over.

"Did we finish last night or did we just stop?" Elaine asks.

"Is there such a thing as an end?" Paul says.

"I hope so."

"Who wins?" he asks.

"It can't continue," she says. "None of this can continue." She finishes her drink and quickly has another. Her face goes white. "Do you want a divorce?"

"Do you?"

"I asked you first."

"Why are you asking me that?"

"I have to," Elaine says.

"No. Not really," he says.

"Which is it—no or not really?"

"No," he says.

"Do you want to go off with her?" Elaine continues.

"Who?" he asks nervously.

"Whoever she is."

"No," he says. "Is there somewhere else you want to be?" he quizzes her.

"No," she says. "There's nowhere. There's nothing."

They drink, they eat.

Paul unzips his pants; pills roll out of the pocket.

"What're those?"

He recognizes the bright colors. "Mental candy, mood enhancers," Paul says, wondering how the magic trick worked, how the palm kisser got the pills out of the gold vial and into Paul's pocket.

"Where'd you get them?"

"A guy on the train gave them to me," he says, picking pills up off the floor, counting, eight, nine, ten.

"Mr. Wash Your Bowl?"

"Exactly." Paul shows Elaine a palmful. "Different colors for different effects. If you're crabby, you take an orange; if you want bliss, eat a blue. Red is for energy. You can take a few at a time."

"What happens if you take too many?"

"You get overwhelmed and maybe a headache, but then you take a couple of aspirin."

Elaine picks out an orange and a red. She swallows them with the last of her drink.

Paul sits on Elaine's side of the bed, naked except for a shirt and tie. He takes a bottle of nail polish out of the night table and proceeds to paint his toes—fire-engine red.

"Should we go and talk to somebody?" Elaine asks.

"What could someone tell us?" Paul asks, working on his little toe. "Everything we're doing is wrong—we're lousy parents, criminals. If anyone knew us, they wouldn't like us."

He's got one leg crossed over the other. Elaine's view is up under his shirt—his balls, his bandage.

"What is it with you anyway—the shaving, the nail polish, the nightgowns?"

"Exploring parts of myself that I'd otherwise ignore."

"It scares me," Elaine says. "I find it weird and scary."

"Haven't you ever been tempted to do something that others might find unusual?"

Elaine doesn't answer. "It's important to try and be normal, as normal as you can possibly be."

The phone rings again. They freeze. They listen. Elaine wonders if it's Sammy, homesick Sammy.

"Just calling to say good night. Are you in there?"

"Pat," Paul says, identifying the voice.

"Did you two already go to bed? Nighty-night," she says. "Sleep tight."

"Let's get the children back," Paul suddenly says. "Their rooms are ready, everything is ready, waiting. Let's go and get them." Paul imagines getting into the car and driving over to Mr. and Mrs. Meaders, banging on the door and insisting that they surrender the little pervert. He sees himself pulling up in front of Mrs. Apple's house—tooting the horn and plucking Sammy from his sleep; in effect kidnapping their own children and bringing them home.

"It's one-thirty in the morning, and you're drunk," Elaine says. "We'll get them tomorrow, when it's light, when we can see what we're doing."

There is a silence. They doze.

"It's so good to be alone," Elaine says.

"We can be ourselves."

"We can be nothing."

"Are you feeling anything yet?" he asks.

"No. What colors did you take?"

"Green and orange."

"Green—what's that do?"

"Not much, apparently," Paul says.

"Maybe you have to take them for a while before they work," Elaine says.

"Like how long?"

"Antidepressants take three to five weeks."

"We only have a dozen," Paul says.

"Well, maybe that's what it takes," Elaine says, noticing that Paul's big toe, with the hairy knuckle, looks interesting painted red.

Paul is dreaming. He is dreaming that he's ice-fishing, he's holding a long line that goes down into a hole. There is a tug. He pulls on the string—his own head pops through the ice. His lips are blue. "What took you so long?" he says to himself. His eyes open.

The bed is wet.

Paul panics. His thoughts race—the tattoo guy hit a nerve and has rendered him incontinent. He is forty-six years old, neither young enough nor old enough to wear diapers. He starts to cry; a pathetic rush of fear bellows out. "Oh, God, I think I wet the bed," he says. "Oh, God!"

Elaine wakes up. "What?"

"I wet the bed."

She feels around; the bed is damp.

"There's something horrible wrong with me," Paul sobs.

"You drank too much," Elaine says. "You fell into a deep sleep. You had an accident. Everything does not require a diagnosis."

She gets up, pulls the sheets back, and looks at Paul. He is still in his shirt and tie. He is not wet. She smells the bed. "It's not you," she says.

He cries.

Elaine looks up. "The roof is leaking," she says. "It's rain-ing."

Paul can't stop crying.

"It's the hole," she says.

He looks up. A drop falls.

"Move the bed," she says.

He gets up, and they push the bed off to the right. Paul takes the damp bedding off and stuffs it into the hamper.

"I'm sorry," he says, still sobbing, great gulps. "I'm sorry."

"It's late, Paul. It's very late," Elaine says, remaking the bed.

Elaine can't sleep. She goes downstairs, gets her tools, and fixes Daniel's doorframe. Reconstructive surgery. Putty and glue. Waiting for it to dry, she reads the book Pat gave her, *How to Fix Almost Anything*—there's a handwritten card from Pat tucked into page forty-three, the laundry section: "Elaine— My ideas don't come from nowhere. My ideas aren't always my own." The page is about how to remove a coffee stain. Elaine remembers splashing the coffee, taking off her shirt, Pat slip- ping the pot holder under her head. Fine. Everything is fine.

When the glue is dry, Elaine repaints the frame around Daniel's door. She washes her paintbrush. She cleans up after herself.

In the middle of the night, Elaine is sitting on the sofa in the living room. She is thinking about what she wants. She is reading an alphabetical list of occupational titles: candy puller, elephant trainer, fatback trimmer, feather washer, felt finisher, female impersonator, field attendant, fig sorter, film inspector.

The cop car whisks by, siren silenced; red light flashes over the walls, flickering like fire.

Elaine is not alone.

NINE

THE WRECKING BALL WAKE-UP. A hard knock shakes the house. They don't so much hear it as feel it—slapping them out of their sleep, pushing the air out of their lungs.

Elaine rolls over. "Wrecking ball," she says as it slams into the house a second time.

Paul sits up. "Are we safe? Do they know we're in here?"

"What do you want to do, wave a white flag out the window?" Elaine says, turning onto her back.

Paul goes to the window and waves frantically at the men in the backyard. "Were you expecting them this morning?"

"I wasn't expecting anything," Elaine says.

One of the guys waves back. "They see us," Paul says. "They know we're in here. We're okay."

Again the ball slams into the house. Elaine wonders what would happen if it came crashing through the bedroom wall. She pictures the swinging ball, like a black bomb, coming toward her; she imagines jumping on it, riding away, like Tarzan or Jane, legs wrapped around the hard metal, fingers clutching the chain—white knuckles. She gets out of bed.

"You're in a weird mood," Paul says.

"What?"

"You're standing in a puddle of pickle juice."

She looks down. There are jars surrounding her—artichoke hearts, olives, debris from dinner—an odd altar to appetizing. She's knocked over the bread-and-butter pickles, green juice has splashed her toes.

The wrecking ball slams the house again, percussion, punctuation, punch line. The capers dance in their jar.

"Get me a towel," she says to Paul.

Nude. Bent over, gathering wrappers and jars, sorting trash from leftovers, her thin belly and breasts hang, everything is a little loose on the bone. She catches Paul looking at her, taking inventory. "Can I help you?" she asks.

He hands her the towel.

She wipes the floor, puts on her robe, and goes downstairs.

Paul is in the bathroom, staring at himself. Things are beginning to grow back. His body is covered in rough fuzz, itchy bristle. Pimples. He applies hydrocortisone and decides that he will leave himself alone, no more experimental grooming. So what if his head looks like he's wearing a broken halo, a ring of chestnut stubble, a crown of thorns? What's the big deal if his chest hair turns into silver-wired topiary, if he becomes dotted with liver spots and his leggy down disappears, revealing shining varicosities? He checks the tattoo—still spooked every time he sees it. It's crusty now, the hair is growing back—sharp pubes, like bristles, poke out of his skin. Soon the inky line of ivy will be buried, it will be hidden in a forest, it will be something you always know is out there, lurking.

He is thinking about Henry, and the date. He is thinking about McKendrick and how he's got to drop off the tapes. He is thinking about work, about the corner office, new carpet, a new chair. He is thinking about aging, about failure and reinvention. He needs to get back into the game, to be on top, to win.

Paul looks in the mirror. He cannot leave himself alone; he cannot surrender to nature. Everything that you can't see, everything undercover, he will skip, but his head, his exposed dome, he will continue to groom—a shaved skull is a kind of power play, mental nakedness, brain display. He sprays his head with shaving cream and scrapes it clean.

Elaine comes in, she pees, she flushes.

These are the moments Paul likes, moments of intimacy, of familiarity. At Pat and George's they took turns; somehow they weren't comfortable going into the bathroom together. "You were really good last night when I wet the bed," Paul says to Elaine.

"There are six men out back," Elaine says. "The yard is full of rocks. Let's not forget to tell them about the hole," Elaine says.

"I wonder how long it will take?"

"They seem to be moving quickly," she says, walking out.

Elaine's mother is downstairs, pouring herself a cup of coffee.

"Morning," Elaine says, finding her there.

"The lock on the front door is broken," her mother says.

Elaine shrugs. She's not surprised at how other people are able to float in and out as if they have special powers—can walk through walls and travel great distances at a blink, etc., whereas Elaine is always earthbound, stuck.

"You should get the lock fixed," her mother says. "You don't want just anyone to be able to waltz right in."

"It's on the list," Elaine says.

"Would you like some coffee?" her mother asks.

"I made it an hour ago," Elaine says.

"I'm sure you did," her mother says. "It's not really strong enough for me. Can I pour you a cup?"

"I'll get it myself."

Her mother wanders into the dining room and stands near the plastic wall. It's as if a curtain has been pulled around the scene of the accident, a blanket over a corpse, in an effort to be discreet, to spare everyone the upset, the embarrassment.

On the other side of the plastic, there are men working—muted voices, hammers.

"Is this a good idea?" her mother asks.

"What?"

"Adding on to the house?"

"We're not really adding on," Elaine says. "We're repairing. We had a fire."

"Should I be thinking about renovating my house? Is this something I should be doing?"

"It has nothing to do with you," Elaine says.

"Your father talks about fixing up the house so we'll get more money out of it. We're not going anywhere, how are we going to get money out of it? Besides, what do we need a bathroom downstairs for? If someone has to go, go upstairs in private. I don't have to be informed every time someone goes."

"It has nothing to do with you," Elaine repeats.

Her mother points at a pillow on the living room sofa. "Where'd that come from?"

"I don't remember," Elaine says.

"Yes you do."

"No I don't."

"Bloomingdale's," her mother says.

"Pier One," Elaine says.

"I knew you'd remember," her mother says. "I could use a couple of pillows like that. Do you think they still have them?"

Elaine shrugs.

There is a sound outside, an incredible clatter, like a thousand things falling at once.

"What's that?" her mother asks.

Elaine looks out the window. "Lumber. The wood has arrived."

A man presses against the plastic wall; his nose makes a dent. "Excuse me," he says, his breath making a wet mark. "Excuse me." He tries to get Elaine's attention.

Elaine turns toward the plastic. "Yes," she says.

"Sorry to bother you." His voice is gurgly, as if he's speaking underwater. "Have you got some ice? I hit my hand."

"Oh, sure. Of course," Elaine says, "we have plenty of ice." She goes into the kitchen, fills a plastic bag, wraps it in a kitchen towel, and goes back into the living room. She is standing on one side of the plastic, the man is on the other. She tries to lift it from the bottom to pass the ice under—but it's tacked down. He's pulling from the top to no avail.

"Stand back," he says, penetrating the plastic with a sharp blade. His hand juts into the living room, the fingers purple and swelling.

"I think you might have broken something," Elaine says, handing him the ice pack.

"I wouldn't put it past me," the man says.

"I meant to tell someone," Elaine says, speaking directly into the trapdoor. "There's a hole in the master bedroom ceiling; it leaked on us last night."

"I'll send a guy in."

"Thanks," Elaine says. "If you need more ice, just holler—I've got a freezerful."

"Do you want me to leave this open?" the man asks, gesturing at the trapdoor.

"Close it," Elaine says, thinking of the dust, of Sammy.

"Hello, stranger," Elaine hears her mother say. "Long time no see. Have you got a kiss for your grandmother? Well, I've got one for you."

The image of Daniel in the kitchen, being kissed by her mother, floods Elaine with a peculiar rush of discomfort. She thinks of the fat woman from the magazine, the woman whose legs have to be held open in order to be fucked, she thinks of her lipstick in the Ziploc bag in Daniel's drawer and wonders what it means.

She hurries into the kitchen and glares at Daniel.

"How'd you get in?" she asks.

"Door," he says.

"Did someone leave it open?"

"Lock's broken," he says, looking at her strangely.

She nods. She doesn't know how to talk to him.

"I need Polaroid film," he says, "for a project."

She imagines him taking photographs of fat women on the streets of Scarsdale, riding his bike to Mamaroneck and Yonkers, prowling for bulk, waiting outside the Weight Watchers office, hunting down chubbies at Overeaters Anonymous meetings, using his allowance to buy film, to buy Twinkies and HoHo's, to bribe the fat girls to show him their padded parts.

"I need some coffee," Elaine says.

"I need film," he says.

Need this, need that. Need ice. Need film. "Then get it," she says.

"What's your problem?" he says.

What's yours? she wants to ask.

He goes upstairs.

Elaine waits for the eruption. She counts the seconds.

"Who went in my room?" he yells less than a minute later.

"It's not your room," Paul shouts from the bedroom. "It's my room. I own this house."

"You went in my room? Why did you do that? Why would you go in my room?" Daniel runs down the hall, screaming.

"Why would you put a lock on the door?" Paul hollers.

"Because I didn't want anyone to go in my room."

"That's why we went in your room."

"Because of the lock?"

"You bet."

Elaine wonders if she should go upstairs and moderate. "We bought you a new comforter," Elaine calls up the stairs. "We were trying to fix things up for you and Sammy."

"You sure fixed it," Daniel shouts.

"Whose shirt are you wearing?" Paul asks Daniel.

"Not yours, that's for sure."

"Who the hell do you think you are?" Paul shouts. "What kind of monster are you?"

"I am not a monster," Daniel yells back.

"What the fuck are all the Ziploc bags?"

"Evidence."

"For what, what are you trying to prove?"

"I don't know," Daniel shouts. "I don't know, I read about it in the junior-detective book. You don't own me," he yells, crashing down the steps, pushing past Elaine, heading for the door.

"Where are you going?" she asks.

"Out," he bellows.

"Look," Elaine says, "if you want more privacy, all you have to do is say so, but no padlocks on the doors. If there's a problem, let's talk about it."

Daniel stops. He turns to her. "Dad is a lazy fuck, and you're pathetic," he says.

A switch flips. She goes from being the concerned and confused mother to pure rage. Daniel is everything that Paul is and worse. She hates him.

She takes off her shoe and hurls it at him. "Brat."

Daniel runs out of the house.

Elaine's mother starts to say something.

"Shut up," Elaine says, before she can get a word out. "Just shut up."

Her mother makes a gesture like she's zipping her lips.

Paul comes down. "Did we handle that well?"

Elaine's mother clucks.

One of the men knocks on the door. "You have a hole?" he asks, stepping in.

"Upstairs," Elaine says, "in the master bedroom—look up and you can see the sky."

"What's the suitcase for?" Paul points to a suitcase by the kitchen table—Elaine hadn't noticed it before.

"I can't take it anymore," Elaine's mother says. "A woman of my age, of my position, deserves more." She pauses. "I'll stay in one of the boys' rooms. You can talk all you want, you can fight, you can make love, you can kill each other for all I care, and I won't say a word."

Elaine imagines her mother upstairs, discovering the lump in Daniel's bed, lifting the mattress. Her mother flipping through the stack of *Chunky Bunch* magazines.

"The house isn't ready," Elaine says.

"It's ready enough for you," her mother says.

"Mother, please."

"Your father isn't being nice. Why should I stay where I'm not wanted?"

"It's your house, you don't have to be wanted. And Daddy does want you, but you're driving him crazy."

"I'm driving him crazy. I'm driving him. What about what he's doing to me?"

"What do you want from him?"

"Some attention. I want someone to pay some attention."

"Maybe you have to pay attention to him first. If you pay attention to him, he'll pay attention to you—that's the way it goes."

"That's manipulative. I am not a manipulative woman."

Elaine rolls her eyes.

"I'm not. Are you telling your own mother that she can't stay in your house?"

Paul leaves the room.

"Where are you going?" Elaine shouts after him.

"Getting ready for Sammy's soccer," Paul says.

"I thought you were just picking up."

"I thought I should go and watch—isn't that what parents do?"

"You don't usually watch."

Paul doesn't respond.

"Did you call Nate's mother and ask her about packing Sammy's stuff? Did you tell her that he's coming home?"

Paul doesn't tell her that he called from upstairs, that he arranged for Sammy's return, arranged for an extra date next Wednesday afternoon, and got a great high-concept blow job over the phone—"I want you to feel my mouth sucking your prick, your balls rubbing my face, my finger on the edge of your asshole." The finger on the asshole was the unexpected bit that did it; he shot off instantly, splashing the wall of the walk-in closet where he was hiding with the cordless phone.

"It's taken care of," Paul says.

"Does she get to stay here?" her mother asks.

"Who?" Elaine asks, distracted, thinking about Nate's mother, her good hair, her big boobs.

"Her," Elaine's mother repeats.

"No," Elaine says, realizing that her mother is talking about Mrs. Hansen. "Mother, just stop it. Go home, go back to Daddy."

"You're sending your mother away. I knew you would. I always knew that eventually you would send me away."

"Not away. Home. You want something from me. You're the mother, and you act like the child. I want something from you: I want to be the child."

"You want to be the child." Her mother snorts. "You're

forty-three years old with a husband and two children of your own; you're not a child."

"Fine, if you're not going to take care of me, then go away." Elaine isn't sure what she's saying—it half makes sense and half makes no sense, but she's saying it. She feels the need to say something.

"Do you want some coffee?" her mother asks. "Should I make a fresh pot?"

"Yes," Elaine says. "Yes, I want coffee."

"See you," Paul says. "Anything you need, anything I should do while I'm out?"

"Just bring Sammy home," she says, opening the door, letting Paul out, checking the broken lock.

There is silence.

Elaine sits at the kitchen table, drinking a cup of coffee.

A horn beeps. The guy upstairs working on the hole calls down, "There's a car out there, waiting for someone." Elaine goes out. A station wagon is idling at the curb. "Is Daniel here?" the driver asks.

Elaine shakes her head. "Not here," she says. The station wagon is driven by a complete stranger, it's filled with kids she's never seen before. "What is this?" Elaine asks.

"Scout trip. Any idea where he is?"

She shakes her head, none.

"Don't worry," the driver says cheerfully. "We'll find him."

"All right, I'm going," her mother says, picking up her suitcase as soon as Elaine comes back into the house.

"Okay, talk to you later," Elaine says.

"You do whatever you want," her mother says.

"I'll talk to you later, Mother," Elaine says.

"Whatever," her mother says.

"I'm too tired," Elaine says.

"Think of other people, Elaine," her mother says, walking out.

The workman comes downstairs. "It's patched for now," he says. "We'll get in there and really do the work on Monday— it'll hold over the weekend."

The house is empty. The wrecking ball is leaving. It is being taken away, guided back down the driveway.

The morning is gone—burned off, like fog.

Elaine opens the refrigerator, pulls out bits and pieces of things, condiments and crackers. She pours herself a glass of wine; she thinks of Mrs. Hansen, who didn't come today. She hopes everything is all right; she wonders if she should worry. Elaine sits at the kitchen table, daydreaming. She pictures herself as a different person in a different life. She sees herself in places she can't even point to on a map, high in the thin air of the Himalayas, wandering the hills of Tuscany, traveling under a new name, making no reference to her life before.

Every day Elaine thinks of disappearing. She will leave and take nothing with her—"You have yourself" is what people say, and that's what stops her. She fears she is nothing. Nonexistent.

The cop is in the kitchen. He arrived unannounced. He stands in front of where she's sitting at the kitchen table, a white foam cervical collar around his neck.

"You're home," he says.

"Last night," she says, coming out of her daydream/travelogue.

"How was it?"

"Fine."

"Did you sleep well, or were you up reading all night?"

Elaine is puzzled.

"You need me," he says, moving in.

"What happened to your neck?" Elaine changes the subject. She gestures toward the foam cuff, thinking of an ox in a yoke.

"Fender bender," he says. He comes closer. His knees press against her leg. "I can tell you want me; I've known all along."

She stands up, banging against the table—things rattle.

"Remember when we first met? I saw you the next morning, crawling naked across the floor, I saw you stand up with dirt on your belly. You put on a coat, and then you answered the door. I've been watching you ever since."

"Watching me?"

"Keeping an eye out. I've noticed a few things, like with your recycling, you don't separate colored glass from clear, your plastic from your paper—I could give you a citation for that." He squeezes her breast. "Go upstairs," he says.

"They'll be home soon."

"Hurry," he says.

His uniform is sculpted to his body, his body is all muscle; every time he moves, another bulge pops out. The sight of his erection pressing against his tan trousers is what gets her. It rises like a pornographic emergency, engorged, trapped.

He undresses her. He doesn't ask. He is persistent and rough.

"How old are you?" she asks.

"Twenty-six."

He takes off his gun belt and lays it down on the dresser. His body is smooth, muscular, and hairless. She is confused, conflating Paul's hair, Pat's breasts, the cream of skin.

"Should I handcuff you?" he asks.

"Do you think it's necessary?"

"Will you resist?"

"No," she says.

His nipples are tiny and hard, like pink match heads. "Bite them," he says, and she does.

He pulls a handful of condoms out of his pocket. "Pick a color, any color."

"Red," she says, and watches him roll it on.

He is huge, his penis is hot and pink and raw like a doggy dick.

He fucks her, harder than Pat, harder than Paul. He is cold and a little cruel. She thinks of Pat, soft, enveloping. She thinks of Paul, the deep familiarity, assorted stubble, flabby ass, a roll around the middle.

"Fuck me," the cop says. He is stronger than she is and a little scary. "Fuck me," he says, pushing off the headboard and slamming into her. "I want you to fuck me."

They are on the bed, they are in Elaine's own home. "I'm fucking you," she says, holding his shoulders. "I'm fucking you."

Elaine sees Pat standing silently in the doorway—she's not sure if what she's seeing is real.

"Fuck me," the cop says. "I want you to fuck me."

Pat goes to the dresser, pulls the gun out of the holster, squats in her version of a police pose, and aims at the cop. "Freeze."

He rears up, thrusting deep inside Elaine.

"You get off her. You leave her alone," Pat says.

The cop looks at Elaine.

She has closed her eyes, her face is contorted, waiting for the shot.

He pulls out. Elaine's eyes pop open. She sees his stiff penis, the bright red condom, shiny with her juices.

"Are you all right?" Pat asks. "Should I call the police? Should I shoot him?"

Elaine shakes her head.

"I am the police," the cop says.

"Did you let him in? How did he get in?"

"Who the hell are you?" the cop asks.

Pat waves the gun at the cop. "I'm asking the questions now," she says. "I'm giving the orders."

"The lock on the downstairs door has been broken since the night of the fire," Elaine says, sitting up.

"Get dressed," Pat tells the cop.

He pulls on his clothes. Despite the disturbance, his cock is still stiff, the condom is still on. He's young, he's a cop, he thrives on scenes like this. He has trouble zipping his pants.

Elaine starts to cry. She sits on the edge of the bed, sobbing.

"When you didn't come over last night, I was worried," Pat says. "I stopped by to check on you."

"Give me the gun," the cop says when he's all zipped up, when he's got his holster strapped on again.

Pat hands him the gun; he puts it away and is quickly down the steps and out the door.

"I feel so alone," Elaine says.

"I don't know what to say," Pat says. She looks around the room. "I can see your Martha Stewart," she says, pointing to the magazine on the night table.

"I can't take it anymore," Elaine says.

Pat leaves.

Elaine cries. She wails, primal pour, the pain of a lifetime, every disappointment, every failure, every missed opportunity is mourned. She cries, and then abruptly she stops—it's enough, it's all she will allow. She looks at the clock; it's almost three. Elaine peels the sheets off the bed, dresses, goes downstairs, throws the sheets into the washing machine, pours the detergent in, and sets the machine on normal.

Outside: an atomic blast of light and heat. The sun is high, the air is hot. She squints. The car is gone—Paul has taken it to the soccer game.

"Fuck." Elaine throws her keys down in the driveway. She brushes it off. She takes off running one way, then turns and runs the other. She runs in a circle. Her heart races. There is no air, nothing to breathe. Bile rises in her throat. Blind panic. She retches. She is afraid she is being etherized, atom-smashed—blasted out of existence.

She runs toward Pat and George's. The Nielsons' driveway is empty, both cars are gone. She scours the streets, searching, thinking she will find Pat. She finds nothing. She rushes to the train station—down the steps to the platform. Empty. Elaine waits—wondering what she will do when the train comes, will she get on it, or throw herself in front of it? She walks back up the steps and down the street. She is headed in a certain direction—the vocational school. The air is heavy, the trees and grass bright green, flush with fresh growth. There's a yellow-and-black symbol on the side of the building—FALLOUT SHELTER. Another sign in a wire-threaded window—SAFE HAVEN.

Elaine pulls at the doors. "Open," she screams. "Open." It means nothing to her that the parking lot is empty, that it's Saturday and school is not in session, the doors are locked. "Shit, shit, shit." Guidance. She needs Bud Johnson. And where is he now? Parked outside some garden apartment with the hood up, working on his car? Elaine kicks the doors, she smacks the brick with her bare hands. "Damn it," she yells. "Fucking goddamn it."

Two halves of a prefabricated house are parked on the grass beside the school, cracked open, split like an English muffin. She steps into one, loses her footing, and accidentally slams her hand against the wall—it goes straight through. The Sheetrock is like cardboard. She punches the wall again intentionally—bam, bam, bam, like a hole punch. There is a hammer on the floor and a box of nails. She goes to it, slamming common nails into the wall, hammering until she is spent, until she has nothing left to say, until she has spelled out FUCK THIS two feet tall. She throws down the hammer and walks away, a vocational vandal, a thief, a woman run amok.

"What do you want?" she asks herself aloud. "What do you want? You tell me," she says. "You tell me." Without thinking, she has taken herself home. She walks past her own house; the car is back in the driveway, Paul is home. She walks up and down the sidewalk, not sure what happens next.

Sammy is in the front yard at the peak of the hill, witnessing her obsessive parade, back and forth, up and down. "Mom," he calls, and at first she doesn't answer. "Mooommm," he tries again, louder.

She looks up, confused. "Mom," he says again, as if reminding her of who she is.

"Oh, hi," Elaine says.

"What're you doing?"

"I went for a walk."

"You were talking to yourself," he says.

She nods. "I was having a little conversation."

"What do you want?" he asks, repeating her incantation.

"I don't know," she says. "What do you want?"

Sammy shrugs.

"Where's Daddy?"

"Inside."

"What are you doing out here?"

"This is the house that hurt me," he says.

Elaine climbs up the driveway and puts her hand on Sammy's shoulder. "Have you seen your room? Come on, I'll show you," she says, guiding him toward the front door. "I had it all cleaned up, scrubbed top to bottom, no dust, no dirt."

Sammy shakes his head. "No."

Out of the corner of her eye, stuck on the branch of a bush, Elaine sees the red condom—like a red flag, hung out to dry.

"My balloon," Sammy says, making a dive for it, pulling it off the bush. The condom stretches and snaps, splitting at the rim, flying off the branch.

"No," Elaine says, grabbing it from him.

"It's my balloon. It's mine, I found it."

"Where did you find it?" Elaine asks, trying to find out who stuck it on the bush.

"Down there," he says, pointing to the street.

"It's a dirty balloon," Elaine says, stuffing it deep into her pocket. "Come inside and we'll find you something else to play with."

Sammy pouts. Elaine opens the front door and leads him in—she is thinking about the cop and the broken lock, wondering if it's something she can fix herself.

Elaine shows Sammy what the workmen have done. She shows him the plastic wall. "See how it's sealed off? That's to keep the dust out. And if you walk around out back, you can see—we're going to have pretty French doors and a deck. Won't that be nice?" She speaks in a chirpy voice that's entirely unfamiliar.

Sammy nods solemnly.

In the kitchen, Elaine pours glasses of lemonade; she drinks hers quickly and refills it, adding a splash of vodka when Sammy's head is turned.

"Everything all right?" she asks. "Are you breathing?"

Sammy doesn't answer, he just stands there.

Elaine digs out the fix-it book and her tools. She sits on the floor in front of the open front door, fiddling with the lock. Sammy stands next to her. She studies the diagram. "How was soccer?" she asks, trying to make conversation.

Sammy shrugs.

"Did you score?"

Again he shrugs.

"Did your team win?"

"Not because of me," he says.

Elaine examines the lock—the strike plate and the bolt are not hitting in the right place, and the cylinder seems misaligned. She unscrews the mounting plate and returns the cylinder to its original position. It works. The door opens and closes and locks. She's pleased with herself. "Now no one can come in unless we invite them," Elaine tells Sammy as she closes the door.

"Open it," Sammy cries.

"Why?"

"Open it," he says, panicked.

She opens the door. "Let's go find Daddy," she says, changing the subject.

"Don't close the door," Sammy says.

"Okay, but when it gets dark out, we have to close it, all right?"

Sammy nods.

Paul. He hears them coming. He gets up off Daniel's bed and meets them in the upstairs hall. "The wrecking ball is gone," he says.

"It was a rental," she says.

"The backyard is dirt," he says.

"They're digging for the deck." Elaine takes a deep breath; the house still has the non-scent of the cleaning company.

Sammy's toe taps the baseboard in a repetitive rhythm, banging out coded communication.

"Where have you been?" Elaine asks.

"In Daniel's room," Paul says.

"Doing what?"

"Thinking."

He leans against the wall. Paul doesn't tell Elaine that he took a look at the molding around Daniel's door and that she did a really good job putting it back together—he doesn't tell Elaine that he's impressed with her craftsmanship.

"The walls look lighter," he says, referring to the layers of grime peeled away by the deep cleaning.

Elaine nods.

Paul and Elaine are in a peculiar place where they really can't do much for each other; they are going forward, lost in themselves—each awkward in a different way, each with reasons.

Paul looks up at the ceiling. He doesn't tell Elaine that he's been in Daniel's room crying; he doesn't tell Elaine that he wishes it were his room, that he wishes he were twelve again and could have another crack at everything. Paul doesn't tell Elaine that he's worried about work—he doesn't even understand what work is anymore—he's worried about money, he's screwing Mrs. Apple and doesn't have a clue what it's all about, and that there's this thing with the date that scared the hell out of him. He doesn't tell Elaine that he can't believe that last night they knocked down the door and raided their son's room, and he can't understand how Daniel turned into someone he can't talk to and how Sammy is so sweet and so adorable and Paul is horrified because he can't even take care of him. And Paul knows Elaine is suffering, and he doesn't know what to do for her. Paul doesn't tell Elaine that he doesn't feel like an adult, that he has no idea what it means to be a man, that in fact he's a total jerk. Paul doesn't tell Elaine that he doesn't know what to do—so he sat in Daniel's room crying and then he pulled out the fat-girl porno magazines and jerked off.

"Did you have an okay day?" Elaine asks. "Was the game good?"

Paul bows his head, he glances at Sammy. Paul doesn't tell

Elaine that when he got to the soccer field, the game was already going and that he didn't recognize Sammy right away—Mrs. A. had to point him out, and Paul joked that it was because Sammy was wearing different-color socks than usual. Paul doesn't tell Elaine that he stood next to Mrs. A. with a hard-on during the whole game and that they whispered tempting and tortuous things back and forth, verbally screwing each other for an hour and a half until the woman next to them walked away snorting in disgust and they realized that maybe they weren't whispering. Paul doesn't tell Elaine how uncoordinated Sammy was, how he missed the easiest shot, how all his teammates jumped on him—literally—and how Sammy had an asthma attack and no one could find the puffer. And so Sammy sat on the sidelines wheezing for the last quarter and then Paul drove him around in the car with the air-conditioning on for another hour, waiting for things to settle, afraid to bring him home like that. Paul doesn't tell Elaine that he took Sammy with him to McKendrick's house to drop off some tapes he picked up for him at the sleaze store near the office, and when the old guy opened the door he'd said, "They're watching me. Be careful."

"Who's watching you?" Paul had asked, thinking the old guy was losing it.

"Feds."

"Why would the feds be watching you?"

"Because I'm special," McKendrick hissed. "Come in, come in," the old guy said.

Paul handed him the tapes. "Just a little something I picked up for you."

"Goodie," the old guy said, then he goosed Sammy's ass. And while Sammy didn't seem to mind, it drove Paul crazy. Don't touch my kid, he wanted to say, don't lay your filthy hands on him. "Time to go," Paul said, tugging Sammy's sleeve, pulling him out of the room.

"They're across the street," McKendrick said. "Wave on your way out."

"What's he talking about?" Sammy asked as they were leaving.

"Old people get a little weird," Paul said as they walked down the flagstone path. Across the street Paul saw a plain parked car with dark windows. He had the strangest sensation that someone was taking their picture—he could almost hear the whir of the auto-wind.

Paul doesn't bother to tell Elaine that when they finally pulled up to the house, Sammy wouldn't get out of the car and Paul wasn't sure what to do, whether to force him or lay a trail of Cheerios and hope that he'd eat his way inside. Paul waited for a few minutes and then just left Sammy sitting there with the car door open. Paul doesn't say that when he went into the house and Elaine wasn't there, he was worried that she'd left for good. He doesn't say that he doesn't know what they would do without her.

Paul doesn't tell Elaine that he's aware that almost anyone else would think it's a perfectly lovely Saturday but that he's scared, absolutely petrified, and he doesn't know why. Instead he says, "Phone rang a little while ago and I didn't get it."

"I'm sure the machine picked up," Elaine says.

Sammy steps into his room and checks everything out: toys, books, bed.

"Are you all right?" Paul asks Elaine. Paul doesn't tell Elaine that about half an hour ago he looked out the bathroom window and saw her walking back and forth in front of the house, muttering to herself, her hair hanging in front of her face, like a lunatic.

"I'm worn out," she says.

"Rest," he says.

"The hole is temporarily fixed," she tells Paul. "The sheets are in the wash."

Elaine follows Sammy into his room. "Everything up to snuff?"

"Open the window," Sammy says, and she does. She lies down on Sammy's narrow bed, her head against the comforter, buried in blue sky, clouds. "Tell me everything," she says, and Sammy starts to spin a story about a giraffe, a monkey, and a little boy. Elaine falls asleep. She drools.

Sammy lies on a small rug near the open window curled into a C. He naps—dreaming lightly.

It is Saturday night.

Elaine wakes up and goes looking for Paul—he's down-stairs folding laundry. "Sheets are dry," he says. "I pushed the bed back to its original position. Hopefully, there won't be any more leaks."

"Hopefully," Elaine says. "What are we supposed to be doing tonight?"

"Dinner at the Montgomerys'," Paul says, "but Joan called to say they canceled, they're in bad shape, a complication with the crazy kid. She seemed annoyed—what will we do, Saturday night and all of us on our own? Should we do something without them? Can we get a reservation anywhere?" Paul does a good imitation of social desperation, the panic of people left without plans. How dare the Montgomerys . . .

"Did Daniel come back?" she asks.

"Not yet." Paul sits at the kitchen table. He has made himself a drink. He sips. "And Jennifer will be here in half an hour," Paul adds. He pulls a Baggie out of his pocket, takes out his rolling paper, and turns out a neat and narrow joint.

"Not in the house," Elaine says.

"Come on," Paul says, "it's Saturday night." He opens the door to the basement and coaxes her halfway down. "Do it with me," he says, flicking his lighter, taking a deep drag. The stairwell glows. Paul hands the joint to Elaine. "We have to get Daniel back," Elaine says, blowing smoke.

Paul nods and takes a hit.

"I fixed the lock on the front door," Elaine says. "Now no one can arrive unannounced."

For Elaine, pot is like a prism, a kaleidoscope turning things; objects and emotions fragment, stretch, and slow, everything looks a little different—mentally muted, visually more intense.

"What do you want to do tonight?" Paul asks.

"I wish we could just be normal. One normal happy family," Elaine says, drawing a deep hit.

"And if not that?"

"Could we do nothing? Why do we always have to do something, why does something always have to be happening?"

"What about Daniel, should we call those people"—their name intentionally escapes him—"and have them send him back?" Paul asks.

"We have to go and get him," Elaine says. "We have to bring him home."

"Mom," Sammy calls. "Mom?" There's a pause. "Dad," Sammy calls. "Dad?"

They each take a last hit, and Paul pinches the joint, putting it out. "Ollie, ollie, oxen free."

"You're awake," Elaine says, coming up the stairs.

"The front door is closed," Sammy says.

"It's okay," Paul says.

"Where were you?" Sammy asks.

"Downstairs," Paul says.

"Did you have a good nap?" Elaine asks.

"You snore," Sammy says.

"Would you like some cran?" Elaine asks, pouring juice.

The phone rings.

"It's Joan," Paul says before anyone answers.

Elaine picks up. "Hello?"

"Henry and his date are going to scale the rock-climbing wall at his gym, and then they're going to the movies in Yonkers. They're planning to eat popcorn for dinner," Joan reports, as though popcorn for dinner is shockingly decadent, unforgivable.

"And what are you going to do?" Elaine asks.

"I'm not sure at all. Ted keeps telling me to calm down. But I don't think I've spent a Saturday night at home since I was fifteen."

"Look at it this way." Elaine hears Ted in the background. "At some point in your life, you're going to be spending Saturday nights at home again. Why not just relax and see what the evening brings—you never know."

"I can't stand it," she says, bickering. "I'm not ready to stay home. What are you and Paul thinking?"

"We're just going to keep at it, we have so much work to do on the house," Elaine says, relieved to have a good excuse.

"Well, let's talk tomorrow and compare notes," Joan says.

Someone pounds on the front door.

Paul lets Jennifer in.

"Door's locked," Jennifer says.

"Elaine fixed it," Paul says.

"Handy." Jennifer sniffs around. "It smells good in here. Did you spray something? Burn a reversing candle?"

"Tell him that," Paul says, pointing at Sammy, who's walking around holding a wet washcloth over his nose and mouth.

"We had it washed, scrubbed floor to ceiling," Elaine says.

"Scrubbing bubbles," Paul says, thinking of the thick white foam.

"What's your mom doing tonight?" Elaine asks.

"Homework," Jennifer says. "Secretly she's thrilled dinner

got canceled, she's 'sick to shit' of obligations. What's the plan
around here?" Jennifer asks.

"We're going to get Daniel," Elaine announces. "We'll be
right back. Are you guys okay for now? You're not starving, are
you?" Elaine asks. "Can you wait?"

"We're fine," Jennifer says, looking at Sammy.

"Not hungry," he says, his voice muffled through the
washcloth.

"Actually, I'm hungry," Paul says, grabbing a stack of
Oreos.

"Give me one," Elaine says as they're backing out of the
driveway. The munchies have descended.

A buzz. A little high, vibrating. As Paul drives, Elaine
pulls the Oreo apart, licking the middle, scraping it with her
teeth, eating the cookie.

Their teeth are quickly coated, caked with black cookie
crumbs like tobacco stains that stick like mud on the gums. If
they smiled, they'd look like Halloween hoboes.

"Are you stoned?" Elaine asks.

"It was just one joint."

They pull into the Meaderses' driveway, and what seemed
like a good idea, a show of parental prerogative, now seems
asinine.

Elaine sits in the car, paranoid—wishing she hadn't
smoked, thinking they smell like pot and scotch, thinking she
looks strange.

"Are you getting out?" Paul asks.

Together they walk up to the house. Paul rings the doorbell. He giggles. "Don't you wish we could run?" Paul says.
"Make it like a prank? I want him to open the door, stick his
mealy head out, and then I'd like to pelt him with tomatoes or
roll the yard in toilet paper or something."

Elaine hates Paul, he's an embarrassment, a liability. "Behave," she says.

Mr. Meaders opens the front door.

"Hi, how are you?" Paul says, his words coming out in a jovial burst of laughter. "Sorry to arrive unannounced."

"We've come for Daniel," Elaine says. "We'd like to take him home."

"Is he expecting you?" Mr. Meaders asks.

"We thought it would be best if we didn't make a big deal out of it," Elaine says.

Paul and Elaine step into the house; it's like stepping back in time. The colors are browns and golds, deep greens and blues, the colors of 1957, of Ozzie and Harriet. Mr. Meaders is wearing a cardigan, and Mrs. Meaders comes out of the kitchen with an apron tied around her waist. She puts a basket of rolls on the table.

"Oh, bad timing," Elaine whispers to Paul. "They're about to eat."

"The boys are upstairs in Willy's room," Mr. Meaders says.

Elaine leads Paul and Mr. Meaders on a march up the stairs. Going up, her legs are rubbery, as if she's stretching with every step.

Mr. Meaders knocks on the bedroom door. "Daniel, your parents are here."

Elaine sticks her nose in, pressing her face close to the door. "Time to go home," she says cheerfully.

There is no response.

"I don't think he's inclined," Meaders says.

They stand in the hallway. Meaders checks his watch. "Seven twenty-two," he says. "Supper's at seven-thirty."

"Could we have a moment?" Paul asks, and Meaders backs off, descending the staircase, hands thrown up in the air as if he's being held at gunpoint.

Paul taps on the door, then opens it. Willy Meaders's room is a generationless homage to being a boy—two twin beds, trophies, sports posters, hockey sticks, a trombone.

Daniel sits on one of the beds, his back against the wall. "We want you to come home. Dad is sorry about the lock," Elaine blurts.

Daniel stares at the fish tank.

"Sammy's back, and Jennifer is there. We're having a family night at home; we might rent some videos or just play a game—like Monopoly." Paul talks, not quite knowing what he's saying. "How's that sound?"

Daniel stares. He absently picks through loose bits of tile from a mosaic project.

"We're fixing up the house. It's going to be great," Elaine says.

"Look, I'm sorry about the lock. To be honest, it frightened me. It was like you'd become a stranger, I lost my head," Paul says. "I'm not perfect."

"None of us are," Elaine elaborates.

"I'm trying to talk to you honestly," Paul says. "Give me a break here, would ya, pal?" He stops and looks around at the posters on the wall, the fish tank bubbling, Willy Meaders sitting in the desk chair. Paul can't believe that the little Meaders is stupid enough to just sit there—doesn't he feel uncomfortable? He just sits there staring at them dispassionately as though they're a movie.

Finally Paul glares at him and says, "Willy, could you please excuse us?" and the boy leaves.

"You're making a scene," Paul tells Daniel. "How do you think it looks—your mother and I having to come here and beg you to come home?"

The longer it takes, the worse it gets. Moment by moment the situation becomes exponentially more humiliating.

"You're embarrassing us," Paul says. "It's almost seven-thirty, the Meaderses want to eat their dinner. You know how serious they are about things like that."

Paul is climbing the walls; he wants to box Daniel's ears,

knock his block off. He wants to haul off and yell, "Get in the fucking car right now, or I'm going to kill you."

Elaine sits down hard on the opposite bed; the bed groans. She is about to cry; in fact, she starts to cry, but knowing that it will only cause more trouble, it will only make Daniel less inclined to come home, she quits. Paul and Daniel look at her. She sniffles.

"What's for dinner?" Daniel asks.

"What would you like?" Paul asks.

Daniel doesn't answer.

"Where's your stuff?" Paul is trying to speed things up. "Is this yours?" He picks dirty clothes up off the floor. "Do you have a suitcase?"

Daniel points to the closet. Paul drags out an old Samsonite.

"Do you have things in this dresser? Where're your socks and underwear? Do you have other shoes? Jeans? T-shirts?"

Paul throws things into the suitcase.

"Do you have a dopp kit?"

"A what?" Daniel asks.

"Toiletries?" Elaine says, still on the bed.

"A toothbrush. It's in the bathroom, should I get it?" Daniel asks.

"You don't need the toothbrush," Elaine says. "We have one for you at home."

"What about your books, your schoolwork?" Paul asks. Daniel stuffs books, scraps of paper, sports magazines, into his knapsack.

"Ready?" Paul asks.

Daniel picks up a tile ashtray, three-quarters finished, gritty grout overflowing the rows. He hands it to Elaine. "This is for you," he says. "I made it for no real reason."

"Thanks," Elaine says, taking the ashtray, genuinely touched by the ugly artifact.

Paul, the escort, goes first with the suitcase; Daniel, the prisoner, is in the middle; and Elaine follows up, pressure from behind to make sure Daniel doesn't take a wrong turn, doesn't change his mind and bolt.

Mrs. Meaders stands by the swinging door to the kitchen holding a platter of food.

"Good-bye," Mr. Meaders says, tucking his napkin under his chin, not getting up.

"Take care," Mrs. Meaders says.

"See you tomorrow," Willy says.

Daniel's place has already been removed from the table.

"Thanks for everything," Paul says as the procession leaves the house. "It's been a rough time. We really appreciate all you've done."

"Thank you again," Elaine says, closing the door behind her.

Elaine is sweating. Whatever buzz she had before is gone. She feels as though they just put one over—on whom, she's not sure: the Meaderses, Daniel, themselves. Inside the house Paul and Elaine talked a good game, but it's immediately clear they can't live up to the promises. Not that they promised so much or that everything they said was a lie—more a fantasy.

"Monopoly, yeah, right," Daniel says, stretching out in the backseat. "We don't even have a Monopoly game."

"Don't we?" Paul says. "I thought we did."

"The Meaderses were having liver. Liver and onions. I hate liver," Daniel says. "Could we order some pizza and maybe rent movies or something?"

"Sure," Paul says.

"Of course," Elaine says.

They drive to the video store. Paul borrows the phone and calls the pizza place while Daniel picks out horrible movies: *The Price of Misfortune* and *BadZone—A Place You Don't Want to Go with Anyone*. At the pizza place Elaine jumps out, picks up the pizzas and two six-packs of Cokes. They make one last stop for ice cream. "Mint chocolate chip," Daniel screams at his father across the parking lot.

Paul waves back at him—"Gotcha."

The sky is fading fast, dropping down into a deep navy blue. Pulling into the driveway, the headlights land on Sammy and Jennifer sitting outside on the kitchen steps.

"I thought the house was fixed," Daniel says when he sees them.

"There are still a few problems," Elaine says.

"Sammy's afraid to go inside," Paul says.

"Retread," Daniel says.

"Hi," Elaine calls, getting out of the car. "We're home, look who's here."

"The Scout returns," Jennifer says.

"Is that supposed to mean something?" Daniel asks.

"It means hi," she says.

"Pizza anyone?" Paul says.

They all go into the house. "Don't close the door," Sammy says.

"Did you hear about the two-digit snacker?" Daniel asks Jennifer.

"Who?" Elaine asks.

"Montgomery kid," Jennifer says.

"Shhh," Elaine says, not wanting anyone to talk about it.

"Like we haven't heard," Daniel says.

"Who's the snacker?" Sammy asks.

"The Montgomery kid—he bites the fingers off little boys like you and eats 'em," Daniel says.

"Fake," Sammy says.

"Real," Daniel says.

"Sit and stay," Jennifer says.

"Stop," Paul says.

Paul puts the pizza boxes on the coffee table while Elaine lays out plates, napkins, Cokes, and Daniel pops in the video.

"The less violent one first," Elaine requests, thinking of Sammy—more than impressionable, he's like a sponge, absorbing everything.

They dig in. Sammy pulls the cheese off his pizza. The opening sequence unfolds. A lost soldier with machine guns slung over both shoulders barrels through the forest.

"Nate's dad has lots of guns," Sammy says. "Bigger guns than that, guns he got in Vietnam."

Sammy pronounces "Vietnam" with what Paul thinks of as the redneck, Republican, or Nixonian intonation—"nam," like "ma'am."

"Interesting," Paul says, curious to hear more about Gerald, the mystery man, the silent type, former Green Beret.

"What's Vietnam?" Sammy asks, again pronouncing it wrong. The hair on the back of Paul's neck rises.

"Vietnam," he says, correcting him. "It's a country in Southeast Asia."

"Mr. Meaders used to live in Washington. He was going to be in the IRA, but then something happened," Daniel says. "He's a total math whiz, he even won a math prize."

"It's IRS, not IRA," Paul says, struggling to straighten things out, to unseat these men from the thrones his sons have set them on. "And Meaders is a weaselly numbers cruncher."

"I could live with the Meaderses," Daniel says blithely.

"For how long?" Paul asks.

"As long as I want," Daniel says.

"It's costing us more than twenty thousand dollars to fix up the house," Paul says. "That's a pretty penny."

Elaine looks at him; talk about pathetic. What do the boys care about what it costs to fix the house? They're kids, what do they know from twenty thousand dollars?

"Nate does push-ups. He tried doing them on me," Sammy says. "It was a special kind; you lie on top of the other boy and you do push-ups. I couldn't breathe. He punched me."

On-screen, helicopters search for the missing soldier, one of the choppers blows up, another crashes into the side of a hill, blood splashes across the windshield.

"Mr. Meaders whacks off twice a day, to keep himself fit," Daniel says. "That's what his father taught him. Frequency solves urgency."

"My mother has a vibrating bed," Jennifer says. "One of those Craft-Magic things they advertise on TV. It's deeply adjustable—head, feet, up, down, higher, lower. She calls it her luxury. She says, 'I'm going to go up and lie on my luxury.' "

Elaine is hearing things she doesn't want to know. "Everyone's got something," she says, shaking her head, emptying her ears.

Daniel takes another piece of pizza.

"How many is that for you?" Elaine asks.

"Only my fourth," he says.

Paul belches. "Leave room for ice cream," he says, kicking off his shoes.

Elaine gets up to clear the plates. She trips over a tennis shoe. Pizza crust falls to the floor.

"Shhhhh," Paul hisses.

"Sorry," she says, apologizing reflexively.

She looks at Paul, Daniel, Sammy, and Jennifer, woven onto a pile on the sofa, spilling over onto the floor. Paul stretches out to fill Elaine's spot. It's as though it's fine, as though it's well and good to burn down the house, fix it, and move back in, as though nothing has happened, as though nothing has changed.

Something has to change. Someone has to notice.

Elaine carries dishes into the kitchen.

She doesn't go downstairs, unscrew the fuse box, plunge

them into darkness, and then turn around and march back into the living room and say, Okay, cavemen, it's my turn now, listen up—I want to be cooked for and cleaned up after. I want to be accommodated and paid attention to, instead of always worrying about how I'm failing you. I want to think about what I'm not getting here. Let's take a moment.

She thinks of Paul, of Pat, Bud Johnson, the cop. Everyone is fucking her, everyone is getting what they want except Elaine—Elaine wants relief, and Elaine wants attention. She wants someone to respond to her, not because they get something out of it, not because it fills some pathetic need of their own, not because they want something back, but just because. . . .

She thinks of Mrs. Hansen, who she hasn't seen or heard a peep out of all day; she wonders if it's too late too call.

"You're such a good cookie," Mrs. Hansen says. "I'm just having a bad day. Tomorrow I'll be fine. I'm glad you called, glad someone noticed." There's a pause. "What are you doing home? It's Saturday night."

"The Montgomerys canceled at the last minute."

"Oh, baby, I bet that got everyone in a twist."

"Yep," Elaine says.

"Something with the boy."

"A complication," Elaine says.

"What about your two? Where are they?" Mrs. Hansen asks.

"We're all here," Elaine says. "Everyone's home. They're on the sofa watching TV."

"Good," Mrs. Hansen says. "That's the way it should be. See you tomorrow. Good night."

Paul's roach, the end of his joint, is on the counter, next to the car keys, pushed back—out of sight. Elaine peels open the gluey paper and eats the pot. She chews it; it's a little burned, a little like lawn, like twigs. She eats it—it's evidence she feels compelled to get rid of. She has some nervous compulsion to keep the house clean, to put something in her mouth. There is a distant memory of hash brownies, escape. The pot sticks in her throat. She eats some ice cream to wash it down. She pours herself a glass of wine. She is still thinking of the cop, of Pat. She should call Pat, but what would she say? What did you and George do when the Montgomerys canceled? Idle conversation, cheap chatter. She finishes her snack, pours herself a glass of wine, picks up a disposable camera, and wanders around the house, taking pictures. She goes into the living room and watches them staring at the TV. Images, colors, flicker across their faces. She aims. She snaps. Flash. Flash.

"What are you doing?" Paul says. "We're watching a movie."

"Documenting," she says.

"Very funny," he says.

The movie ends, no one wins, everything goes up in smoke.

"I'll drive Jennifer home," Paul says, putting his shoes back on.

"I'm so glad you were here. We don't see enough of you," Elaine tells Jennifer as she's opening her wallet, taking out a twenty.

"Hush money?" Paul asks.

"Baby-sitting," Elaine says.

"You didn't go out," Jennifer says, refusing the money.

"You baby-sat the whole family," Elaine says.

"I ate pizza and watched a movie. I put no one to bed, I didn't call poison control, the pediatrician's pager, or the parents at a dinner party—forget it."

"It's Saturday night," Elaine says. "I'm sure you had a hundred better things to do."

"It was a night off for me," Jennifer says, following Paul out of the house. "Deeply relaxing."

"Back in a flash," Paul says, picking up the car keys.

Elaine is afraid to be home alone even though the boys are there—she imagines the cop is still out there, still hard. The condom is in her pocket—she doesn't know what to do with it, save it like a caul, a scrap, the skin of her infidelity, or take it out and toss it in the Dumpster.

Elaine tries to sit somewhere in the living room where he wouldn't be able to see her. She sits in the corner holding the portable phone. If he comes back, who will she call?

Sammy wakes up. "Where am I?"

"You're right here at home," Elaine says.

"Is the door closed?"

"It's nighttime, and the door is closed," Elaine says.

She shakes Daniel's shoulder. "Come on, Scout, up to bed." Daniel babbles something about making a left turn at the what'd-ya-call-it tree, losing the route of the trail.

"You're talking in your sleep," Elaine says.

"No I'm not," he says.

She tucks both boys in and goes down the hall to her room.

They are home, back where they belong. Elaine hears the car pull in, the engine turn off, she hears Paul come into the house, she hears him whistling downstairs, making a drink. He comes up, offers the glass to her.

"Nightcap?"

"Pass," she says, pulling her nightgown over her head.

"Twelve-twenty and all's well," Paul says, unzipping his pants. "Kids asleep?"

"In comas," Elaine says.

"I'm so glad to be home," Paul says, sliding in next to her.

"Door locked?" Elaine asks.

"Bolted, chained, and I threw the sofa in front just in case."

TEN

SUNDAY MORNING. Two dogs knock over a trash can, dragging garbage across the grass. Squirrels jump from tree to tree, a cat slinks around the corner of the house, someone's sprinkler kicks on—things bubble beneath the surface.

Elaine is awake, alert, vigilant. She hears everything: the cracks and creaks, the shifting of the foundation, the even engine of Paul's breathing. She has been up half the night, afraid to go downstairs, afraid the cop is out there, watching. She had a strange dream and woke up thinking Paul was Pat. In the middle of the night, she sat up and took a look. Paul was Paul. The splash from the streetlight, the spill of the moon, gathered on Paul's shiny dome, giving his scrubbed skull a blue glow. A vein in his temple pulsed, his eye twitched. Elaine took a deep breath, turned over, and went back to sleep. She dreamed that every morning when she woke up someone different was in her bed: Pat, the cop, the workman with the broken fingers, the architect, Ted Talmadge. Every day someone new was pressed up against her—naked. Elaine dreamed she had no way of stopping it, she dreamed that she had no control.

Again Elaine woke up. Again she looked; still Paul. She got out of bed, walked down the hall, and checked on Sammy.

"Leave me alone," Sammy said in his sleep.

Standing over him, she cast a shadow across the bed, a dark cloud over the comforter's blue sky. She stepped back.

"Don't close the door," he mumbled.

"Door's open," Elaine said, leaving.

Elaine went back to bed and lay there, waiting.

A noise: tires, the slam of a car door, the sound of her mother's voice. "Try the kitchen door."

Her father asking, "Do you have a key?"

"If I had a key, why would I send you around to the other side of the house. Blow the horn."

There is a single shy beep, simultaneously splitting the air and struggling to be unobtrusive.

"More," her mother says.

The beep is followed by a second solid blast.

Sammy staggers into Elaine's bedroom. "Grandma's here," he says. "She beeped right under my head."

"Why don't you go down and let her in?"

He is in his pajamas, rubbing his eyes, a sleepy boy. "I don't like her," he says. "She squeezes too hard."

The horn blows again.

"I'm not here," Sammy says, crawling in next to Paul, pulling the covers over his head.

"All right," Elaine says. "All right."

Paul stirs in his sleep.

"My parents are here," she tells him. He rolls away.

"House of sleepyheads," her mother says, pushing ahead of her father and into the house. "Good thing we didn't call before we came."

"It's Sunday morning," Elaine says.

"It's nine o'clock," her mother says.

"We brought brunch," her father says. He is holding bags of groceries and a white bakery box tied with string.

"You've already been to the store?" Elaine asks.

"I'll tell you a secret," her mother says. "When you get older, you need less sleep."

"You need less of everything," her father says, putting the bags down.

"I brought your father so you can see for yourself," her mother says.

"See what?"

"Exactly," her mother says. "I want you to see how he is." She says it right in front of him.

"She thinks I *am* something," her father says. "The fact is, I just am, and that annoys her."

"The kitchen, by the way, looks very nice. Do you want to show your father what you're doing with the house?"

"We're not finished," Elaine says.

"Well, I want him to see something," her mother says, leading her father into the living room. "Look at this sofa, these pillows. Everyone has to do something about where they sit." She sits down, patting the cushion next to her. He sits beside her. "You can feel it," she says. "The stuffing goes, you sink lower and lower until it takes a crane to get you out. This is how it is on our sofa. Some Saturday night I'm going to sit down and not be able to get up—it makes me think I'm an old woman."

"You are an old woman," her father says.

"Not that old." She peels herself off the sofa with some difficulty and goes back into the kitchen.

Elaine sits next to her father. "You haven't been here in a long time," she says, realizing that she hasn't seen him in months. He looks older and a little frail.

"I like it at home," he says. "Your mother always wants to get out of the house. She just wants to go, I don't think she cares where. Go, I tell her. Go without me. For thirty-five years I left the house every morning; now I want to stay home."

"He just sits there. Some days he just sits all day," her mother throws in from the kitchen.

"So what if I sit? What's wrong with sitting? I earned the right to sit."

"You didn't call me yesterday after I left," her mother says to Elaine. "You have to be careful what you promise people."

"I didn't say I would," Elaine says.

"You said, 'I'll talk to you later.' " Her mother goes on, "I call you every day."

"You call me because you want my attention—you want a lot of my attention."

"That's my way of *paying* attention. You're always disappointed in me, I can never do enough."

"The feeling is mutual."

"Elaine, I am the way I am. I'm almost seventy years old. The only way I'm going to have a personality transplant is if, God forbid, I have a stroke; otherwise, this is what you get. Would you like some coffee? I brought some of my own from home. I grind the beans every day."

"Are you depressed?" Elaine whispers to her father, hoping her mother won't hear.

He bends toward her. "How would I know?" he whispers back.

"Do you feel unhappy?"

"I feel nothing," he says. "Sometimes a twinge in my back, a little bursitis, but other than that, nothing." He pauses. "It isn't always perfect. Your mother still wants perfection. She still wants everything she never had," he adds loudly. "She won't die without it."

"I will die without it, that's the problem," her mother says.

"Mother, what do you want?" Elaine calls into the kitchen.

"Everything. I want everything, all the best, and you should want it, too."

Her mother sweeps into the living room—a force of nature, her determination evident in the flare of her nostrils, the flash of her eyes, the tightness of her lips. She is fierce. "Where's your family? Why haven't they come down? Rally the troops," her mother says, clapping her hands.

Elaine goes upstairs. Sammy is still in the bed. She uncovers him. "Time to get up," she says.

"No," he says.

"Yes," she says.

Paul is in the bathroom, staring at himself in the mirror.

"You look at yourself more than anyone I know," Elaine says. "What do you see?"

"Decay," Paul says. "The early signs of rot."

"Breakfast is ready," Elaine says.

"I'm almost done," he says.

There's a little pile of pills on the dresser—mental candy. She can't remember which color does what. She picks two, orange and blue. She dresses. Sammy still has not moved. Elaine goes to make the bed; she pulls the sheets up over him, pretending he's not there. She fluffs the pillows. "Paul," she calls. "Paul, there's a problem with the bed."

"What now?" he asks, not realizing it's a joke.

"There's an inexplicable lump in the middle. Maybe you can do something about it."

"Can't it wait?"

"I don't think so," Elaine says. "I think you ought to deal with it before breakfast."

"Give me a minute," he says, "and I'll take a look."

Sammy giggles.

Elaine knocks on Daniel's door. She pretends her hand is

a horn, she pretends that she's playing reveille, she blows hard. "Rise and shine," she says. "Chow's on."

"Where are your filters?" her mother asks when Elaine returns.

"In the drawer below the toaster oven—on the right."

Elaine could go blind and no one would notice. She's memorized where everything is. She could navigate the house for years before anyone caught on. The problem would be something simple, like laundry.

Paul bounds down the stairs, his flat feet clomping like hooves. "Morning," Paul says. "Long time no see. How've you been?" Paul slaps her father on the back.

"I saw that Robertson got Van Kamp," her father says to Paul.

"Only after they gave up Raleigh," Paul says. "And Donaldson is out on his ass."

"Yeah, where'd he go?"

"Organic farming," Paul says.

"Jumped ship?" her father asks—he's the retired guy talking to the working guy, looking for a taste of the old life, a sip of the juice. Paul tries to give him some.

"No, he's gone into organic farming," Paul says.

"I've never heard that one before," her father says. "What does it mean?"

"He gave up everything and started a chicken farm."

The conversation stops, and then her father tries again. "Do you still talk to that other fella?"

"Which one?"

"The guy with the . . ."

"Henry?" Elaine says. Her head hurts—maybe orange and blue were a bad combination. She takes a couple of aspirin.

"That's the one—how's he doing?"

"He's gotten into rock climbing," Paul says.

"What's that mean? Why don't I understand what you're talking about?"

"It's very literal," Elaine says. "He left his wife and has a new girlfriend, and they've been going hiking."

"Oh," her father says. "I thought you were talking in some kind of a code."

"He can get a little paranoid," her mother says. "Where's your dining room table?"

"Elaine axed it," Paul says.

"Mom," Daniel yells downstairs. "Where's my plastic cast?"

"Your what?"

"You know, the white mold I made at Scouts."

"Your plaster cast?" Elaine corrects. She remembers it. She remembers finding it on Daniel's desk, she remembers Paul smashing it, thinking there was some hidden treasure buried within. She remembers dusty white smoke rising, rubble, small pieces on the floor.

She looks at Paul. He goes to the bottom of the stairs.

"Maybe you left it at the Meaderses'," he says.

"No," Daniel says. "It was here. You didn't take it, did you?"

"Just because you can't find something doesn't mean I took it."

"Paul," Elaine says, stopping him before it gets worse.

Her parents stand in the kitchen—oblivious.

"Weird," Daniel says, coming to the top of the stairs.

"It happens," Elaine yells. "Chow's on. Get Sammy."

"Samster, the hamster boy," Daniel says. "Come and get it."

"This is great," Paul says as they squeeze in around the kitchen table. "Elaine doesn't usually make a real breakfast."

"Don't touch me," Sammy says, sitting down.

"It's early for tomatoes, but I'm a sucker," her mother says, loading her plate.

"A sucker for anything that costs double what it should," her father says, digging in.

"Does anyone need me to make eggs? I can make eggs if anyone wants them. I brought a dozen."

"This is fine," Elaine says. "We're fine."

"Could someone pass the onion?" her father says.

"Now, that's what you shouldn't be eating," her mother says. "All day it'll repeat on you."

Elaine listens to her parents "not fighting—talking." She has the sensation of something pecking at her, pinching, biting off pieces of her flesh. She hears her mother's voice and hates it.

"Sam, come here, I have something to show you," her father summons Sammy.

"Don't go," Daniel says. "He's going to make your ears excrete money."

"That's a big word," Paul says.

" 'Money'?" Daniel says.

" 'Excrete,' " Paul says.

Daniel squeezes the two halves of his bagel together—cream cheese oozes out.

The phone rings, it's Joan. "Will you be home later? I have a little something for you. I was thinking of dropping by at around six. How does that sound?"

Elaine watches her father pluck a quarter from Sammy's ear.

"Excrete," Daniel says.

"Fine," Elaine tells Joan. "Great."

In the living room, after brunch, Elaine's father pulls a cigar from his shirt pocket.

"Since when do you smoke?" Paul asks.

"It's his new passion," her mother says.

"For years I was too busy to enjoy anything. That's what retirement is about, discovering pleasure," he says, clipping the tip.

"We just had the house cleaned," Elaine says.

Her father slides the cigar back into his pocket. "I'll wait," he says. "I'll have it later, in peace."

Elaine watches her father lower himself onto the living room sofa; he's a little stiff, unsure of himself.

Her mother goes to him. "Are you tired?" she asks. "Would you like to lie down for a few minutes before we go home?" She puts her hand on his forehead and then sweeps it back through his white hair. Elaine has never seen her mother behave this way before—solicitous.

"I'm all right," he says, waving her away.

Her mother bends and kisses her father. She gives him a long good one right on the lips, and Elaine is shocked. The kiss is so tender, sexual, surprising. Elaine's parents are lip to lip in her living room, and she's watching them with her eyes popping out like she's a kid—grossed out.

"Come on, old man, I'll take you home," her mother says, helping her father off the sofa.

"All right, old woman, let's go," he says.

"I put the leftovers in your fridge. You have plenty for tomorrow," her mother says.

"Thanks," Elaine says. She can't bring herself to hug or kiss either of them. She is glad her parents are leaving. They have frightened her. They can go home and do whatever they want, but here in her house she doesn't want them being affectionate, she doesn't want them getting along, she has no concept of them that way.

"Willy's here," Paul says, looking out the window.

Daniel opens the door.

"You got lucky last night, leaving before the liver," Willy says, stepping in. "Organ meat, can't be beat."

Paul and Elaine are still sitting in the living room.

"Hello, Willy," Paul says over his shoulder.

"Hello," Willy says.

And no one says anything else.

"What's going on?" Willy asks.

"My grandparents just left. We're all kind of burned out," Daniel says. "Come up to my room."

Elaine pictures the two of them fondling the Ziploc bags, flipping through fat-girl magazines. "Why don't you go outside? It's such a nice day, play outside."

Despite the distractions, Elaine is thinking about yesterday, about Pat yelling "Freeze," about the cop with the red balloon, about the way she went racing to the school, looking for the guidance counselor. She thinks about the hammer and nails. She fixates on the idea that the police will investigate—they'll find the hammer with her fingerprints and bust her. She feels a sense of impending doom; something is about to happen, something she's not going to like.

"I've got to go out for a minute," she tells Paul. "Be back soon."

He looks at her.

"What?" she says.

"You tell me," he says.

They stare. Bastard, bitch, prick, cunt.

There is the constant fear of being found out, exposed. What does he know? What is she getting at?

"I just need a minute alone," she says.

"You *are* alone, Elaine, everyone has gone on their merry way."

"Just let me go," she says. "I'll be right back."

"Take the videos," he says.

"Can I go?" Sammy asks. "I want to go."

There's a pause.

"Sure," Elaine says. "Of course you can go." She offers Paul the same opportunity. "Would you like to come along for the ride?"

"Absolutely not," he says.

Elaine goes. She gets in the car and goes with Sammy.

She passes Pat and George's house. They are home, both cars are in the driveway. She hovers in the middle of the street, idling with no particular plan in mind. She hovers until she feels conspicuous and then steps on the gas. She wonders why everything seems catastrophic, why she's always holding her breath, waiting for something to change her life.

"Where are you taking me?" Sammy asks.

"Video store."

"Why are we going this way?"

"For a change," she says.

"Are you kidnapping me?"

"What are you talking about?" Elaine asks.

"I don't know," he says.

"Well then, stop it," she says.

They return the movies, and on the way home Elaine swings by the vocational school.

"Have I been here before?" Sammy asks.

"Have you?" Elaine pulls into the empty lot and parks. "I have to check on something, about the house." She plants an explanation in Sammy's brain, something Sammy can repeat if Paul asks what they did. "Stay here," she says, getting out of the car.

"Why?"

"It's really dusty, you won't be able to breathe." She is intentionally scaring him and hating herself for it.

"Hurry," he says.

"I will."

Elaine scurries across the grass to the split sides of the prefab house. She steps in. Her theme has been elaborated upon. Her FUCK THIS now reads FUCK THIS WHOLE FUCKING THING. And someone has woven string, a deep-red yarn, around the nails, connecting the dots. And someone else—she assumes—

has gone at it circling the phrase with black Magic Marker and, in a wobbly hand, offering the evaluation BAD ATTITUDE B-.

There must have been a party last night, a conclave of youth on the loose. Elaine looks for the hammer, the nails. Gone. All gone. She hopes they are being held in Allied hands. She hopes no one called the cops.

"What were you looking for?" Sammy asks when she gets back into the car.

"Details," she says. "Whenever you do something, you have to be sure to get the details right."

Paul. Paul is home alone. He is in front of the TV watching an extra videotape he bought for himself when he was shopping for McKendrick. Amateur porn: *Neighborhood Women*. There is something about the cheesy homemade quality of it that he finds appealing. He thinks of the date, and of Mrs. A. He closes his eyes and thinks of Elaine. He pictures himself lying out on the new deck, drinking, listening to the sound of the neighbor's Weed Whacker. He imagines Elaine giving him a little lap dance where the neighbors can see. He thinks of the lap dance, the deck, the warm air of a June afternoon. It's exciting up to a point, and then it isn't. He thinks of Elaine and wonders what's going on with her—has she done something? He swells with generosity. Goodie. Goodie if she did it, goodie for her if she got herself out of the house and got herself laid. He's engorged with the idea, generous to a point, and then he's wondering who it might be—could it be Henry? In a fit of jealousy, mad at Paul for doinking the date, could Henry have taken a dive with Elaine? Paul tries out a few other men—George, Mrs. Hansen's husband, the contractor—and decides that, yes, it's Henry, that's the one who makes the most sense.

When Paul hears Elaine come in, he turns off the TV, he holds the Sunday paper on his lap.

"What are you doing?"

"Reading," he says.

"Anything good?"

"Not really."

He gazes at her. "That was nice with your parents," he says.

She nods. "Things are getting back on track."

"We should try and enjoy ourselves a little," Paul says. "How about an early movie in Mamaroneck with the boys? Or a walk, we could walk down to the water?"

"It smells," she says. "There was an article about it in the paper: bacterial growth, a terrible smell."

"Remember . . ." he says, thinking back to the night when they first moved here, the night they went to the movies and on the way home stopped down by the water, smoked a joint, and the cop came.

"Yes," she says, knowing what he's thinking.

He stands up. He reaches for her hand. He leads her upstairs.

"The boys were in Florida with your mother," she says.

"It's good to have them home," he says.

"Where's Daniel?"

"Somewhere outside with Willy," he says. "And Sammy?"

"Sitting on the front step," she says.

Paul and Elaine are upstairs fucking. A quickie—the kind of thing they used to enjoy.

Elaine is dry.

"Have you got anything? Any kind of lube?"

"Just you," she says.

"Oh," he says.

He licks her.

She sucks him.

They fuck. Elaine is on top.

"Mom," Sammy yells upstairs. "Mom, the people are here."

"What people?" Paul asks.

"The people," Sammy shouts.

They keep fucking.

"They're here," Sammy says.

"Hurry," Elaine says.

"Help me," Paul says. His hands are on her hips, he's pulling her down, pressing her against him.

"This isn't about me," Elaine says, panting.

"What do you mean?"

"Just come, so we can find out who's here."

"Dad," Sammy whines.

"Coming," Paul bellows.

He comes. Elaine pops up off him and goes to the window. "It's Joan and Ted," she says.

"Did you come?" he asks, pressing against her from behind.

"I don't know."

"You don't know?"

Another car pulls up. "What's going on?" Elaine wants to know.

"How could you not know if you came or not?"

More cars arrive.

"Hurry," Elaine says as they're dressing.

"Surprise!" Joan throws her arms up in the air as Elaine and Paul come out the front door.

"Surprise!" Elaine says, imitating Joan.

"It's a housewarming," Joan says. "I planned it last night. We were just sitting there with nothing to do. The whole gang's coming, isn't that great? Catherine and Hammy are back, and they're desperate to see everyone—they haven't seen a friendly face in a week."

The trunk of the car is open, and Ted is struggling to pull something out. "Joan," he says. "Joan, can you give me a hand?"

"I wasn't sure what you did or didn't have, what might have gotten damaged in the fire, so I brought everything," Joan says.

"The house isn't really ready," Elaine says. "The deck isn't finished."

"You're home, that's what matters," Joan says.

Paul interrupts. "Is Henry coming?" He needs to know. He's been obsessing about Henry, Henry and the date, Henry and Elaine, Henry on top.

"Any minute," Joan says.

The Nielsons' car pulls up. "It's George, one of the little M's, and . . . who's that? That's not Pat," Joan says.

An unidentified woman is at the wheel.

"My cousin Lois," George says, opening the passenger door. "She's visiting from Syracuse." He hands over a pitcher of martinis. "She drove. I didn't want to bruise the gin."

A man Elaine doesn't know asks, "Are we staying in front or going around back?"

"The back is full of rocks," Elaine says.

He plunges the sharp stake of a bamboo torch into the ground.

"Our friends from Pelham, I asked them to join," Joan says, nodding toward the slightly younger couple. "We had plans for tonight," she whispers. "And I just couldn't cancel; I hate it when people cancel."

"Drinks? Who would like a drink?" George holds the pitcher high. "When it's empty, it's yours to keep," George says. "A housewarming gift from Pat and me."

"Actually, we owe you a gift," Elaine says. She's been thinking that they need to get the Nielsons a really big thank-you present. What would do the trick? Something she can order from a catalog; Pat would appreciate that.

George shrugs. "Whatever feels right."

"Where's Pat?" Joan asks. "We can't have a party without Pat."

"You know how women are," George says, leaving the line dangling.

Elaine wonders, Did Pat tell George? Does he know more than he's letting on?

"Henry's here," Joan says. "Now, where's Paul?"

Paul hates Henry, he hates Elaine, he hates everybody. He meets Henry down by the curb and hands him a drink.

"How was rock climbing?" Elaine asks.

Henry smiles. "It was fantastic."

When the Montgomerys arrive, they all stop talking, they stare without meaning to.

"We're so glad you're here. How are you?" Joan asks before the Montgomerys are even out of the car.

Catherine and Hammy get out; their eleven-year-old daughter climbs out after them, she stares at the ground. Catherine and Hammy smile and wave, their hands traveling back and forth through the air, as if they're washing windows. "How are all of you?" they ask.

"Would you like a drink?" Paul gestures with the pitcher.

"Fill 'er up," Hammy says, closing the car door.

"We're so sorry about canceling last night," Catherine says.

"It's been a hell of a week," Hammy says.

"We missed you all so much," Catherine says. "We couldn't wait to get home."

"Back where we belong," Hammy says.

They've said the right thing; they've said nothing at all.

"How are you really?" Elaine asks again, privately, a few minutes later.

"How could I be?" Catherine says.

"You must be so relieved to have it over with," Joan butts in.

"It isn't over, it's just begun," Catherine says, and stops herself. She shouldn't say more, more would be too much. She sips her drink. "It's a mean martini."

"It's the onions," George says.

"Isn't it surprising none of us have had cancer yet?" Joan says, and no one knows what she's talking about.

Mrs. Hansen and her husband cross the street. "Fruit in vodka," Mrs. Hansen says, handing Elaine a large, foil-covered bowl. "My old standby. I've been soaking it all night."

Mrs. Hansen's husband, the hubcap, circulates through the crowd, presenting himself to everyone as "The Invisible Mister."

Liz, Jennifer, and a friend of Jennifer's cut through the yard. "We walked," Liz says. "It's further than you'd think."

"I haven't walked in years," Joan says.

Jennifer introduces her friend, Robert, a straitlaced kid except for a set of Frankenstein-like bumps or welts across his forehead. She leans toward Paul. "See the ridges above his eyes? He has barbells under his skin. Subcutaneous decorative jewelry—implants. Isn't it great? Way more subtle than piercing. You sort of see it and you sort of don't."

Paul stares.

"It's going to be wonderful," Catherine says, coming around the corner of the house. "French doors and a deck, who could ask for more?"

"Lots of people," Ted says.

They are suspended in a strangely golden hour, that odd expanse of time at the beginning of the summer when afternoons are elongated, holding off the dimming of the day.

Sammy and the Montgomery daughter playing with walkie-talkies. Elaine overhears Sammy ask, "What are you wearing?"

"A tiara," the girl says.

"And what's under it?" Sammy asks, not knowing what a tiara is.

"Hair," the girl says.

Daniel and Willy have George's little M by her wrists and ankles. They swing her through the air—she squeals. One of her shoes falls off.

"Are you hurting her?" Paul asks.

"Willy, it's time to put her down and say good-bye. Time for you to go home," Elaine says.

Ted gets into his car and toots the horn to get everyone's attention. The friends gather round. Joan and Ted are grinning, so proud of themselves, clever—good at the game.

"We have a little something for you," Joan says to Elaine and Paul. "From all of us."

Ted pops the trunk.

"The pièce de résistance," Joan says.

"Could someone give me a hand?" Ted asks.

George steps in, and he and Ted pull a big black orb from the trunk.

Elaine sees something black and round and thinks of the wrecking ball, the hard knocking against the house.

"A Weber kettle," George announces, in case anyone doesn't know.

"Top of the line," Ted says. "We wanted you to have the real thing."

"Let's get some legs on it," Ted says, reaching into the trunk for the missing parts.

"Welcome home."

"To new beginnings," Catherine puts in, and they tap their glasses together; the tinkling clink of good glass for a moment sounds like the music of a wind chime.

"It could have happened to any one of us," Ted says. "And that's the truth."

Elaine and Paul look at each other for clues. Elaine finally sputters, "We're overwhelmed. Thank you, thank you so much."

The men set up the grill, filling the kettle with coals. Henry hands Paul a can of lighter fluid with a red ribbon on it. "Fire it up," he says.

Paul remembers squirting the fluid against the house, streaks of it splashing the back wall and evaporating. He remembers the excitement, the anxiety. He remembers coming home, after the fire, late at night in the dark, finding the house still standing. "My aim isn't always true," Paul says.

"It all depends on how full your container is and how hard you squeeze," George says.

"Go on," Ted says. "Hop on the horse."

And with the other men standing by, Paul squirts the stuff on the briquettes.

Henry strikes a match, a quick, fiery burst. He throws it in, and a flash of flame rises from the kettle.

"Bravo!" Joan says.

Showing off, Ted squirts a little more stuff onto the fire, and the flames shoot higher.

"Don't get reckless," Joan says. "That's how accidents happen. That's how this whole thing started."

The men hover around the grill, waiting for the coals to turn. The women press hamburger meat into patties.

George goes into the house to make more martinis; Elaine follows him in. She's come for something, she had a reason, she just can't remember what. It's dark. She turns on a few lights.

"Is Pat all right?" she asks.

"Fine," George says, stirring the pitcher. He pours himself

a drink. He downs it and pours another. "She's fine." He adds a splash of vermouth to the pitcher. "That's the benefit of being the bartender," he says. "You get to sample the elixir. Where did Elvis die? All day I've been wondering, did he die on the throne?"

"Is this a joke?" Elaine asks.

"No," George says. "I'm just trying to remember if he died on the toilet."

Mrs. Hansen raps on the window. "Music," she shouts. "We need some music if we're going to dance." She's wearing a dandelion chain like a crown on her head—the Montgomery daughter made it for her.

George glances around the room for the stereo, for something to turn on.

"All that's here is TV," Elaine says.

They pull the TV stand close to the window, put it to a music station, and turn up the volume.

Outside, images flicker across the bushes.

"It's like we're in a movie," someone says.

"Martinis, get your martinis here," George calls as they return to the crowd. He taps his glass against the pitcher, ringing it like the ice-cream man.

The man from Pelham lights the bamboo torches, and the scene starts to look like a jungle party, a tribal gathering. The yard throbs with the smell of citronella, the scent of meat cooking taints the air. Cars drive by, slowing as they pass.

"This is perfect," Jennifer's friend tells Paul. "You're inverting the phenomenon of the backyard, playing the interiority of the back against the exteriority of the front—substituting private space for public, not worrying who might see, what they'll think. It's a radical gesture."

"Whatever you do, don't marry him," Mrs. Hansen whispers to Jennifer. "He'll reduce you to rubble."

"What happens next?" Elaine asks Catherine.

"You don't want to know," Catherine says.

Elaine squeezes Catherine's arm—giving her the go-ahead to continue. Liz and Joan stand by ready, waiting to hear.

"The only way they'll treat him is if they treat the whole family. We'd have to move up there and go into residential family therapy."

"You'd move?" Joan asks, missing the point.

"And if you don't agree?" Elaine asks.

"The state may try and charge him as an adult."

"They couldn't really do that, could they?" Joan says. "It seems kind of extreme, doesn't it?"

"He ate somebody's fingers," someone says.

"There but for the grace of God go I," George says, flipping hamburgers. The men have been listening in.

Hammy's lip trembles.

The light fades, big birds gather on the electric lines. They call to each other.

"Listen to the birds," Elaine says. And they all do.

"It's a wonderful life," Mrs. Hansen says.

"Who's to judge?" Mrs. Hansen's hubcap says, raising his glass. "We all have so many damned opinions, so much we think we know. We don't know anything."

They are all so glad to be back together again. They feel the warmth, the heat, the flicker of the flames. None are what they seem, none are what you think, none are what you'd want them to be. They all are both more and less—deeply human.

"I'm so happy to be here," Catherine says; then she begins to cry and runs into the house.

"It's been a week," Paul whispers to Elaine, who hasn't for a minute forgotten. "Almost this time of night. I squirted the stuff and lit the flame, I fanned the fire and you kicked the grill," Paul says.

"We started the fire that burst the bubble that burned the house and so on and so forth," Elaine finishes the tune for him.

"Do they know what happened?" Paul asks.

"I don't think so," Elaine murmurs.

"Are you embarrassed about the grill?"

"A little. Aren't you?"

"Dinner is served," George says, taking the burgers off the fire.

The children come out from around back covered in dirt. They've invented a game called Making Clouds that involves spinning in circles and kicking up loose soil—they're filthy.

"What were you thinking?" the parents ask, smacking at their children, beating the dirt off their clothing. The children, dizzy with delight, woozy from spinning, laugh hysterically and fall down on the grass.

Catherine is back. She's washed her face, powdered her nose, and taken some sort of little pill that the doctor ordered.

"Whatever does the trick," Mrs. Hansen says, laying a line of mustard down her dog.

"Delicious," Joan pronounces, and they all agree. "I'm so glad I had the idea."

It is dark now. The light of the fire, the glow of the torches, plays off their faces, staining them an orangey yellow. The adults have Mrs. Hansen's famous fruit in vodka, and the children make themselves silly and sick on s'mores—sandwiches of chocolate, toasted marshmallows, and graham crackers. "Excrete," Daniel says, mushing everything together, repeating his theme for the day. White sticky stuff oozes over his fingers.

"How many have you had?" Elaine asks, wondering how he'll sleep.

"Didn't count," he says.

"Were the burgers cooked enough?" Liz asks. "I ate mine, but I thought it was raw in the middle."

"Would anyone like an after-dinner drink?" Paul asks. "What goes good with hamburger?"

"Brandy," George says.

They sit on the grass, drinking, having a look at the stars. "Isn't it nice to sit outside?" Ted says. "We're never just outside for no reason."

"Especially in the dark," Joan says. "I hate being in the dark."

There is the wash of headlights across the party, a car pulls into the driveway, the door slams.

"That's Pat," George says.

Crossing the grass, she calls ahead, "I'm off schedule."

"We're finished," Elaine calls back.

"You missed dinner," Joan says.

"Would you like a drink?" George asks his wife. "I just made a fresh pitcher."

Elaine goes into the kitchen to get Pat a glass; Pat follows her. The cabinet is empty, the glasses are all dirty, the only thing on the shelf is a Curious George mug. "I have very little to offer you," Elaine says.

"I'm sorry I left so abruptly yesterday." Pat presses against her. "I'm a little in love with you."

Elaine washes a dirty glass. "Wine? Martini? Seltzer?"

"What are we going to do?" Pat asks.

Elaine slides away from her. "Paul and I are fixing the house, we're making everything good again. There's nothing else to do," Elaine says, handing Pat the empty glass.

In the yard, there is the sound of crickets and the whoosh of someone's sprinkler kicking on. "He's going to have the best grass," Paul says.

"There's something cursed about that house. No one stays," Liz says. "It's always turning over."

"Who lives there now?" Joan asks.

"Someone with a baby," Elaine says, sitting down again. "That's all we know. We see them wheeling him around sometimes."

"There's the Big Dipper," George says, pointing up. And

they watch the sky. It is bigger than they are, and it is calming, and they are quiet.

"There goes the space shuttle," Daniel says as a plane passes.

"Really?" Sammy asks.

"Not really," Liz says. "It's a plane out of La Guardia, a night flight to Europe filled with bankers, movie stars, and runaways."

They all take a few deep breaths. They drain their glasses, stretch out their arms and legs, and say, "This is so relaxing, I am so relaxed. For the first time in a long time I feel as though I don't have a care in the world."

Mrs. Hansen's hubcap pulls out a pack of sparklers and gives one to each person.

"To summer," they say, lighting up, tapping the sparklers against each other, toasting. The sparks are bright white, phosphorescent, clean and clear. They are a sweet explosion firing the night, evaporating in the air. "To all things bright and beautiful."

"Touché," Ted says, sword fighting with Paul.

And then they have had enough.

"Big day tomorrow," George says, bringing things to a close. "Back to work, back to school. I almost forgot—your things are in my car." He goes down to the car and returns with a box of clothes. "Back to you," he says.

Under the torchlight Elaine can see that they are perfectly pressed. "Thank you," she says to Pat. "For everything, always."

"Damn knees," Ted says, trying to get up off the grass.

"Call you tomorrow," Liz says, walking off with Jennifer and Robert.

In the end, the goal is to be left with something: a spouse, children, even parents if you can manage it. The goal is not to be left alone, not to be left old, poor, and on the street. Everyone thinks it could happen to them, everyone worries that they might drift so far from reality as not to be welcomed back— think of bag ladies, men living on steam grates, the Montgomery boy. Everyone secretly knows that it's something that could happen at any moment—an error or an accident.

Paul and Elaine are left alone with the grill.

"What now?" Elaine asks.

Paul looks at Elaine.

"Any ideas?"

They could do it again. It would be harder to explain a second time around. They would have to do a better job, they would have to make it spectacular and inescapable, they would have to be committed.

"Put the lid on it," Paul says. "It'll burn itself out."

"And the torches?"

"They'll be out by morning," Paul says.

The boys appear out of the darkness, and all four of them— Paul, Elaine, Sammy, and Daniel—go on a hunt, scouring the field of debris, gathering glasses and plates, knives and forks, ketchup, mustard. They carry things into the house, they go from the dark into the light. Everything is fiercely illuminated—they struggle to adjust.

Sammy covers his eyes.

"The mayonnaise is still out there somewhere," Paul says, sending Daniel on a reconnaissance mission, back into the night.

"It turned out okay, didn't it?" Elaine says to Paul as she's loading the dishwasher. "We have such nice friends. I don't think they want to hurt us," Elaine says—and it comes out sounding strange.

"Why hurt us?" Paul wonders.

"Because that's what people do, they constantly try to knock each other down and mow each other over." She adds the soap.

Daniel returns with the jar of mayonnaise, blades of grass

stuck to the rim. "The top is missing in action," he reports, his mouth rimmed with marshmallow glue and graham-cracker crumbs.

"Thanks," Paul says, slipping the mayo into the refrigerator topless.

"Nine o'clock, baths and bed," Elaine announces to the boys. She's determined to have tomorrow go right. She's taken a lesson from Pat: plan ahead. "Tick-tock, I bought you each an alarm clock." She gives them to the children like gifts. "All set, ready to ring. Breakfast in the kitchen at seven, attendance will be taken."

Later, as she's tucking Sammy in, his skin still warm from the tub, his hair still damp, his smell still the milky sweet of a child, she lets her head dip into his neck, she breathes deeply. "Good night," she whispers in his ear. "Sleep tight, pray that nothing knocks or bites."

ELEVEN

ELAINE IS MAKING PANCAKES.

Paul comes into the kitchen showered, shaved, ready to work. "No fat," he says.

"No lumps," she says, stirring the batter.

There is a hiss as she sprays the frying pan. "No stick," she says. Elaine pours batter into the pan. It spreads into small circles.

"Don't burn the blueberries," he says.

"Why would I?"

She has set the table. She has poured glasses of orange juice and milk. She has made a pot of coffee using the grind that her mother left her. She is determined to make things good again.

"Coffee?" She has an apron around her waist, her hair in a bun. She is their Aunt Jemima, their Mrs. Butterworth—she is cooking.

Elaine has had a revelation: She doesn't have to wait for something to happen; she can make something happen. She has some control. If she doesn't like the way things are, she can change them. That's why she's making breakfast. Pop-Tarts are no longer an option. She's hoping that the boys haven't yet unlearned what they learned last week. She's hoping that she can take advantage of the habits of other people's houses. She's playing a home version of the When in Rome Game. She has taken a lesson from Pat: act normal.

"Are they up?"

"I hear water running," Paul says.

Sweat breaks out above Elaine's lip. She feels thin, wobbly, dehydrated.

"Are you all right?" he asks.

She was sick in the night. For two hours, she sat in the bathroom, wondering which end would erupt first, hoping not both at the same time. Paul was good; he held her forehead, he brought her a cold washcloth and a drink of water. "What do you need?" he asked. "What can I do?"

"I felt poisoned," Elaine tells him this morning. "I think it was the hamburger."

"Who brought the hamburger?"

"Joan," she says. Elaine can't decide whether or not to mention it to Joan when she calls to thank her for the grill. Would it be impolite to ask, Was anyone in your house sick last night?

"Don't tell her," Paul says, reading Elaine's mind. "You're the only one who got sick; the rest of us are fine. I doubt she was trying to kill you."

Elaine shakes her head. The idea that Joan was trying to kill her had never occurred to her.

Paul comes to the stove, he stands over her, watching her cook. "Don't let the fruit get gooey."

She slaps the spatula into his hand and walks away. "Flip 'em when the bubbles pop," she says, trying to maintain the momentum, the good cheer of a Monday morning. She sits at the kitchen table and puts her head between her legs.

She sees Sammy's shoes first—red sneakers. "Good morning," she says. "Did you sleep well?"

"The alarm scared me," Sammy whines. "Why can't you wake me up?"

"It's your job to wake yourself up, you're a big boy now," Elaine says, talking into her knees.

"Two pancakes or three?" Paul asks him.

"Three," Sammy says.

"Why are you bent over?" Daniel quizzes as he walks in— black Nikes in the lead.

"Just taking a moment," Elaine says, lifting her head.

Paul is at the stove. He has tucked a dish towel under his chin in an effort to keep himself clean. He is serving the children first and then himself. "Can I get you anything?" he asks Elaine. "A pancake? Some toast?"

"You're burning the pan," Elaine says, seeing smoke rise from the stove. "Turn the fire down."

"Is there any caviar?" Daniel asks. "Caviar is good on pancakes, right? Isn't that how it's served, on little pancakes?"

"Blinis," Paul says. "The little pancakes are called blinis."

"It's not a breakfast food," Elaine says. "You should never ask for caviar—it's rude. Always wait until it's offered, and then just take a little bit. It's not something to be piggish about. It's a delicacy."

"I thought fish was good for you—brain food. Willy's sister eats a can of tuna every morning, and she gets straight A's." Daniel rolls up a pancake like a tortilla and stuffs it into his mouth.

"Use a fork," Elaine says.

"Pass the syrup," Paul says. They eat as though they have always eaten breakfast at the table together, as though it's nothing out of the ordinary. There is no rebellion, no threat of a coup or a sick-out; no one is demanding Pop-Tarts in bed.

"It's so bright in here I almost need sunglasses," Daniel says.

"It's shiny," Sammy says, sweeping a pancake through a slick of syrup.

"It's a bright and shiny day," Elaine says. "A perfect day, inside and out."

The workers arrive. They strap on their tool belts at the curb and let their hammers dangle. They come carrying cups of coffee and bags from Dunkin' Donuts. Elaine hears them outside talking about lumber, talking about what they did on Saturday night—bowling, movies, dinner at a sister's house, kids. She likes the sound of their voices, she likes listening in.

"Are we going to live here forever?" Sammy asks.

No one knows what to say—what's forever?

"We're not planning on going anywhere," Elaine says.

"Why?" Paul asks.

"Nate's moving."

"Really?" Paul says. Where is Mrs. Apple going? Will he go with her? And why is he the last to find out? "Where?" Paul asks.

"Somewhere," Sammy says.

"Exactly where is somewhere?" Paul leans in; he wants to shake Sammy until the words fall out of his mouth, exact quotes. "How do you know that Nate is moving?" he asks. His intensity is a giveaway.

Sammy shrugs. "I made it up," he confesses.

"You made it up? Why? Why would you do that?"

Sammy shrugs again. Dipping his finger in syrup, he licks it.

Elaine watches this display, she watches Paul. "Too bad," she says.

The phone rings. Elaine picks up.

"Good morning, Elaine, it's Bud Johnson calling from woodshop. I just wanted to see how you're doing."

"Can I call you back in about twenty minutes?" Elaine asks.

She is annoyed. She's annoyed with Paul and Sammy and whatever this weird game is about Nate's family. She's annoyed with Bud—where was he on Saturday when she needed him? To hell with all of you is what she feels like saying.

"Who was that?" Paul quizzes.

"What do you care who?"

"Why don't you want to tell me? Why don't you just say who it was—is it a secret?"

"No, Paul, it's not a secret. Do you have a secret?" She waits. "Am I allowed a life of my own? You certainly have one. I don't quiz you about who you talk to at the office, do I? Consider this house my office," she says.

"So that was a work-related call?"

Elaine nods.

"Contractor?"

"Yes," she says.

"I don't think so," he says. "The contractor is right outside. I saw him go by a minute ago."

Elaine doesn't respond.

"Architect?"

Sammy spills his milk; a white flood spreads across the table, soaking the place mats, running over the edge onto the floor. "Sorry," he says.

Paul and Elaine have done it again. They have done exactly what they don't want to do, reverted to their standard behavior—acting like jerks. The kid had to spill his milk to create a distraction.

"Don't worry," Elaine tells Sammy. "It's not your fault. It was a bad glass."

"Bad glass," Paul says, mocking her.

"Is everyone finished?" Elaine asks. "Are we all done?"

"Just tell me who that was," Paul says.

"No," she says, clearing the table.

"I can't believe you're being like this—it's so unlike you."

"Thank God I'm being unlike myself," she says. "There's hope yet." She turns her back to him and does the dishes.

"Okay, I'm an ass," Paul says on his way out. "That's the truth. The pancakes were great, Elaine. Really good." He pulls the dish towel out from under his chin. "Come on, guys," he says to the boys. "I'll drop you on my way. Do you have your stuff?" The boys cram things into their knapsacks. "Wasn't that a good breakfast? Didn't Mommy do a good job?"

"Fuck off," Elaine hisses.

Sammy burps.

Kissing the children good-bye, sending them out into the world with a peck and a pat, Elaine is learning how it's done. "Good-bye," she says, "good-bye, good-bye," closing the door behind them, quickly.

"Feel better," Paul says through the glass. "I'll call you later."

Elaine is fighting a foul mood. Despite her morning flurry of activity, her insight, her determination to stay upbeat and positive, the smallest things bring her down. As soon as they are gone, she steps outside. She has taught herself a new trick: Whenever she starts to sink, to get caught in a whirl, she must do something different, anything, it doesn't matter what, as long as it's active. She steps out of the house; the world opens in front of her. She stands on the kitchen steps, breathing deeply. Elaine wants so badly for everything to be good that she doesn't care how awful she really feels.

The workman with the crushed fingers waves when he sees her. His fingers, taped together with white adhesive, cut through the air, like a flag of surrender. "You were right," he says. "They were broken. Shows you what a hammer can do when you really swing it."

Inside, the phone rings.

"Your mother told me to call," her father says.

"Is Mom all right?" Her father rarely calls unless there's a problem.

"She told me to tell you for myself how nice it was to see you and what beautiful boys you have."

"Where is she?" Elaine can't help but think something must be wrong.

"Gallivanting," her father says.

"Tell her to call me when she comes in," Elaine says.

"I don't have to tell her, she'll do it automatically. Your mother is entirely predictable and I never can tell what she's going to do next, that's what keeps her beautiful. She's always a surprise."

"Okay, Dad," Elaine says, having heard enough. "I'll talk to you later."

While she's got the phone in her hand, she calls Joan to thank her. For what—food poisoning? "It was so nice of you," Elaine says. "Such a warmhearted gesture."

"It was a good idea, I'm glad I thought of it," Joan says.

Elaine's Call Waiting beeps. "That's my other line—gotta go."

It's Bud Johnson again. "I had a break between classes. I thought I'd try once more. Is this a good time?"

"It's fine," Elaine says.

"I went over your tests." He speaks with the seriousness of a specialist.

She holds her breath waiting for the diagnosis, waiting to hear that she has cancer or some other kind of career-counseling failure.

"Well," he says, hedging, "I think the results explain why you're so unhappy in the house all day, all alone."

"Yes," Elaine says, still waiting.

"You're a people person," he says.

She's still waiting, thinking there's more.

"People make you happy. You feel better when you're with people. Yes?" Bud says.

"Yes," Elaine repeats, giving Bud Johnson's word enormous weight. "That makes sense." She doesn't like to be left alone. When Paul and the boys leave in the morning, she feels as though she's under house arrest, they are free to go and she has detention. "I like people."

"I thought so," he says proudly. "Should we meet again?" he asks. "Should we put our heads together and talk about where to go from here?"

"Sure," she says. "Why not?" She won't say no to anything.

"How about Wednesday afternoon?"

Elaine hangs up. She has to step outside again. Once more, she is in a whirl, a dangerous spin. With the regularity of a cuckoo clock, she steps out onto the kitchen steps. Every hour there is more light, things glow as though the intensity of the day is being turned up; the grass is fluorescent green, what's left of the geraniums are a vibrant red, and the forsythia along the driveway is spilling Technicolor yellow across the gravel. Elaine thinks she smells honeysuckle. She remembers, as a child, plucking the flowers and sucking syrup.

It is getting hot out. Hot and humid. The men in the backyard are hammering, hard and fast, working to get as much done as they can before it gets too hot, before something happens. There is the threat of a storm later. She knows. She read it in the paper.

Elaine wanders from the driveway to the curb. She looks down the sidewalk—the concrete footpath cuts through the landscape, stretching out in front of her for miles.

"Don't go anywhere," Mrs. Hansen calls from across the street. "I'm on my way over."

*　　*　　*

Self-improvement. A renovation of the soul. Paul is on his way to work. He wants to be a better person. He wants not to run, not to cave in under pressure, not to sweat the small stuff; he wants to live without fear, not in a constant state of inexplicable panic. Perspective and priority, efficiency and competency. He is always tripping over his own feet. He is his own worst enemy. He wants to do better.

And he wants not to hate Elaine.

Why is he such an asshole? What does he get out of it? Is there pleasure in pulling the rug out from under? Does it make him look bigger, better? What does it mean to cripple yourself, your wife, and your children with bitterness, with spite, with envy, with the overwhelming energy of your anxiety? Does he want them to fail? Will that make him feel good? Will it make him feel safer if they never pass him, if they're never more than he is? Isn't the goal to raise children that have more and do more than you? Why not inspire them, elevate them, encourage them? It has to be easier.

Sammy spilled his milk—it was Paul's fault. Paul was causing trouble. Everything is Paul's fault. He takes a breath. He coaxes and coaches himself. It's fine, he tells himself, it's better than you think. The house is getting fixed, the weekend was nice, the family is back together. And despite how strange things have been, Elaine appears to feel somewhat warmly toward him. She appears to have hope. They are gathering a second wind, a new lease on life.

He continues talking to himself. It's Monday morning, you're on the train, on the way to work. You ate pancakes for breakfast, you walked your boys to school, you had a good time, you played a game they invented—You Call It.

They started off in a line arranged by height, shortest to tallest, with Sammy in the lead.

"Age," Daniel called out. "Oldest first," and they switched places, filing themselves accordingly.

"Funniest walk," Sammy yelled, and they did their odd walks, waddling down the sidewalk like a family of palsied ducks.

"IQ," Daniel called, and they stumbled out of order, weaving stupidly, crashing into each other, all of it part of the joke. Sammy laughed wildly.

"Fattest to thinnest," Daniel called, and Paul took the lead.

"Bluest eyes," Paul said, and Sammy stepped in front.

Father and sons, brothers, boys, men.

"Don't play without me," Sammy said when they dropped him at school.

"Wouldn't think of it," Paul said.

Daniel and Paul stood at the bottom of the school steps, watching Sammy go in, and then they walked on. There were things Paul wanted to ask Daniel: Do you really think Meaders is something special? Does Willy strike you as a little weird? How serious is the Scouting thing? And what's the deal with you and the fat girls? A thousand things he wanted to know, but he asked nothing, opting to savor the moment, the relative calm.

On the train, the palm kisser, Mr. Mental Candy, comes up from behind and sits down next to Paul.

"Did you eat your candy?"

"Most of it."

"Favorite color?"

"Couldn't really tell the difference," Paul says.

"Try two of something, that'll show you. Want some more?"

Paul puts out his hand. "Is it addictive?"

"Only if you like the way it makes you feel," the palm kisser says, filling both of Paul's hands.

"What's that mean?"

"You should come visit me sometime. Take a dip in my pool."

"Out in the country?" Paul asks, sliding the pills into his pocket.

"Or at the office. I'm in the water a lot. It helps me think. I tread water while I make decisions. I like to stay fluid, liquid, calm. I have a lap pool in my office—we're on the first floor."

"Any thoughts on desk chairs?" Paul asks, seeing that the guy obviously has a certain flair for things.

"Some are better than others," the man says.

"What do you sit on?"

"A cushion," the man says.

Paul nods. Why did he ask?

The train pulls into the 125th Street station.

"We're almost there," Paul says.

"You are your own beginning. Every day, every hour, every minute, you start again. There is no point wishing you were someone else, you are who you are—start there," the palm kisser offers.

"I was just thinking the same thing," Paul says.

The palm kisser looks at him, checking to see if Paul is teasing.

"Seriously," Paul says. "Something right along that line—odd, isn't it?"

"Or not," the palm kisser says.

The train pulls in. "Grand Central Station, New York City," the conductor announces.

The palm kisser bends. Paul thinks he's going to kiss Paul's hand again, maybe put his head in Paul's lap. Paul pulls away, abruptly. The palm kisser bends and picks a quarter off the floor. "Accept the things you find," he says.

Paul hurries off the train.

Monolithic skyscrapers push out of the ground, steely and

strong. Shafts of light cut between the buildings, punctuating the boulevard. Park Avenue is like a Grand Canal filled with shining black town cars—gondolas of good fortune. Every morning the streets are filled with Pauls—scrubbed and polished men in thousand-dollar suits thinking they are something. One hundred thousand offices, a million windowless cubicles, creativity and commerce. The metropolis hums—sings of the spirit, of the romance of trade, of the glory of the great game— things bought and sold. Paul is flooded with the anticipation of doing a good day's work.

He takes off his jacket, hangs it over his shoulder, using his finger as the hook, and strides up Park Avenue. He makes a right onto Fiftieth Street.

She is there, waiting outside the building. He doesn't notice until it is too late—he swerves, he goes out wide on the sidewalk. He walks past the entrance, pretending he doesn't see her. He walks around the block. On Friday, he dismissed her. He phoned her and told her it had to stop.

"Why are you calling me?" she said. "Are you afraid to see me?"

"No," he lied. "I'm calling to tell you that I can't see you, I can't talk to you, I can't do this anymore. It's too much."

"What makes you think you can just call me up and say something like that, that you can dictate the way things are going to be?"

"I'm not dictating."

"What about me? Don't I have a say in this?"

He didn't say anything.

"You don't boss me," she said. "I do what I want—that's who I am."

"This is not a negotiation," Paul said. "I have to go now." He hung up, drenched in sweat.

Paul comes around the corner again, sticking close to the edge of the building, hoping all she wants to do is scare him, hoping she'll be gone when he gets to the door.

She's still there. Waiting. She calls out, "Forgot where you work? Thought I'd just disappear?"

"It's Monday morning," he says, as though that gives him some immunity. "You're not supposed to be here," he clarifies.

"Free country," she says.

"Henry's very upset," Paul says. "You're not being nice to him. You should call him."

"He's not the one telling me to fuck off," she says loudly.

Paul tries to slip past her and into the revolving door. She blocks his way.

"Stop it," he says. "I have to go to work. You're harassing me."

"No," she shouts, snapping like a thing suddenly sprung. "You're harassing me." She speaks sharply enough that heads turn.

"Leave the girl alone," someone says.

Cold panic, Paul sees the way things can get turned around.

"I'm going to work," he hisses.

She presses into the revolving door ahead of him, turning to face him, talking through the glass. He goes around twice, hoping she'll finish quickly, hoping to lose her along the way.

"What makes you think you can dictate the way things are going to be?" she says, repeating her Friday line.

"I'm not dictating," he says, his breath fogging the glass. "I'm simply telling you that I can't see you anymore."

"You don't make the rules," she says.

"Leave me alone," he whispers as he slips out of the revolving door and into the marble lobby. "Go away."

She follows him. He ignores her. He makes himself steely. He gets into a crowded elevator. She crams in after him. This is exactly why it has to stop. She has no control, no reason, no logic. She rides up. Paul's tattoo is suddenly itching, burning as though it recognizes danger. He worries what she'll do when they get to his floor. Will she get off when he does? Will she follow him, biting at his heels? Will someone have to call security? Will he have to have her removed like a malignancy? Will she ruin everything?

At the forty-fourth floor the doors open. Paul gets off. She stays on.

"See you later," she says as the elevator doors close.

"Would you like a muffin?" his secretary asks.

Paul stares. He has no idea what she's talking about.

"A breakfast muffin? Corn, blueberry, bran?"

He shakes his head no.

"A doughnut then?"

"I had pancakes," he says, and goes into his office.

He needs a moment to gather himself. He calls Mrs. Apple. He dials and hangs up. He can't talk to her; he knows he will blurt—Why are you moving? He will accuse—Why am I the last to find out? He will defend—I'm just wondering about my time, trying to plan my days.

How can he ask without seeming to have formed an attachment, without seeming to cling, which is the one thing that isn't allowed? No expectations. No attachments.

Paul looks out his window. Across the street the windows are being washed, an urban ballet, men on a rig, descending— harnesses, ropes, safety belts.

His secretary buzzes. "You've been summoned," she says. "Down the hall."

"Pardon?"

"Mr. Warburton has asked to see you."

Do they fire people on Monday mornings? He thinks of

the palm kisser's advice: begin again. He stands up, dips his hand into his pocket, and pulls out a fistful of pills. With no idea of which is for what, he takes three—yellow, red, blue—figuring he's covering all the bases, primary colors.

The big guy is behind his desk, jacket off, sleeves rolled up, his tie thrown over his shoulder. He's pushing paint around on a glossy white piece of fingerpaint paper. He raises his hands, flashing his palms at Paul. Dipped in red, the lines of his palms are thrown into relief—heart, health, long life. "The sensation is incredible," Warburton says, squirting paint through his fingers. "This is what work should be about, getting your hands dirty. I'm doing the quarterly report." Using his index finger, he cuts an arrow through the red. "Things are going up," he says.

"Looks good," Paul says.

"It's so much fun," Warburton says, grinning, and then he gets serious. He wipes his hands on a paper towel. "Have you given any thought to our discussion last week?"

Paul raises his eyebrows. He doesn't want to give anything away, doesn't want to assume, presume, or be disappointed. "Which discussion?"

"The empty office," Warburton says.

Paul nods. "I'm looking into desk chairs. I'm thinking a cushion might be just the thing."

Warburton gives him the nod. "Will a cushion be high enough?"

"I may need a pile."

"Whatever it takes," Warburton says, and then he's back to painting. "Whenever you're ready it's yours. And by the end of the week I'd like to have your thoughts on fat. How do you make people think fat is good?" He stops. He meets Paul eye to eye. "Have you heard the stories about fat substitutes and anal leakage? Are they true? I want you to investigate, personally."

Paul sits at his desk in an anxious stupor. He conjures the sensation of good work, productivity, and pride, the dream of the office. Images move through his mind, flashbacks, juxtapositions: the boy with the barbells in his brows, the date, the palm kisser—"Every minute is a new beginning." Paul looks at his watch; several new beginnings tick by. He takes out his paper and paints. He dips in.

A package arrives; his secretary buzzes. "B and B Office Supply. Shall I sign for it?"

Paul steps out of his office. "Don't sign anything. Don't open anything. Send it back. I didn't order anything." He thinks of ticking packages, Unabombers, mercenaries, girls gone mad, men at work with blown-off fingers, with stumps and stubs. "It's not worth the risk."

"You asked for it," the messenger says, trying to hand the package to Paul.

Paul refuses, he hides his hands behind his back. "I did not," Paul insists. As he's insisting, he remembers that he did order something last Friday, a portfolio for his watercolors. He remembers them saying they'd send it on Monday, but he can't say that now, he can't undo what's already being done; it's gone too far. He remains indignant. "This is a scam."

"Whatever," the messenger says. "I'll take it back. No skin off my dick."

"That's right. You'll take it back," Paul says, storming back into his office.

He sits at his desk. He cannot call Mrs. Apple, he cannot call Henry. He cannot go out for lunch; he is afraid she is out there, still waiting.

"I'm going to grab a sandwich," his secretary says. "Can I bring you anything?"

"Some soup would be good," Paul says. "Some crackers and a bottle of water."

"The prison diet. How about a bowl of gruel?" she teases.

He gives her a twenty. "My treat," he says.

Later, when the call comes, he will think it is the date, he will think it is a game she's playing—impersonating the school secretary.

"Okay, very funny," he'll say. "I'm hanging up now. Don't call back again. This is a place of business. This is not a joke."

And the phone will ring again immediately.

"This is an emergency, Mr. Weiss. I'm calling about your son Samuel."

"Enough is enough. Not funny."

"Mr. Weiss, there is a situation here at the school. The principal is on the phone with your wife now; the police have been called."

"What?" Paul will say, sobering.

"This is an emergency, Mr. Weiss. You are needed here at the school. We hope to have the situation under control shortly, but it would help to have both of you here."

"It's Monday afternoon, I'm in the city, at work. It'll take forty-five minutes, minimum."

"Mr. Weiss, never in my thirty years as school secretary have I had to make a call like this, and never in my imagination, if I had to make such a call, would it have gone this way. I'm telling you something is wrong. Get in a cab!" she says, and hangs up.

Paul calls Elaine—the line is busy.

He washes out his paintbrush, puts on his jacket, and dials again. The machine picks up; he hears the sound of his own voice. Everything has fallen out of order. "Are you in there? Elaine? Pick up," he says. "Pick up, pick up," he says, his voice increasingly panicked. "They called from Sammy's school. Did they call you, too? Elaine? Where are you? I'm getting in a cab. I'm on my way. I'll meet you there."

In the elevator, going down, he worries that she is still out there, waiting. The coast is clear; he is out the door and into a cab. He is on his way as fast as he can, his chest squeezing, chemicals coursing through.

"Hurry," Paul tells the driver.

It is not an accident. If there had been an accident, they would have said so. If Sammy had had an asthma attack, they would have told him. Accidents and asthma don't require the police. The school secretary was so strange, so cryptic and insistent. It makes no sense. It must be something Sammy said or did. He must have insulted a teacher, stolen something, or pulled a fire alarm.

Suddenly, it occurs to Paul that it's not Sammy at all; it's Elaine and Paul. It's a setup. A sting. The police have been called—"it would help to have both of you here," the secretary said.

Show-and-tell. Smokey Bear. Fire prevention. The fire department must have paid a visit to the school. They must have given a lecture on not playing with matches. And Sammy must have spilled the beans. He must have told them the story about his mother sitting in the yard saying she couldn't do it anymore, his father coming home and finding nothing to eat. He must have told them how his father squirted the stuff against the house and how his mother kicked over the grill and how they all went out to dinner and ate steak and ice cream and how his father said, "Fuck the fat." He probably told them about driving home, seeing the fire engines blocking the street, then going to the motel, and how he woke up in the middle of the night not sure where he was and how his parents were in the bathroom talking. And then he must have told them how they drove home in the dark, how they slept in the car—how they lied.

Paul never thought Sammy would be the one, but that explains it, that explains it all. "It would help to have you both here. . . . The police have been called." The less they tell you, the worse it is.

Busted, framed, hung out to dry. They're going to arrest them—Paul and Elaine.

He wishes to hell he'd never given the cell phone back to Henry. He wonders if you're allowed to make calls from the back of a police cruiser. He wonders if you're really allowed only one call from the station after they arrest you. If you are, he would call Tom again. Not Henry, George, or Ted. Tom. Tom was so nice, so calm, so good about things the other night. He makes a deal with himself: As soon as he can, he will call Tom, and everything will be all right.

Will they handcuff him? Will people see them being taken away? Will it be thoroughly humiliating?

"Bet you don't take many people all the way out here." To distract himself, he makes conversation with the driver.

"More than you'd think," the cabdriver says. "I'm taking you, aren't I?" he adds, as if to prove Paul is just another sucker.

"You're taking me to my son's school," Paul says, as though there's a difference. "It's an emergency."

Paul plays a guessing game—how much will it cost, more or less than a hundred? He takes out his wallet and checks his cash supply. Will he need more? Will he have to stop? Later, Paul will think about the ways he wasted time, the things he ignored. Later, he will feel bad about everything. He will think it's all his fault.

"Hot for the beginning of June," Paul says.

"This is nothing," the driver says. "Just wait a couple of weeks, you'll be wishing we were back in January."

Paul rolls the windows down as far as they'll go. He looks straight ahead. He can't see through the Plexiglas divider. He is woozy, carsick. It will be over soon.

"People always want what they don't have," the driver says. "Why is that? Why aren't they ever satisfied? Human nature?"

*   *   *

Elaine is already gone.

The phone rang, an interruption. She stood over it, waiting to see if it was something she had to respond to. Incoming calls were almost always about other people's needs, rarely about what someone can give, mostly about things that can be taken.

She checked her watch—just after one.

"Mrs. Weiss, it's the Webster Avenue Elementary School. We're having some difficulty this afternoon. We need you to come down to the school." A bell rings in the background.

The school office—forgotten lunch money, an unsigned form, head lice.

"The principal asked me to call. She asked me to stress the urgency of the situation."

Elaine pictures Sammy gasping for air, powerless, terrified. She remembers him as a toddler, looking at her as if to ask, Why is this happening? "Fix it," he used to say. "Fix it." Halfway through the message, she can't stand it anymore; she picks up the phone. "Do you have his puffer?"

"Mrs. Weiss?"

"Yes."

"Did you get the message?"

"I just picked up," she says.

"One moment. I'll put the principal on."

"Do you have his medication?" Elaine implores. "Is he breathing?"

"It's not the asthma," the principal says, taking the phone. "He's having a problem with another student. They're in the cloakroom and won't come out."

Elaine is relieved—he's breathing.

"There's some question as to who's holding who and if they're armed."

"Armed?"

"The police have been notified. My secretary has called your husband—he's en route."

"I don't understand," Elaine says. "Where is Sammy?"

"He's in the cloakroom," the principal says. "Please hurry."

The day twists, it turns, it starts in one place and ends in another. Elaine is moving backward and forward simultaneously. This is something Elaine can't control. She doesn't get to choose, to say yes or no.

She calls Paul; she gets his voice mail. "Are you there? Are you hiding at your desk? Are you out for lunch? Are you having an affair?" She stops and starts again. "We got a strange call. Something is happening to Sammy."

She hangs up and tries his secretary; she gets voice mail. "Fuck you. Fuck everyone." She runs out of the house.

A single police car is parked in front of the school.

Two by two, in long narrow lines, the children are being led out of the building and up the sidewalk to the farthest edge of the playground. It is a practiced procedure, like a fire drill or an Easter parade.

"Hold on to your buddy," the teachers call out.

Excited by the unexpected disruption, the children giggle, they wiggle, they dance.

"Don't let go," the teachers say. "Hold tight."

Elaine rushes up the front steps. The janitor blocks her. She tries to duck around him. Children are streaming out on either side. He holds up his broomstick, brandishing it like a sword. "This is an emergency evacuation," he says. "You can't go in."

She turns, spinning full circle, sweeping through a whirl of anxiety and indecision. Behind her is the semicircular driveway, the parking lot filled with cars. In front of her is the red-brick two-story school building. And Sammy. She hurls herself forward. The janitor puts his body between Elaine and the door. The children keep coming out, squeezing past them. He shakes his head no.

"I was called here. Let me in. I need to come in. I need to speak with someone."

"I'm sure they'll be with you directly," the janitor says.

Another group of students slips out.

"What grade is that?" Elaine asks.

"That's the fifth grade," the janitor says.

"Where is the fourth grade?"

"I don't know where anybody is," he says.

It is hot. She is panicked. She sweats profusely. "I'm the mother." She tries to sound authoritative. She stops one of the teachers. "Who's in charge? Where's the principal?"

The teacher points to a side door. Before the janitor can do or say anything, Elaine is in. It is cool and dark. There is the echo of a hundred small feet racing down the cinder-block halls. Controlled chaos. She sees the principal in the hallway ahead of her. The same bulletin boards that a few days ago were filled with hope and promise, celebrations of the future, things to come, now seem cold and menacing: RITES OF SPRING, SUMMER SAFETY TIPS.

"Where is Sammy? Where is my son?" Elaine yells.

The principal waits to answer until they are closer. "We believe they are in the cloakroom," the principal says, leading Elaine back outside.

"Believe?"

"Well, that's where the teacher saw them go."

"Can't someone go in and look?"

"We can't take any chances. He told us to go away. He threatened to shoot."

"Who?"

"Nate Warshofsky," the principal says.

"Nate?"

"I called his mother. She's not home. She doesn't have a job, does she? There's not a work number for her, is there?"

"No," Elaine says.

The principal is old. A couple of years ago there was a petition to force her to retire. Elaine fought against it. She thought the principal's age, her kindness and good faith were impressive qualities. She liked the way the principal ran the school, like a family rather than a corporation. The principal is shrinking; she is only about four foot ten. Her silver hair is twisted into a bun; it sits on top of her head like a brioche.

"When did this start?" Elaine asks.

The principal looks at her watch. "Less than an hour ago. I hoped we could handle it ourselves. Over the PA I asked Nate and Sammy to come down to the office. I said we would talk about things. I got no response. I went down the hall and knocked on the door and asked if I could come in. That's when he said, 'Go away, idiot.' I had Mrs. Goldmark, the teacher, try, and he threatened her even more explicitly."

Elaine looks bewildered.

The principal gestures to her breasts. "It's an issue."

Elaine nods.

"And so I called the police," the principal says, as though that's what logically follows.

"Did you offer them anything?" Elaine asks.

"Like what?"

"They're little boys. How about asking if they'd like to come down to the kitchen and have ice cream? I bet that would get them out right away. They both love ice cream."

"The boy is armed, people saw strange lumps under his clothing, he's got your son Sammy in the cloakroom. It's a hostage situation."

"Surely you have ice cream in there somewhere," Elaine says, not letting go.

"Let's not minimize the situation," the principal says.

"The batteries on the bullhorn are dead," the school secretary informs the principal. "But I found this." She waves a cone, like the kind cheerleaders use. She turns to Elaine. "I spoke with your husband; he's on his way." The secretary holds a clipboard filled with class lists, charts, plans, pressed close to her chest.

Elaine overhears the librarian talking to the gym teacher. "Why doesn't someone just march in there and tell him to behave? Hell, I'll do it. He's not going to shoot me," the gym teacher says. "I'll put him over my knees and give him what for—the trouble he's causing."

"The word no means nothing today," the librarian says.

Two more police cars pull up.

"What's the story?" the top cop asks.

The principal defers to the teacher, who apologizes in advance. "I'm a little rattled," Mrs. Goldmark says. "I've never seen a gun before."

Elaine can't help but notice that she's got huge breasts—tits like torpedoes, high and hard, mounted on her chest. Elaine doesn't remember her having a chest like that before. She guesses it's new. You get what you pay for—more for the money.

"It was a perfectly normal day," Mrs. Goldmark says. "They'd just come back from lunch and were settling down—they're always a little wild after recess. I noticed Nate was wearing a long-sleeved flannel shirt. 'Aren't you warm?' I asked him. 'No,' he said. 'I'm hot, like I'm on fire, like I'm going to explode.' And then he laughed. 'Well, take a layer off,' I said. Then I turned away and wrote something on the blackboard. Next thing I know, he pulls out a gun, points it at Sammy, and says, 'I'll show you what history is.' " The teacher continues, "Then he grabbed the little girl next to him and kissed her."

"She'd never been kissed before," the school secretary says. "She's with the health aide now."

Elaine is listening to what they are saying, fitting one line into the next like Legos, trying to get it to add up. She stares; Mrs. Goldmark and her torpedo tits look like something out of a James Bond movie—and her roots are coming through, black beneath the blond.

Mrs. Goldmark goes on, "He told us all to get out of the room, and then he led Sammy into the cloakroom. He's definitely got something under his shirt—I don't know what, but there's something there. I instructed the children to remain calm, to collect their things, and to file out into the hall. They ran like maniacs."

"Did he bring anything unusual to school? Was he carrying anything this morning?" the cop asks.

"They all have knapsacks and gym bags," Mrs. Goldmark says, shaking her head. "The ones who go back and forth between parents sometimes come with suitcases."

"What's the status of the school?"

"We're evacuating, I've called for an early dismissal, we've ordered buses and crossing guards, and we've activated the telephone tree to notify parents."

"Which window is the classroom?"

The principal points to one on the first floor. "Four-B, fourth grade, second section."

The cop rubs his head. "I'm not very good with kids. I always say the wrong thing. How old are they?"

"Nine," the principal says.

The cop gets on his radio. "We're going to need backup down here. Find Macmillan and tell him I'll him call from a landline in a couple of minutes. I'm going to need to use your phone," he tells the principal. "I'm gonna call the Bomb Squad, and if I go on the radio with this, every nut-ball in hell will be here in ten minutes." He turns to the younger cop. "Search it, room to room. Start on top and keep it very quiet, no radios, no talking. Make sure all the kids are out. Check closets and bathrooms, too. And then we're gonna need a zone out here, block it off. There's tape in the car."

"Who are you?" the cop asks Elaine.

"I'm the mother."

"Which mother?"

"Sammy's," Elaine says. "I came to pick Sammy up."

"The good boy or the bad boy?" the cop asks.

"The good boy," the teacher says.

Etherized by anxiety, Elaine's breath is light, shallow, at the top of her lungs. She is dizzy; her hands tingle.

It is morning. They are sitting at the kitchen table, eating blueberry pancakes. "Pass the syrup," Paul says. They eat breakfast, as though they've always eaten breakfast at the table together, as though it's nothing out of the ordinary. Sunlight floods the kitchen. "It's so bright in here I almost need sunglasses," Daniel says.

"It's shiny," Sammy says.

"It was a perfectly normal day," the teacher says.

The school secretary pops her trunk and takes out a pair of binoculars. "I'm a birder," she says, slightly self-conscious. "I keep them in my car." She takes a quick peek and then hands the binoculars to Elaine.

"Which window?" Elaine asks, not sure she wants to see.

"That one."

Elaine sees nothing. She adjusts the focus and sees chairs knocked over, things spilled, upset, as if people left in a hurry. There is a border of alphabet, cursive letters running around the top of the room, like decorative trim. On the blackboard is a paragraph that goes nowhere, an unfinished sentence. There is a map of the world and a globe on a stand.

"I'd like for this not to turn into a circus," the principal says, leading the cop into the school.

A yellow cab pulls into the driveway. The horn beeps. And beeps again, demanding, self-important, wrong-headed.

It's Paul.

"Elaine," he calls. "Elaine. Do you have any cash? I didn't stop for money."

She hands over her wallet.

"I'll need a receipt," Paul tells the driver. "Eighty-six seventy," he says, getting out of the car. "The whole way out I was playing a game with myself—How much would it cost? I guessed it would be about seventy-five. I gave him a hundred and ten. Was that enough? Too much? What do you think?"

Elaine can't answer—the sight of Paul drives her further in. "Nate and Sammy are in the cloakroom," she tells him, her voice flattened by the facts. "Nate has a gun. He has bulges under his clothes."

"Bulges?"

"Mysterious lumps. They're calling the Bomb Squad."

The radio crackles, and Elaine thinks of Sammy and Daniel in the backyard, the grass, the garden, the roots of trees, dirt in the Dumpster. Sammy and Daniel playing with walkie-talkies— what are you wearing? Red socks.

The younger cop is busy wrapping yellow crime scene tape around everything. It is the same kind of tape the fire department used at the house. He ties tape to the trees, the bike rack, the flagpole. He asks the passersby to take a step back, to give them some space.

Paul and Elaine stand inside the tape as though they are the thing being contained, quarantined, sealed off. They stand in the middle as though they are "it."

As much as the tape is to keep others out, to draw a line, a border, Elaine feels it is there to hold her in, to keep her corralled.

"I thought they were going to arrest us," Paul says. "I

decided the whole thing—calling me at work, telling me to hurry, saying they needed us both—was a sting operation. I thought Sammy told them about the fire."

"Everything is not about you," Elaine says, raising the binoculars to her eyes, looking again.

"Can you see anything?"

"Pencils and pens. Notebook paper on the floor."

"Where would Nate get a gun?" She passes the binoculars to Paul.

"Gerald has guns," Paul says. "He goes to war camp on weekends. He shoots people with paint pellets."

"How do you know?"

"I know," he says, looking in.

Far away, there is the sound of sirens.

The top cop comes out of the school. "Let's keep this area here a quiet zone. All I want the boys to see out that window is their parents and an empty parking lot. And no radios, kill all the radios."

"My husband," Elaine says, introducing Paul.

"This isn't a holdup at 7-Eleven. It isn't like some irate employee at the post office went off. These are nine-year-olds," Paul charges.

The cop looks at Paul. He waits.

Paul tries again. "What seems to be the exact nature of the problem?"

"Last we heard, the boy had a gun aimed at your son's head," the cop says. "How well do you know the other boy? Does he have a history of mental illness?"

"We wouldn't know," Elaine says, looking at Paul.

"Any idea what could have prompted this?"

"We had a little fire at our house," Elaine says. "Sammy's been staying at Nate's."

"For how long?"

"Just this week."

"Do the boys get along?"

"They're boys," Paul offers, as though that explains it. He doesn't elaborate. He is thinking of what Sammy said that morning about Mrs. Apple moving.

"Nate kind of runs the show," Elaine says, looking at the cop. "He's not always nice."

"When was Nate mean?" Paul asks.

"I'm just saying there's some tension between them. Nate peed on Sammy the other day."

"He missed," Paul says.

"When you dropped Sammy at their house, you told me that Nate opened the door, said something crappy, and ran away," Elaine reminds Paul. "And Saturday, when Sammy came home, he said something about Nate making him do push-ups. It sounded weird, but I was tired, I didn't really pay attention," Elaine confesses to the cop. Mentally, she berates herself. She should have known something was wrong, she should have paid more attention, she should have been vigilant, ever on alert.

A television truck pulls up. Its antenna crawls into the air. The school buses start to arrive. Parents, having been notified via the telephone tree, are flocking to the school. There is a traffic jam as cars circle the block.

The secretary chases the principal around the parking lot. "You're needed at the top of the hill. They're boarding the buses, but they don't know what to do with the students whose mothers couldn't be reached. Can they send them home to empty houses?"

"There's only one of me," the principal says, throwing her arms up. "I'm doing the best I can."

"Are they handling this right?" Paul asks. "Can't they just shoot him with a tranquilizer dart?"

"This isn't *Wild Kingdom*," the secretary says.

In the distance, children are shouting, playing games, a ball is being tossed around. It is a perfect summer afternoon.

The Good Humor man has set up at the top of the hill. A Frisbee flies. The normalness of their behavior seems surreal, distracting, disrespectful. Elaine wants to scream, Don't you understand what is going on here? He's holding a gun to my son's head.

In a parked car, a dog barks.

She thinks of Sammy homesick in the middle of the night. Sammy in his Superman pajamas asleep on top of Paul and Elaine. Tender Sammy.

Nate's mother arrives. Elaine sees her coming. She sees her running across the parking lot toward them. And in the distance Elaine sees the cop, her cop, directing traffic. She thinks of Sammy, the cop, the red balloon.

"I was at aerobics. I got home. There was a message." She is out of breath, pink, flushed. She's still wearing her gym outfit. "I haven't showered," she says. "It was hard getting through."

"Mrs. Warshofsky?" the cop asks.

She nods.

"Apparently your son has taken another boy hostage. We believe he is armed. We need some information—are guns kept in your house?"

"My husband is a war buff," she explains.

What does that mean—a war buff? Elaine imagines asking Nate to let them change places, to let the mothers stand in. She imagines being in the cloakroom with Susan. What would they do—pull each other's hair? Elaine imagines slapping Susan, punching her, scratching her, clawing. It's all your fault, you fucking aerobic idiot.

"How many guns? What kind?" the cop is asking.

"Half dozen, assorted?" Susan looks at Paul. She is his Mrs. Apple. He is her Friday Fun.

"What other kinds of explosive devices does your husband collect: rifles, shotguns, grenades? Any ammunition of other types? Land mines? What does your son know about weaponry?"

"Where is your husband?" another cop asks.

"At a convention in Minneapolis. I don't have the number. He's supposed to be calling tonight."

"Does your son know how to fire a gun?"

She nods. "Yes."

Elaine is imploding, erupting internally. He knows how to fire a gun. Who are these people? What is happening here?

"What was he wearing this morning?" the cop continues. "Was he carrying bags with him? Do you know what the content of his bags would be? There are reports of bulges or lumps on his body or under his clothing. We're just trying to figure out what he's got with him in there."

Paul is struggling to say something. Elaine watches him. She remembers last week rushing from lunch with Liz to Pat's, rushing to get to the school play by two o'clock, sitting on the gray metal folding chair. She remembers watching the back of Susan's head. She remembers Nate as a hunter in the play—Sammy was a rhino, and Nate shot him.

"Could we send someone over to your house to take a look around?" the cop asks.

"Of course." Susan drops the keys into the cop's open hand. "There's a gun case in the family room, and then there's something in the dresser upstairs, on the right, under the socks."

"Do I need a search warrant?" the cop asks.

"She gave you the keys to the house," the top cop says.

"Sammy was a rhino, and Nate shot him," Elaine says. She feels herself start to cry. A small sound leaks out; she presses her fingers to her mouth and pushes it back in.

Paul doesn't know what to say. "We'll get it straightened out as quick as we can, and then we'll go home."

Elaine shakes her head. She doesn't believe anything Paul says.

The three parents are inside the tape, in the zone. Paul is in the middle, pulled in both directions. They are all there, in the same place at the same time.

Elaine stands with her fingers pressed to her mouth, afraid it's all going to fall out, endlessly spew. All she can do is press it back, push it down, swallow it.

It is clear.

Everything is out from under.

She knows.

Elaine wants to walk, to run. If it weren't for Sammy, she would turn and go, she would be already gone. "What have you done?" Elaine asks. "Have you done something awful? Is that what this is about? Is that her?"

Paul stares at the classroom window.

"I am very uncomfortable," Elaine says, mechanically. "I don't want to be here. I don't want to be here anymore."

The TV crew is interviewing the cafeteria lady. "Sammy likes my baking, my snickerdoodles. We're one of the few elementary schools that still cooks our own food. All the others are heat and eat. I've been here since 1972. . . ."

The Bomb Squad arrives in a station wagon. Two plain-clothes cops and two German shepherds get out. The dogs are panting, they are excited. Their penises are pink and pointy. The cops take black boxes out of the back; they pull on special uniforms. The dogs sniff everything.

"I feel sick," Elaine says.

On the hood of a car the principal sketches a map of the school. On a piece of lined notebook paper, she draws a detailed layout of the classroom.

Nate's mother steps forward, striding across the parking lot and onto the grass. She stands outside the classroom window. "Nate, can you hear me? It's Mommy. This isn't a game, guns are not toys. Come on out, and I'll take you to FAO Schwarz. I'll buy you anything you want. Sammy is your friend. I'm sure you don't mean to upset him." She pauses. "It's three-thirty, Nate. Time to go home. You know what's for dinner? Fish sticks. And tartar sauce. You know how much you like tartar sauce." She yells at the building. Her voice echoes off the brick, slapping back at her. "Five minutes, Nate, I'll wait five minutes."

Elaine has started to move away. Without knowing, she has taken several steps back; she is drifting close to the edge, the yellow tape.

At the front of the crowd, Elaine sees Joan with Catherine Montgomery—their expressions frighten Elaine.

Daniel arrives with Willy. He ducks under the tape. "Mom?"

Elaine pulls him to her. Daniel's arms stay flat at his sides; it's the middle of the afternoon, they're in public, strangers are watching. Elaine squeezes him tight. "I hope I'm not a horrible mother," she says. "I may act distracted, but I do care—I care enormously. I care about the two of you so much that it's almost unbearable—do you know that?"

"I heard Nate's got a gun," Daniel says. "I heard he made a bomb."

"No one knows," Elaine says.

An ambulance pulls up and parks across the street. At a certain point it becomes hard to pretend that nothing is going on.

"Did you see all the people, Joan and Catherine? And Mrs. Hansen should be home from the dentist soon," she tells him.

The school bell rings, pealing, screaming, slamming off the walls of the empty building like an alarm. It scares the hell out of everyone.

"School's out," Daniel says.

"Excuse me," Paul says to the top cop. "Excuse me, I'm wondering if you could get this whole show to back up a bit. This is one of those games that kids play, and it's gotten a little out of hand. He's probably too embarrassed to come out. He's probably nervous as hell. You're making it hard to walk away. Could you ask them, could you ask everyone to take it back?"

Paul runs pathetically from person to person, begging them all to do something, urging them, imploring them.

"Patience is the key," the cop says. "There's nothing to be gained from rushing people to places they don't want to go."

"I just want it fixed," Elaine says.

The newscaster goes out live. "A disturbed little boy, a desperate cry for attention. A mother stands outside a school, pleading with her child. A hostage crisis."

"Can you shut up? Just shut up? You're making it worse. This is a private moment, and you're turning it into snack food," Paul shouts at the reporter.

"Understandably very agitated, the father of the boy that's being held hostage." The reporter speaks in a hushed whisper. "Two nine-year-olds in an afternoon showdown."

The heat continues to build. A thick breeze blows back the leaves, sweeping Elaine's hair off her face.

Jennifer has slipped in and is standing next to Daniel. Mrs. Hansen arrives with a wad of cotton still stuck in her cheek. "I came as soon as I heard."

Inside the classroom there is a dull thud, like the bang of a bass drum, a flash that catches the eyes outside. The cops duck behind parked cars, they draw their weapons, they aim and brace, ready to fire.

Inside the room there is a spray of sparks, a fountain of light, cascading colors.

"Fireworks," Elaine says, looking through the binoculars. "Fireworks," she says, remembering the time when the boys were with Paul's mother in Florida and Elaine and Paul stayed home and smoked crack. Elaine had the sensation of being a fountain, the fountain in front of the Plaza hotel. She was a Roman candle, a ball of light, a fantastic flame.

"Hold your fire," the top cop calls.

There are more small explosions—firecrackers snapping, a

couple of loud cherry-bomb bangs. And then there is a flood of yellow smoke. A sulfurous eruption, a urine-yellow cloud billowing, swelling, rising. Nate has opened the windows and tossed out smoke bombs. A diversionary tactic. When the smoke clears, the venetian blinds have been dropped and drawn.

The breeze shakes the blinds, they rattle—slithering snake.

For the moment, Elaine is only a witness. "There's smoke," she says. "Smoke isn't good."

"He's got asthma," Paul tells the top cop. "He can't breathe smoke."

The cops are too busy to listen. They are suiting up, putting on bulletproof vests, gas masks, riot gear.

Elaine looks out at the crowd.

Pat is there now, huddled with Joan and Catherine. "What can I do?" Pat mimes.

Elaine shakes her head—nothing. There's nothing she can do.

"This is exactly what I was saying," Paul tells the cops. "You'll scare them. You're scaring me. Right now, you and your men are frightening me. You're dealing with a nine-year-old, not some Middle Eastern mastermind. This is out of control."

"You can't guess what they're carrying," the cop says, tightening the strap of his vest.

"It's true, Gerald has all kinds of strange catalogs," Susan says.

"Remember the boy on Long Island who brought anthrax to school?"

"We have extra vests. If you want to put one on, you'll be covered if he fires out."

"He's not going to shoot us," Paul says.

Susan puts on a vest.

"This is not a movie," the secretary says, hiding behind her car.

"I don't care," Elaine says, refusing.

If Elaine were home, this would be one of those moments, time to do something different. She would step out of the house, she would stand on the steps, breathing.

A white truck pulls in. The back door opens, and men in high-tech uniforms pile out, carrying ropes and rifles.

"Is that the SWAT team?" Paul asks. As each new thing happens, the craziness compounds.

The top cop huddles with the SWAT team and the Bomb Squad, consulting the principal's diagram. "I want to close this situation down as quickly and quietly as I can." He makes his plan and then turns to Paul, Elaine, Susan—the parents. "We're going to send a little robot in. He's remote-control-operated, outfitted with a camera and a microphone so we can talk to the boys. He's unarmed. It's both an investigatory procedure and a negotiation tool."

"Does he have hands? Can he carry something?"

"Like what, a note?" the cop asks.

"Sammy's puffer," Elaine says, reaching into her purse, pulling out the spare, and handing it to the cop.

She watches them unload the robot from the back of the Bomb Squad station wagon. They set up a bank of four video monitors and walk the robot up and down the parking lot, testing the system. Before he goes in, the cop puts the puffer in the robot's claw.

One of the guys from the Bomb Squad, suited up like a scuba diver, waddles up the school steps carrying the robot in front of him as if it's a toddler.

He opens the front door and puts the robot down inside the school.

"Video up," the cop says, and four monitors fill with a robot's-eye view of cinder-block walls and bulletin boards. The picture is grainy, hard to define; the images look as though they're being transmitted from thousands of miles away, sent home from the moon.

The robot scans right and left.

"Let's go." Someone gives the signal, and the operator sends the robot forward.

"Take the first left and go down the hall," the cop whispers—high tension.

Elaine stares at the video feed; she fixates on the robot's claw, clutching Sammy's medicine.

In a gesture meant to be comforting, Paul reaches for Elaine's arm. He touches her—she shudders. "You frightened me," she says.

"Sorry."

Suddenly, the monitors go to what looks like a close-up of tile, a linoleum zoom.

"What happened?"

"Dunno," the operator says.

Two men from the SWAT team and the Bomb Squad guy go up the steps and into the school. A helmeted head appears on the monitors in extreme close-up. "The robot fell down," someone whispers into the microphone. "He tripped." The report booms out of the speakers, spilling across the parking lot.

The robot is set upright and is once again on his way. As the robot gets closer to the classroom, the cop starts to sing; a synthesized sound, like bad karaoke, comes out of the robot's speaker. A mélange of Simon & Garfunkel. "And here's to you, Mrs. . . ."

"We want to warn the boys that R2D2's coming. It shouldn't be a surprise," one of the cops says.

"Did your kids like *Star Wars*?" the operator asks.

No one answers.

The robot pushes open the door to the classroom. "Hello. Anybody home?" The camera scans. The picture is dim. The robot moves toward the cloakroom.

"Can we get a little light?" the cop asks.

The operator flicks a switch that turns on a light on the

robot's head—like a coal miner's helmet or an old-fashioned super-8 movie light. The picture zooms in on Sammy and Nate in the cloakroom, Nate with the gun.

"Hi, Nate, my name is Bob. That was a great fireworks show. I love fireworks." The robot speaks in a synthesized voice. "Do you mind if I come in?" The robot rolls forward. "I brought some medicine for Sammy."

"Does your son have unusually developed arm muscles?" the cop asks, watching Nate on the video feed.

"No."

"See those bulges under his shirt?" the cop asks.

"Canisters," a Bomb Squad guy says. "And there seems to be some wiring. Would your son know how to make a bomb?"

"I have no idea."

"Would you like to talk to him?" The cop hands her the microphone.

"Nate, it's Mom. Can you hear me?"

"You sound weird," Nate says. "Like the robot."

"That's our anonymous voice of authority," the cop explains. "We use it in situations where we have multiple negotiators. It gives us universal sound, a united front, and we don't reveal anyone's identity."

"Can you make it normal?"

The operator flicks a switch.

"Nate, it's Mom. Is that better? It's enough already. It's getting late. They have to lock up the school for the night. Everyone wants to go home and watch TV. Don't you want to go home?"

"I'm not going home," Nate says. "No one is going home."

Sammy leans forward. "I want to go home." He looks into the robot. "Fix it," he says.

"He's wheezing," Elaine says. "You can hear it?"

"Nathan, Sammy is sick. He needs to take his medicine now," Susan says.

The robot's claw extends, handing Sammy the inhaler. They watch while Sammy exhales and then inhales; they can hear the dull fart of the puffer expelling its stuff.

"Thank you," the robot says. "Is there anything that you need?" The robot pauses. "It's a beautiful afternoon, why not pull the shades up?" The robot moves toward the windows.

"Get out," Nate yells. "Get out of my house."

"What's on your mind, Nate?"

Nate grabs Sammy.

He raises the gun.

He pulls the trigger. Slow motion. Video feed. Black-and-white fragments.

Sammy.

His knees go out from under, his head snaps back, like he's dodging, but it's the bullet hitting his head, pushing through skin, scalp, skull, taking out bone, hair, brain— Sammy.

The bullet—the crooked, shattering, caplet—exits, landing on the floor with a small plinking sound that no one hears.

Sammy falling.

Nate, knocked back, bangs against the wall. He waves the gun wildly.

Outside, they hear the sound of the shot in stereo, real and recorded, muffled through the walls and windows of the school and oddly amplified by the robot's microphone, a big metallic bang exploding over the speakers.

They watch it on TV.

Close-up.

Sammy.

Daniel charges the building. He goes for the side entrance. No one is moving fast enough to stop him.

The air is thick and still; there is the suspension of time, long beats of waiting. Seconds stretch.

Elaine moans, low, animal, deep.

The newscaster whispers, "One has the sense that something awful has just occurred. Shots have been fired. A little boy may have been hit. This is quickly turning into an afternoon tragedy."

Susan blows into the microphone, her voice tentative, floating over the parking lot. "Nate? Hello? Hello? Is anybody there?"

Daniel is in the room. He appears on the monitor, screaming at Nate. "You little fucking jerk. You pathetic putz. Such a fucking asshole." He lifts Sammy up. "Get the fuck out of my way."

More shots. The monitor goes black.

"Nate?"

Elaine turns. Her arms are raised up—near her ears, terrified, protecting. She moves to run—the opposite way. A fireman catches her and points her in the right direction.

"We've lost audio and visual"—an official report.

And then Daniel is coming out of the building, holding Sammy in his arms. The front of his shirt is bright with blood. He's staggering. "Help me," he bleats. "Help me."

There is a stampede. Paramedics race across the parking lot. The SWAT team descends from the roof, breaking glass, crashing through windows; heavy hooves pound down the hall, moving on all fronts simultaneously. It is as though they could do nothing until something happened, and now they do everything—all at once.

Paul is rushing toward Daniel.

"I can't carry him," Daniel says, collapsing into Paul, knocking him down, like a football tackle.

The medics sort out the heap. They lay Sammy and Daniel out in the parking lot, between the yellow lines. They are cutting away Daniel's shirt, they are looking at Sammy's head.

Radios crackle. "We're gonna need a medevac chopper to shock trauma. We have a white male, nine years old, with a gunshot wound to the head."

"His head," Elaine says, stunned. "He shot him in the head."

"He has a hard head," Paul says, pulling himself up. It's the stupidest thing he's ever said.

Paul and Elaine are at the edge of a human circle. They can't get closer; no one will let them in.

There are ten men bent over Sammy, men on their hands and knees, crawling.

"Pulse?"

"Rapid, one sixty-two."

"Blood pressure?"

"Trying to get it."

"Respiration?"

"Fast."

"Can we get something to pack it with?"

"There's bone missing."

"Where's the chopper?"

"ETA six minutes, landing on the lower school playground."

"Oxygen."

"Can I get a line in?"

Fragments, bits and pieces.

"Did they find the eye?" someone asks.

There is no response.

It is beyond their control. Out of their hands.

"Why aren't they asking us any questions?" Elaine says to Paul.

Paul has no answers.

"This one's fine," one of the paramedics says. Daniel sits up. "It was his brother's blood." His shirt is off. They're giving him oxygen. They're checking the other parts of him. "He's fine, just a little shocky."

"He's fine," Elaine says. "I heard them say he's fine."

Paul shakes his head.

Not Sammy.

"Should we bag him? Intubate?"

"Can we get an EKG?"

"He has asthma," Elaine tells a paramedic. "He uses a puffer. And he can't take penicillin, it gives him a terrible rash."

"What was the ammo? Hollow-point?"

"We don't know."

They stand helpless.

"Is he breathing?" Elaine asks, pleading, as she watches the paramedics squeezing the plastic ball.

"He's getting air."

"Could someone call my mother?" Elaine asks softly.

"Nate?"

The Bomb Squad has Nate. They're moving him to the playground at the top of the hill carefully—afraid he might explode.

They set him down in the outfield near second base.

Someone from the Bomb Squad approaches, takes out a pair of scissors, and cuts off Nate's shirt.

Nate, the boy bomb, has cans taped to his torso, cans taped up and down his arms: Raid, Magic Sizing, Reddi Wip, Easy-Off, Cheez Whiz. Cans and wires.

The trained dogs sniff him.

"Don't move."

People run up the side of the hill to see what's happening.

His mother is held back behind a line.

The area is sealed off.

"Arms and legs spread wide."

The man from the Bomb Squad cuts up one leg of Nate's

pants and down the other. Nate's pants fall away; smoke bombs roll out of the pockets. Nate is on the playground in his underwear, a steak knife taped to his leg.

"He's got wires running from can to can, and it looks like three kinds of tape—silver duct, some sort of a black fiber, and what looks like regular old Scotch Magic. The cans appear to be attached by a white wire that ends in an outlet—I think he's done it with some sort of extension cord." The man pushes down Nate's socks with a pencil. "There's two sets of double-A batteries around the ankles."

"Check him for a timer." The squawk of the walkie-talkie.

"I hope they don't have to detonate him," an ambulance driver says. "In 'Nam, they medevaced a guy with a live grenade embedded in his head. It hit him and didn't detonate. The doc came out to the chopper pad, shot him full of morphine, and we set him off—like smashing pumpkins. Kaboom!"

"No timer."

"Go ahead and cut the wires."

The man from the Bomb Squad snips a wire, separating the spray starch from the Reddi Wip. Nothing happens. He reaches out and slowly pulls a piece of duct tape off Nate, peeling the cans away from Nate's skin.

Nate whines.

"Neutralized. Disarmed."

The chopper comes in over the hill. They hear it before they see it, thumping through the air.

Smoky red flares mark the spot.

It lands, kicking up a hot, dry wind.

"Stay with Mrs. Hansen," Paul yells at Daniel over the din.

The door slides open.

One, two, three, they lift Sammy off the ground. The

medic holds the IV bags in his teeth, the oxygen tank under his arm. Whatever is not attached falls away, wrappers, scraps.

Sammy's head is swathed in an enormous wad of white gauze. There is a bandage over one eye. The other eye is open, pupil dilated, fixed as though it has seen something horrible.

"You did a good thing," Paul says, draping his jacket over Daniel's shoulders.

"Go," Daniel says.

Elaine is pulled into the helicopter after Sammy. She sits curled into the half seat by the door, the rivets of the low ceiling brushing her hair.

"It's all right," she tells Sammy. "You've had quite a hit in the head, but you're fine. Everything is fine."

The medic checks Sammy's vital signs. His helmet hides his face; he speaks into his headset. "Pulse one-twenty. Respiration shallow." He pumps the blood-pressure cuff.

Paul is last on board, crammed into a corner.

The door is slammed closed, locked. The whir is louder now, wings bladishly beating, a deafening metallic din.

The chopper takes off, thrusting up, hovering above four-square, hopscotch, a diamond painted yellow.

Rising.

Pulling back on the scene.

"Chopper four, we are en route."

They are up and away, over the trees, clear of the wires, looking down on the familiar, a crooked cartography, houses, streets, the neighbors' yards, home. They are looking in on themselves from a peculiar perspective—everything in miniature, their lives made small.

Elaine is holding Sammy's hand; it is flaccid, unresponsive. He's getting whiter and whiter, and the gauze is staining red. When no one is looking, she pinches his finger, hard. Nothing happens.

"Pressure is falling," the medic says, pumping.

The sun glints off something metallic, a split second of shattering light.

Shiny, Elaine thinks.

They are into the blue.

Paul checks his watch—it beeps. Four forty-five.

Elaine looks at him. "It's over," she says.

ACKNOWLEDGMENTS

For their enormous generosity of spirit, I would like to thank: Sarah Chalfant, Jill Ciment, Gregory Crewdson, Marc H. Glick, Amy Hempel, Erika Ineson, R. S. Jones, Randall Kenan, M. G. Lord, Rick Moody, Karen Murphy, Marie V. Sanford, Helen Schulman, Laurie Simmons, Andrew Solomon, Ben Taylor, Liza Walworth, Rob Weisbach, Karl Willers, and Andrew Wylie.

For a much needed and much appreciated grant given at just the right moment, I thank the Guggenheim Foundation, and for the great gift of time, the Corporation of Yaddo.

And always, my family.

A. M. Homes is the author of the novels *The End of Alice,*
In a Country of Mothers, and *Jack,* as well as the short-story
collection *The Safety of Objects* and the artist's book *Appendix A.* Her fiction has been translated into eight languages, and she is the recipient of numerous awards,
including a Guggenheim Fellowship and a National Endowment for the Arts Fellowship. Her fiction and nonfiction appear in magazines such as *The New Yorker* and
Artforum, among others, and she is a contributing editor at
Vanity Fair, Mirabella, Bomb, Blind Spot, and *Story.* She
teaches in the writing programs at Columbia University
and The New School and lives in New York City.

This book was set in Garamond 3, a typeface designed by the Parisian type cutter Claude Garamond (1480–1561). This version of Garamond was modeled on a 1592 specimen sheet, which was produced from types thought to have been brought to Frankfurt by Jacques Sabon (d. 1580).

Claude Garamond is one of the most famous designers in printing history. His distinguished romans and italics first appeared in *Opera Ciceronis* around 1544. Garamond's types have been revived in this century, due to their elegant yet clean and open design.